MARK H NEWHOUSE

The Devil's Bookkeepers Book 3: The Noose Closes

Newhouse Creative Group

Dear Reader

This is the finale to *The Devil's Bookkeepers 1: The Noose* and *2: The Noose Tightens.* I recommend you read Books 1 and 2 to learn the origins of this suspenseful story about love, friendship, and courage in a Holocaust ghetto, a time of terror. The series follows the timeline of the tightening of the Nazi noose around the Lodz Ghetto in Poland, beginning in 1941, as described in *The Chronicle of the Lodz Ghetto*, translated and edited by Lucjan Dobroszycki (Yale University Press, 1984). Some character names are real, while most attributes, conversations, and their reactions are fictitious since little is known about the authors who wrote this record of the suffering they and those they loved experienced. The dialogue incorporates some of their anonymous entries and is my attempt to imagine their responses to the extraordinary circumstances they struggled to overcome. While the characters' behaviors and relationships are figments of my imagination, unfortunately, the historical facts are real. If only we had recordings of what was said as the nightmare unfolded around them.

Some chapters open with the *Chronicle* excerpts. Thank you, Yale University Press, for allowing me to use these. I've retained most of their wording, tone, and even errors to preserve the 'chill factor' as people vanished without explanation, and hope flared only to be extinguished by terrible uncertainty. Of approximately two hundred thousand human beings who suffered in the Lodz ghetto, less than five thousand survived despite the controversial efforts of the ghetto Chairman. Two of these survivors were my parents. I dedicate this work to them, the grandparents

1

and relatives I never knew, and all victims of hate and genocide past, present, and future. The Holocaust is not only about Jews during World War Two, but a warning and call for tolerance that must echo for all time to all people. I hope this story will inspire you to read the original *Chronicle of the Lodz Ghetto*, a remarkable "message in a bottle," written under the noses of the Nazis. My mission is to help make more people aware of this incredible record and the horrors of hate. The Holocaust is the shadow that haunted my life. I hope this story has that effect on you, so we may all say,

"Never again to anyone, anywhere."

With love,

Mark

NOTE: The entries are presented in italics. While edited for content, they retain their original format, including grammatical and punctuation errors.

ABOUT THE COVERS:

The photographs on the covers are among the few my parents were able to bring with them after surviving the Holocaust. I was deeply torn about using them, but hope they honor the memory of my relatives and my parents. The young girl's face on Book 1 is one of Mom's sisters, a beautiful girl with eyes that haunt me. Book 2's cover is of Mom holding me after I was born in Germany, thankfully, two years after the war ended. Book 3's cover is of one of Mom's younger sisters, whose smiling face makes me ask how could any civilized people want to destroy such innocence and hope.

SINCERE THANKS TO:

My fantastic editor, author and professor of literature (retired), great friend, Louis Emond. I couldn't have finished this without your encouragement. Thank you to early readers, William S. Russell, Edna Maker, Neil Campbell, and Heidi Berri. I'm sorry this suspenseful trilogy kept you awake at night. It did me as well. A big thank you to my friends at Writers 4 Kids and the Creative Writers Group, whose emotional responses and suggestions were so helpful.

Thanks to my sons, Josh and Keith, for their patience and ideas. A special thanks to Keith for spearheading Newhouse Creative Group with such energy and caring. Perhaps nobody was more impacted by this 'insane' project than my wife, Linda, who endured years of watching her husband pounding at the keys to tell a story he wished he didn't have to share. More than anyone else, she knows I had no choice.

Finally, thank you to the readers of *The Devil's Bookkeepers 1 and 2*. Your kind reviews and emotional reactions forced me to return to the Lodz ghetto and finish the story of the men and women who, like my parents, suffered the incredible suspense as the Nazi noose closed around them and those they loved.

I'm honored to be able to bring this story to you and hope you will want to learn more by reading the original *Chronicle of the Lodz Ghetto*. Only education can end hate before it ends us.

BEFORE

L ODZ GHETTO, POLAND
SEPTEMBER 14, 1942
The period of September 5-12, 1942, will leave indelible memories among that portion of the ghetto's population on whom fate smiles and who survive the war. One week, eight days that seem an eternity!

One week, eight days that seem an eternity?

Our apartment, one room, the only window blacked-out in faded drapery, stank of sweat. In my chair, in darkness, I was unable to ease my pain by getting drunk. There was no alcohol, barely any food in the ghetto. Not that I was hungry, not that I wanted to live. Why live? Why struggle against the Nazi noose tightening around us when Miriam, my young wife, and Regina, my precious child, were gone. My loves ripped away from me, taken to some farm in Poland for God knows what purpose.

I'd defended our ghetto leader, Chairman M.C. Rumkowski, the Eldest of the Jews, believing he would give up his life before he would let the Germans take our children. They were the only treasure left to us. They kept us alive, but he gave them to the Nazi wolves. How could he bring himself to demand that we give up our children? He declared it was for the greater good, the only way to save the ghetto from far worse. What could be worse? Only a devil could tear out our hearts with such a cruel demand.

When there is nothing else, there is work. I forced myself to go back to the Jewish Ghetto Administration, where I was employed with a small group

4

recording daily events for our Chairman. He established this chronicle, he said, because it would be evidence someday when he would be judged. I wondered how the future would judge his actions. How would the future judge us all?

Chairman Rumkowski insisted that ghetto residents must work. He argued that maintaining smooth-running factories, proving our value to the enemy, would save the ghetto. Would it? It didn't matter what I thought. To survive, my mission had to be to support his efforts, even if I felt a gnawing fear that his efforts to enforce Nazi decrees were only delaying the inevitable. Many people resented our leader, calling him, in secret, of course, a German-appointed dictator and a Nazi collaborator. In our slum, sealed in by barbed wire fences and armed sentries, surrounded by Jew-hating Germans and Poles, what choices did he have? What options did any of us have? His strategy was the only one that made sense when faced by a military insulating us from all news of the outside world.

I dressed in my soiled shirt and pants, no longer caring about my appearance. I felt for my identification documents in my jacket breast pocket. In the chaos of that horrific night when I lost Miriam and Regina...was it only a week ago...we had been roused from our beds with banging on our door and inhuman shouts. Chased into the street, the Gestapo, anyone, could have stolen my identification, denoting my status as a ghetto administrator. That card protected us. Or so I thought.

As I left our flat, a tomb for my dead soul, to return to work on the Chairman's chronicle, others trudged the streets with zombie-like indifference. No crying, no moaning, no cursing the Nazis. Being starved by our oppressors, our battered shoes barely left an impression on the muddy roads. We were 150,000 slaves making our way to the Chairman's factories under the watchful eyes of his police. He justified their brutality with warnings that the Gestapo was poised to take over if the Jewish police failed to enforce their decrees. We went to work fearful we could be snatched off the street at whim, swept like trash to an unknown destination. Jews in the ghetto vanished and were never heard from again. Miriam and Regina...would I ever see them again? Julian Cukier, our former Chronicle leader, dear Professor Rosenfeld, whose writing turned nightmares into poetry...and young Oscar Singer, the gadfly who had irritated us all with his wild urgings that we fight the enemy even if it meant our destruction. I missed him too, even if he had stolen my Miriam's heart.

CHAPTER 1

The Administration building in Balut Square showed no sign of the latest tragedy. The protesters that once crowded our largest open area no longer appeared after being forcibly dispersed by Chairman Rumkowski's club-swinging police. The garish yellow stars painted on the doors, even in my dazed mind, burned like fire. How did the Germans dare brand us with what was once the emblem of the great Hebrew nation? It was a knife in our hearts I barely felt anymore. I was semi-conscious, addled brain, escaping the present. Even the towering Jewish guards at the door no longer aroused fear. The surrender of my papers was automatic, as was the door guard's examination. He returned my documents and let me by without a word of greeting.

Another guard, wood club in his hands, stepped barely one pace back.

If these officers of Chairman Rumkowski felt anything, if they were still human, they hid it well beneath their coats and official caps. But even they could not conceal the yellow stars on their armbands and on the front and back of their garments. No Jew was allowed to escape the yellow stars that marked us as subhuman in this barb-wire enclosed holding tank, whose purpose was unknown to those penned inside.

A light burned in Rumkowski's office.

I admired the Chairman's work ethic. Even recently married, the 'old devil,' as Miriam called him, was in his office when he could be in his lavish apartment, 'shtupping' his much younger wife, Regina...my daughter's name. It had to be an omen. He would bring my Regina back to me, my daughter, with the same name as his new wife. "God bless the Eldest of the

Jews, our Chairman, our savior."

A German soldier marched across the hallway. The sound of boots, the glint of his rifle, forced me to avert my eyes to the floor.

I shivered at the memory of making love to Miriam and hearing her break my hopeful interlude with, "How can we bring a child into a world such as this?" Was she right all along? Nazi wolves were among us. Black and sleek, heavily armed, while we starved and cowered at their footsteps. How did this happen? I'd asked that question so many times but never found a satisfactory answer. Had Rumkowski accepted our slavery as the price for his family's survival? Was he beguiling us to serve the wolves so he could shear us when it was the right time? Singer and Miriam believed the worst of him. Until that night, the night he demanded our children, I refused to question his devotion, especially to our children...our children.

Through tears in my eyes, the light in the Chairman's office glimmered with hope. *He's working on finding our children. He's a good man, a great man. He swore to protect our children, and that is what he is doing here now.* "Thank you, dear Chairman Rumkowski," I whispered, believing he could hear the prayers of a desperate father. I would try anything, even appealing to a God who had cotton in his ears when it came to the Jews. I leaned toward the door, eager to hear any sound, laughter, tears, anything.

There was nothing. *The Eldest's working on it. Soon, I'll see Miriam and Regina. Soon. Everyone is wrong. He is a savior, not the devil, as many hiss, but behind his back.*

I pushed open the door to the Archives Department. Deputy Neftalin's office was dark. I intended to ask our immediate supervisor if he knew to what province the last trucks carried away our children. Though Henryk Neftalin was a bachelor, he'd understand my hunger to know where my wife and child were. He'd always helped before...before that terrible speech by the Chairman shattered all my hopes. I was shocked when the Eldest of the Jews shouted in the microphone, "Give me your children!" It boomed from the amplifiers all around the square: "Give me your children! Give me your children!" My jaw throbbed where the soldier's rifle butt struck my jaw. I tasted blood as Miriam walked to the truck where Regina had been deposited by the soldier who found her hiding in our flat. My child being carried away, and Miriam refusing to let her go by herself. *Oh, God! Think of something else. Where is Neftalin?*

The Archives. A large chamber; empty shelves. The outlines of where the books stood were marked in the dust. As God said, "from dust to dust...ash to ash?" Even the Huns were not soulless enough to burn books into ash...only to separate our children from their loving parents. But only temporarily. They promised they would return them when the war was over. Soon.

I'm early, as usual, I thought, pushing open the door at the rear of the Department of the Archives. The entrance to our workroom was almost invisible behind the tall shelves. The Chairman had selected this location so we could work without German officials buzzing around. "If they discover what you are doing, you'll face imprisonment, deportation, or worse," Rumkowski had warned me on that first day. *What can be worse than the loss I recently suffered?* A light came from the half-open door. Someone was in the room.

CHAPTER 2

"Y ou're early," I said when the rays fell on the figure in the shadows. "Turn on the light. You frightened the hell out me, sitting in the dark."

"It's been a week. I wondered if you were coming back," Jozef Zelkowicz said, pulling the light chain. "Jews vanish, and I wasn't sure...never mind."

The naked bulb in the ceiling cast an orange tinge on the walls. The Chairman's portrait, grave face commanding work and loyalty, was the only artwork permitted.

I removed my coat and placed it on the back of the cushion-less wood chair. Rosenfeld and Cukier's chairs...vacant. I cupped Rosenfeld's pipe bowl in my pocket. It was silly, but the broken pipe reminded me of the professor. It was the only thing I took from his apartment, that soulful, demolished, monument, all that was left of my elderly friend. Someday, I would return the pipe bowl to him. He'd laugh at the foolishness of my keeping it so long. I refused to believe he was dead. Jews disappeared, and nobody knew where they were.

Zelkowicz placed his hand on my shoulder.

The touch of his hand, the expression on his face, dredged up my recent loss. I fought to restrain tears. I wanted the comfort of not remembering. I focused my eyes on the scratched conference table and the hideous typewriter that dominated it like the monster it was.

"Do you want to talk?" Zelkowicz asked, the creases on his face more prominent than usual. "I suppose not. I would not want to talk either after such a cataclysmic thing."

10

I was relieved when his hand lifted from my shoulder. It was not until much later that day that I read what he wrote about the incident. I immersed myself in my role as the group's typist. My pounding fingers on the hard-to-press keys, the loud sound of the miniature anvils striking the pages, carbon paper between them, deafened me to the echoing, pleading voices of Miriam and Regina tormenting my brain. I hated typing on that stubborn machine. Now, it was a relief...until I typed Zelkowicz's final paragraph in his entry dated September 14, 1942:

The populace's strange reaction to the recent events is noteworthy. There is not the slightest doubt that this was a profound and terrible shock, and yet one must wonder at the indifference shown by those—apart from the ones who were not directly affected and who would return to normal life at once—from whom loved ones had been taken. It would seem that the events of recent days would have immersed the entire population of the ghetto in mourning for a long time to come...

Didn't Zelkokwicz see I was mourning? Didn't he feel the pain I had in every part of my body and soul? You don't need tears and shrill wailing to declare your loss to the uncaring public and deaf God. I swallowed my anger and found where I left off:

It would seem that the events of recent days would have immersed the entire ghetto in mourning for a long time to come, and yet, right after the incidents, and even during the resettlement action, the populace was obsessed with everyday concerns— getting bread, rations, and so forth—and often went from immediate personal tragedy right back into daily life.

When there is nothing, there is work. Why didn't such a learned man understand? I forced myself to continue, bile rising in my throat.

Is this some form of numbing of the nerves, an indifference, or a symptom of an illness that manifests itself in atrophied emotional reactions? After losing those nearest to them, people talk constantly about rations, potatoes, soup, etc.! It is beyond comprehension! Why this lack of warmth toward those they loved?

"Lack of warmth?" Simmering, I forced myself to read on:

Naturally, here and there, there are some mothers weeping in a corner for a child or children shipped from the ghetto, but as a whole, the mood of the ghetto does not reflect last week's terrible ordeal. Sad but true!

It was signed Jozef Zelkowicz. It should have been signed, "Cold-blooded." We rarely signed our entries. Was he proud of it? I closed my eyes, overcome by anger. "I feel the pain," I wanted to shout into his face, but what was the point? Why should I care what a pompous fool thinks?

Singer, the 'gadfly,' would have excoriated Jozef's assumption that hunger made us forget the children we held in our arms. I typed his sanctimonious review verbatim, though it infuriated me how little he understood that the root cause of our dead emotions lay in our disbelief and helplessness. The clatter of the keys was a violent rainstorm drowning out all sound, thought, memory. As I typed Jozef's analysis, the thoughts of one who had lost nothing in the upheaval, a dull drum throbbed behind my eyes. I typed and typed, praying my work would not end, even for nightfall. Though I was convinced the chronicle was meaningless, solely for the Chairman's vanity, it was all I had. I did not even have the relief of revealing my anguish. Zelkowicz was right. Everything about our lives was sad, but unfortunately, true. Yet, like most people in the ghetto, I held onto hope that the war would soon end, and we'd be reunited with our loved ones. That's what kept me going. If we could hold out a little longer...a little longer.

CHAPTER 3

SEPTEMBER 1-19, 1942
WEATHER
During the first twenty days of September, the weather was lovely and sunny, with only a few brief showers.

"Weather?" Heilig asked, eyeing me anxiously from across the table.

I'd lost the steam to attack him again. I found it unsettling that I, the logical engineer, had gone for him with fists, pounding his stomach until he doubled over and spat out that Singer had died in Warsaw. I apologized but suspected he was wary of my losing control again.

"Why do we waste our precious time on the weather?" Heilig asked Zelkowicz, avoiding eye contact with me.

I studied Bernard Heilig, our youngest member, comparing him to Oscar, Dr. Oscar Singer, for whom he was taking over. There was no comparison, though he had finally revealed the two were cousins. Singer was a reckless, long-haired scoundrel capable of anything, even trysts with a friend's wife…holding that same friend's newborn baby while… No, I didn't want to think about that. My soul was tortured by such thoughts. Heilig had to be my focus. "The Weasel," I called him because of his lean and timid appearance. Darting eyes, narrow, sly, promised not one morsel of the hope Singer represented …hope of escape from the barbed-wire enclosed ghetto and the armed Nazi sentries. Those robotic guards viewed Jews unfortunate enough to venture near the wire, or who placed themselves there deliberately (yes, deliberately) as clay ducks in their shooting gallery.

13

I was interrupted by Zelkowicz asking, "Ostrowski, are you alright?"

My mind strayed frequently. Being reported lax or ill, I could lose this job. Rumkowski hammered into us with every speech that those who did not, or could not work, risked 'resettlement.' I had to remain in the ghetto to await Miriam and Regina's return. They must find me here. "The weather, you ask? Note the last sentences of my entry."

Heilig recited them by heart. I envied his photographic memory, but imagine not being able to forget all that had befallen us since the ghetto was established by the Nazis a little more than two years ago? How could anyone live with such memories? But, not being Singer, he did not possess the passion, the emotions, that made our gadfly relentlessly poke holes in our leader's policies. Singer had also questioned including weather in our daily records. I repeated to my newer colleagues what I said to him, Cukier, and Rosenfeld at the start of our dangerous enterprise, "The weather impacts multiple aspects of our lives here in the ghetto." I leaned close to Zelkowicz. "It is also a disguise for what we include in a document that is forbidden by the Nazis."

Zelkowicz, who resembled Rosenfeld in some ways, creased face, tired eyes, stooped-over shoulders, nodded slowly. "Yes, that makes sense. Unharvested fields in a rare period of conducive weather suggest manpower shortages, I suppose. Is that what you mean?"

"Nobody will read this shit in the future," Heilig grumbled.

He sounded like Singer, but without the charm. "The Chairman reads every entry daily. It is our duty to our benefactor to portray things in their most positive light." I remembered our Chairman, the Eldest of the Jews, looking up at me from a pile of papers on which he was placing checkmarks after our first tense interview. His words were inscrutable to me then: "One day, we will be judged." It was for his posterity that he wanted this chronicle. It was for how he would be judged by the future that the Eldest of the Jews accepted the risk of having our work discovered by the Nazis who worked and prowled in the same building. And, as Singer had argued, it was for this judging that we were compelled to support Rumkowski's actions...even when he issued that life-changing command,

"Give me your children."

"Ostrowski? You drifted off again. You were talking about the weather," Zelkowicz said, a worried look on his face. "Perhaps, you should go home...."

"No!" I glared at him though he didn't deserve it. I grabbed a sheet of paper. It was the month's entries for Deaths and Births. Why did I have to randomly grab that? My hands shook, but I forced myself to type:

DEATHS AND BIRTHS

On September 1—56 deaths, no births

On September 2—46 deaths, no births

On September 3—62 deaths, 2 births (1 boy, 1 girl).

A girl? I felt such joy at Regina's birth. She was a candle of hope for Miriam and me. Children are hope. Tiny pink toes wiggled free of her thin coverlet. The same blanket I draped over her in the closet..."Play hide and seek. Shhh." Type! Type.

On September 4— 35 deaths, no births.

"Where are the records for September 5 and 6?" I shouted for no logical reason.

Heilig and Zelkowicz searched their piles of departmental notes and shook their heads.

I dug in my pile and found a report to the authorities, our euphemism for the German Ghetto Authority, from the Burial Department. Why was I filled with a sense of relief? I calmed behind the typewriter, my one trusted friend, and poking a letter at a time, finished the list as if it were one of Singer's play scripts or Rosenfeld's philosophical articles:

On September 5 and 6—93 deaths, no births

On September 7—47 deaths, no births

On September 8—53 deaths, no births

On September 9—68 deaths, no births

On September 10—72 deaths, no births

On September 11—51 deaths, no births

On September 12 and 13—68 deaths, no births

On September 14—29 deaths, 1 boy born

A boy? Moses? A boy who might lead us from bondage. There had to be more pages. I rifled through the sheets of paper.

On September 15 and 16— 29 deaths, no births

On September 17—26 deaths, 2 boys, 3 girls born

2 boys? 3 Girls? I didn't want to think of Regina, but there were girls born? I typed: *September 18—16 deaths, no births.* "Where are the rest?" I pulled through the pile again. "No more?" I'd run out of reports. I looked up. Heilig and Zelkowicz were staring at me as if I were a lunatic in an asylum.

"You were reading out loud," Zelkowicz said.

Heilig was silent. Was that pity in his eyes?

"I'm sorry. I didn't realize I was disturbing my learned friends...."

"It is alright. We all have a right to go slightly insane." Zelkowicz bit his lip. "You have been at this for a long time. I can't imagine how you bear the weight...."

"The suicide reports. I'll do them now," I interrupted, holding out my hand. It was still extended when the door burst open.

CHAPTER 4

I jumped to attention at the sound of the door opening. We were ordered to greet any German with a formal salute or face "severe punishment." Their intrusions, unannounced, had become frequent. I sagged with relief when I recognized Neftalin. I had not seen the Deputy for nearly a month, and he looked different from the spit-shined bureaucrat who had interviewed me. His slicked-back black hair was marred by strands of gray. His coat, fur collar not yet confiscated as were all furs, showed wear on the elbows. His eyes, once eager, full of light, looked weary, black smears around them. "I have news," he said before I could ask about Miriam and Regina.

"Another deportation?" I asked, fearing the worst.

"No. God forbid. We had a fire."

Zelkowicz came closer. "Another one? There have been several fires lately."

"I wish the whole damn slum would burn," I muttered.

Neftalin glanced at me but said nothing, perhaps knowing not to confront me at this time. The others may have warned him of my instability. More likely, he read it in my eyes.

Heilig, pen over paper, looked hungry for news. "Where was the fire? Was it serious? Did anyone die?" How many of his neighbors burning to death would satisfy the Weasel's lust for something different to report about?

Neftalin removed his hat. "I would say it was the largest in the history of the ghetto."

"Where was it?" Heilig repeated.

Damn ghoul. I hated the sight of him.

Neftalin leaned against the wall. "It started in an apartment house, 12 Jakuba Street."

"When did it start?" Heilig asked, writing furiously on his pad.

"Around noon. The Jewish Fire Department was called."

"They're useless," Heilig muttered. "No horses allowed to Jews, not even to pull our antiquated fire wagons."

"The German Fire Department soon arrived." Neftalin wiped his brow of sweat.

That awoke me. "The Germans came to fight the fire?"

Neftalin smiled as if welcoming me back after a prolonged absence. "The fire threatened neighboring buildings, including the workshops."

Heilig gave a bitter laugh. "They didn't give a shit about the apartment building, but the factories they need."

"For their snowsuits," Zelkowicz said. "They're freezing their balls off in Russia." He chuckled. "Hitler should study history better. He'd know about Napoleon's fate. We shouldn't be making snowsuits for the Nazis. We should be making burial shrouds."

I shot Jozef a warning look.

Neftalin didn't look happy either but remained silent.

"Were the factories saved?" Heilig asked.

"Yes, but Hans Biebow, head of the German administration, showed up with criminal investigators. Our Chairman was there as well."

Heilig stopped writing. "Rumkowski was there?"

The Chairman hadn't made a public appearance since his terrible speech: "Give me your children." Rumors were that he was terrified of his own people. Others claimed he was a prisoner of the Nazis, forced to do their bidding or face brutal consequences. He now had a wife, a hostage, the authorities could use to keep him in line.

Neftalin rubbed his chin. "It was the largest fire I've ever seen. It was not fully extinguished until four-thirty in the afternoon. Thankfully, nobody was killed."

18

"Amen," Zelkowicz said.

"Amen," Neftalin echoed. "Thank God."

"That no one died or that their precious factories weren't damaged?" I let out.

Neftalin looked at me as if he knew this was uncharacteristic, something Singer, our resident cynic, might have taunted. "Engineer, I suppose in these strange times we should consider ourselves blessed that our factories were spared. God knows what the authorities will do if these fires persist."

"God and the Germans," I said.

"Yes, God and the Germans." Neftalin pulled up his collar and left the room.

"And the Chairman. He knows." I heard Singer's familiar refrain echo, though he was long gone from our chamber.

As I walked home, I inhaled the smoke rising from Jakuba Street. It was thicker than the usual from the factory smokestacks. It also stank. It must have been some destructive fire, I thought, smiling at the hope that someday soon a spark placed in the right location might engulf this ghetto, the jealously-guarded property of the Reich, and send it to the hell it deserved. Singer had derided the Chairman's policies aimed at forging the ghetto into a manufacturing hub for Hitler. He accused Rumkowski of being deluded, self-serving, a collaborator, interested only in saving his own life and wealth. He had passionately urged us to rise up against our oppressors, but I argued back that we had no weapons. The wolves kept us starving, too weak to fight. "Fight without guns! Use the legendary Jewish ingenuity to sabotage them at every turn! Use explosives, fists, resistance. Use your bodies...alive, dead...resist in the face of their bullets." How reckless and foolish I thought he was. How disturbed I was when my sweet wife echoed his criticism of the Chairman's policies. I couldn't imagine their connection. I was blind, blind to everything.

The smoke was thicker, the air acrid, pungent. The apartment building was a body bent to the ground. Bricks were strewn, wood blackened, the few bits of personal property still allowed to its residents were burnt to ash or smoldering. Everything was too hot even for thieves to steal. There were black streaks on several neighboring buildings. Lacking alleyways, the fire jumped, a voracious cat, from its first feeding ground to vulnerable neighbors. The black teeth marks were everywhere, even on the doors of the factories, but the yellow stars were still conspicuous on their wood skin. "Fire can be our weapon," I heard Singer urging, and for the first time in a month, I walked home feeling a little hopeful. When the bells rang again in the dark of night, I prayed the flames would not go out until every Nazi was burned to ash.

CHAPTER 5

MONDAY, SEPTEMBER 21, 1942
NORMAL WORK ON THE DAY OF ATONEMENT
Great appreciation and gratitude were felt for the especially good and substantial midday meal—a potato and pea dish cooked with bones—that was served to mark the holiday...

Yom Kippur, the sacred Day of Atonement, was canceled by the authorities. God didn't care. So, why should I give a damn? I had no family with whom to worship, and the Nazis had burned down our synagogues. Our benevolent hosts wanted to destroy the last string attaching Jews to this life, our faith. Even I, an atheist, muttered God's name in my sleep, as directionless, I was merely existing. Without Miriam and Regina, I had no one I shared my life with except the two men to whom I was chained by our bookkeeping.

"Yom Tov," Zelkowicz exclaimed when I had barely one foot in our workroom.

"A good holiday to you," I said, removing my coat. Feeling cold, I put it back on. Rosenfeld always complained of the cold, rubbing his hands together until I'd given him gloves I'd taken from a corpse on the street. Such flashbacks that popped up spontaneously upset me. Was I becoming insane? "You're here early, Jozef," I said, not knowing what else to say.

"I have nowhere else to go. I remember when I was a boy, my brothers, and I...." He gulped hard. "I had two brothers. Older. They're gone."

I should have said I was sorry but couldn't. New grief trumps old pain.

21

"Anyway, my father used to scream at us from the rooster's crowing to get up and get dressed for shul. He'd yell so loud to get us to the synagogue that I hated holidays. Yom Kippur was the worst." He laughed. "Not only did he force us to fast from sunrise to sunset, or he would scream at us again, but we had to stay in synagogue all day. Can you imagine not eating all day and having to stand and sit and stand and sit and stand and sit all day too? I tell you it was torture."

"But you took it," I said, reminded how we Jews take everything without rising up against our tormentors. My own father, a rabbi, forced me to pray daily until I escaped to college. Even then, he pressed me to follow in his footsteps, become a rabbi. He filled me with guilt. I grew to hate him. I hated him so much that I didn't care when, abruptly, the letters I sent were returned, "addressee unknown." I didn't work very hard when I couldn't find out where the Germans sent him when Lublin was evacuated. Jews disappeared...

Zelkowicz shook his head. "No, I rebelled. In fact, and I know you won't believe it, I took off one time and got myself laid. Don't look so shocked. I was once as young as you."

Rosenfeld would never have spoken like this. I felt an unexpected warmth for this man I considered a stranger, an easily forgettable replacement for my departed Professor. "You got laid on Yom Kippur?" I hadn't laughed in a long time.

Zelkowicz leaned closer, a rotting gum odor coming from his mouth. "Why not? I hated Yom Kippur. It was hypocritical that my father prayed all day after screaming at me, my brothers, and my mother, God bless her soul. And then, the very next day after admitting all his sins, apologizing to God, he did all the same things again. I was young and idealistic. I saw this as hypocrisy. You understand?"

"Yes." I backed away. His breath reminded me too much of decaying corpses.

"Why should I be forced to pray for forgiveness? He was the sinner, not I. I had nothing to atone for...not until I shtupped that girl on the holiest day of the year. What was her name?" Jozef laughed again. "I'd like to thank her."

I wished I could thank Miriam for all she had done for me and apologize for having failed her, failed to protect her. I will, someday soon, I thought. "I never liked Yom Kippur either," I confided.

"Nobody does," Jozef replied. "But now that the Nazis have taken it away from us, I feel different about it. I realize it is important to fight for our faith."

"Maybe, you should get laid again?" I cast him a wicked smile.

"It wouldn't hurt." He sighed. "But seriously, will you do something for me? As a friend?"

I nodded.

Jozef stood. He took my hands, and in a voice that reminded me of my father when I was a boy, a voice tinged with tears, he sang softly, "Baruch atah Adonai Elohenu Melech haolam sheheheyanu, vekeyimanu, vehigianu lazman hazeh." He looked at me. "Please, say Amen? Humor an old man's lunacy?"

"Amen," I said.

He released my hand. "Do you know what that prayer means?" he asked.

"Yes." It was the prayer I said when I tried to reach God's ears months ago. "Blessed are thou, O Lord, our God, King of the Universe, who has allowed me to live to this day."

Jozef clapped his hands. "The atheist remembers?" He put his hands on my shoulders. "By saying this prayer, you acknowledge that God created you. It is by his consent that we live and die, not by our own will." He gazed deeply into my eyes. "No matter how others make us suffer, even now, we need always remember we must not destroy what God creates. Do you understand?"

This stranger was lecturing me? I had a hilarious thought: he is afraid I'm going to kill myself and become another nameless statistic in our chronicle. Doesn't he understand I have to stay alive? Miriam and Regina have to find me here when they return, so why would I not fight for every breath of life? I was about to respond when the door opened. As always, I froze.

Heilig entered. A rare smile on his face revealed several teeth broken

23

when he was tortured by the SS, or so he alleged. He looked at me and said, "A shipment of large machines arrived for the carpentry shops."

I stared into the Weasel's face. What did it mean? I gave him a curious look, and he nodded his head. Was it possible? Earlier, Singer had hidden in a shipment of sewing machines when he was smuggled from the ghetto. But he said that others trying that subterfuge were captured, executed. Their bodies had been left hanging from gallows in the square, a warning to others. Heilig mentioned, "large machines." I looked at him again, but Jozef was too near. *Trust no one. But Heilig looked excited. Could Singer have returned?*

Heilig held up a sheet of paper. "Don't you understand? We've just received large orders from the military for fur coats."

I was disappointed. I'd hoped the Weasel's emphasizing of "large machines" meant Singer was back. If anyone could find Miriam and Regina for me...

Heilig laughed. "Fur coats! It's almost over! The Huns are freezing and getting their asses kicked in Russia. All these new fur uniforms imply they are sending thousands of reinforcements. They need us to make their damn coats, or they'll all freeze to death."

Jozef smiled. "For once, Father, I have something for which to atone. I wish every goddamn German suffers the worst death possible, and Hitler too."

"Amen," Heilig said.

"Amen," I said, picturing a tundra covered in thick snow, German bodies in our white coats, staring up with dead eyes at the star-lit sky. "Please, God, please, hear us at last?"

CHAPTER 6

T UESDAY, SEPTEMBER 22, 1942
No sooner had the wounds of the horrible last ten days ceased bleeding than dreadful news again swept through the ghetto. The local authorities have been ordered to evacuate a large part of the ghetto within a few weeks...

Zelkowicz stopped writing. "I must move again," he said. "They are removing most of the Marysin quarter from the ghetto."

"You live in that area?"

"Where do you live?"

"Near the cemetery."

"A safe place to live," Heilig let out a bitter laugh. "That's one place they can't do without."

"Even the Germans would not desecrate the dead," Jozef said.

"Do you actually believe they respect our Jewish dead?" Heilig asked.

Jozef sighed. "No. They respect nothing. But the cemetery grows larger as it welcomes more of our brothers and sisters."

Heilig looked thoughtful, a small map spread before him. "This area they are shutting off from the ghetto houses many of our factories."

"May I see that?" I leaned over the map. "You're right. Why would they seal that area off from the ghetto? The new shoe factory, the tailoring shops, and metal shops are located there."

Jozef peered over our shoulders and then straightened up. "You are missing the main point." He pointed his finger, a black bruise visible under his filthy nail. "This area is the largest cultivated area in the ghetto."

I looked again. "This is a big loss if it's true."

"It used to be a garbage dump," Jozef said. "It took great effort to turn it into fertile soil." He shivered. "The wolves are trying to starve us to death. I may lose my home, but that is no matter. This is a loss we can't make up."

"The Chairman won't allow it," I said. *But he'd allowed them to take our children.*

Jozef sucked at his teeth. "I saw the Chairman himself supervising the relocation of more than 5,000 residents from the area."

Heilig hissed, "Anything to save his skin."

"We'll have to see how this develops. Meanwhile, you may move in with me. If you like?" Loneliness made me offer that.

Jozef looked as if he was fighting tears. "Thank you. The Housing Department designated housing for me."

That chilled me. I don't know why. "Jozef, I insist. The company will do me good." It would only be until Miriam and Regina returned.

"I do not wish to inconvenience you."

"Jews must help each other," I said, thinking of Rosenfeld's ransacked flat.

As Jozef and I walked to my apartment that afternoon, I heard a train approaching the Marysin station. Jozef looked too weak to survive a long train ride to the northern farmlands. Miriam was stronger and would protect Regina. I couldn't wait until this damn war ended, and I'd hold my child again.

As we reached my tenement, Jozef turned to me and said, "I hope you don't mind snoring?"

CHAPTER 7

L ITZMANNSTADT GHETTO
SEPTEMBER 25, 1942
Absolutely nothing is known about the fate of any people resettled from the ghetto. After the last resettlement there is no one in the ghetto over the age of 65 or under the age of 10.

Zelkowicz never mentioned my role in helping him escape from the deportation. Had he remained in his building, like others there, he would have been transported to rural farmlands. It was not a cozy partnership. He was not someone who compromised but insisted on having his own way, even in what had been my flat. To be fair, he warned me that he snored loudly. Strangely, I found that, at first, reassuring. Analyzing my reactions, it was because his snoring, the sound of breathing, was an affirmation that we were both still here, still alive. Perhaps most annoying were his efforts at counseling, which I should have appreciated, but resisted. "There's nothing wrong with me," I said yesterday after his needling.

"You are mourning. It's natural to mourn your loss."

"You 'mourn' the dead. Miriam is not dead. Regina is not...neither of them are. I am not mourning!"

Jozef smugly replied, "Of course, you are right. Yes, of course."

There was no escape from Jozef. At night, in our one-room flat, we were locked together. The curfew and blackout imposed by the Chairman, and now, Zelkowicz, transformed my flat into a prison cell. "Let's discuss something else," I suggested.

Jozef, 'Mr. Cheerful,' sitting in Miriam's chair, muttered, "While I am thankful for your help, I sometimes wonder if I would be better off had I joined the others and volunteered for resettlement."

I'd have been better off. "The devil you know is better than the devil you don't," I said, wishing he'd go to sleep and leave me in my misery.

"I suppose, but you've heard many are getting sick here." He leaned forward. "My friend, typhus is spreading. In our crowded conditions, quarantining those already ill is impossible."

"I'm sure the Chairman is aware and will act accordingly." I shifted in my chair.

"Haven't you heard? The emergency medical services are to be abolished. The disease is running rampant. It will exterminate all of us if not checked soon."

"You're exaggerating," I said, but in the back of my mind, I theorized how typhus, tuberculosis, and other diseases were ideal weapons for the Nazis to finish off their troublesome Jews.

Jozef pulled out his shirtfront and pointed to a brown stain. "Filth, my friend. That is our enemy."

I hated feeling dirty, but cleanliness had become impossible with a shortage of water and soap. "There's a war on. Or haven't you heard?"

Jozef scratched at his stomach. "Warm weather makes perfect conditions for typhus to spread, but I tell you, filth is the true cause of the plague. We live in filth, sleep in filth. We eat without cleaning our vegetables. There is no hot water to wash them. After slaving all day in the factories, people don't wait for food to be cooked. Out of hunger, we consume half-cooked, filthy food. Filth. That, my friend, is the real cause of typhus and many of our ailments."

"The cure then is simple," I said, tired of his griping.

"Nothing is simple here. You should know that." He scratched his stomach again. "Do you expect the Germans to provide us hot water and fuel for cooking? No. But without that, and not being able to wash our bodies and clothes, we are in the throes of an epidemic that could wipe us all out." He pulled at his soiled shirt. "The Chairman has clean clothes and hot water, I can assure you." He spat on the floor. "I would be better off on a farm in the north. This waiting for disease to slowly, painfully eat you is far worse than farming." He looked at his hands. "My hands have never been in soil. I wonder how it would be to work the land as our ancient Hebrew ancestors did. I don't think it would be so terrible."

I pictured Miriam and Regina in bright sunlight picking fresh vegetables from the fertile soil somewhere in the north of Poland. I saw Miriam's hair and her lovely back as she stooped over the earth, a filled basket at her side. I heard Regina giggle with joy as she played with a shovel. "If that is where they are sending them," I said, the vision shattered by the imagined sound of a convoy of trucks entering the ghetto and pulling up to warehouses guarded by Gestapo with rifles and dogs.

"What do you mean?" Jozef asked, looking at me as if I were crazy.

"Nothing," I replied, wondering how much my new colleague knew about the mystery trucks. There had been reports of convoys of military vehicles, arriving at night, loaded to the top with clothing and shoes. Singer said he spied on these trucks. Miriam helped unload them. Rumors triggered questions about where the tons of items came from. The worst speculations were countered by the arrival of a handful of postcards from resettled residents. These brief notes relayed good news about abundant food and comfortable housing conditions our former residents were enjoying in the farmlands. I wanted to believe in those postcards. But how could I explain the thousands of shoes and undergarments, men, women, children's, baby's, all with signs of use, secretly unloaded from the trucks?

"Typhus is my greatest fear. Typhus and rats," Jozef murmured and soon was snoring.

I remained awake. If I closed my eyes, I might see Miriam running her sweet hands, palms flat, over a child's pair of trousers spread out on her worktable. Logic and mathematics told me the atrocity I suspected was not humanly possible. Even the Germans, with their advanced technology and their obsessive hate of us, were incapable of engineering such an impossible feat, an unprecedented genocide of unimaginable proportion. Jozef was worried about typhus? I was staring in disbelief at the remote possibility

29

that Hitler had managed to harness German ingenuity, its brightest, if warped, minds, to the task no other enemy had ever accomplished, the total eradication of the Jewish people. "Damn it, Singer, where did those clothes and shoes come from?"

"Only the Nazis know," Singer said.

"You're still awake?" Zelkowicz asked, punctuated by a loud yawn. "I must have dozed off."

"Your snoring keeps me awake," I lied. "You snore like an old horse."

Zelkowicz laughed. "Impossible. You know Jews are not allowed to grow old or own horses anymore."

CHAPTER 8

L ITZMANNSTADT-GETTO
SEPTEMBER 27, 1942
In his recent speech, on the 19th of this month, the Chairman alluded to the ghetto's loss of its former autonomy, but he did not go into detail, and he offered no commentary.

"You can't say that." I read the rest of Heilig's article. "The Chairman reads our entries daily." I doubted he still did. With everything going on, how would he find time to read our scribblings? Why would he bother?

"Are you serious? He finally admitted he has lost control. He admitted what my cousin, God rest his soul, often argued to deaf ears."

Zelkowicz looked frightened. "Why now? Why would he say this now?"

Heilig sneered, "The devil was alluding to the recent resettlements. He admitted that he gave the instructions for all the deportations until now."

"You have no evidence of that," I said.

"His own words are the evidence," Heilig shot back at me.

"Okay, but what of this sentence you've composed: 'This was a hard and painful blow to the Chairman, for he felt helpless before a variety of events which had borne the imprint of his will.' Isn't this conjecture on your part?"

"I think that properly states his current situation as I remember his speech." He gave me his insolent smile and said, "You do remember I am blessed with photographic memory?"

How could I forget when he continually bragged of his gift. I was about to re-enforce our duty, to put our entries in the most favorable light, when

I heard the door open. "Attention!" I shouted, jumping to my feet.

At first, it appeared no one was there. Then Neftalin, looking disheveled, entered.

"Are you alright, Deputy?" I asked, concerned by his dazed appearance.

Neftalin glanced at me, then at the others, and then back at me. "My friends," he began and stopped.

"Henryk, are you alright? What has happened?" I remained seated, fearing more bad news.

"Change is afoot. I pray it is but a bump in our long road. I don't know. I honestly don't know." Neftalin shrugged his shoulders, seeming to sink into his coat.

"Will you sit?" I asked.

"I know there are some who deride his policies, question his authority." He shot his eyes at Heilig. "Your cousin, young Oscar, God bless his soul, was often critical. Yes, I know. I even understand. But you know, when the Chairman spoke, when people saw his face on posters, it calmed their dread. Yes, they feared him, but they saw the Eldest's power as a bulwark against far worse threats."

"What is worse than dictatorship?" I heard Singer ask. *Not now, Oscar, I replied. Not now.*

Neftalin pointed at the Chairman's portrait, the only object hanging on our wall. "All this time, this poster could have been a swastika or the hated one's face...I don't say his name."

I knew he meant Hitler. Our hated enemy's portraits, backed by the Nazi flag, or fronted by lines of goose-stepping soldiers, thousands of hands raised in salute, had begun to appear in public places within the ghetto, supplanting the Chairman's image. How could an entire nation worship a man who looked nothing like the super-race he claimed Germans to be? Another puzzle in the many I had not the brain any longer to solve.

Neftalin pointed his index finger at Rumkowski's portrait, a copy of the one I'd cowered under when I first stood in his office, but smaller. I'd grown used to his imperious stare, the wild white hair spreading out from under his felt fedora. That day, clutching his summons, I felt as if there

32

were two sets of his hard eyes hypnotizing me to obey his power.

Neftalin's finger shook, his voice quivered. "People believed in his power and authority. That gave them hope. Yes, they feared his strength but were grateful the Germans had given him that authority. Can you understand that? Am I not making sense?"

I nodded.

Heilig and Jozef were silent.

Neftalin aimed his eyes at me, our club's presumptive leader, now that Julian had vanished. "The authorities vested their power in him. Everyone knew that. Time and again, he interceded, and they saw the results. Remember the retarded boy who threw the brick at the tram?"

I shook my head. I'd blocked much out, my head still throbbing from some blow I'd received…I saw the rifle butt magnified as I tried to duck from its full impact. The pain of my jaw, a constant headache, and the purple bruise reminded me of that night when I lost them. "He promised to protect our children," I wanted to scream at Neftalin. "I'm sorry, I don't remember…."

"How can you forget such a thing? They were going to shoot 200 of us at random. There was a German officer on the train when the rock smashed his window." Neftalin looked angry. "Everyone forgets the good he does."

"Yes. I recall that now."

"And well, you should. We should all remember how this time, and so many others, our Chairman bravely fought for us. He saved 200 Jews from randomly being selected to be shot because a retarded boy threw a rock at a tram."

Heilig muttered, "He was the master of the ghetto."

I shot him a warning look.

Neftalin stared at Singer's cousin as he had often stared at Singer. "Yes, the authorities made our Chairman sole master of the ghetto. That is how he worked miracles. Do you think that was a bad thing for us?"

I had no answer.

Heilig was scowling. Singer would not have let this opportunity pass without arguing that collaborating with the enemy isn't fighting them.

Neftalin sighed. "We will soon see, I'm afraid. Things have changed. As of today, the Chairman no longer runs the factories. The Germans have seized control and are already reducing the number of employees and increasing the hours the rest of us must work. All holidays are now days of work. All. No excuses." He handed me a proclamation. "Little by little, we are losing our freedom, which not all of us appreciated before."

"Do you know how many employees the Germans will terminate?" I asked, understanding the implication for those no longer vital to their production. Was our work vital?

Neftalin chuckled. "Always the numbers man, even after all you've been through? No, they are keeping us in suspense. But I assure you that soon everyone will, in some way, feel the impact of greater intrusion by the authorities in every aspect of our lives. Even those that hate him the most will pray for the days of our Chairman's wise administration."

Neftalin's warning was prophetic. On September 30, all workers in the ghetto, in all departments, were ordered, in a circular signed by the Chairman, to work twelve hours daily: 7:30 a.m. to 8:00 p.m., with one hour off for lunch, and on Saturdays, from 7:30 until 2:00 p.m. The final line on the proclamation was, "and I will dismiss without notice all employees who fail to observe these instructions."

"And so it begins," Zelkowicz said. "Nobody can work twelve-hour shifts for very long. How will they get their food? They will go home and drop into their poor excuse for beds, exhausted and starving. If the typhus doesn't get them, this will."

Heilig raised his fist in the air. "The workers will rebel. They'll strike. At long last, they'll say enough!"

"Do you think so? It's a fool's dream. Do you think the authorities will be as lenient as the Eldest of the Jews?"

"Then they'll slow down production. Some deliberately, others from hunger, exhaustion, and illness," Heilig said. "What can our Chairman do about that?"

"His policy has always been those who do not work are expendable. We all know what that means. The workers know too. No, the best solution to all our suffering is the end of this damn war. But as long as that is out of our control, we must make everyone aware of the dire consequences of not pulling one's weight." I thought of Rosenfeld and Cukier, the former lost to me because of his age, and the latter because of health. I remembered my shock at seeing a large 'A' stamped on Cukier's chest, a secret he kept from us. That 'A' haunted me. It meant he was branded to someday soon be removed from our ghetto…my friend. My hand reached in my coat pocket for Rosenfeld's pipe bowl. I glared at Heilig and said, "No, in this department, at least, we will adhere without question to whatever demands are made of us. No more discussion."

Grumbling, Heilig went back to his work.

Jozef nodded his approval.

I fed the 'monster' three sheets of paper, carbon paper inserted in between. I couldn't risk being deported when I was sure the need for increased production of military goods, and the sending of more of our laborers to other parts of Poland and Germany was evidence the Nazis were losing the war. I felt the end was near, but always the numbers man, I shivered that our population had dropped to 89,446 after 20,000 Jews had been deported from the ghetto in one month. I couldn't believe such a feat was possible. The implications were frightening. If I could be assured that I would be reunited with my wife and child, I would gladly have climbed onto the trains, but nobody could tell me where they were. Nobody knew where anyone who left the ghetto now was. I had no choice. I had to find a way to remain here, even if everyone else was removed. I searched for places where I could hide if the resettlement actions began again. I was becoming another Singer, the playboy, the black marketeer, my wife's seducer, restrained by no moral barriers, guided solely by my determination to survive for my family.

CHAPTER 9

"**S**UNDAY, OCTOBER 4, 1942

  The Mortality Office reported today that 56 people have died in the ghetto. This number includes..."

I stopped typing and turned to Bernard Heilig. He was reading a different memo. How could he do that after writing about the latest unprecedented atrocity? Didn't anything touch him? *Are we all dead inside? Is that how we cope?*

"Are you alright, Engineer?"

"I'm fine, Doctor," I said and realized I'd mistaken Zelkowicz's voice for that of my lost friend, Rosenfeld. "I'm sorry, Jozef."

"It's understandable. Just when you think the worst is over, the authorities do something else to upset the apple cart."

I aimed my eyes at Heilig. "Nothing affects him."

"Different people have various ways of dealing with such traumatic experiences. I am sure he is also dealing with the horror, but in his own way." Jozef touched my shoulder. "None of us speak much of the past. To live on, we try to forget...." He choked up. "I must get back to work."

I watched him return to his chair, the same seat which had been my friend's throne. I thought no one could take our eldest member's place. When Jozef looked up, I realized I'd let down my guard and was starting to be fond of him. "Does anyone know who the victims were?" I asked, unable to see the men's faces from the rear of the crowd in the square. I no longer feared hearing Singer's name among the executed, now that I believed he was dead. That was small consolation for what we had been forced to witness. My mind reverted to a few hours ago. There was a knock—to be exact, three barely audible knocks—on our door. Anyone knocking once was unusual, but seeing a woman enter our room nearly kicked me back in my chair.

She remained by the door, eyes peering around the room.

"Are you in the right room?" I asked.

"Is this the Chronicles?" She looked down at her shoes, which I noticed were stuffed with paper, scraps hanging off the back of her flat heels. "Deputy Neftalin sent me. You are all summoned to the square." She pulled her coat tight around her thin frame.

"Thank you, Miss," I replied.

"Mrs."

"Mrs."

"It must be another of his damn speeches," Heilig grunted, weasel eyes studying our visitor.

With Singer, the playboy, I would have worried about lustful thoughts, but his cousin seemed little interested in the opposite sex. He never shared his exploits as his cousin had done…until Miriam. "Will you accompany us?" I asked.

"Are you the one called Engineer? Bernard Ostrowski?" Her eyes probed my face. Blue, almost gray eyes.

"I am."

"My name is Pola Levinski. I was directed to report to you."

"Neftalin sent you?" Now, I studied her, wondering why the Deputy had sent a woman into our male den.

"I'm from Warsaw." She glanced at me. "We better hurry. There will be time to talk later."

Warsaw? I ran to catch up with her. "How did you get here?"

"I see friends there," Heilig said, and before I could protest, he shot off in the direction of three men I did not know. I wondered if they were also 'friends' of Singer, black marketers, smugglers, or worse.

Zelkowicz caught up to us, breathing heavily. "Now, I not only snore like a horse, but I also breathe like one."

"Look there," Pola interrupted, a hard look on her face.

In the distance, over many rows of heads, on the elevated wooden stage, beams of wood, uniform in height, rose, naked trees, toward the sky.

"Oh, God." I counted. "There are twenty." My body tensed.

Zelkowicz's lips moved in silent prayer.

I'd forgotten about the woman. "They wouldn't dare. Not this many."

Pola said, "They're capable of anything."

I looked at her, but an announcement blaring through speakers on the square forced my attention to the front.

German soldiers with rifles, others with machine guns, took aim. If we voiced protests or dared to rush the Nazi officials lined up on the stage, or our Chairman in his tweed coat and fedora hat, looking lost among the Aryan masters, they were ready.

A series of automobiles rolled past a machine gun station. They were followed by four military vehicles.

"What the hell is going on?" I couldn't see who was dismounting from the rear of the trucks. Then I counted eighteen men being marched up the wood stairs to the platform. Though I knew none were Singer, since he was killed, I strained my eyes but could not see over the crowd. I did not believe even the Nazis were capable of such an outrageous act, but then remembered they had hung three men, one a teenager, before in public. But eighteen? Surely, they would fear the effect of this barbaric act on the crowd. Would they risk incensing us to rebel against them with our pent-up hate? Would their troops, though bristling with weapons, risk a tidal wave of violence such a brutal act might unleash against them? Did they possess enough bullets to quell a spontaneous uprising from tens-of-thousands of Jews who, though bare-handed, might tear out their eyes and throats before they gunned us down? Who was I kidding? We had been starved and beaten, so our brains were mush, and our muscles had atrophied. We were zombies without the strength to be a threat. We hadn't fought for our children.

"They're slipping the hoods over their heads," Pola rasped.

"Eighteen?" I couldn't believe it. "Don't look," I cautioned.

"I've seen worse."

"Baruch atah Adonai," Zelkowicz whispered his useless prayers.

Others were moving their lips, eyes closed, but many were directing stone-dead eyes at the stage. I wondered if any saw my eyes. What did they look like from the outside?

There was a loud command.

The nooses were being slipped around the men's necks. Most of the victims were standing on their own, but several were held up by guards. I noted the yellow stars on the guards' armbands. "Oh God," I let slip from my parched lips. "Not so many."

The thousands of souls trapped in this limbo stared in silence, many praying for some reprieve, many resigned to yet another unspeakable tragedy.

I clutched to hope. Even after the sharp command came blasting through the loudspeakers, I didn't believe it would happen. At the gasps from the crowd, my eyes shot to the sight of eighteen pairs of legs struggling to reach the blocks of wood that had been kicked from under their feet. I reeled backward, on legs that could have been those dangling on the gallows.

Pola stared at the gallows in icy silence.

I couldn't do that. I also couldn't face Pola. The expression in her eyes and on her lips reminded me of what I'd seen on my young wife Miriam's face the night I accused her of loving Singer, the night I made her hate me. "How could you suspect me of betraying you?" Miriam had spat at me. The letter, Singer's damn farewell letter. He'd placed it in my coat pocket before he escaped the ghetto. He said he loved her…Regina too…and then had the nerve to say he loved me as well. He could have been one of these unfortunate souls dangling in front of me…but no more. I turned my head. Pola was there.

Pola's look of ice-cold rage didn't matter. This woman worked for Neftalin, perhaps for the Chairman. She delivered their message that brought me out here to witness this mass execution. I began to walk to our building, unconscious of how many others left and how many remained.

Unlike the first public hanging I'd witnessed, I did not intend to revisit the site. I forced myself that first time to return to the surreal scene…searching the victims' contorted faces, praying none were Singer. No need this time. Someone was walking next to me. I expected to see Jozef. "What is it? May I help you?"

"I've been assigned to your department," Pola replied.

"No," shot out of my mouth.

CHAPTER 10

T UESDAY, OCTOBER 13, 1942
A DELIVERY OF POTATOES
On the night of October 12, shipments of potatoes arrived here unexpectedly, and in amounts unprecedented for the ghetto. 118 loads arrived, and thus, overnight, the ghetto was faced with difficult problems...

"This is one for the books," I said after Pola read the memo from the Department of Food Supply. "We complain when we're starving and now gripe when we're swimming in potatoes. Are Jews ever happy?"

"We haven't enough storage facilities," Jozef muttered.

"That's not the problem. The Department lost most of its manpower," Heilig said. "Every worker not deemed essential has been terminated, most resettled." He laughed. "Our Chairman should call out his police force, the Order Service. That department is growing by leaps and bounds. He enlisted every able-bodied man. Surely, they are capable of dealing with a few potatoes. Imagine our most virile officers chasing after runaway potatoes." He burst into laughter.

"The police have more important matters than dealing with potatoes," I said. "I think Rumkowski is fearful he is losing control over the criminal elements. That is why he is beefing up his police." I held up a proclamation. "I will read this to you. 'A warning that concerns every inhabitant of the ghetto:' is the heading in bold letters."

"Is it about the potato invasion?" Heilig joked.

I shot him a stern look. "This is not a joking matter, as you will see when

41

I finish reading this. If you don't mind?" Seeing he was cowed, I continued, "Recently, there has been an increase in robberies, a serious offense against the wartime economy, and two...."

Heilig cut in, "Get to the point. The Chairman harps on criminal behavior in every speech. What is new here? At least, the invasion of potatoes is different."

I was losing patience with Singer's cousin. "Very well, here it is: 'Effective immediately every instance of theft will be punished with the harshest possible penalty.'"

"That is nothing new," Heilig said. "Idle threats. The Chairman has said all this before."

"The proclamation is signed by Biebow, the German administrator," I said.

Jozef, who had been silent, muttered, "The Chairman's name has been removed from the factories as well."

"Even in Warsaw, we heard of your Chairman," Pola said. "We heard he was a highly respected administrator."

Zelkowicz looked uneasy. He had cornered me earlier and asked if I could do something to get our newest arrival removed from our midst. "I have nothing against women," he said, "but having her in our chamber will limit our discourse." He bit his lip. "Of course, you understand."

"Treat her like a man," I said but was also uneasy about having a woman with three men who had grown accustomed to a female-less society within our workroom.

Jozef shook his head. "My god! The room stinks of men. How will she be comfortable? Why does she want to be with us?"

I thought of Pola's expression, stone-like, during the mass execution. "I don't think we need to worry about her," I laughed. "I'm more worried about you." His nerves were severely frayed. I felt he was cracking under the strain of all that was happening to us.

Jozef stormed away, but I caught him muttering, "Next, you'll invite her to live with us."

"Right." I hadn't even surveyed her appearance, other than her over-sized shoes stuffed with paper and eyes whose intensity I couldn't get past.

Heilig grunted. He showed no inkling that a woman joining our team was of interest. "The damn Chairman is a legend," he said in a mocking tone.

Jozef frowned. "We have a woman present," he said, pointing his nose at Pola.

Heilig studied Pola for several seconds as if he had not noticed that she was a female.

I was about to interject when Pola spoke, "You need not concern yourselves with my gender. We are all the same here. Treat me as you do all your members."

"I can't do that," Jozef said. "I was raised as a gentleman."

Pola smiled at him. "Dr. Zelkowicz, my survival here in Lodz depends on being employed. If you cannot work with a woman, I will be deported again. As you know, newcomers are the first to leave."

"Again, you said?" Jozef frowned.

"Pola came from Warsaw," I supplied, hoping this would end the matter.

"You were in Warsaw? Rumors say it is worse there than here," Jozef said.

I thought I saw Pola stiffen. "It is difficult to compare one suffering to another."

Heilig whispered, "My cousin, Oscar Singer, was there. Do you know him?"

I sprang to attention. I was waiting until I had an opportunity to be alone with Pola to ask about Singer.

Pola shook her head. "There were more than 600,000 Jews in the ghetto, so who knows who is there?"

"600,000? I thought it was only 300,000," I mumbled.

Heilig smirked. "You should know, Ostrowski is our 'numbers man.' He reduces everything to statistics and ice-cold measurements. He is a calculator and unable to feel—"

"Damn you, Heilig!" I sprang from my chair.

Heilig backed away from me, his fists raised.

Pola shouted, "Jew fighting Jew?"

I faced the wall, ashamed, and said, "Forgive me." In control again, I sat down at the table.

Heilig, fists still raised, sat back on his chair. "I only wanted her to understand how different we all are."

Pola shot back, "This damn war has erased our differences."

Jozef nodded. "You're right. We've all lost loved ones." He looked at me and added, "We all have the goal of surviving so we may see our departed friends and relatives again when this war ends."

I glanced at Pola, but her face revealed no clues about her inner thoughts. I sensed she did not want to talk about Warsaw and her past. At least, not yet. I didn't blame her. I couldn't speak about Miriam and Regina without choking, tears ready to explode. Perhaps Heilig, the Weasel, was right; numbers are safer. "Mrs. Levinski, you said 600 thousand Jews have been herded into the Warsaw ghetto. Not 300 thousand, as rumored?"

Heilig's eyes rolled up in his head, but he remained silent.

Pola frowned. "It seems impossible the Germans could manage that." She looked at me. "More than 250,000 were removed this summer."

"Impossible," I said, unable to fathom the enormity of this mass deportation. "Where did the Nazis put so many people?"

Pola shrugged. "Nobody knows."

Jozef's voice was emotionless. "How many are in our ghetto still, Engineer?"

"89,000," I replied.

Jozef nodded. "Don't you see? Don't any of you see? 300 thousand, 600 thousand...if the Nazis could do it to Warsaw...." He didn't finish.

Pola's face showed no emotion. "Did you really think Lodz was immune?"

I noted her closely cropped hair, brown with touches of burnt red, and her arms, legs, and torso...she was so thin...almost a stick-figure. How did I not notice that before?

CHAPTER 11

T UESDAY, OCTOBER 20, 1942

Jozef was still living with me, a blessing, and a curse. Having to
host him and working twelve-hour shifts kept my mind from
straying into depression and insanity, plaguing so many in our ghetto.
Being employed, with memos streaming into our baskets, gave me hope
that, despite the increasing intrusiveness of the German authorities, they
needed our skills and labor for their war. A week after their unprecedented
public execution, even that was fading from my consciousness. I welcomed
the routines of our task, the blessed lack of surprises by the German
oppressors.

Walking to Balut Square, I no longer glanced at the twenty gallows. The
Germans no longer bothered to have them removed, perhaps as a warning
to us, their subjects. The fact that no one seemed to know why these men
were executed added to the message's potency. No more labor strikes. No
more throngs in the public square. No more fires.

"What do you think her story is?" Jozef asked as we walked in the mostly
barren streets toward our building.

"Who?"

Jozef stopped walking. "Who? There is only one woman in our room.
Who."

I hardly thought of Pola at all, let alone as a woman. "Oh. I don't know.
She's very competent, though."

"She's hard. For a skinny girl, barely five feet tall, she's gutsy."

"I guess she had to be, coming from Warsaw." The rumors had died down about what happened in the most populated Jewish ghetto in Europe.

"She never talks about her past," Jozef said.

"Neither do you."

He stopped walking again. "Tuberculosis," he said. "My wife coughed herself to death."

"I'm sorry. I shouldn't have asked."

Jozef scratched a scab on his face. "It was long ago."

"I'm sorry." Another sad tale to add to the many I'd collected during this war. "My wife and daughter were taken...." I couldn't finish.

"I know, my friend. We all know. The night after Rumkowski's speech."

"I tried to save them. I taught Regina 'Hide-and-seek.'"

He looked puzzled.

"I taught Regina to hide in the closet...under a coverlet...dirty laundry piled over her...." I stopped again. Did I really think that would work? Fool! Damn fool! About so much.

"I understand. Don't talk anymore."

We walked the rest of the way in silence, but he planted the seed of curiosity in me. I wondered what mysteries—we all had them—our newest member was concealing.

Before the steps of the Jewish Ghetto Administration Building, German guards with rifles had replaced Rumkowski's guards. We handed them our papers and waited for what seemed an interminable time as they scoured our valuable passes before they left us barely enough room to squeeze between them. I could grab a rifle...No, I could not. Regina.

I tried to arrive in our chamber earlier than the rest, but waiting for Zelkowicz to recite his prayers, something he did in a hushed voice every morning, delayed me. "Why don't you pray with me? It will make you feel better," he'd say.

Most of the time, I'd ignore him, but this morning he was more insistent than usual. "Your Miriam, did she not pray?"

Please, don't bring her up, I thought, giving him a look that I hoped would warn him to drop this subject.

46

"Would she not want you to pray?"

"To a God who doesn't listen?"

"God listens. It is man who does not. God said, 'Thou shalt not kill.' Does Hitler listen?"

"I'm tired of this, and we're late, as usual. Ever since you moved in with me, I'm late. Not only does God not listen to me, but you don't either."

I settled into my chair. Pola and Heilig were already sorting reports from the multiple departments, warehouses, food distribution points, and factories according to their importance. I grabbed a memo and winced. It was signed by Hans Biebow. "Crap," I said, "Listen to this. It's official now:

SIGNS IN THE GHETTO

In accordance with a Ghetto Administration directive signed by Biebow...now all signs and signboards of any kind in the ghetto may only be in German.

Jozef reached for the memo. "I saw they were painting over and tearing down anything written in Hebrew, Polish, or Yiddish. It will be such a loss...like our books."

"Rosenfeld predicted this. He said the value of our factories would make the Germans salivate to annex us, to Germanize Lodz...Litzmannstadt." I said, realizing again how much I missed my wise friend. "Did they try this in Warsaw?"

Pola shook her head. "I think this is unique. Your Chairman has made the ghetto a prize possession, but don't fool yourself, that does not extend to the Jews here."

Heilig sneered. "Just as my cousin, Oscar, argued. He urged us to fight."

I interrupted, "We have no weapons. Unlike Warsaw, we are totally sealed in. Not even your cousin could get back in."

"I don't understand," Pola said.

Jozef sounded like the teacher he was, gently explaining how Hitler, recognizing the industrial value of Lodz, had stocked the surrounding Lodz city proper with Germans and Germanized Poles. "We are in an envelope made of barbed wire, trigger-happy Nazi sentries, Gestapo, and antisemitic inhabitants, all eager to cash in on Jewish scalps. Nothing comes in or out of the ghetto without the approval of the authorities, unless in caskets."

"And yes, Pola, it is unique. Dr. Rosenfeld, one of your predecessors...a dear friend (I felt myself choking up) said many times that in all of history, he had never read of any place being so hermetically sealed off from the rest of the world."

"So, that is why you didn't fight?" Pola asked.

"How did Warsaw get weapons?" I asked.

"I don't know." Pola rolled her tongue in her cheek. "I wasn't involved. I was pregnant."

"Mazel tov! Boy or girl?" Jozef asked.

Where was her child? Did she know more than I knew about the destination of her husband and child?

"I lost the baby."

It was as if I saw her as a human being for the first time. "I'm sorry," I managed to say.

"I didn't know," Jozef said.

Heilig was silent.

Pola stood and aimed her eyes at me. "It is okay. How can we bring a child into a world like this?"

I fell back onto my chair. Those were the exact words Miriam said one night when we had just finished making love. "No more talk," I said. "We have work to do."

Jozef remained standing. I'm sure he felt awkward about what he'd said.

Pola returned to her chair, but her eyes were aimed at me as if she knew I was fighting my emotions.

A brief memo caught my attention. My God. The shoes! It was finally on paper. I gazed in disbelief: "250,000 pairs of shoes."

CHAPTER 12

SATURDAY, OCTOBER 24, 1942
MARRIAGES
There have been no marriages in the ghetto since the September evacuation. But now, prospective parties are being notified that, as of next week, the Chairman will personally perform marriages.

"I guess this is his demonstration of power. You can bet the Nazis aren't happy about this," Heilig said after he read the entry he'd written.

My mind was on the memo I'd discovered a few days ago. My hands had shook as I'd held the yellow sheet of paper and read the words, "250 thousand pairs of shoes, some of which can serve as material for repairs." It was finally out in the open. One listing by a departmental head, either accidentally or deliberately, included in a long record of how only workshop employees were being issued replacement shoes on a needs basis, confirmed what Singer had reported to me. Had this departmental manager realized what this implied, would he have included it? The factories were now under the direct control of Germans. Every document had to pass their inspection. I imagined this department head debating with his conscience, knowing the risk he was taking by including this one clause.

"There are no Negroes in the ghetto." Heilig burst into laughter.

"What did you say?" I asked, unable to focus, obsessed by the memo of October 20.

Pola's eyes were on me. "Is something wrong, Mr. Ostrowski?"

Of all the people I'd worked with, I thought she was the most observant.

If anyone suspected what I was planning, it was this painfully thin woman from Warsaw. "Heilig, you said, 'Negroes.'" I pretended to be interested.

Heilig recited the memo from memory. "Precinct VI of the German Police has inquired of the Chairman whether there are any Negroes or mulattoes in the ghetto."

Jozef remarked, "Hitler hates them both. Remember how he reacted when that American...what was his name?"

"Jesse Owens," Heilig rattled off.

"You remember everything," I said, wishing my mind was so focused. Since Miriam and Regina were taken away, I felt as if my thoughts were straying, flashbacks of the past appearing when I should have been focused on the present. The memo about the shoes changed that. It was all I could think about.

"My memory is a blessing and a curse," Heilig said, giving me a strange look. Did he suspect?

We were interrupted by Deputy Neftalin with news that three women, escapees from a labor camp in Poznan, had been lodged in Central Prison. "The Chairman hoped to learn what is happening in the German labor camps, but they are now prisoners of the German authorities." Even the frustrated look on Henryk's face did not penetrate my brain after reading that memo, that damn memo that appeared to confirm my worst fears. Where could the Nazis come up with 250 thousand pairs of shoes? Why would a departmental head state, "some can serve as material for repairs?" Why would he not say they were "new," or at least "wearable?" Burning questions.

"Engineer, are you here?" Neftalin asked. He patted my shoulder. "Come and see me later. We will talk in private." He frowned and left the room.

The others were staring at me. "Heilig, you were talking about Negroes in the ghetto." Why was Pola eyeing me? I had to remain alert, but my body was tense with anticipation as night neared, and there would be limited moonlight. It was the Sabbath night, when all the Jews rushed home for a little time with their families. The Germans knew Jews could be trusted to not cause trouble on the Sabbath. I would use that against them. "So, what did the Chairman reply?"

Heilig laughed. "The memo says, 'The Chairman was able to report that there are no Negroes in the ghetto.' Of course not. Have any of you ever seen one Negro or Mulatto in all your time here? The Huns are stupid. Their hate makes them blind." He tossed the sheet of paper on the pile. "You have to wonder how such stupid people can keep a war going so long against the rest of the world."

Pola handed me a memo under the table.

I read it in silence. "A female worker in a ghetto sorting office found a gold necklace in an old piece of clothing." I looked at her. Our eyes met. Why did you hand me this, I thought, ducking back to read the rest, "The woman turned the valuable item over to the management." The last sentence sent a chill through my body: "This is not the first case of valuables being found in clothes that were shipped here for use within the ghetto." I folded the memo.

Pola watched as I shoved it in my pocket. She must have realized its significance. She must have wondered why I did not share this new evidence with the others.

Jozef let out a low moan. "I can't bear much more of this."

Pola shot her eyes away from me. "What is it, Jozef?"

"Someone jumped from the upper platform of the bridge on Koscielny Square," he said.

Heilig snapped, "So what? We should be used to suicides by now. We don't even report them."

"Shut up, Heilig," Pola said, her eyes murderous. "Go on, Professor. What has upset you about this?"

Jozef sniffled into his handkerchief. "She was 45 years old. My wife would have been her age on the same day."

Heilig let out a low groan. "How could I know that?"

"Shut up," Pola shot at him again.

Jozef glanced at his handkerchief.

Cukier had used a nose rag. I remembered the tell-tale spots of blood. Was that what Jozef was looking for? In the time he had lived with me, I

51

realized he was a hypochondriac. He had a right to be. He revealed that his wife died of tuberculosis. Cukier had fought it, coming to the office every day no matter how ill he was. Had he succumbed at last to the scourge of the ghetto? Had the Nazis snatched Julian from us when they seized all our sick...and our children? Would we ever know? Was I to lose Jozef next?

Jozef's sad eyes were aimed at Pola. "It says this woman's husband, 46 years old, leaped to his death from the fifth story of a building a day earlier."

"She followed him into heaven," Pola said without emotion.

I often thought of doing that, but Miriam and Regina were alive, not like this poor woman's husband. Was Pola's husband alive? She never spoke of him.

Jozef rolled his eyes. "She first attempted suicide near the barbed wire fence. She did not succeed because the sentry was not willing to shoot her."

"When you want them to shoot, they don't. When you wander too near the German's precious fence. Bang! You're dead," Heilig muttered.

Pola didn't shut him up this time. She just shot him a glance and refocused on Jozef.

Jozef was staring at the shaded square on our wall where, until recently, the portrait of the Chairman had hung. "When two of a family end their lives in such close proximity, we must ask, what is the cause?" He looked at me. "We are instructed to insert that all such acts are borne of 'insanity' or 'mental illness.' Engineer, is that not what you direct us to do?"

He was accusing me. "It was what we were instructed," I replied, but it sounded a lame excuse. It was an insult to degrade the memory of those who died. There was one cause: the blame lay with the Nazis, not with those driven to take their lives. "We were instructed," I repeated, almost as if appealing to Zelkowicz for atonement, forgiveness.

Jozef looked angry as he read the last line of the tersely worded obituary from the Jewish police investigator: "The couple's two children were taken away during the evacuation in September."

It was as if Jozef plunged a knife into my heart.

CHAPTER 13

I knew Jozef's Sabbath routines. All I had to do was wait until dusk without giving clues of what my mind was plotting for tonight. Pola was observing me. I sensed it, so I greeted her curious eyes with what I hoped was a reassuring smile. Full smiles were rare in our circumstances. When we laughed, it was not from joy, nor amusement, but from the ridiculousness of some scrap of news, from the bitter irony of our situation: long waiting lines at the cemetery, an unmanageable flood of potatoes, naked people waking up to discover their staircase was stolen for fuel as they slept. All were ludicrous breaks from our reality resulting in bursts of laughter, irrational, illogical, laughter. Laughter that left us hollow when it ended.

"Why don't you come with me, my friend?" Jozef asked when we reached the intersection of Zgierska and Wesola Streets, where we parted each Sabbath eve. "Pray with us? It will soothe you. It does for me."

"Thank you. I can't." I didn't tell him I prayed silently every day, although I did not believe in God. It was better to hedge my bets in the unlikely case some deity did exist.

"Miriam would want you to pray."

"Please, stop?" I dreaded another lecture, a delay.

"Perhaps, someday?"

"Perhaps. Good Sabbath, my friend," I said, knowing this could be the last time I might see him if the Nazis got wind of his small gathering. Why did I choke up? I didn't even like him, the hypochondriac, the fuss-budget, the snorer. "Go with God," I said.

He looked triumphant, a broad smile. "God's blessings on you and your family, Bernard."

Before he dragged me with him, I walked away as if heading for home. With dusk approaching, the chill of late October, most ghetto inhabitants, lacking warm clothing and without coal for heat, were shivering in their ratholes. A small minority, such as Jozef, were huddled in some basement or hidden room, risking imprisonment, praying to the God who was deaf to our pleas. Knowing our Sabbath is a day of rest, the Germans, eminently practical, reduced their guards to a skeletal crew. I counted on that.

I veered toward the site of the warehouse where Miriam had worked.

Ever since I read the memo about the shoes, I was obsessed. The note Pola had slipped to me about a gold necklace discovered while sorting clothing sealed my determination. I had to know.

The size of the brick warehouses dwarfed most buildings in the ghetto. Within their walls was the evidence that would prove or disprove the virulent rumors about the fate of our family and friends. The evidence I already had collected was enough to convince me that some were dead — but so many? I could not conceive how this could be managed. The logistics of what would constitute mass extermination — unthinkable — the logistics were insurmountable. I had to see for myself. 250,000 used shoes? No, not believable. But, if it was real... it would portend a nightmare.

I found a narrow alleyway.

A German sentry sidled over to the side of the warehouse. He propped his rifle up against the wall and lit a cigarette.

Damn him! He looked bored. How could he think Jews were too cowardly to merit his full attention?

I saw a corner near the westernmost building.

The guard's cigarette...quite a bit to go.

I scurried to the corner of the boarded-up building, an abandoned tenement. The authorities had shut down all the buildings around the warehouses and factories to protect them from the plague of fires and threat of sabotage. The area was a 'no-man's-land' where large signs in

German warned that trespassers would be shot.

Out of breath, gulping air, I smelled the smoke. From the factory chimneys nearby? From the fires? I didn't know. I struggled to suppress a cough that could reveal my presence. It was nearly dark. Crouched in the shadow of the building, my eyes were on a boarded-up window on the lower floor of the warehouse. A metal spoon stolen from Kitchen 2, the Kitchen of the Intelligentsia, was in my coat pocket. I didn't dare risk being caught with a knife or fork. The spoon handle would suit my purpose and could not be evidence that I possessed a weapon in the event I was brought to trial. Trial? The image of eighteen men hanging from gallows in the square flashed before me. I nudged closer to the building. I would not join those swinging from gallows. A bullet would be better. No. I must live.

The guard stubbed out his smoke. He replaced his helmet on his head and slung his rifle on his shoulder. He took his time walking the perimeter of the warehouses. He didn't even finish his circuit. No need. "The damn Jews are cowering in their shitholes for their Sabbath. Let the bastards freeze. Blessed are the authorities who allow the Jews to observe their blasted Sabbath, so we can relax our guard." I imagined the guard's thoughts as he unslung his rifle, dragging it along barely off the dusty ground until he could again lean its weight against the wall. Without a superior to check him, the young guard removed his helmet and fished in his pocket for another cigarette.

Before he lit it, knowing his mind was focused on getting his match to ignite on the striker, I made my move.

Eyes on the guard, I scuttled to the east side of the factory. Hidden by the wall from the window, I wrapped my fingers around the lowest wood plank. I pulled. Harder. I felt the board move, but rusted nails kept it attached to the frame. I slid the spoon from my pocket and wedged the handle between the board and the rotting window frame. Got it. As I pried the board loose, something pressed into my back.

CHAPTER 14

I always contemplated that my last images, if faced by death, would be the faces of Miriam or Regina. A gun barrel in my back, I only thought of the spoon in my hand. Some weapon.

The gun barrel pressed harder.

"Move," a voice hissed. "Speak, and I'll kill you." He grabbed my shoulder and shoved me hard toward the rear of the warehouse. My hands were still raised, the spoon clutched tightly. If he let the gun barrel slip one iota, I would turn and smash the handle in his damn eyes.

As if reading my mind, he pressed the gun deeper and hissed, "Don't try anything." His hand gripped the back of my neck. "You're a fool, a goddamn fool."

He pressed my face against the back wall of the building.

Why didn't he shoot me? He's not a guard...he didn't want to risk the noise. A robber? A thief? I could make my move. I tightened my fingers around the handle of the spoon. Go for the eyes or throat? The head can duck...the throat is less mobile...but a spoon handle? If I used enough speed...enough force...my fist tightened on the metal spoon.

"Damn you. What the hell are you doing here?"

I recognized the voice. "It can't be. You're dead."

"Face the goddamn wall."

"You won't shoot your goddaughter's father, you bastard." I turned around, and he shoved the piece of pipe into his coat pocket. "It wasn't even a gun! You should be dead." At that instant, I wished he was rotting in hell.

"For everyone else, I am dead," Singer said. Was he smiling under his scruffy beard? He looked different, grime around his eyes and jaws, bones showing, sharpening the shape of his face. "You could have been shot if the sentry saw you."

"So you risked yourself to save me? You heartless bastard. We needed you." I was choking on my words. "They're gone. Miriam…Regina. You bastard! You said you loved them. How could you abandon them? I could kill you…."

A knife appeared in Singer's hand. "You can kill me later, but now we have to get out of here."

"I'm not leaving until I see what's inside this warehouse."

The knife was against my throat. "You won't kill me," I rasped, about to move away from Singer's blade.

Singer's words came slowly, each word a dagger. "You should believe I will kill you. I will not hesitate if it is your life against the thousands I may save." He tried smiling, but there was no warmth in it. "I have been inside…."

"You're lying."

The knife drew blood from my neck and still pressed into my flesh, so I couldn't speak. Singer's eyes, once aglow with the lustiness of bachelor life, were gray and sinister. In his eyes, I saw he was capable of slicing the blade across my throat.

Singer hissed, "Please, don't test me. Now, move to the other side of the street without making a sound. I'm behind you."

He didn't have to threaten me again. The ice in his voice and eyes, the blood on my hand when I touched my neck — when he moved the knife from my neck to behind my back — were enough. I stooped down and, with him behind me, scurried silently behind the nearest building across from the monolithic warehouses.

Singer said, "Turn around. We're hidden here." He lowered the knife. "Now, I will do the talking, and you will listen. Once the Germans lose this war, we'll have plenty of time for chit-chat."

"How did you escape Warsaw? Heilig said you were killed. Does he know you're alive?"

"No. That much I will tell you, so you don't go beating up my poor cousin again."

"You know about that?" How could he conceal himself after knowing what I did to the Weasel? God, I hated Singer for so many things.

"My engineer resorting to violence? I wish I'd been there to see that."

"It's your fault it happened. It's all your fault." My hands balled into fists.

"You've changed. We've all changed." Singer removed his hat. Part of his hair was missing. "It was a graze, but it saved my life."

"You were shot?" Why did I feel anything for him?

"Ah, so you do still care?"

I detected a hint of his rakish smile. "No, you sonofabitch, not after all you've done. How could you?"

Singer glanced between the boards. "I have no time now to explain. I know why you're here."

"How do you know? Who told you?" I had my suspicions.

"Listen, I've been inside this warehouse. The rumors are true. There are ceiling-high rooms of shoes...men, women, and children. First, the shoes are separated men from women. Then sorted by color...."

"I don't care about that. Are the shoes new?"

"They are only good for the leather."

"You're not lying?"

"I'm insulted you think I would lie to my dearest friend."

"Don't say that! I trusted you."

"That's why I left. But never mind. There is little time. What you want to know is if the shoes are new. I've answered you." He put his hand on my shoulder, but I threw it off. "Engineer, you would not believe the woeful state in which these shoes and clothing come to the warehouses."

"Miriam told me of a truck she helped unload...."

"There have been thousands of trucks."

My heart sank, but I had to ask, "Where? Where are all these things coming from?"

"Do you really not know?"

"Miriam? Regina? Rosenfeld? Cukier? Do you know where they are?"

Singer put his hand back on my shoulder. "We don't know where any of them are."

This time I did not push his arm away.

"My friends risk their lives to learn what happened to those uprooted in Warsaw. We know the Germans have established labor camps throughout Poland, but we have not been able to penetrate any as yet." He lowered his hand. "I promise. Well, you know…what I promise."

"Please, Oscar? Please? Find them for me. I know you love them. I know you love them." I stared hard into his face, my own words tormenting me. "You do love them, don't you?" It was as if I were twisting a knife into my heart.

"More than I thought possible…and you, my foolish friend."

"No. No." Before I could hurl epithets at my betrayer, Singer was gone. I was paralyzed, uncertain of what I should focus on. The sight of the austere-looking warehouses, expansive, taller than most buildings in the ghetto, was like seeing malevolent giants staring down at me with hateful eyes. "Probe inside, and we'll kill you and all your friends and family," the giants warned.

I felt a pang from the thin cut on my throat. My finger touched the small nick and came up with blood. I pressed my thumb against the tiny wound. "I cut myself shaving," I'd say. On legs rubbery from my encounter with Singer, I hurried back to my flat, rehearsing what I would say to Jozef.

When Jozef saw me, he asked if I'd eaten.

I thought that was strange but was relieved he did not ask me for an explanation for where I'd been. Seeing his eyes staring at me from behind a candle, I said, "I was visiting an old friend in the cemetery."

"Did your friend give you the answers you require?"

There was a kind look on his face, but it sounded as if he was playing some sort of game with me. Did he know? Was he Singer's informant? The irascible master-writer, whose prose often brought me to tears, was the last person I'd suspect of spying for the devious Singer. That made him the logical choice.

CHAPTER 15

L ITZMANNSTADT-GHETTO
OCTOBER 28, 1942

Four days had gone by since I'd risked my life to answer a question that had been burning inside me after I detected the cryptic sentence about 250,000 pairs of used shoes. It was also four days since I was threatened with murder by my daughter's godfather, my wife's lover, Oscar Singer. An excursion which was to answer one vital question left me with many more and unable to trust anyone in our small club. One of these colleagues, I was convinced, was a spy for Singer, so I couldn't trust any of them. I also didn't rely on myself to keep Singer's return from death a secret. With his knife at my throat, he demanded that until the soon-to-come end of this war, he had to play possum. Why? Who asks questions of a madman who just drew blood from your neck?

I was relieved not one of my coworkers asked about my cut. As long as it didn't appear as if I cut my throat in a suicide attempt, it was not a big deal. Perhaps they knew already. Were they all in on it? Jew, not trusting Jew, was one of the costs of Nazi oppression. "So, how was your first big assignment?" I asked Pola, thinking she was staring at me. "Did you enjoy the wedding ceremony?"

Jozef leaned back in his chair. "I would have liked to see that. The Chairman has given us hope."

"It's a false hope. Performing weddings does not mean he has power." Heilig said, puncturing our balloon as usual.

Jozef whirled on Heilig. "What do you know? This is a giant step. Since the authorities banned all religious rituals, nobody has been able to be married. Our Chairman bravely took the role of chaplain and made it possible to be married in the Jewish tradition, risking his position and more."

"He changed the ceremony to comply with the German edicts," Heilig said. "He never should have bent to their will."

"Stop! I've had enough arguing for one day." It was as if Singer had returned, which he had, giving me one throbbing headache. "I want to hear what Mrs. Levinski has to say about these weddings. She was there." I glanced at Pola. "I'm sorry. Bulls are bred to fight."

Pola didn't laugh. She pulled out several sheets of handwritten notes. "Yesterday, the first seven couples were married in the auditorium of the former Rabbinate at 4 Koscielny Square."

"He dared to use the Rabbinate's auditorium?" Heilig said. "I'm surprised. Maybe he is finally asserting himself."

"Please, Pola, go on?" I shot Heilig an annoyed look.

"After 6:00 p.m., in the beautifully lit hall, the Chairman seated himself at a table covered with a green cloth. A typewriter was on the next table."

"We could use another one here," I muttered, staring daggers at the monster with its stubborn keys. "I'm sorry. Continue, please."

"The couples were called into the room, accompanied only by witnesses. Invitations were checked by the door."

"He's cautious," Jozef said.

"Did he do the Jewish ceremony?" Heilig asked, looking skeptical.

"I think he did as much as he could," Pola replied. "He told the couples that the new marriage ceremony had been 'adapted to the needs of the present situation.'"

"That's double-talk for complying with Nazi demands," Heilig said, a sneer on his face.

Pola shook her head. "He said the most critical parts of the wedding ceremony are the vows and the blessing. He called everything else, 'remnants of an old tradition.'"

"How convenient. I'm sure the Germans would love for us to cut out all the 'remnants' of our old traditions."

I was surprised. It wasn't Heilig voicing his sarcasm, but Jozef. "I suppose he also abandoned the ksuba, our 'out-dated' wedding contract?" He looked at me. "Would you abandon your contract with Miriam?"

"Jozef, he didn't abandon it, but it was changed. As he said, we have no gold, diamonds, or other valuables, so the old contract was, as he called it, 'fiction.' But he did have the contracts," Pola said, smiling benevolently at our senior member.

"What of the canopy? I stood under it with my Rosa..." Jozef's shoulders shook.

"Why don't you go into the next chamber?" I suggested, recalling that Miriam and I had only a civil service. She wanted a religious ceremony, but her parents, as much as they would have wanted a rabbi to marry us, insisted she had to leave before it was too late. Perhaps, I thought, if God had been asked to bless our marriage... what a thought for an unrepentant atheist. Oh, God, I wish I did believe in you. Better than that, I wish you believed in me.

Jozef shook his head. "Pola, continue, please. You must forgive an old man."

Pola smiled. "No forgiveness necessary."

I hadn't seen her smile much. She had tiny dimples under her eyes that I'd never noticed.

"There was no canopy nor other traditions. I missed the breaking of the glass for good luck." Pola turned the paper over.

"There is no good luck in the ghetto," I said.

Pola looked surprised.

"Did the couples have wine? We always sip wine from the same glass. It is a sign that we are now one. Never to drink from life separately again."

"That tradition was changed," Pola said.

"Even that is not allowed us by the wolves," Jozef shouted.

"No. It was the Chairman," Pola replied. "He said, 'with rampant disease and epidemics in mind,' he ordered a separate glass for each couple. It was for health reasons."

Jozef nodded. "Very wise. Filth and contamination cause typhus."

"Good job, Pola. Anything else?" I watched her scan her notes. Her handwriting was small and neat, a bit compressed…like her personality, I thought.

Pola nodded. "I think the Chairman sounded sad during the entire ceremony. In fact, all the brides and grooms also seemed subdued. Natural under the circumstances. The Chairman asked if they had gold rings, but who has gold?"

I recalled my mother's gold ring, a thin, dull strip, but enough for Singer to barter for a dress for Miriam. I laughed inside at how I'd regretted trusting Singer with it, fearing he'd gamble it away or spend it on a whore. As things turned out, either of those might have prevented Miriam from falling in love with him. Her face when he walked into our door carrying that dress. His face, uncreased by war, barely visible in our flat's candlelight, appeared mysterious. Yes, he was a mystery man, a quality for which young girls like Miriam hunger, especially when married, not by choice, to a human calculator. "So, no rings, either?"

"Two couples had fountain pens with gold nibs," Pola said. "There was quite a bit of discussion, but the Rabbi, acting as a consultant, ultimately agreed that the pens could be used instead of rings."

I stared at my fountain pen. The nib was missing. "That's funny, but also sad," I said, musing that I would settle for anything if I could get my Miriam and Regina back.

"I forgot the gifts," Pola exclaimed. "Good thing I take notes."

Heilig popped up. "You should have sent me. I have a photographic memory."

God, I hate him, I thought. "You mentioned gifts. Were there any?"

"The Chairman had been giving away coupons for rations," Jozef said. "Those were abolished."

"That's what he did this time as well, but he apologized that each coupon was only good for one loaf of bread. You should have seen the radiant smiles on the couples' faces…for one loaf of bread."

Miriam had crawled on the floor for the crusty crumbs of a roll I'd stolen from the Kitchen for the Intelligentsia. The sight of her scooping crumbs into her hand from the roach-infested flat broke my heart. When she asked in her child-like voice — she looked and sounded like a child in those days — if she could eat a bit of it, I could only nod my head. I fought tears seeing her eyes imploring me for those crumbs. "In these times, a loaf of bread, a whole loaf, is a blessing," I said. "It is manna from heaven." Why was Pola staring at me again? I didn't want her, or anyone else, to pity me. I bucked up, suppressed my emotions.

"There was one more thing. The newlyweds did not wish to waste this rare time with the Chairman."

"I'll bet," Heilig said. "Nobody sees him lately."

And I'd thought Singer was annoying. "Heilig, we value your comments, but could you please remember the mission our benefactor has set for us." I gave him an authoritative stare. "None of us can afford to lose our position."

That threat shut him up.

Pola looked almost sorry for Heilig. "As the Chairman was about to walk out, the newlyweds approached. He waved his bodyguard aside and asked what they wanted. One couple asked for a new apartment."

Fat chance. I wanted that for Miriam, but like all my other prayers, that went unanswered too. "I wish them luck with that request."

"The others also asked for favors, mostly material. The Chairman smiled and asked his secretary to note the requests so he might take care of them later. He closed his coat and leaned on his cane when one of the brides smiled timidly. She had watched silently as the others entreated the Chairman for gifts he most likely cannot provide."

"What did she ask for?" I asked, barely here.

Pola aimed her eyes at me. "She asked for new shoes."

A chill shot through me. Was Pola Singer's spy? They had both been in Warsaw, but she denied knowing him. Was it possible not to know someone as dynamic and conspicuous as Singer? "Write your report, please. It is positive news for once."

CHAPTER 15

Heilig burst into rude laughter.

CHAPTER 16

S UNDAY, NOVEMBER 1, 1942
A SUICIDE
Solomon Malkes, the head of the Information Department and one of the ghetto's most senior officials, committed suicide by jumping from a fourth-floor (window)...Malkes had recently been in a state of severe depression that dated from the deportation of his mother. The suicide had a profound effect on the ghetto.

"This last sentence, 'The suicide had a profound effect on the ghetto,' Jozef, what does it mean?" I asked.

"He was a top official, so we must honor him in some way," Jozef replied.

"Why?" Heilig asked. "The sonofabitch took his own life. We don't honor suicides. We hardly mention them anymore."

"He was a top official," Jozef insisted. "How can we ignore the loss of a top deputy to our Chairman?"

"No one is more important than anyone else, Jozef," Heilig said. "That is my point."

"That denies reality," Jozef said, looking at me for help.

I decided to let the bulls fight it out.

"Do you want to encourage more suicides?" Heilig charged. "We have too many already, so why honor such a deed? It will unleash an epidemic, bodies falling from every window in this goddamn place! It's raining human undesirables! Grab your umbrella! It's raining...Oh wait, we have no umbrellas. The authorities have them all."

"All this over one sentence," Pola remarked and went back to reading through her piles of memos. "Men."

I went back to my typing.

Everything was quiet. The noise of the keys had become a refuge from debates that resolved nothing. Was the population of Lodz capable of feeling 'a profound effect' at anyone's death? Was I?

Heilig shattered the solitude. "This almost snuck by me. The Chairman will be so pleased."

"What now?" I asked, wondering what good news had attracted our resident ghoul's attention.

"All the prisoners, mostly smugglers, have left the ghetto," Heilig replied.

"That is good news. We have something we agree on," Jozef said. "Criminals are one thing we have more than enough of here."

Pola reached for the memo.

What was her interest? Her eyes looked angry. Should I ask her? "Do we know who these prisoners were?" I asked, wondering if Pola knew someone mentioned in the report.

Jozef looked at Heilig. "Was Chmol Rozenberg taken?"

Pola's eyes shot up.

"Did you know him?" I asked.

"No," she replied.

"You did not know him?"

She shook her head.

"I know of him," Jozef said. "He and his gang of smugglers tunneled into the food warehouse and stole sacks of sugar. The thieves stole sugar from our mouths."

"Sugar is like gold here," Heilig muttered.

"Everything is like gold here," Jozef replied. "Well, Chmol and his like are gone now. Good riddance, I say."

"You, men, miss the point," Pola said.

"I don't understand," I said, sensing hostility. "None of us knew any of these crooks. You said you don't either?"

"I don't."

"Then why should we care about prisoners who steal food from our children's lips?" I asked, thinking of Regina. "What difference does any of this make?"

"Engineer, you read, but are blind."

"Don't call me blind," I shouted. Miriam accused me of being blind to so many things, so many damn times. I was blind to her and Singer. "I'm sorry. The pressure is getting to me." I saw the shocked look on Pola's face. "Please, accept my apology?"

"I'm sorry too," Pola said. "We've all been through a lot. I shouldn't have said that."

An apology from her? "No. Please, tell me what your concern is about this memo?"

Pola leaned closer. When Miriam used to do that, I smelled the sweet scent of her hair. I inhaled nothing from Pola's hair. We were all so dirty. One shower a week…if we were lucky. "See this first sentence."

"Read it aloud," Heilig said. "I want to know what you say I missed."

Pola's finger pointed out the words as she read aloud, "A motorized squad appeared at the Central Prison early this morning and took the prisoners."

"The Germans are the only ones with cars," I said.

Pola nodded.

"Oh, God," Jozef said softly, "The Nazis have them." He rubbed his hands together, as Rosenfeld had done so many times. "I missed that. We all missed that." He looked at me. "I said, 'Good riddance,' but I didn't realize the Nazis have them."

Heilig grabbed the memo. "Let me see that."

I grabbed his wrist. "Don't ever do that again," I hissed at him.

"What the hell is wrong with you?" He pulled his wrist away.

"Never grab anything from Mrs. Levinski again."

"I just wanted to see for myself!" Heilig stood and grabbed his coat.

I stood. "Sit down. We have work to do."

Pola's voice broke through, "I don't need anyone to defend me."

I let out a sigh. "Heilig. Please, sit back down? I'm sorry. My nerves are on edge."

Heilig looked uncertainly at the coat in his arms, then replaced it on the back of his chair. "I should not have grabbed it from her. I was upset that I missed that detail. I'm sorry, Pola."

Pola nodded.

Now that things were calm again, I saw she had moved back away from me. I didn't have much time to think about that when Jozef said, "Listen to this report from the Paper Workshop."

I couldn't imagine why a report from the paper factory would be of interest but was grateful for anything that erased the memory of what just happened.

Jozef said, "This is strange. I think it is good news for a change."

"That would be a welcome change," I said, settling back in my chair, casting a furtive glance at Pola, who was locked on Jozef, her back facing me. Was she angry?

"It says, 'A large collection of the latest in toys has recently been produced. Several million such toys are to be manufactured,'" Jozef said.

"Let me see that, please?" I asked, reaching for the official document. I read it feverishly. "Millions of toys," I said, "Millions of toys!" Tears burst from my eyes. I tried to wipe them away but failed.

Jozef said, "They're making them from paper and trash items it says."

I didn't care if they were made of shit. Millions of toys meant children. My body was racked by my effort to keep from crying.

"Damn you," Pola said. "You're all emotional powderkegs. Don't men ever cry?"

I trembled uncontrollably. God had heard my prayers, the prayers of all of our despairing parents. The Germans had ordered millions of toys. Regina was safe. Our children were going to get toys.

CHAPTER 17

T HURSDAY, NOVEMBER 5, 1942
COMMITTED TO PRISON
Eleven men from the camp at Radogoszcz have been transferred to Central Prison. The person reported as remanded from Litzmannstadt on the 3rd of this month is a 6-year-old boy of unknown background: he is suspected of being of Jewish descent.

Pola shook her head. "A six-year-old boy. Nobody knows who he is?"

I noticed Pola seemed softer of late. I thought her more vulnerable, but still with a hard shell. I took her concern as no more than the act of kindness she might have shown a dog or cat, or some stranger in similar distress. "It is a hard world," I said, "but there is always hope."

Pola said, "For cigarette-lovers for sure. We've just received trucks full of cigarettes, and new ration cards will be issued next month."

"That should calm nerves around here," Heilig said. "Remember the riots outside the distribution centers a few months ago? It was worse than the uproar over potato peels." He laughed bitterly. "We have sunk to new lows."

I was not going to let the Weasel's pessimism upset the others. The news of the toy order had provided me with new optimism. Why would the Germans place such a large order amid war if not for our precious children? It confirmed their promise that our wives, friends, relations, were all safe in the rural farmlands, working on supplying food to their military and embattled population. The large orders for snowsuits also confirmed that Hitler's dream of conquering the Soviet Union was not yet accomplished.

"How many cigarettes?" I asked.

"Here is our numbers man again," Heilig taunted. "Tell me, Ostrowski, what is our latest population here in paradise?"

Pola shot him a disapproving look.

"Don't you see, it's for my record. For all our cigarette lovers. If our population has dropped, which it has because of all our recently deceased and our deportations, these nicotine-starved citizens will enjoy larger rations of their precious smokes. So, Engineer, what is our latest population?"

"88,630. We had twenty deaths yesterday." I rattled off the figures without having to search for the memo. I was becoming another Heilig when it came to such statistics.

"That low?" Jozef asked, looking concerned.

"Don't forget we had one birth yesterday," Heilig nearly sang. "A lovely baby girl."

I didn't react. I had too much hope to let the Weasel get to me today.

"More good news," Pola said. "They're increasing our ration. Starting tomorrow, we will get 150 grams of meat and 100 grams of sausage per week."

"It's a miracle," Heilig said, "Bless our generous German benefactors. Hail to our saintly Aryan brothers and sisters in their cozy bastions far from this shithole they have lavished upon their Jews."

"Shut up! Shut up, Heilig," I shouted. Then I heard the door. "Attention," I croaked, praying the authorities hadn't overheard my angry outburst.

We all jumped to our feet, except Heilig, who muttered, "another false alarm," until he saw it wasn't. He rose just as a Gestapo officer's hat met my eyes.

We just had good news, I prayed silently, don't do this now? Please, God?

The officer stood aside, and a tall man in a black leather coat sauntered into the room.

At the sight of the leather coat, I froze. 'S.S. officer' was written on his weather-beaten face and his contemptuous survey of our room. Behind him, several feet behind, a man in a black suit stood. I almost didn't recognize Neftalin, the Chairman's deputy. He looked as if he were praying that the officer would not notice him. "What do you do here?" the officer asked in German.

Neftalin said, "Oberfuhrer, these men are essential—"

"All of your Jews are essential," the officer cut in. "We are well aware of this from your Eldest of the Jews." His hand, his black leather glove, balled into a fist. "I asked you what these Jews do here?"

"Yes, Oberfuhrer," Neftalin said. "They maintain our productivity by keeping all our manufacturing and export/import records."

"That is all?" The officer leaned forward and grabbed a sheet of paper, thankfully from my pile, a sheet covered with numbers. "This is important to the Reich?" He dropped the page on the floor.

I remained immobile and hoped the others were as well.

"You." He pointed to me, perhaps because I was closest. "How does this work of yours help the Fatherland?"

I looked at Neftalin. He shook his head slightly.

"Do you speak German?" The officer's eyes were skewering me.

"Yes, Oberfuhrer, but not well. We are learning as decreed—"

"Fine. How many in your department?"

"Four, sir."

He aimed his eyes at Pola. "Are you from here?"

"Yes, sir," she replied.

The officer stared at her and then turned back to me. "I am waiting."

"Yes, sir. We keep records to assure full satisfaction of orders from the military and government. Without such records, we would not be as productive—"

"Enough. It takes four to do this paperwork?"

The officer had become an eagle appraising his prey. I was flustered.

"Yes, Oberfuhrer. There are more than 30 departments and factories. This is our brain."

The officer's eyes landed again on Pola. "One less is one less mouth to feed," he said.

Neftalin interjected, "It's a small department, sir."

"Yes, it is." He aimed his eyes at Jozef. "It may be smaller yet." He signaled the guard and turned to the door.

I didn't breathe until five minutes after he left. I saw the others were still standing, looking as uncomfortable as I felt. "I never encountered such a chill from a human being before," I let out, once sure the unnamed officer wasn't returning.

Heilig nearly fell to his seat. "That's the point, he's not human. None of them are."

"Why was he looking at you so intently?" I asked Pola, who looked shaken. "Do you know him?"

"No."

I wanted to ask more but had learned she was not responsive to questioning. "Jozef, are you not well?" He was leaning on a chair, both hands gripping the top.

"I was a piece of meat to him. I am the oldest here."

"I am the only woman," Pola said. "You will not be the one taken."

"Enough." I looked at Pola. At that moment, I knew I could not lose her, too, nor could I lose my irascible roommate. Heilig? I wasn't sure about him. Yes, I was. "None of us are leaving here," I said. "The Chairman will fight for us because he needs his witnesses."

Heilig laughed, that insane, bitter laugh of his. "Rumkowski fights only for himself." He peered at me. "You, of all of us, know this. Did he fight for our children?"

"Oh, God," Jozef exclaimed. "Which of you wrote this? Which of you?" He began to read, his voice shaking, "The workers who sort the old clothes...."

"I wrote it," Pola said.

Jozef shook the note at her. "How? How could you write this? There is no evidence. None."

"Calm down," I said. "May I see this entry?"

"See. See. Oh, God. Where? Do you know this for a fact?" Jozef asked, almost in tears.

"Yes."

"How? How do you know this? It has been rumored forever, but...but...."

I read the entry and sat down. "Is it true?"

"Yes. Our friend verified it."

"Our friend?" So, Pola knew Singer. I had suspected as much. All liars. "I will type it as is."

"Will the Chairman let you get away with it?" Heilig asked.

"I don't know, but the future must learn what we learned today." I looked at Pola to see if she showed any sign of remorse. She looked sad. I typed the entry:

The workers who sort the old clothes delivered to the ghetto frequently turn up valuables such as jewels, gold objects, and foreign currency. All such items are duly handed over to the authorities.

I stared at the entry in numb disbelief. Valuables in used clothing? The implications were terrifying.

"Are you alright?" Pola asked, seeing I was not typing, not writing.

I didn't reply.

"What the hell?" Jozef exploded. "Can you believe it? The Chairman is hosting another concert?"

"Yes, I believe it," I said, "And I'll bet he's going to give another speech." I placed the last entry on the table. Workers found jewels, gold, and currency in old clothes. Finding that note was like finding a burning lump of coal. But Pola was staring at me. I had to hide my emotions. I didn't trust her. I didn't trust anyone.

CHAPTER 18

M ONDAY, NOVEMBER 16, 1942

"Doesn't anyone have good news?" I asked after a long night of listening to Jozef snoring. I had taken to my trusty wood chair. God knows how long until that is gone too, I thought, as I bundled myself up in whatever rags I still possessed against the cold wind. With so few people remaining in the ghetto, I thought of asking Zelkowicz to find other digs, but I could not face my flat each night alone with Miriam's remembered face…Regina's little face. No, I'd rather be tortured by Jozef's snoring than their faces hovering before me like ghosts in the night.

The door opened.

Damn! "Attention," I shouted, and we all, including Heilig, leaped to our feet.

"I'm sorry, my friends," Neftalin muttered. "I was in a hurry to bring you news about the resumption of concerts. Were any of you at the House of Culture? We have not had a concert in months. This is a big deal for us."

I remembered how Julian Cukier, our departed leader, enjoyed the concerts. In the end, his incessant coughing had deprived him even of that respite.

"You, Engineer, you should bring your beautiful…" Neftalin paused.

All eyes were focused on me. I trembled but said nothing. The vision of Miriam in the dress Singer had gotten for her from one of his black market 'connections,' her eyes when she first saw him…that started it all. But she looked so lovely. Everyone was looking at me with envy as we entered the grand lobby. "What? What did you say, Henryk?"

"I'm sorry, Ben. In the excitement...I forgot your loss." Neftalin looked contrite.

I nodded. "Please, continue? We can all use some good news for a change."

Heilig spoke up. "How could they do a concert when so many of our finest musicians have been deported, and the concertmaster has died?"

"It's my understanding," Jozef added, "that the musicians are no longer excused from working in the factories."

Neftalin shook his coat of snow. "You're right, of course, the musicians can only play in their spare time, and the deportations have taken their toll on the orchestra. That makes the resumption of concerts even more of a triumph of our Chairman." He buttoned his coat as well as he could with several buttons missing. "You all should attend. The Chairman announced that regular concerts will be performed from now on."

Heilig sneered. "I suppose the Eldest of the Jews made a speech?"

"Why not? All the ghetto leaders and factory managers were present. He has not made a public address in months." Neftalin dug in his pocket. "I'm sorry, Heilig, my notes are not as good as your memory." He unfolded the slip of paper. "He spoke of the food problem. He said we should not expect any more potatoes for now."

"Back to potato peels," Heilig said.

Neftalin ignored him. "He mentioned that he is establishing a female police force."

"He is looking for women police?" Pola asked.

Why did her interest in that alarm me? My eyes shot automatically toward her.

"Why do we need female police now? We don't have enough with the S.S., Gestapo, Kripo, and let us not forget our own Order Service?" Heilig asked. "We're drowning in enforcers."

Neftalin looked uncomfortable. "As you know, the ghetto has received nearly 600 orphaned children...."

I looked up. "I didn't know," I said, looking at the others. "What is this about?"

Jozef cheek twitched. "We didn't want to upset you."

"You hid this from me? Henryk, what is this about?"

"In the last week, we've been sent many children. They are from all over. Orphans."

"Orphans?" I didn't ask about the parents.

"Many are from Warsaw." Neftalin bit his lip. "At any rate, we had no means to cope with such a storm of unprotected children, so the Chairman, in his compassion, is hiring and training women to work with them."

"Where are these little ones being placed?" Pola asked, looking at me with soulful eyes.

"We have managed to place 624 of these parentless children with foster families." Neftalin shrugged. "The project is in progress." He looked at me. "We have adolescents that need male guidance and protection."

Why was he telling me this? Regina will be coming back any day after Miriam is no longer needed for farming.

Pola said, "I'm willing to take in a child."

"Given your circumstances, I don't think that will be approved." Seeing her pained expression, Neftalin added, "If you wish, I will not prevent you from applying."

I aimed my eyes at her. What made Pola ineligible to help a child? She lost one of her own. I sympathized with her. I missed Regina more than I could have imagined, but my situation was temporary. Why would she be denied a child if she wanted one?

Pola stood. "I understand. I will abide by your advice." She glanced at me, and our eyes met. Were there tears glistening in the corners?

CHAPTER 19

MONDAY, NOVEMBER 23, 1942
PEOPLE ARE SAYING...
A rumor is about in the ghetto that the Ghetto Administration has granted permission for the establishment of a movie theater. A similar rumor circulated two years ago, but the wish did not come true then and will not come true this time either.

Pola asked if she could serve as our link to the new women's police force. I hesitated to agree to this, sensing she might want to enlist and escape from the clutches of her three male co-conspirators. I could understand that. I'd be uncomfortable with three single men...single? What was I thinking? I'd let her do as she pleased. "So, how many of these women officers are there?" I asked, always the numbers man.

Heilig and Jozef stopped their work. I suppose they too suspected her motives.

"More than 50," Pola said. "They were on the street for the first time today."

Heilig shook his head. "And what were our lovely officers wearing?" He sneered. "For my reports, of course."

I was surprised he showed any interest in women at all. He may have been Singer's cousin but was nothing like that rakish scoundrel.

Pola smiled at the Weasel. "The young girls wore special green uniforms — short trousers, short jackets, and round caps, all made from the same material with yellow stripes. They bear the insignia of the Order Service on one arm." She breathed into his face, "Satisfied?"

Heilig backed away.

Good for her, I thought.

Heilig laughed nervously. "At least they don't have weapons," he said. "Imagine women with weapons?"

"They have nightsticks," Pola said. "Just like their male counterparts."

"Really?" I asked.

"Why would they need clubs?" Jozef asked. "We have too many club-swinging police already."

"528 in the precincts, and approximately 1,100 in total," I said, rattling off the numbers from the latest accounting."

"So, why do we need so many women?" Jozef asked.

Pola looked thoughtful. "Men are leaving the ghetto every day. The Chairman may want to assure that the loss of his male officers doesn't result in a crime wave."

"That makes sense," Jozef said. "He always rants and rails about how if crime gets out of control, the authorities will swoop down on us like vultures and pick off the last Jews from the ghetto's rotting bones."

"So God created Eve," Heilig said, bursting into insane laughter.

"I'm sorry, Pola." I wished I had the authority to fire the Weasel, who was so annoying. Even if I could, I'd never do that. It would be signing his deportation papers to an unknown destination. *The devil you know is better than the one you don't.*

"Oh, this is more shit," Heilig exploded. "Now, we're banned from using any electrical appliances."

"What appliances?" I asked. "We have no electricity."

"It's the hot plates," Pola said. "The authorities claim that the rash of power outages and fires are caused by the illegal use of hot plates."

"I saw squads of Kripo, the German criminal police, racing from house to house last night on my way to shul," Jozef said. "They were carrying anything that uses electricity: hot plates, irons, anything they could find. They were armed with guns and rifles."

Heilig leaned closer. "Rumors are that using an electric light during the day is now a capital offense. Is this an exaggeration?"

"I wouldn't put that past them," Pola said and ducked back into her work.

Heilig sidled toward me. His mouth emitted a strong odor, but I didn't back away. "They think the hot plates are behind the power failures that are hitting their factories. They believe it's sabotage."

"Is it?" I asked, remembering the fires that had impeded production for weeks. "Is Singer behind this?"

Heilig shrugged his shoulders. "How would I know?"

What the hell did that mean? I was about to interrogate the Weasel when Pola burst into laughter. It was so rare that we all looked.

Jozef asked, "So, what is so funny?"

"A rumor is spreading that the Chairman has gotten permission to open a movie theater," Pola said.

"A similar rumor has spread for at least two years," Jozef said. "It would be wonderful, but it did not come true then and will not come true this time either."

"You're a pessimist," Pola said but was smiling at our eldest team member.

"I'm a crotchety old realist," Jozef replied. "A movie theater in our slum is a dream, like the end of this damn war."

Pola settled back in her chair. She slid it toward me. "My husband used to love taking me to the cinema. Did you go too?"

"Once. My wife was...she was very young."

Pola looked puzzled.

"Her parents gave her to me...to protect her." I choked on that phrase. "I failed to protect her...Regina. Miriam. That was my wife's name... is her name. She's fifteen years younger than me."

Pola looked surprised.

"You didn't know?" I thought Singer, Heilig, or Neftalin had given her all the details.

"Nobody speaks of the past here." Pola looked at her hands.

I saw a thin band on her finger where the coloring was lighter than the rest of her skin. She looked so vulnerable for a change that I said, "Perhaps, one day, we should take a little time and talk."

She didn't answer, but said, "My favorite movies were when two strangers, both suffering some kind of pain, eventually learned to trust each other."

I pushed my chair back to its original position.

Pola didn't move. "I didn't say they fall in love," she whispered.

I glanced at Jozef, then at Heilig. Had they overheard? The word 'love' hit like the crash of a cannonball. Surely Heilig heard? But no, both were engrossed in their writing. Where were they when I needed them? When I looked back at Pola, she was reading a memo as if nothing had happened. Perhaps, nothing had?

CHAPTER 20

F RIDAY, NOVEMBER 27, 1942

It was a week of tension. Pola said little to me after that brief, but disturbing allusion to what I decided was her love of romantic movies. I must have misread her. She had no interest in me other than as a colleague. On the one hand, I was relieved, but I was also lonely. I'd grown used to nestling my body next to Miriam. How such a tiny body could exude such warmth in our frigid flat was a puzzle. It was cold without her. Though now I shared that bed with Jozef, his face turned to the boarded-up window, and I turned toward the only chair left to us. I should have asked him to move, but any company was better than none.

"Good morning, all," I said, grateful to see none had vanished overnight. Heilig yawned.

Pola gave me a faint smile.

Jozef settled in his chair, still wearing his coat. With the collar turned up, he reminded me somewhat of my dear Professor Rosenfeld. The pipe bowl was still in my pocket. Someday, I would return it to him, I promised myself, a bit of silliness that gave me comfort. "What is the news?"

Heilig removed his glasses. "They're moving the Straw-Shoe Workshop to Poznan. They assert it is easier to transfer the workers to the new location than to keep shipping materials from Poznan to our factory here."

"I suppose that is logical," I said, wondering why he looked concerned.

"If they can do that with this factory, they can do it with others," Heilig said.

"There are rumors of mass resettlements," Jozef said. "For once, our young colleague is right. This could be a harbinger of what the Nazis are planning for us."

"What do you think, Pola?" I asked. She'd been silent since we arrived.

"They shipped 250,000 Jews out of Warsaw," she replied.

"I believe our Chairman is correct and that our factories are too valuable for the authorities to want to terminate their service," I said.

"I don't know," Jozef said. "Something may be afoot. We lost nearly 16,000 in resettlements in September." He handed me the official census.

I examined the paper. A more disturbing figure hit my eye: only two people had been resettled here in August, and our population had dropped to 88,036. I decided to keep my concerns to myself and to monitor this trend. Why alarm them?

For lunch, we were served cabbage soup. We had been served cabbage soup all week. When I asked why the sudden change from potato soup to cabbage, the server looked me in the eye and said, "We are fortunate to have this." It was tastier than the thin potato soup, but after a week of it, you can imagine the problems it caused to my digestive system. I was not alone in my reaction. The others shifted uncomfortably on their chairs in our cubby hole after every lunch. It was during one of Jozef's escapes to the only toilet in the building allowed to Jews that Pola leaned toward me.

I was caught off-guard, or I might have moved away. "That soup is quite potent," I said, praying I did not embarrass myself — farting.

Pola gave me a furtive look. "Jozef goes to shul on Friday nights?"

I nodded.

"You walk home alone?"

"Yes."

"Where does he leave you?"

"Why do you want to know?" Of all the stupid things I could have said. I wished Jozef would hurry, but suspected he was suffering from cabbage soup issues.

Pola laughed. "Don't be so frightened. It is just a walk."

I nodded. "Near the abandoned hospital." I had a flashback of the

Germans chasing everyone out of the now-vacant building, Jews jumping from windows. Some patients being clubbed unconscious by the collectors of our weakest citizens. No one had ever heard from the patients again. There were reports of massive gunfire in the forests. "The one on Wesola Street."

Pola moved back to her pile of memos.

Nothing else was said. In my brain, the conversation kept playing.

"689," Jozef said.

The sound of a number broke through my thoughts. "What is that?" I asked.

"We had 689 die this month. 397 men and 292 women. That makes 689. Does it not, Engineer?"

I didn't reply. I had no answers for anything anymore.

Heilig didn't return after lunch. I assumed he had rushed to his rathole with the cabbage malady. I was distracted, my thoughts swerving back to Pola's conversation. I worked the rest of the afternoon, one eye on my typing, another searching for some sign from her that I existed, that she was thinking of me. I was thinking of her, secretly appraising her, comparing her to Miriam. But how could she compare to my young wife? No woman could. Pola was my age, possibly older. Her hair was nearly black and stringy, where Miriam's had been similar in color, but thick with curls. The smell of my wife's hair when we met reminded me of honey.

I could not see Pola's eyes. When I closed mine, I saw Miriam's wide eyes, hazel, almost gray in candlelight. In the dim light of memory, I saw her body, curved, fair-skinned, child-like. The woman next to me was thin. Her face had appeared hard, without warmth. How could I possibly feel anything for a woman who looked as if she was made of sticks?

"Good-night, my friend," Jozef said when we reached the corner of Wesola and Zgierska, the ghost of the old hospital shaking me from my conflicted inner thoughts. "Are you certain you won't accompany me to the shul tonight?"

"You ask that every week," I said.

"And someday you will say, yes. So, I will keep asking." He gave me a warm smile. "My friend, there is an emptiness in all of us. Even you, my most logical friend, must someday find something that fills that void inside you."

"You're a good man, Jozef," I said. "Your friends are waiting."

"Go with God," he replied, and at long last, began to walk to the rathole in which a small group of Jews risked their lives to try and reach our deaf God.

"Go with God," I whispered, hesitating, actually thinking of running to join him. A short trot and all would be resolved. I was sweating. Why? I was trembling. She wasn't coming. I didn't want Jozef to see me waiting, so I walked to the corner, feeling unbearably alone.

CHAPTER 21

T UESDAY, DECEMBER 1, 1942
WE HAVE LEARNED
From sources in good standing with the (German) Ghetto Administration that no resettlements are anticipated before the New Year...

"That is good news. Is it not?" Jozef said.

He recognized my sullenness, but could not have known the cause. When Pola did not show up Saturday night for the concert, I was filled with conflicting emotions — asking what I expected, what did I want. I came up blank. I felt more empty because of it. I ached to confront her, but work came first.

When Pola arrived in our workroom the next day, she gave no sign that anything was wrong between us. I didn't understand. I wasn't sure I wanted to. Miriam would return soon, and whatever this was, once I saw my wife's lustrous eyes, once I held her in my arms, all my doubts would fade into misty memory. "That is good news," I said.

"I have more good news. Work cards are to be issued to all workers between the age of ten and sixty-five," Pola said

Heilig shot in, "Everyone who works is safe. Those who do not produce...no promises."

"You sound like the Chairman," Jozef said.

"Heaven forbid," Heilig replied. "Hey, listen to this, rumors are that there will be a potato ration, and everyone will get ten kilograms of potatoes every month." He patted his stomach. "That will be a relief from all that cabbage. I never thought I'd pray for spuds, even peels."

"Mothers are praying for milk," Jozef said. "There is none anywhere…except on the black market where the price has skyrocketed."

At the mention of the illegal markets, I thought of Singer. "Sugar too."

"I've heard brown sugar will soon be allocated to us, but no more white," Jozef said.

"Of course. Hitler hates anything brown, so he sends it gladly to his Jews," Heilig said and burst into laughter. "Do you get it? It's funny."

Pola suddenly burst into laughter. "Forgive me. I'm not laughing at that." I turned toward her.

"They're doing it. The Chairman promises a motion picture theater." She handed me the notice.

I read the announcement aloud, "a motion picture theater is to be set up to provide working people with entertainment and diversion from daily life." This can't be real? I stared at Pola, confused about her having left me on Wesola Street on Friday night. "It's another disappointment," I said.

"You read it yourself," Pola said. "Imagine seeing a motion picture again."

"The Engineer is right. I'll believe it when I see it," Heilig said.

"It's an official document from the Chairman's office," Pola protested with a rare show of emotion. "Why must you always ruin things?"

"They make promises, and shit comes of it," Heilig fired back. "Movie theater in this slum? More lies and false hope."

Pola turned toward me, her eyes imploring me for help. Was she a damsel in distress? I was not a knight riding on a white horse to her rescue. I aimed my sights at her and said, "People make all kinds of promises they do not intend to keep." I turned away, not wanting to see her reaction.

"I still believe it will happen," she said. "Did not the Chairman promise concerts? Do we not have concerts now?"

Heilig smirked. "Yes, we have concerts. So he can keep his chosen few in line and have a venue for his pep-talks. More damn lies and faked optimism. Only fools believe in his promises. Remember when he promised and promised to protect our children?"

"Enough," I said.

Heilig ignored me, "A movie theater? No. Not here."

I was about to agree that it would never happen when I saw Jozef staring hard at a sheet of paper in his hands. "What is it, Jozef? Are you alright?"

"I turned sixty-six a few days ago," he said.

"Happy birthday," I said. "I didn't know. We could have celebrated."

Heilig laughed. "Yes, celebrated. So few reach that milestone these days. Mazel tov, congratulations." He fished into his pocket. "Here. Here. Take my gift of a ration card for meat and milk that do not exist. Wait! I have a ticket for a motion picture that also does not exist, and never will." He had tears in his eyes. "Oh, God, will we ever see a motion picture again?" His head dropped into his arms.

"We should all sing Happy Birthday to our distinguished colleague," I said and began to sing.

Jozef held up his hand. "Stop! Stop it all of you."

"What's wrong? It's your birthday," I said.

Jozef's voice was plaintive. "Numbers man, they are only issuing work cards for those between the age of ten and sixty-five."

"You're safe here," I said, "We're all safe here."

Jozef laughed bitterly. "Yes, in this room, we are all safe." He looked at Pola. "You look as I remember my wife. I even miss her coughs."

"In heaven, nobody coughs," Heilig said.

"What?" Jozef looked shocked.

Heilig said, "I meant to say, nobody suffers. No Nazis get into the pearly gates."

"What do you know? You're an atheist like my friend, Benny, over there." He leaned toward Pola. "You do know the Engineer is a godless man? A good man, but without faith."

"I would rather know a good man without faith than a man of faith who hurts others," Pola said, casting me a glance.

I realized, without her saying it, that perhaps that was why she didn't keep her promised appointment. A woman who loved her husband understands the thoughts that were battling in my head as I stood on that corner, waiting for her, secretly praying she would not appear. But how can a man so tempted be considered a good man? I settled back to my typing. I wondered if it was she who was the good one, the one who could not betray the memory of her husband.

"So, where do you think they will put a movie theater?" Pola asked.

I burst into laughter. A movie theater in the ghetto? Insane.

CHAPTER 22

THURSDAY, DECEMBER 3, 1942

I shook the snow off my coat but kept it on. The shortage of coal and wood was making us all freeze.

"At least we have the consolation that the wolves are also freezing in Russia," Heilig said.

"Yes, but our fighters in the forests are also freezing," Pola remarked.

What fighters, I thought, aware she appeared to know things that the rest of us did not.

"Heilig is late again," I said.

Jozef, who walked in a good fifteen minutes after me, was stamping his feet. "We need snow to add to our miseries?"

"It's your God who is doing this to us," I said. "My hands are cold. I think I'm getting old." I am becoming Rosenfeld, I mused, rubbing my hands together as he so often did.

"You should be so lucky," Jozef snapped back. "Nobody gets old here. They ship us away to warmer pastures."

The door opened.

"Attention!" I shouted automatically, fearing a German bursting in and arresting the lot of us for neglecting to show the proper respect.

Pola stood and turned to the door.

"What a bitching morning," Heilig said, his hair and hat white with snow.

"You look like a white-haired old man," I said. "Brush that snow off your coat."

"You know the bridge all Jews must cross to get from one side of the street to the other?" He asked.

"It's so Germans may avoid contact with their Jewish vermin," Jozef said.

"Well, the snow blocked it up and made it so slippery that sentries would only allow one worker at a time to cross over. And that was a dance on the ice." Heilig stamped his shoes, the loose sole of one slapping on the floor. "But the joke was on the Huns," he added.

"I'm sure they enjoyed watching Jews break their necks," Pola said.

"You know how the Germans built the tram so their people could race through the ghetto without risk of bodily contact with our inferior race?" Heilig asked. "Well, nature stopped the tram. Their Aryan race was forced to travel on our Jewish streets on foot."

I laughed. "That must have been a rare sight. Germans and Jews walking, sliding on the same streets."

"Not quite. The soldiers, shivering and covered in snow, were given the task to ensure that Germans walked on the roadway while Jews were restricted to the sidewalks. Aryan purity was preserved." He rubbed his mittens together.

I wondered if he'd gotten them off a corpse as I had obtained gloves for Rosenfeld.

"The Germans, to preserve their racial blood, post Gestapo as street guards when they should be fighting in Russia. And we're the crazy ones?" Heilig shook his head. "And never the twain shall meet."

I glanced at Pola. *Never the twain shall meet.*

Pola caught my eyes and asked, "What does this mean: the ghetto is to be designated as a 'labor camp?'"

I reached for the paper, and our fingers touched. Was I more aware of this than she? Her eyes showed no reaction.

"Who is giving us this designation?" Jozef asked.

"It says, 'the highest authorities in Berlin,'" I replied.

"I would say this is good then. Perhaps very good," Jozef said. "Berlin is acknowledging our contribution to their war effort. If that is true, then we will be protected by them, have our conditions improved."

"Mothers may even get milk soon," Heilig said. "The wolves are such humane souls."

I shot him an angry look. "It affirms that our Chairman selected the right path," I said, but how could it be if it cost us our children?

"That is still for the future to decide," Heilig said.

"There is a concert this Saturday at the House of Culture," Jozef muttered. "It will feature Dawid Baigelman conducting light Jewish music."

"The Eldest does it for the elite," Heilig said. "I wonder if the snow even lands on their backs?"

"We're invited to the concerts. I guess that makes us part of the elite."

Heilig gave me an angry look and ducked back into his work.

Pola was looking at me. Did she expect me to ask her for the concert? A woman alone was not acceptable at such events.

She was writing on a sheet of paper with print on one side. Paper was in short supply.

Heilig interrupted my thoughts, "The bridge is going to jam up again. I'll leave now." He stood, and before I could raise any objection, was out the door.

"Jozef, tell that idiot to be careful. There is a rumor going around that every able-bodied man is being taken to construct a highway between Litzmannstadt and Warsaw," Pola said.

"Where did you hear that one?" I asked, shocked by this new gossip.

Jozef hurried out the door.

"Okay, Pola, where did this information come from?"

She handed me a rolled slip of paper. "It says this will result in the evacuation of the ghetto."

I looked at her. "Is this rumor confirmed?"

"Not yet, but if it transpires, the entire ghetto will be evacuated."

"It can't be done. We have nearly 100,000 people here."

"My husband said the same of Warsaw."

"We mustn't tell the others, not until this is verified. Who is your source?"

Pola looked at the door. "Jozef will be back soon. I'll tell you tonight."

I gave her a confused look.

She whispered, "A woman can't go to the Chairman's concert alone."

CHAPTER 23

S ATURDAY, DECEMBER 5, 1942
A CONCERT
Today, as on every Saturday, a concert took place in the House of Culture and, as usual, the ghetto's elite attended.

I thought of not showing up. It would serve Pola right for leaving me standing on a street corner. I'd been full of anticipation, a schoolboy on a first date, but with the conscience of a mature man who knows his wife is going to return. I thought Pola's invitation for me to take her to the concert was typical of her inscrutability. I could concentrate on nothing else, arguing inwardly what my actions should be. One minute concluding, "I will meet her;" the next, determining, "I will abandon her to the snowy street as she did to me."

Did her face flash into view as Miriam's had so many times? No. Did I see a young, innocent, hazel-eyed face? No. So, why did I dress in my suit, wrinkled, worn at the knees and elbows, but still serviceable? Was I planning on something happening? *No. Of course not.* Why did she ask me to take her? *She said it was not proper, not allowed, for a woman to attend a concert alone, but in these times most women are alone.*

After Jozef left me last night for his clandestine Shabbat eve services, I stood in the shadow of the barren hospital. The glass broken during the round-up of patients had not been replaced. There were no replacements for windows in the ghetto. Once windows were broken, residents could only pray they would not freeze to death. Another of our many shortages while concerts were regularly scheduled.

"For the elite," I heard my Miriam, her sweet voice transformed to that of a shrew. A shrew? Not my Miriam. Then whose voice was it that burned through my brain like acid? Were they Singer's words? His ideas? His cynical point-of-view? Was that the result of their hidden love-making? I shut off these thoughts, unable to face the vision of their two young bodies mocking our marriage vows, but understanding how such young bodies and faces attract and entwine. I had to stop this. Focus on Pola. I tried. I tried.

Multiple times, as I walked toward the House of Culture, I stopped. There were fewer Order Service policemen on the streets. Many had been dismissed, subsequently resettled in the rural farmlands. I wondered how they fared lodged with those who had feared and hated them for enforcing the edicts of the Chairman, who enforced the orders of the occupation. There were stories that long-suppressed violence had been unleashed on some of these former policemen by their fellow Jews. Rumkowski had warned, "They will hate you when they find out what you knew."

"I wasn't sure you were going to come," Pola said as I was about to reverse my decision.

"I wasn't either," I replied. Pola appeared shorter next to me, about Miriam's height. I snuck a glance at her clothing. Her dress was rather plain-looking, a drab tan that fell nearly down to her shoes. Miriam's dress, the pearls in a vee, some missing, had forced men to look at her cleavage. Singer had bartered my mother's ring for that dress, but it was worth it. I had said she would be eyed by everyone at the concert. "But I have only ratty shoes," she replied. I glanced at Pola's shoes. They were the same she wore to our office, but the tissue paper she used to fill the back wasn't visible. "You look nice," I said.

Pola smiled. "I'm sorry, I don't have anything better."

"You look nice," I repeated, almost grateful she did not look as young and lustrous as Miriam. I remembered dear Dr. Rosenfeld's face when he first saw my wife...and Singer's eyes. "You really do look nice," I said louder, sensing that Pola was hesitant at entering our last great hall of

Jewish culture. "Shall we go in?" I asked but did not take her hand.

"You don't have to do this," Pola said. "I would have understood if you decided not to come." She looked into my eyes. "I almost didn't...again."

Miriam hadn't understood me at all. I assumed it was because of our age difference, a generation. "Let's go and enjoy the music. Do you like music?" I knew so little about Pola. Does a man ever know about his wife...women?

"My husband was a violinist."

"I didn't know." We walked up the grand stairway. I wondered how so many women still had gowns. They were the ghetto elite. I felt none of the swell of pride I felt walking Miriam up past the snooty ladies in the ornate hallway. Miriam looked beautiful, even with her baby bump....

"Engineer, are you alright with this?" Pola asked, seeing me reach for the banister.

I nodded, my hand gripping the railing.

At the landing before the entrance to the auditorium, Pola whispered, "Do you know anyone here?"

"I recognize some, but many I used to know are gone."

Pola smiled sadly. "Warsaw had wonderful concerts. We had many friends...."

"I'm sorry," I said. "Was one Singer?"

"We will talk later. The concert is about to begin," Pola pushed past me. Miriam would never do that. She was shy around people.

I followed Pola to our seats. From the rear, she looked thinner, her legs were almost sticks. When she sat, I glanced at her breasts, hidden by her buttoned front. Not much there.

The lights dimmed.

Pola's hands were in her lap. I remembered Miriam clasped my hand during the entire concert. I dropped my hands in my lap and prayed the music would erase all of my straying thoughts for at least a few minutes. Wasn't that why I'd decided to come?

A tall man with hair overflowing his hat caught my attention. Even from this distance, I recognized our Chairman, the Eldest of the Jews. He was staring straight ahead. Was that his new wife next to him? Singer had laughed that the "old fart" had met his match, marrying a lawyer. I was stunned the Chairman's wife was named Regina…the same as my child. I believed it was an omen. He would protect her.

"You're tense," Pola whispered. "Do you wish to leave?"

"That's Rumkowski." I pointed out our leader.

"I know. I've seen the Chairman at the weddings you send me to report on. Is that his wife next to him?"

"Yes. Regina." I gulped hard. "That was…is my baby's name."

Her hand touched mine. "I think that is why I was drawn to you. We have a common loss…a shared pain."

I didn't reply.

"Did your wife like music?"

"She loved it."

The audience burst into applause. Dawid Bajgelman was walking to his platform.

"He looks older than when I saw him tour in Warsaw," Pola whispered.

"We all do."

I noticed she didn't remark about the grandeur of the House of Culture. Miriam had gawked at the proscenium arch over the stage. I guessed the ghetto concert hall was not remarkable when compared to the vaulted ceilings of Warsaw's cultural centers. Did she have an inkling of the miracle the Chairman wrought in getting this building, his dream, spared by the Nazis?

Bajgelman held up his baton and then lowered it. He turned to the audience and hesitated, searching the front rows.

In the stage lights, I saw the gray of his complexion, the wrinkles that had transformed him to an old man leading half an orchestra in a ghetto with an unknown future. "I dedicate this wonderful event to the memory of those no longer performing on this stage."

The Chairman, who had stood and faced the audience, sat down.

"The music is beginning," I said.

The music came from all around us. I recognized Bela Keler's Overture. It was the same as the first time I brought Miriam to the concert.

Pola's eyes were closed, as Miriam's had been.

The orchestra next played Popa's Suite Orientale. I recognized it as being the same as during that first concert. I closed my eyes and was transported to the Far East. Miriam had placed her hand in mine. Pola's hands were still in her lap.

"It's lovely," Pola whispered at the end of the suite.

A man walked to the front of the stage. He lifted a violin to his chin. He began to play the mournful sounds of a tune I did not recognize. The violin made a sound like a voice crying.

Pola's palm dropped over mine.

When I looked, there were tears in her eyes. I didn't pull my hand away.

Pola trembled. She'd said her husband played the violin. Placing her hand on mine was a natural reaction. Nothing more. I wondered if she would remove her hand once the orchestra joined and drowned out the tearful wail of the violin.

She did not.

I did not. I couldn't.

CHAPTER 24

MONDAY, DECEMBER 7, 1942

"Good morning," I said to Heilig and then repeated my greeting to Pola, hoping the Weasel couldn't detect any change in my demeanor toward her.

"Good morning, Engineer," Pola replied. "I hope you enjoyed your weekend?"

I gave her a quick smile. Thankfully, Jozef, always a few minutes behind me, stumbled in at that point.

"This damn snow and ice. I wonder how cold it is in the north country where they are sending our people? I'll bet they have fuel for heat." He leaned backward and then forward again. "My old back is killing me. You have to walk so gingerly or fall on your ass. The slippery roads and the lack of heat are making me into a cripple."

"Stop complaining. That is all Jews do. We gripe when it's cold and then when it's hot. You sound like an old gossip, a yenta." I burst into laughter.

Jozef stared at me. "What are you so happy about?" He glanced at Pola.

Pola shrugged, barely looking at me.

What the hell was I laughing about? I looked at Pola and knew. "I don't think you'd like farming much," I said to Jozef.

"Perhaps not, but who farms in snow and freezing cold? All our departed are enjoying warm hearths and hot cocoa while it is winter outside. The joke is on the Germans who must provide food and fuel to keep their farmers fit for the next season." He looked at me. "I'm getting old, my friend, from this damn weather. Would a farmhouse be so bad?"

"I must remain here, for Miriam and Regina," I said, and glanced at Pola. Her face offered no insight into her thoughts.

Why did I say that? Was I trying to put up a wall between us? I thought back to Saturday's concert. Her hand in mine…it felt good. It had been a long time since I held a hand…felt anything other than loneliness. As the orchestra continued to take us from our desperate ghetto, I had felt her hand pulsing and prayed she would leave it there.

"This is wonderful news," Jozef said. "The Chairman's appeal has met great success. His commission has found foster homes for 720 orphaned children."

I glanced at Pola.

"That is good news," she said.

"Note who is taking the credit," Heilig mumbled.

"He deserves it," Jozef replied. "Who else could arouse people to take in more hungry mouths in their beleaguered homes?"

"Who makes us starve?" Heilig replied. "His family and friends, and yes, even we, dine in luxury while everyone else starves. Did you know they held another damn concert this past Saturday? All the stuffed shirts and their bitches attend every Saturday. How is it possible when even potatoes and milk, milk for babies, are only available on the black market and for prices that are fitting for caviar and champagne. Both of which I'm sure Lord Chaim and his family are basking in while we—"

"Enough, Heilig," I rasped, feeling attacked for being one of the elite who attended the concert. "The fact is that 720 orphans now have homes because of his efforts. You can't deny facts."

"Numbers! You are always with numbers," Heilig said. "Do you not wonder why we have so many orphans sent like baggage to our ghetto? Where do they come from? Where are the parents? That is what we should be investigating, great journalists that we are."

Pola looked up. "Do you really want to know that? Do any of us want to have more misery heaped upon us? Heilig, their parents are dead or vanished. It is all the same. It is the lives we have now that we must save.

The wolves are not defeated. They may never be." She choked up. "The children are safe. God bless them. Please, let it go?"

I wished I could embrace and comfort her but couldn't risk it. I addressed Heilig instead. "Bernard, in other times, I would be the first to mourn the parents of these children, now given hope. I would lead the charge for a thorough and unyielding investigation. You have been here long enough to know there is nothing we can do. Nothing. Accept what is and pray for no worse. Pray for no worse."

Jozef said, "He is right. Even in this good news, there is a distressing counterpoint: there are more than 300 children still housed in hostels."

Pola looked up. "Young children?"

I picked up the longing in her tone. Was I feeling that longing as well? *Regina will be back. I can't give that up.*

Jozef replied, "Most are older adolescents. Plans are to place all the younger ones with families and leave the older ones in the hostels when they're not working."

"Those poor children," Pola said, looking at me.

"We have work to do," I replied.

The others settled back into their tasks. I tried, but my mind drifted back to the concert and its aftermath.

After the concert, when the lights returned, Pola withdrew her hand. I was grateful nobody saw our hands clutching. I was about to stand when the room grew silent. The Chairman made his way onto the stage, helped by Neftalin, and supported by his cane. His steps were more faltering than when I'd seen him on the day of that infamous "Give me your children?" speech. I wanted to leave, skittish his voice would roar me back to that terrible night. But it was not the same voice. No emotional appeal, no dramatic flair. His address was surprisingly short. He first thanked the conductor and orchestra for their performance "under such trying circumstances." He then praised his managers and administrators for their loyalty but reiterated the need to improve productivity. "Those who choose, or who cannot work, will be dealt with," he said. Everyone knew what that meant. After that, he let out a rare smile and concluded with his promise that there would be more concerts in the future for those who serve the ghetto so well.

"May I walk you home?" I asked Pola, after the concert, more from obligation than anything else.

Pola studied my face. "I enjoyed tonight. I enjoyed it more than anything since my Hershel…

"Your husband?"

"Thank you, Engineer. You have done enough."

"Thank you. I enjoyed it too."

"Did you?"

"Yes."

Pola smiled. It made her look younger. It may have been the snow falling around us like glitter. "My slave driver of a boss has given me an assignment for tomorrow. I am to cover the Chairman marrying fourteen couples."

"He must be a tyrant," I teased.

"You are," she teased right back. "I find it rejuvenating seeing these young brides and grooms bursting with optimism. I suppose that is why the Eldest of the Jews risks the ire of the authorities by conducting these ceremonies. Weddings give hope for the future."

"Are you inviting me to a wedding?" I asked, pondering how to respond.

"We all need a shot of hope once in a while. So, yes, I'm inviting my tyrant of a boss to a wedding."

"I haven't enjoyed myself like this for a long time," I said, staring into her eyes as if for the first time. "I thank you for the company and the invitation. I need to think it over."

Pola nodded and then smiled. "Opportunities don't always come. Who knows how long the Germans will allow these weddings to continue?"

I looked at Pola and said. "Sometime I will go."

She shook her head as if she didn't believe me.

That ended the evening. One of the nicest I'd had in a very long time.

But that was already in the past. I glanced to where Pola was working. Maybe, one day, I thought and dove back into my work.

CHAPTER 25

FRIDAY DECEMBER 11, 1942
**A SPECIAL DISTRIBUTION POINT FOR THE ORDER
SERVICE AND FIRE DEPARTMENT**

*The members of the Order Service and the Fire Department are to have two
special distribution points; ...these two services will receive all their rations
there...This is a very welcome reform since there have always been altercations in
the cooperatives and other stores whenever the Order Service men and firemen
wished to pick up their rations without waiting in line.*

Heilig was late. Jozef was at the Personnel Department, where there was
news of a census of all office workers. I was alone with Pola and felt
uncomfortable. She did nothing to make me feel that way. She was all but
ignoring me. I did not know how to break the ice. "Are you angry I did
not accompany you to the wedding ceremonies?" I asked, afraid the others
would arrive and sense the tension.

Pola looked up. "No. You have the right to do as you please."

This wasn't going well. Why did I care? What was I looking for? There
was something still hard-shelled about her, yet I'd seen evidence of a warm
human being beneath that aloof exterior. "I don't know why I didn't come
with you."

"It takes time to get over a loss such as you've experienced."

"What loss? I've lost no one." How could she believe I lost my wife and
child? "I'm sorry. I snapped at you."

"I understand. Your wife and child...how old was...is she?"

"My wife is…twenty…."

"Your daughter. Not your wife."

"Two…two and a half." I bit my lip. I couldn't remember how old my own child was.

Pola reached for my hand. "It is too soon for you. I understand. I really do. It took me a long time to want to live again."

"After you lost your baby?"

"And after they took my husband." Pola sighed. "They broke his hands. He had beautiful hands. He could wring the most heart-wrenching sounds from a violin."

"You don't have to talk about it now."

"I would like to."

I settled back to listen when the door burst open. "Attention!" I shouted the greeting as ordered by the Chairman, and we both jumped from our chairs.

"God damn them! God damn them all!"

It was Heilig. He leaned on the wall, his face hidden. "Oh, God, my eye!" Pola raced to his side. "Please, move your hand?"

"I can't. Oh, God. How much more can I take?"

"Please? Move your hand. I have taken care of many injured men and women." Pola attempted to pry his hand loose, but he pushed her away.

She had tended many injured? Was she a nurse? Another piece of the puzzle. "Heilig, let Pola help you. That is an order!"

"Order? You are not my boss! The damn Nazis are our bosses." He swatted away at Pola's hand.

I leveled my voice. "Heilig, if you don't let her look at your eye, I am going to call Neftalin and have him send you to the hospital. Now, stop being a child. Let Pola examine your eye." I gripped his wrist. "Now, move it off your eye. And yes, I will call Neftalin if you disobey."

"You're a bastard," Heilig growled, but let me lower his hand.

"It's bleeding," Pola said. "He should see a doctor."

"No. If the Chairman learns I can't work, you know what happens." Heilig was pleading.

Pola gently lifted his eyelid. "How did this happen? Did the Nazis do this?" She tore a piece of her blouse. "I think you should see a doctor, but I'll try and clean it up for you. I can't promise anything."

"Shall I get some water?" I asked.

"Yes. See if you can find some."

I headed for Neftalin's office. I kept my eyes straight as I passed the German police. When I got to the Deputy's office, I tapped on his door. When there was no answer, I pushed it open. A water carafe was seated on his desk. I took the cloth and poured some water over it. I was about to leave when Henryk walked in. At first, I didn't think he saw me. He looked despondent as he pushed his door closed. When he saw me, he asked, "What are you doing here?"

"Heilig had an accident. I need to wet this cloth." I held up the makeshift bandage.

"Is he alright?"

"Are you? You look upset."

Neftalin sighed. "How are you bearing up, my friend?"

"May I ask something? As a friend."

A frown crossed Neftalin's face. "You want to ask if I know what happened to them. I wish to God, and I swear this, that I could answer your questions." He dug into his desk and pulled out a few small postcards. "These arrived from a women's labor camp near Munich. These other postcards are from people's relatives from some other Polish provinces. Sadly, we have only a few. You know the postal service has been problematic. I'm sure there are more postcards to be expected." He smiled. "It is a good omen."

"I have not heard from Miriam since that night. Can you find out where she and my daughter are? It would be a great favor." I must have looked very small and pitiful, begging like that, but had to ask. The emptiness was gnawing at my soul. I had nowhere else to turn.

Neftalin nodded. "I will try." He stood, a signal that our audience was over. "How is the new woman working out?"

"She is very competent," I said. "Her husband was killed." How much did

Neftalin know about Pola?

Neftalin walked toward the door. "She was imprisoned as well. I'm sure she told you about it all." He opened the door. "Now, get that cloth to Heilig. Let me know if he needs medical attention. God be with you."

"You'll look for Miriam?"

"I said I'll try. You know more than most how precarious our situation is." He closed the door.

I felt like barging back into his office and demanding his help — screaming of my agony, my loyalty. I saw the hard face of his door and knew there was nothing more I could do. Neftalin was as frustrated as the rest of us. *Damn, the cloth is dry.* I walked back to our room. "Where is Heilig?" I asked, glancing at his chair.

Pola looked frightened.

"Where is he?"

"He left. I tried to hold him. He pushed me away and ran out."

"His eye? How bad was it?"

"I couldn't tell. He may lose it."

"The goddamn Germans," I hissed, slamming my fist on the table.

"Benny, it wasn't the Nazis."

"What are you talking about? Who else would do such a thing?"

"It was an accident. Heilig was standing on a long line for his rations when a group of Order Servicemen charged to the front. Some people, some waiting for hours, reacted. There was a lot of shouting and then shoving. The Order Servicemen swung their clubs to quell the fighting."

"They caused the commotion by pushing ahead."

"Heilig was in the wrong place. He was struck in his eye."

I fell into my chair. "Poor Heilig. Desperate men do desperate things," I echoed the Dr. Rosenfeld refrain.

"We're all starving. Some blame your Chairman for their misery. They hate the police that enforce his laws."

"Are they his laws? Do you believe he wants to do these things?" I asked.

"The point is, he does them."

I looked at the pile of papers on the table. The stack of the Chairman's proclamations grew each day. "Would you like to go to the concert tomorrow?" I asked. "It would be my honor to escort you."

The door opened slowly. I was about to shout, "Attention!", but saw it was Zelkowicz. I'd almost forgotten about him. "Where have you been?" I asked. He had a strange expression on his face. "What is it? Has something else happened?"

Jozef looked at me. "Do you remember the German inspector who came here a short time ago? Yes, I'm sure you do." He removed his hat and placed it on the table. "They are letting go of more than 700 office workers."

My eyes shot toward Pola, our last hire.

Jozef removed his coat and scarf. "I'm the oldest here."

"No! I'm not losing any more of my friends. Goddammit! No more." I slammed my fist on the table.

Jozef picked up a sheet of paper and began to write up his report from the Personnel Department. "Where will they find 700 office workers?"

Pola slid her chair toward me. "Yes," she whispered.

CHAPTER 26

MONDAY, DECEMBER 14, 1942
PEOPLE ARE SAYING
The entire ghetto is saying that a delegation of the Swiss Red Cross will be coming here.

"That is wonderful news," Jozef exclaimed, rubbing his hands together to keep warm. "Once they see this shithole, the world will be told of our dire conditions, and we'll be rescued. God bless the Red Cross."

"It's just a rumor," I said but was hopeful since most rumors came true. Some took time but eventually became a reality. I wondered how those who started the stories got their information. The Chairman tried everything to crush them, especially those that spread bad news.

"It is hopeful," Pola said, giving me a smile. "We must never abandon hope."

Jozef poked me in the ribs. "That is why I still pray to God, and so should you, my atheist friend."

Pola helped Jozef with his coat. "Jozef, I will let you pray for all of us."

Jozef looked at her. "Not another atheist?"

"No. Who else could have invented music but a God?"

"You should attend the Chairman's concerts," Jozef said. "Take the atheist with you. Maybe then he'll believe in God too."

I laughed inside, musing how Pola and I were fooling the old man. I looked forward to our next concert. I had not looked forward to anything for a long time. "Yes, Mrs. Levinski, I would love to take you to one of our

Chairman's concerts," I said and bowed to Pola, who gave an exaggerated curtsy as Jozef watched our idiotic antics.

"I think you two are finally going insane," he said and then frowned. "A little companionship would do us all good."

He was right. I couldn't wait for Jozef to leave for his Sabbath services the next morning. "Are you sure you don't want to come with me?" he asked at the door.

"No, thank you. I think I'll take you up on your suggestion."

He gave me a curious look.

"The concert. I'll write a first-hand report about the Chairman's cultural event."

"Perhaps, Pola will take my advice too," he muttered and pushed the door shut.

It was fun to pull the wool over his eyes. He was practically shoving Pola on me, not having an inkling that this was our second concert together. *Why am I concealing this? There is nothing to hide. We're friends. We're helping each other get over terrible losses.* Nonetheless, it was fun to think that we were fooling Jozef and everyone. Unlike the first concert, when I drove myself crazy debating whether I should meet Pola, this time, I was excited, eager to see how a different repertoire would move my companion.

The second program was almost an exact repetition of the previous week. The conductor, Beigjelman, hinted at the reason for this by complimenting his orchestra members for meeting after their "grueling daily labor." I knew what obstacles our brethren had to overcome to be on this stage after slaving in the Chairman's factories ten to twelve hours per day. It was a miracle they wanted to rehearse after such demands on their bodies.

"I'm glad you consented to this," I whispered to Pola, who settled back in the cushioned chair, a luxury.

"I always loved music. It takes me back to a happier time."

"Me as well." I sat back in my chair as the first swells rose toward us, wings of an invisible bird carrying us away from the filth-caked world of the ghetto.

Pola's eyes were closed, her finger swayed with the melody. She was conducting the orchestra, her face more peaceful-looking than I'd ever witnessed. There was a beauty in her relaxed features I had not noticed before. Not the lively luster of Miriam, the way I remembered her, so innocent, so young. But when Pola allowed her jaws to lose their tension, her lips to be less tight, it was pleasing to look at her. With her eyes closed and her lips formed into a contented hint of a smile, I glanced at her several times. Her eyes caught me, I'm sure. Finally, when a violin solo filled my heart with its mournful cry, I moved my hand over hers, in her lap.

Pola did not push my hand away.

I sat that way through the rest of the concert, removing my hand only when the lights came on. Neither of us said anything about it, but her eyes were not angry for a change when the Eldest of the Jews was helped up to the podium and again addressed the crowd. First, he praised the factory managers, and then, hitting his stride, he launched a tirade scolding all who shirk their duties. I barely heard. I was thinking about what made me move my hand over Pola's. It had felt pleasant to hold someone's hand again, but was it just to grasp anyone, or was it because it was Pola's hand?

"He always says the same thing," Pola said, once we were away from anyone I might know. I wasn't ready to be seen with someone other than Miriam. "He compliments those who are loyal and offers thinly-veiled threats to those who oppose him. It's always the same."

"He's had to face the same problems all along," I replied, noticing she was walking with me, not on her own, as in the previous week. "He must deal with obstructions from many quarters, including socialists, criminals, and immigrants who have no loyalty to our community."

"Not all immigrants are malefactors. Why must he be so repressive?" Pola's eyes darted from one side of the street to the other.

"What are you looking for?" I asked.

"Nothing. I'm just cautious, a woman alone."

That made sense. "You're new here, but the Chairman believes, and I do too, that if the Germans see any signal that we can't control our own people, they will come in with their brutal force. That would be a nightmare. My old friend, Dr. Rosenfeld, predicted that the Germans would use every means to ensure that our productivity is maintained."

"We heard of your Chairman's success in Warsaw," Pola said. "His factories are a model for all of us. Unfortunately, in Warsaw, it may be too late."

"Here too. Singer said our value to the Germans was our salvation but also our curse."

"How so?"

"He was an immoral rascal, but quite astute." I left room for her to admit she knew him, but she said nothing. "Oscar theorized that making Lodz valuable to the German war effort, we might delay the inevitable, the resettlement of all Jews from the ghetto."

"That makes sense. It appears to be working."

"It's a two-edged sword. By convincing Hitler of our importance, we risk him lusting to take over our facilities. That is why he has annexed Lodz as part of Germany. Lodz is no longer shown on maps as part of Poland. In fact, Hitler had it renamed as Litzmannstadt."

Pola looked distracted.

"Enough. I'm boring you with my history lesson. Did you enjoy the music tonight? You've heard most of it before."

"I can hear the same song a thousand times, and it still transports me to another place and time."

I saw her smile, and then she took my hand. She was leading me toward the side of the roadway. I let her. I barely heard when she said, "Benny, there."

The building's windows were boarded up.

I looked around. I thought of pulling away. I didn't. I didn't ask why or where Pola was taking me. I saw a door near the rear of the abandoned structure. Planks were nailed across it.

Pola led me to the side of the building. I waited for her to turn toward me. My heart was beating hard. *What do I feel? Why did I follow? Is it lust? Hope? Do I love her? No. Can I love her? I don't know. I don't care.*

I was so lonely, so lost. Pola's hand in mine had pulsed with life, warmth. I had hoped the war would end soon; now, I didn't know if it would ever end. I had expected to have Miriam and Regina back with me…now, I was unable to see their faces…all was fading…all was fading. At night, lying awake, Jozef snoring, I saw only eyes, more gray than hazel, floating in a face that was a blur, Miriam's eyes, but as if reflected in a puddle. So, I followed.

"Benny," Pola whispered, "Please, forgive me?"

Forgive? For what? I felt a gun barrel in my back.

CHAPTER 27

The gun barrel, pressing hard, forced me to the door of the building. "Who are you? What do you want? I have nothing for you to steal." "Inside." The gun pushed harder.

From a corner of my eye, I saw Pola shove the door open and step inside. "It's clear," she whispered.

"Get in."

"Singer, is it you?" I thought of twisting away from the gun but wasn't sure it was him.

"Face the wall. Don't try to see my face."

The gun was still there. I trembled, thought I might pee myself.

Pola pulled the door closed. She stood sentry by the window, peering through the planks.

"Don't move."

"Who are you? You're not Singer."

"I have very little time. I need you to shut up. Don't say anything. I'm moving the gun, but have a knife. Face the wall, and you will be released."

"Who are you?"

"A friend. If you see me, you'll be putting yourself in danger."

"Are you a friend of Singer?"

"He is one of us."

"Is she?" I sounded angry. I had the right.

"Yes."

"What do you want?"

"We need your help. You are in a position where you may learn things that could help our cause."

"I'm not a fighter. Singer knows that."

"We're not asking you to fight. It's impossible to smuggle weapons into Lodz. Yesterday, a Polish smuggler was captured by your Order Service and turned over to the Kripo, the German criminal police. The net is tight around you."

"Then what do you want?"

"Singer says you can be trusted."

"That's more than I can say of him," I spat.

"He said you'd have something to say, but I should ignore it because you are at heart a good man."

"Did he tell you I have a wife and daughter? Did the sonofabitch tell you he's my Regina's godfather? Did he tell you that?"

"It is for their sake that you must help us. Your ghetto is living on borrowed time. We believe the Chairman's efforts to save the Jews of Lodz are doomed to failure."

"You're wrong. The Germans need us. They are sending us order after order. Ask her, she can tell you. What do you need me for when you have her? She's more than stealthy enough to be your damn spy."

"You did not tell him?"

"Tell me what? What other secrets is she hiding?" How could I have fooled myself again?

"I'll let her tell you herself," the voice said.

"I don't want to hear her." How could she do this to me? How did I fall for it?

"As you wish. Recently, your chairman ordered 35,000 pairs of wooden clogs."

"Shoes? Is that what this is about?"

"Just listen." Pola read him the memo.

"I said I don't want to hear anything from her."

"Shut up and forget about yourself for a minute," the man rasped. "Read the damn memo."

Pola came closer. "35,000 wooden clogs have been produced within the ghetto in less than two weeks."

I was losing patience, my face pressed against the wall, my back aching. "There has been a shortage of shoes. So what? If you let me go, I won't report this kidnapping," I said.

"Please, listen. Singer said you were stubborn but would eventually listen."

At his name, I became quiet.

Pola was close enough that I could smell her breath. "Benny, the memo goes on."

"Don't call me that. Just read the goddamn thing and let me go home to Jozef. At least I can trust him."

"You can trust me," Pola said.

"This is bullshit," the man shouted. "I'm going to get shot by a Nazi while you two have a lover's quarrel."

"We're not lovers," I hissed.

"Just finish reading it to him."

Pola's hair was almost touching my face. "Please, let me finish this. Trust me?"

I didn't answer.

"The memo goes on: 'Not even the ten percent quota could be met, since not enough leather soles were available.'"

"Nothing new here. Nothing is available," I said.

"We're almost there," Pola said. "Because of this shortage, the Chairman succeeded in obtaining permission from the authorities to manufacture 35,000 pairs of clogs for the ghetto."

"Problem solved," I said. "Tell Singer, I send my love." I started to pull away from the wall. I felt a sharp point in my back. "I'm standing still."

The blade moved off.

Pola sighed. "I'm almost done. 'The Used Materials and Sorting Point supplied the necessary material: the tops were to be made chiefly out of knapsacks.'"

It was as if a bullet hit my brain. "Knapsacks," I said.

"Yes," Pola replied.

"You're sure of this?" I asked. "Used knapsacks?"

"Yes. The shoes are already made. 35,000 pairs."

I didn't ask where the knapsacks came from. I didn't have to. "You can put away the knife," I said. "What do you want me to do? As long as I'm here, waiting for Miriam and my daughter, I'll do what I can to help."

"Please remain facing the wall," the man said. "If you don't see my face, you will not have that information should you be tortured by the Gestapo or S.S."

"Thank you. I'm sure my friends told you I'm not a brave man, but an engineer."

"You've been risking your life every day, but no, we don't want to put you in more danger. What we want is information. As head of your department, all we ask is that you keep us aware of anything that could help us against the wolves."

"I ask again, why do you need me when you have her?"

The man sighed. "Pola is here temporarily."

I felt sick to my stomach. Temporarily? Where was she going? Why did I give a damn? Like Singer and Miriam, she had betrayed me.

"We must have you to replace her. If you learn of anything that can help us, we'll be grateful."

I nodded. "I'll help you. I want something in return." The man was silent. "I want to know if my wife and child are alive."

The man placed a hand on my shoulder. "Don't turn around. We all want to know that," he said. "Sometimes, I think the lucky ones are the ones who know the fate of their loved ones."

"Will you do that for me?" I asked.

"Our agent will watch for you on Zgierska and Wesola Street. If you have news, hold your papers in your right hand. You are left-handed, Singer said."

"Where is Singer?" I asked, wishing it was Oscar in this building with me.

"You'll see him soon," the man said.

"You'll keep your promise?" I didn't get a reply. When I turned around, very slowly, fearful still of the knife, I saw he and Pola were gone. My head throbbing, I walked to the door. I couldn't go out. Sagging against the rough surface, I felt like crying. I'd been betrayed again, led into a trap by a woman I was growing to trust…a woman…I almost made a terrible mistake. I almost kissed her.

CHAPTER 28

MONDAY, DECEMBER 14, 1942
AN ORDER FOR 50,000 PARIS OF INSOLES MADE
FROM BAGS

I dreaded going to work. I didn't want to see Pola. The pain of her betrayal was impossible to describe. My head ached, my thoughts were murderous. I was trapped in a room with three people I didn't trust, didn't like. I hated one of them. She had hurt me.

When I walked alone back to my flat after that terrifying encounter with the unnamed fighter, I searched the streets. I feared a Gestapo officer had followed and was about to leap upon me for associating with a spy ring. "Damn, Singer! Even from some far-off lair, he is ruining my life." Ruining my life? What life? I dragged myself up the staircase to the third floor. There was not even a railing to hold me. It was stolen, most likely cut up for fuel. I had laughed so hard at the police report of a few apartment dwellers, naked and staring down at a missing staircase. Who would believe such insanity could happen in Lodz? "Who can believe...she's a damn spy?" No. They're not spies, they're resistance fighters.

That night, I couldn't sleep. Hungry, frightened, and tortured by having been betrayed again, I remained in my chair while Jozef's snoring completed this immersion into hell.

The next morning, walking to the office, my hope for a few moments of solitude was shattered by, "How did you enjoy the concert? Was Pola there?"

"Jozef, I'm exhausted."

"Not from a concert." He gave me a playful look. "So, was she there?"

"No. She wasn't there." I didn't want to say her name.

"It's a shame. You both could use companionship." Jozef shook his head. "I'm past that point, but you're both young. You have your entire lives—"

"Are you serious? What the hell are you talking about? I love my wife. I don't want anyone else." I felt like crying. I thought of the knapsacks and shoes. "They're coming back! Miriam and Regina—"

"I'm sorry, my friend," Jozef said. "I misspoke. You are right. Your Miriam will be returned to you. Soon."

We walked the rest of the way in silence. When we arrived, he turned to his pile of memos.

The memos on my pile didn't interest me. I whipped through them, barely reading. Old news.

"They opened an umbrella factory," Jozef said. "In the first few weeks, it made over 1,000 umbrellas."

"For our tears, I suppose."

"For export out of the ghetto. It's good. It keeps us working."

"Umbrellas to keep allied bombs away. What a war." I imagined our new umbrellas shielding German soldiers in their obscene helmets from bombs falling from allied airplanes.

The door opened. I didn't feel like performing my required duty, but stood and was about to shout, "Attention!"

Pola walked in. She was bundled in her coat, collar up against the frigid wind.

I watched her as if watching a ghost as she walked across the far wall and aimed her eyes at me and then away. I felt Jozef observing us and had to throw him off the scent. "Good morning," I said, sounding half-way cordial.

"Good morning," Pola replied.

"Good morning, Pola," Jozef said, the cheeriest of us three, a rare occurrence. "Did you hear about the umbrellas?"

I tuned them out. I was staring at a notice from the Used Materials and Sorting Point. Of all the departments and factories the Chairman established, this one had to issue a memo today. I rarely received anything from this department, but here it was. On the surface, it appeared to be an innocuous note, an invoice for a large order of shoe insoles, 50,000 pairs. It barely merited attention, but such a large order meant more jobs, more security. But when I reread the note again, I felt a chill. What had that thuggish man, that friend of Singer's, said about shoes being made from used leather? These insoles, the department head had snuck in, were made from thousands of used knapsacks. I crushed the note and tossed it under Pola's foot. I watched her bend to retrieve it.

"Are they trying to starve us to death as well as freeze us?" Jozef exclaimed, rising from his chair and buttoning his coat.

"What now?" I was in no mood for any more bad news.

"They're cutting our potato content in our midday soup from 400 grams to 100! And there is still no milk." He leaned on his chair, so weak he could barely stand. "I'm ready."

"Ready for what?" I was getting used to his constant complaints. They were almost comforting.

"For the farms up north. They can't be worse than it is here." Jozef walked out the door.

I should have run and stopped him, but I had no energy. We were all skeletons with thin coatings of flesh hanging onto our bones. "I wonder if I told him about the used clothing and shoes if that would help," I said, not looking at Pola.

"The fewer people that know this, the better," Pola said.

"I wish I didn't know." I sucked in my lips. "Do you think there can be another explanation than what I'm thinking?"

Pola gazed at the note in her hand. "I pray there is."

"It's inconceivable, humanly impossible. There has to be another explanation."

"They are training more girls to run their hands over the endless stream of clothing to search for valuables."

"No. I don't want to hear it."

Pola glanced at the door and then stepped toward me.

"No. Stay back. I don't need your pity." I held my hands up, ready to push her away.

"It isn't pity."

I looked at her, anger flaring. "You betrayed me."

"I'm sorry. I wish there were another way. We need you to help us." She held up the note. "You already have."

I looked into her eyes. "I'm glad you did what you did." I wanted the next words to be daggers. "For a few minutes in this insane world, I almost fell for it. Thank you."

Pola looked as if she wanted to say something else but gave me a sad look and walked back to her chair.

For the rest of the week, when we spoke, I avoided her eyes and kept my tone professional. For the first time in weeks, I did not go to the Saturday concert. Music would not play in my heart again until Miriam was in my arms.

CHAPTER 29

SUNDAY, DECEMBER 20, 1942

I felt empty Saturday evening, my mind racing back to the music I'd believed was lost to us until I'd attended the concert with Pola. I found such enjoyment in the emotions of the familiar melodies played by our skeletal orchestra and our exhausted conductor, but mostly because I was with her. But after what she did to me, leading me into the hands of that knife-wielding shadowy figure, I couldn't bring myself to venture back to the House of Culture, and certainly, not to invite her to join me. So, it was with impatience that I listened to Neftalin spouting on about the latest concert.

"I tell you things are turning around for us at last. The great Chairman himself sounded extraordinarily optimistic in tone," Neftalin said, sitting at the table.

"Did he mention the rumors of the new resettlement?" Jozef asked.

"He denied it completely. You can rest assured all these rumors are false."

I wondered if we should believe the Eldest. After all, he promised to protect our children…I didn't want to think about it.

"One of our major concerns has been typhus, which is related to the poor sanitary conditions we've had to live with," Neftalin said. "Well, no more. The Chairman ordered inspections of all residences and the establishment of community laundries. Can you imagine?" He lifted up his shirt and gave a disgusted shake of his head. "My friends, clean laundry, and bathing will be mandatory."

"These are good measures," Jozef said, scratching at his overgrown stringy hair.

"Haircuts," Neftalin said. "We have a new barber, and so everyone will have haircuts."

"Women too?" Pola asked.

Neftalin smiled at her. "The Chairman said if it proves necessary, he will pass a decree that haircuts will be compulsory, and yes, even for women. He is determined to rid us of the dirt that causes typhus and other diseases."

I remembered the Neftalin of old, the starched shirt, the pin-stripe suit, the slick, black hair. In his smile, I saw the shadow of what he was less than two years ago. I hesitated, but had to ask, "Did he say anything about our children?" Surely, by now, the Eldest must know where our lovely children were sent.

"Yes. The Chairman is going to employ nine-year-old children in the workshops."

"So young?" Jozef asked.

Pola remained silent.

What did she know?

Neftalin continued, "And, he's setting up areas in each workshop for younger children to remain, under supervision, while their parents are working. They will be fed and cared for until their parents take them home."

Pola looked at me. I think she knew this was not what I needed to know.

Jozef plucked at his chin. "These are all good things, but what about the food situation? We're starving."

Neftalin frowned. "He recognizes food as a problem area."

"So what did he say we should do with this 'problem area?'" Jozef asked. "I've tightened my belt as far as it will go."

"We all have," Neftalin said. "Our Chairman suggested that people should economize on their consumption in order not to be faced with hunger."

"Economize on our consumption? Of what? What more can we economize?" Jozef shouted. "Is he economizing?"

"Jozef," I barked.

"It's true. We're starving, and the Emperor rides in his coach smoking cigarettes," Jozef said.

Neftalin rose from his seat. "You must have faith."

"We need food and fuel," Jozef mumbled. "Faith, we have."

I placed my hand on Jozef's shoulder. "Thank you, Henryk, for the good news," I said. "Any news of…." He was gone before I could finish. "Do you see what you've done? You chased him away with your endless complaints." I turned him roughly toward me, both of my hands on his collar. "We're all suffering here. I'm so damn sick of your complaints. Why don't you complain to that damn God of yours and see if that shit will do something to save his most loyal subject?"

"Bennie," Pola said, reaching for my hand.

I shoved it away and headed for the door. My hand on the knob, I stopped. Where could I go? This room, this job, was all that was keeping me from being sent away. If I left this room before nightfall, there was an excellent chance I would be on the next transport. If I knew it would take me to Miriam and Regina, I would gladly volunteer to leave for the cold north. But with no idea of where they were, and this ghetto being the only place they would come and search for me, I had to remain. I turned to Jozef. "I'm sorry. I…my nerves are shot."

Jozef was sniffling into a soiled cloth. He reminded me of Julian, abruptly coughing and sneezing into his nose rag.

I turned to Pola but couldn't find words for her. I gave her a cold stare and turned away.

In a few seconds, we were all back at work.

Jozef broke the silence. "The Germans have ordered all factories and workers to remain at their posts for Christmas."

"Don't they know we're Jews?" I asked.

"Trust me, that's one thing they never forget," Jozef replied.

CHAPTER 30

FRIDAY, DECEMBER 23, 1942

"Attention!" I shouted as the door creaked open. "My God, Heilig, it's you? Where have you been?" I rushed toward the Weasel but stopped when I saw a patch over his right eye. "Are you okay?"

"All hell is breaking loose," Heilig shouted. "Do not go out. Do not leave this room."

Pola was next to him. "We were worried about you."

"You didn't tell anyone I was missing, did you?" Heilig was wriggling around and looking more like a weasel than usual. "If anyone asks, I was here the whole time." He took off his coat and dropped it on his chair.

I never saw him so agitated, except when I was pounding him with my fists trying to get him to tell me where Singer was. "Calm down. Tell us what's going on."

"I was on Wesola Street, where the old hospital was before they emptied it of all the patients. God knows what happened to them. Nobody's heard from them again." Heilig was glancing at the door. "It was a huge fire."

"Fire?"

"Yes. The whole four-story building went up in flames," Heilig said. "It was like a bomb went off. Fireworks everywhere." Heilig laughed insanely.

Sabotage? Singer? He had called for us to fight the Nazis with everything we had. Fire?

Pola looked confused. "Why would anyone set fire to a hospital? We have so few medical facilities here."

Jozef shook his head. "The Germans transformed the entire building into a highly modern factory. The loss would be felt dearly by them."

Pola frowned. "They took a hospital with patients in it and turned it into a factory?"

Heilig laughed again. "It's crazy, isn't it?"

I heard Rosenfeld answering Pola's question with, "Only the Germans know why they do such crazy things." I had to focus. "How bad was the factory damaged?"

"Destroyed, I think." Heilig sounded happy.

"It was an old building, mostly made of wood," I said, reverting to my past life as an engineer. "They put in new plumbing, wiring, and a freight elevator. Quite an investment."

Heilig said, "I heard someone say it was the second most valuable building in the ghetto."

"Mostly built with German money," I said, eying Heilig suspiciously.

"Oh, yes," he replied. "This fire will really hurt them in their wallets."

I thought it sounded like something Singer advocated. "Do they know what caused the fire?"

Heilig shook his head. "The authorities are going crazy. They arrested the factory director and others. You can bet it isn't going to stop there."

So, they thought it was deliberate. I looked at Pola, but she was staring at Heilig.

"How did it manage to be so destructive?" Jozef asked. "Such an important building, people would see if it was on fire. No?"

"The air raid warden told me he discovered it at about 5:00 a.m., but it could have been burning much earlier," Heilig said.

"It's the German's own fault," Jozef remarked. "Their curfew and blackout regulations would keep anyone from seeing the fire if it did start earlier."

"But isn't the factory guarded?" I asked.

Heilig replied. "Only the outside. Most factories are locked up at the end of the day."

"So, someone could hide in a building until it was locked up," I said. I wouldn't put it past Singer to try such a crazy stunt.

Heilig smiled.

I thought it a strange smile given the circumstances, but waited for him to continue.

"It was the most sensational blaze I've ever seen. It was beautiful," Heilig said as if picturing it in his mind.

"Why were you there?" I asked, wondering if the Weasel was somehow involved.

"I heard the firetrucks. There were at least fifteen trucks from outside the ghetto."

"German trucks?"

"Well, our truck is no match for this kind of fire. I heard our boys say benzine, alcohol, paint, and other flammables were in the building."

As if on cue, a powerful blast shook our chamber.

I grabbed Pola, who looked as if she was about to fall. It was a reflex, but now I was holding her in my arms. I released her quickly. "I'm sorry," I muttered.

"It's okay," she replied.

A second blast made me run to the window. I couldn't see through the boards.

Jozef gripped the table with his hands. "You said the Germans arrested some people?"

"Oh, hell, yes. The Gestapo rounded up anyone they suspected. I mean, this is one of their most valuable factories, and the fire threatened to spread to another important factory next door. So, yes, they went wild. Their firemen fought to save the building from the first report at 5:00 a.m.. They were still there when I saw Gestapo and our Chairman arrive...."

"Rumkowski was there?" Pola asked, a grim look on her face.

Heilig nodded. "Our great leader was driven there by the Gestapo. I can't say he looked happy."

"I guess they suspect it was deliberately set?" I asked aloud what I was sure everyone was thinking.

"Why else would they arrest so many," Heilig replied. "They're hunting for others."

127

Like you, I thought, wondering if reckless people like Singer and Heilig understood what the wolves might unleash on us after such an act. "Not long ago, a rock was thrown at a moving tram with a German officer on board. The authorities threatened to execute 200 Jews chosen at random if the culprit wasn't discovered." I let that sink in.

Pola said, "They carried out random murders in Warsaw. Did they do it here?"

"No. The Chairman found out that a young boy threw the rock."

"A child?" Pola looked concerned. "What did they do to him? They didn't execute him?"

"The Chairman risked his own safety and begged for the boy to be released. He claimed the boy was retarded and did not know what he was doing. We were all sweating. Would the wolves still execute 200 innocent people?" I aimed my eyes at Heilig. "That was a stone striking a tram. Imagine what the Germans will do if they believe this was a deliberate act?"

The sound of explosions lasted all day. The German firemen gave up at 5:00 p.m.. The building was a total loss, but surrounding factories were saved. The entire ghetto was on edge as arrests continued throughout the day. The Chairman was seen at the site of the fire and German police station many times as the investigation into the cause continued.

It was almost dark, and I was alone in our workroom. Jozef left for the soup kitchen, hoping for some potato soup to calm his raging stomach. Pola said a curt goodbye and left. Heilig, I suspected, was back at the fire. He seemed fascinated by the "accident."

I took the task of writing up the report of this devastating fire. Like the Germans, I suspected it was a deliberate act. I thought it was Singer, or one of his shady comrades, finally launching assaults on our oppressors. I had mixed emotions. On the one hand, I was beginning to believe we had to do what we could to damage the German war effort, but on the other hand, feared their reprisals. My entry was written after a final report from the Chairman: *The investigation into the cause of the fire is, of course, being conducted by the German authorities. Although their investigation is not yet complete, they have enough information to know that no one can be held responsible for the fire since it was caused by a short circuit.*

I added a sentence that summarized the widespread feelings in the ghetto: "This finding has afforded the ghetto's population great relief."

"Merry Christmas," I said to the empty square where the Chairman's portrait had once hung. Was the cause a short circuit? Or was that a way for the Germans to avoid admitting that some Jews sabotaged their showcase factory? I doubted we'd ever know the truth.

"The Germans know," Rosenfeld would have said. "Perhaps the Chairman knows too."

As I walked past the ruins of the hospital on Wesola Street, I couldn't help wondering if Singer knew.

CHAPTER 31

T UESDAY, JANUARY 19, 1943
WEATHER
A frost set in suddenly during the night, bringing the morning temperature down to minus 17 degrees. In the course of the day the thermometer rose to minus 8 degrees...

Sleeping in the same bed with Jozef was the only way to survive the brutal cold. We were two nearly fleshless skeletons. Of course, he complained that I sometimes cried out in the night. "What did I shout?" I'd ask. "Miriam, no," he'd reply. It made sense. It had been six months since she had climbed on that truck. I wondered if she hated me. Why else did I not hear one word from her? Not one word about my precious Regina?

"I'm frozen solid," Jozef said. "I'm not working today."

I was too exhausted to argue, so I said, as I did almost every day to him, "You know what happens to those who don't work." And he replied, between sniffles, sneezes, coughs, and farts, "So, a farm in the north country would be so bad?"

I had no answer. Nobody did. Our food allocation for the first ten days of 1943 quashed rumors that we were going to see better rations now that there were only 80,000 of us left in our paradise. The shock came that we were not to receive any potatoes.

"Not one potato. Not one peel even." Jozef read the new ration notice.

We had lived on only potatoes for months.

"How can a man exist on 400 grams of rye flour? That's 100 grams less than last month," Jozef asked.

"We must exist," I said. "What else will our generous benefactors allow us?"

Jozef squinted at the notice. "I need new eyeglass lenses. 200 grams of rye flakes, 100 grams of oil, 300 grams of coffee, 200 grams of artificial honey. Do they have artificial bees too?" He let out a hoarse laugh and then coughed hard.

Why didn't he cover his mouth? Disease was everywhere. People were dying in the snow-covered streets. That was how I found my gloves. This time, I did not hesitate. The dead do not need gloves...nor shoes. Most were found barefoot these days. "Artificial honey, ersatz coffee? German ingenuity. Give them enough time, and they'll solve any problem." Even getting rid of their troublesome Jews, I thought, but still couldn't fathom how they could kill off millions of their vermin. "What else are they granting us?"

"250 grams of marmalade, an equal amount of salt, 10 grams of paprika, 10 grams of baking soda. Who bakes? We have no fuel for heat or cooking." He coughed again. "Here, take the list. I'm going to sleep. You read the rest."

"You're really staying in bed all day?" When he didn't reply, I read the rest of the list, "A tenth of a liter of salad dressing and 5 kilograms of turnips." I heard him snoring. "They're giving us a half a bar of soap." Isn't that marvelous, I thought, we can all take bubble baths.

There was not one mention of meat or sausage.

The trek to the Jewish ghetto administration building was one of great danger. Not from the Germans. They were all tucked safely away in their warm barracks. They knew we were too weak and beaten by hunger, disease, and the frigid cold to be a threat, so only a few sentries in their booths remained on shooting-gallery duty. Even the Jewish police were rarely seen on the streets in the early hours of the morning. The danger now was ice on the pathways. With our bodies too meatless to serve as padding, a fall could fracture our brittle bones. Bodies were left writhing in the cold. Some were left for days, then found without shoes. The needs

131

of the living trump respect for the dead.

I arrived first into our chamber of horrors. I wondered if Rumkowski's office had heat. We had no coal, and there wasn't mention of any fuel in the allocations. There was also no further mention of the factory fire in any reports. We had ended the old year with the fear that the Germans would want some form of reprisal for the destruction of their factory. There had been many arrests and talk of executions, but perhaps because it was Christmas, nothing materialized. Those arrested were released. But the ghetto residents remained in suspended animation waiting for something else to happen.

The same was true of my relationship with Pola. The New Year was here again. I recalled how the previous year I had rushed home to reset my life with Miriam. I was so full of hope and anticipation for the new year. It never happened. Singer's love letter killed that for me. I made up my mind that I would start fresh with Pola too. I was angry still that she had led me on but accepted that it was my fault as well. I had let my loneliness lead me into the trap. I should have known there was nothing between us. There could never be. I had Miriam and Regina. I could be cordial with Pola, understanding of Jozef, and even overlook the annoying mannerisms of Heilig. They were the only family I had here. The New Year would see the end of the war.

Pola rushed into the room. "There has been another roundup," she said, not removing her coat.

"How many this time?" I asked, understanding that 'roundup' was a euphemism for forced, often violent, deportations from the ghetto.

"Nobody knows for sure. They took mostly single men."

"There was a notice that the Chairman was asked to supply a list of 150 healthy men by the authorities," I said, searching my stack of memos. "The Chairman argued with them that he could not do that without hurting productivity and got the number reduced to 80."

Pola leaned close to me.

I pulled back.

"My sources tell me that the authorities demanded more men. Many were dragged from their beds at night."

Her sources? "Are you sure?" I asked.

"The quota demanded has not been filled," Pola said.

"We don't have many healthy people left," I replied.

"They're taking all the prisoners and anyone who ever committed any kind of infraction, but it still won't be enough."

"Your sources. Do they know where all these people are being sent?"

She shook her head. "They claim the men are needed for manual labor, but their destination is not known." She looked at me. "I know what you want. He's working on it."

"I have to know."

Pola smiled sadly. "I'm sorry we don't have an answer for you yet." She let out a deep sigh. "I'm sorry...for what happened. Bennie, it's a new year. Can we start again? I enjoyed our concerts so much. They made me feel alive again."

I didn't speak. I nodded my head.

"Bennie, things are happening. Last night's roundup may continue. Nobody knows. Nobody is safe." She turned back to her work and suddenly let out a laugh. "Did you know there was a celebration in the Kitchen of the Intelligentsia on January 7th?"

"I wasn't invited."

"The report says, and I quote, 'The reception was quite sumptuous.' Sumptuous?"

"I haven't heard that word in this place ever. What was so sumptuous?"

"I'm just quoting from the memo: 'The reception was quite sumptuous and in very good taste. A variety of delicacies, including wine, was served; a truly copious dinner caused the people of the ghetto the greatest surprise.' I would think so," she said.

Wine? I couldn't find any alcohol even to get drunk on New Year's Eve, I thought, and here the elite was dining on "delicacies," "a truly delicious dinner," and wine. "May I please have that?" I held out my hand.

Pola stared at my new gloves as if asking from where I got them. Of course, she didn't ask. "The party didn't end until 2:00 a.m.."

I typed the report as we received it and added one sentence at the end: "The populace has made a wide variety of comments on this odd affair." What the hell if I made that up. I certainly had questions about such a sumptuous celebration while we were starving and freezing to death.

"Bennie, will you escort me to the concert on Saturday?" Pola asked.

I burst out laughing. "Why the hell not?" I replied.

CHAPTER 32

F RIDAY, JANUARY 29, 1943
SIDEWALKS TO BE CLEARED
Because a Kripo (German criminal police) officer fell on a slippery sidewalk (without suffering any injury, however), janitors from the adjacent buildings were summoned to the Kripo (office) and beaten.

"It's about time someone did something about these dangerous conditions," Jozef said, after reading his entry. "I'll break every bone in my body if I ever fall on all this ice."

"They did this because one of their own fell, not to save the bones of old Jews," I said. "And I suppose you're ecstatic because the Nazis beat up our janitors? It doesn't matter that they were starving and freezing cold?"

"Why should janitors be exempt from work? And as for beatings, that seems to be the norm around here."

I knew what he meant. Residents complained that they were accosted by Germans, asked their opinions about various matters, and according to their answers, were then beaten up. "Well, then I suggest you get to work before some official comes bursting in here and sees your lazy ass and decides to take his pound of flesh."

"You're laughing, but the Germans are more brutal by the day. I'm thinking of volunteering for resettlement."

"What? You can't be serious."

"My friend, I'm an old man. My time to be deported is coming, so why not volunteer to be resettled in some rural community? What I wouldn't give for fresh fruit, a piece of potato...an egg. I'm ready."

"You can't leave. Nobody knows what's out there." I thought of Miriam and Regina. "Germans are dragging our people from their beds and beating them for their resettlement actions."

Jozef bit his lip.

"There is something not kosher when they use violence to get people to leave such a paradise."

Jozef looked at me for several seconds. "Damned if you do and damned if you don't." He shook his head. "So, I guess I'll extend my vacation here for a while longer."

I nodded. "I'm glad you're staying, even if you snore like a horse."

"Perhaps, after I go, you will find a woman. They do not snore." He gave me a gentle smile. "My friend, you don't want to spend the rest of your life alone."

I was thinking about what he said when Pola entered our room. She greeted Jozef with a smile and then aimed her eyes at me.

Heilig stomped the snow off his shoes. "He's doing it again. Jozef, you should take him up on this. You're the oldest here."

"What are you ranting about now?" I asked. It didn't take much to set me off.

Heilig sneered. "Our esteemed Chairman, the beacon of egalitarianism, has found a new way to reward his most loyal subjects."

I stiffened. "Are you going to tell us or not? If not, then get to work."

Heilig aimed his weasel eyes at me. "I thought for sure our club leader would take advantage of this new benefit."

My fists balled.

"Lay off him," Pola shot at Heilig, "Bennie is one of us. He does his job as we all must until the time is right. Now, tell us what you are going on about."

Nobody in the room could stand up against Pola when she was on fire. I admired that but was surprised she defended me.

Heilig looked angry but tempered his tone. "I'm sorry, Engineer. I know you are not to blame for this."

I nodded.

Heilig was quieter when he spoke. "None of you knew that the Chairman is offering a select few of his best workers a period of recuperation?"

"What is that?" Jozef asked.

"It means he is giving people who have the right 'connections' employment in the bakery for eight weeks."

"This is 'recuperation?'" I asked.

"Hey, they're each getting a half kilogram of bread for every 12-hour workday plus an additional two kilograms per week," Heilig said. "The price of a kilogram of bread is up to 60-70 marks on the private market. So, yes, this is a great deal."

Jozef was deep in thought. "So, how does one apply for this benefit?"

Heilig laughed rudely. "It is limited to those with the 'right connections.' Not for us commoners."

I watched Jozef sag back into his chair. It wouldn't surprise me if one day his chair would be vacant too.

Heilig was working silently. They all were. I was sifting through my memos when I felt Pola slide her chair next to me.

"After the concert, someone wants to see you," she whispered and slid her chair back.

"Hey, look at this," Jozef said. "We're getting one day off per week, and they're reducing our workdays to only ten hours." His smile quickly turned to a frown. "The day off is Sunday, not Shabbos. Would it have killed them to give us our Sabbath day off?"

I hardly heard the rest of his string of complaints. I was locked on Pola. She had said someone wanted to see me after the concert. At least this time, she was honest, but was it the shadowy figure she called David? I glanced at her, a questioning look on my face. She was busy working. I knew I'd have to wait until the concert was over to find out who wanted to see me. I hoped it was Singer with news of Miriam and Regina.

CHAPTER 33

SUNDAY, JANUARY 31, 1943
TYPICAL OF THE TIMES

Is the fate of young people who are not yet old enough to be employed in workshops. They spend much of their time indoors, not getting out into the open air; their games, even their songs, are accordingly, sad and serious. Their songs are less like children's songs than they are plaints and lamentations over rations, resettlement, and the hard life in the ghetto, of which even the youngest among them are already aware. One has a sister who has been resettled, or a brother, or even a father or mother, and so these children all know the meaning of life in the ghetto. It is not unusual to hear them say: "If we are still alive, then..." Words such as those have a particularly tragic ring when spoken by a child.

"This is beautifully written," I said to Pola after she handed me her entry. I was surprised she showed such emotion. Then I remembered she had lost a child, so, of course, she would be sensitive to children even if she showed little vulnerability to adults.

"It was last night's concert that softened me up." She gave me a meaningful look.

"It was the same music as always," I said.

"They get better each week."

I laughed. "I suppose that is a benefit."

She smiled. "Thank you for taking me."

"Thank you," I replied. I suspected Pola really wanted to know how my meeting after the concert went. I wasn't ready to share that with anyone.

Pola smiled again and returned to her seat.

It had been a strange night. I knew she was enjoying the music, but I was not. My mind was elsewhere. She met me barely a minute before the orchestra leader signaled the first overture. I assumed she did this to avoid my questions. Was the meeting still on? Who was so anxious to see me? Was it David, who had terrified me? When I reached over, my words about to form, she held up a hand before her lips and glanced around our seats. A rock would confide more. I settled back in the ratty cushion and tried to melt into the music. I did not reach for her hand as I had before. She did not place her palm on mine.

After the concert ended, the Chairman, supported by Neftalin's arm, climbed the steps to the stage. His voice sounded strained as he thanked the "valiant" performers, praised the conductor, and then gave his customary scolding to those who shirked work. He made one announcement that caught my attention: all injections of medicine would be done by a distinct section of the Sonderkommando, to eliminate the black market for medicine at exorbitant prices. He elaborated that to qualify for injections, patients would have to line up and get a doctor's prescription.

Pola whispered, "That could take an entire day."

The Chairman added that the following day, those with prescriptions would again need to get on lines and wait their turn to have the medicine dispensed. "And all this," he said, "is because some would profit from the needs of others."

The applause at the end of his speech was subdued.

Pola said, "Some of the profiteers are most likely in the audience."

"He warns us and warns us," I replied as Pola proceeded ahead of me through the aisle. "Why don't they understand the wolves are waiting for such opportunities to make our lives better?"

Pola didn't reply. She buttoned her coat and wrapped her scarf around the lower portion of her face.

I pulled up my collar and tied my scarf around my face. The House of Culture had been warm. Was heat being pumped from one of the few systems that still worked? It made the frigid air and winter wind feel even worse. I did not see one policeman, Jew nor German, on the street. The curfew was suspended for those fortunate enough to be allowed to attend the weekly concerts. Strangely enough, it cut back on the 'incidents' of shootings, which the authorities claimed were provoked by ghetto residents. It was as if this respite from the regimentation of our lives was so appreciated, not even the underground wanted to risk its loss.

"We're here," Pola said. "I can't stay."

"Tell me who I'm seeing?" I reached for her hand.

Pola clutched my fingers. "Don't be afraid. I'll never hurt you again." She pulled her hand away and was gone.

I searched the area, my eyes peering over the scarf. The wind bit at my exposed flesh. I wanted to go home. While the curfew was lifted for concertgoers, there was a risk of being caught out at night by Nazi patrols. But that was not what was keeping me from entering the door.

"Don't be afraid. I'll never hurt you again." Pola's words echoed in my mind. Her eyes, barely visible over her scarf, made me believe her. I searched again and then ducked into the door. "No knife at my throat this time?" I asked Singer.

"Not this time," Singer replied. "I knew you wouldn't scream."

"Did you know I would not try to knock your damn head off?" I asked.

Singer laughed. "Yes, I knew that too. Although I wasn't sure about it. Not after you went after my cousin, Heilig. I never knew you had a temper."

"Miriam also thought I had no emotions. Well, I guess we were all wrong." I sat down on a chair. "Come into the light. I want to see you."

"You want to see if the playboy is still here?" He moved his seat closer. "None of us are the same."

"I expected you'd have a beard," I said, studying his face.

"I had to shave it off. The Germans don't like them. Remember, dear Dr. Rosenfeld? When that German pig forcibly chopped off his beard...that poor old man crying against the wall as if his heart was broken. That's when I knew I had to do something."

"You left Miriam and Regina," I said. "At least you could have...."

"What? What could I have done? Even if I could get them out of this ghetto, something I can't even do for myself at this point, where could I take them?" He leaned forward, his hands pleading.

Singer looked so much older, creases under his eyes, furrows on his forehead. "Your hair is gray now," I said.

"That should make you happy. I'm becoming an old man like you."

"Warsaw," I said. "You could have taken them to Warsaw."

Singer stretched his legs. "Last summer, a group of people, mostly wealthy people from Lodz, paid up to 6,000 marks each to take transports to Warsaw. They went there believing conditions were better than here. My friend, things are coming to a head there. Most of these people are trying to come back."

"I heard you were killed," I shot at him.

"Singer is dead." He pulled a knife from his coat pocket. "I am this now." He pushed it into the tabletop. "My dearest friend, my Engineer, I am leaving the ghetto very soon. I don't know if I'll ever be back."

"Where are you going?" Looking at him, I knew he wasn't the same man. Thinner, weather-beaten skin on his face, dressed in a black coat, he was the knife sticking in the table. Though he was smiling, there was something dark and sinister in his appearance.

"I can't tell you that. For your safety, the less you know, the better." He pulled the knife from the table. "I came to tell you that I love you, and I hope you will forgive me...."

Forgive him? For what? Did I dare ask him the question burning inside me ever since I discovered his note? "One condition."

Singer leaned forward, the knife handle in his fingers.

"Is she with you? You must tell me that."

Singer sat back, a frown appearing where a small smile had seemed out of place. "No. I swear it." He pointed the knife at me. "I don't know where they are." He held the knife's black handle toward me. "If you don't believe me...I will not stop you. Take it."

"And what? Kill my wife's lover?" I shook my head. "You're my Regina's godfather. You were my dearest friend."

Singer pocketed the knife and sighed. "If I swear to you that nothing

141

happened between us, will you believe me?"

Believe him? I hardly knew him anymore.

Singer stood. He looked at me in silence for what seemed a long time. "I have not had many people I loved in my life. I have had people I've hurt, even killed." He pulled up his coat collar. "When I leave here today, I need you to know that I love you. Yes, I love Miriam, and of course, our sweet Regina. But the only way I can make sense of my actions is if you believe I love you. I never wanted to hurt you." He put his hands on my shoulders.

I felt small. He was hardened by the life he led while I had become a skeleton by my life in the ghetto.

Singer gave me a sad look. "If you don't believe me, my sacrifice was for nothing. Do you understand?"

I thought I did. But who could be sure? The earnest expression on his face was convincing. "Yes…I believe you." I held out my hand, and almost inaudibly said, "I love you too."

Singer pulled me into his arms. "I will love Miriam, Regina, and you, my dearest friend, until I am dead. That is my promise."

"I believe you. Can you find them for me?" I asked, holding my brother tight, knowing it might be for the last time. "Please, help me?"

Singer gently pushed away from me. His eyes were infinitely sad, far darker than I remembered them. "You mustn't give up hope. Our resources are small. I have asked for help ever since I learned what happened. You know that."

I nodded.

"I will never give up. This, I also promise you." He put on his hat. "I must leave now. Remain here for a count of 200." He laughed. "I'm telling my numbers man to count. It has become a strange world where I am the unfeeling one and you…."

"I'm not that man anymore," I said.

"I'm not either," Singer said. "Perhaps, someday, the old Singer and the old Engineer will return and sit on the floor and play with our sweet Regina."

"Miriam and I will have you over for schnapps and kugel," I said.

"That will be nice." He walked to the door. "Goodbye, my friend."

"God bless you," I said a second after the door closed.

That night, I don't know how I got home. My thoughts were of Singer. For the first time in months, I prayed to God that he would take care of my friend. Our meeting was all I thought about most of the night and the next day. It filled me with hope but also fear for Singer's safety. I didn't know what he was involved in but sensed it was terribly dangerous. What else would I expect from my reckless gadfly? Why wasn't I more like him?

Near the end of the long day, I leaned over to Pola and said, "Thank you."

"It was a good meeting?"

"Yes. It was a very good meeting." I smiled. "Thank you, Pola."

"You can thank me with another concert," she said.

"Yes. That will be nice," I replied, helping lift up Pola's coat collar.

CHAPTER 34

S ATURDAY, FEBRUARY 6, 1943
   PEOPLE ARE SAYING
   that the death penalty for people who read newspapers is being considered.

"Can you imagine? The death penalty for reading a newspaper?" Jozef said. "Yet another reason to leave this place. We have no books, no radios, and now, not even smuggled newspapers."

"We also have no fats for cooking. But why do we need fats when we have no food?" Heilig let out a laugh.

I heard his insane-sounding laughter more with each passing day. "I think what we should be most concerned about are the rumors about resettlement," I said.

"The Germans need men for manual labor," Jozef said. "Their own men are fighting Hitler's stupid war. Hopefully, losing."

"Which brings us back to why they don't want us to have news," Heilig said. "They don't want us to know their asses are being kicked now that America is finally in the war."

Pola, who had been silent, spoke softly. "I think there are other things they don't want us to know about."

"Like what?" Heilig asked, sounding rude. "What else is more important to hide than having their Hun asses kicked in Siberia?"

Pola stared at him and replied, "Things are happening that we here know nothing about."

"And, you know?" Heilig shook his head. "They're losing the war, and they don't want us to have any hope." He let out his insane laughter again. "I hope they hang Hitler by his balls. Him and all his sick bastard cronies."

Pola shook her head and then turned to me. "There will be news soon that will change everything."

"There already is," Jozef said, staring at a sheet of paper in his hand. "All ghetto enterprises not engaged in work for the German military are to be closed." He looked up at me, fear in his eyes. "The rumors are true. They are closing up our factories."

"Let me see that?" I took the official German document from his hands. "If this is true...."

"It means resettlement," Jozef said.

"And nobody knows what the hell that means," Heilig muttered.

"What do you mean?" Jozef whirled on Heilig.

Heilig said, "What do you think I mean, old man?"

"Heilig, show respect," I barked. "Jozef, ignore him. He's insane, like the rest of us."

Heilig leaped from his chair, which struck the wall and fell to the floor on its side. "You don't know? Tell him. Tell him, Engineer."

Jozef now whirled to me. "Tell me what? What the hell is he talking about?" The fear in his eyes was unmistakable. "What are you not telling me?"

Pola stood up. "Jozef, you've heard the rumors."

"Rumors? What rumors?"

"Pola," I said, trying to restore calm.

Heilig shook his head and laughed again. "I don't believe anyone in this ghetto doesn't know about the clothing and shoes."

Pola shot a warning look at Heilig and hissed. "That is why you are not with us anymore."

What was she talking about?

Heilig shouted, "The Germans don't need their dirty Jews anymore." He was almost singing. "Shut down. Shut down. All shut down."

"Heilig, shut up," I said.

He sang again, "Filthy clothes. Filthy shoes. Truckloads arrive. That's the news." He looked at me, the patch still over his eye. "Pretty funny, eh? I should write that down for our journal that nobody will ever read. What a waste of time."

"Heilig, get out," I ordered. "Get out or shut your damn mouth." I rose from my chair.

Jozef sank back in his chair. "Filthy clothes...shoes?" He looked at Pola. "The rumors are true? I heard of truckloads of used clothing, but it was gossip. It's true, though. Isn't it?"

"There can be many explanations," I began, knowing how fearful Jozef already was.

"Why didn't you tell me?"

His eyes were blazing, painful for me to face. "Such news would have caused panic if it got out."

"The rumors were everywhere. But you knew they were true."

"We don't know what it means," Pola said in a calm voice. "As Bennie says, there could be many explanations."

Heilig laughed. "The bastards have somehow done it. It's genocide a la Nazi ingenuity."

"Heilig, get the hell out of here!" I dragged him to his feet and shoved him to the door.

"Leave him," Jozef shouted.

Shocked by his unprecedented outburst, I kept myself from throwing our garbage through the door. I looked at Jozef.

He was staring at me, his eyeglasses in his hand. "Leave him. He is the only one who told me the truth." He walked over to Heilig and wrapped his arm around the Weasel's shoulder. "Sit down. It will be alright. It will be alright."

Heilig sagged and let go of his coat.

I watched morosely as Jozef led the Weasel back to his chair. He remained by him for a long time, the Weasel calming down until he finally picked up a slip of paper and, as if nothing had happened, began to read it aloud: "The most available food now is rutabagas. People are finding all kinds of useful ways to make meals from this plant."

Seeing Heilig was calm again, Jozef walked up to my chair. He knelt close to my ear and whispered. "You knew and didn't tell me." He then walked back to his chair and began to read his stack of memos in silence.

"When they find out you knew and didn't tell them, they will hate you," Rumkowski had warned that first day in his office. When Miriam discovered how much I knew, as a member of the Chairman's inner circle, she had hate in her eyes. Now, Jozef hated me too. But how could I tell anyone what I suspected? The logistics of such mass murder, literally extermination, were impossible for my logical brain to accept. The only explanation was that for some reason, the Germans were providing all Jews in their new homes, uniforms, and shoes, so they did not need their rotted clothing and shoes. That would make laundering easier. It would help stem diseases. Yes, uniforms had to be the answer. The other explanation was impossible, unthinkable. There was no evidence. Lodz was sealed off from the world, so how could I spread the panic that would destroy all hope?

"Engineer," a soft voice penetrated my muddled thoughts. "It's not your fault. Nobody knows...."

Heilig burst into raucous laughter. "A concert? The Chairman is having another concert tonight. Shall we all go? My friends, shall we all listen to music? Rome burns while the Emperor plays with his fiddle."

"Do you still want to go?" Pola asked. "I understand if you don't."

I gazed into her eyes. Why weren't they hazel? "More than ever," I replied.

CHAPTER 35

MONDAY, FEBRUARY 8, 1943
PEOPLE ARE SAYING
that working and living conditions in the ghetto will become even worse because the workday will be increased from 10 to 12 hours, and Sundays, now free, will once again become workdays. As compensation, the working population is to receive soup twice a day.

"They're trying to kill us," Jozef said. "It's as simple as that."

"Conditions are bad all over," I said. "The workers who came back from manual labor on the Frankfurt/Poznan road are in such poor condition that they may not survive. But at least, they came back."

"The doctor prescribed one meal a day containing meat for them," Heilig said. "I'm surprised the Chairman is willing to waste our precious meat on these lost souls. Remember his speech last September when he demanded we turn over our sick and our children…." He stopped talking. I guess he saw the look of horror on my face. "I'm sorry, Engineer. My mind…I'm sorry."

Pola looked at me, sympathy in her eyes.

I bit my lip. The Weasel was going insane. Such people can't be held accountable for what they say. "I'm glad he's caring for them," I said.

Jozef said in a soft voice, "As Jews, in our worst suffering, we must still care for our fellow man."

I nodded. Jozef had said very little to me since he learned I had withheld the truth of the used clothing. We slept in the same bed, but he walked to work alone. I realized the only reason why he walked back after work with me was that he was afraid of being stopped and beaten by the German thugs who roamed our streets, spreading fear.

"Matches."

"Heilig, what did you say?" I asked.

"There are no matches. How the hell can we light candles, cook, get heat without matches?"

"We get home in the dark. Now, no matches?" Jozef sighed. "When God created light, he didn't count on the Nazis to extinguish it."

I didn't want to get into a philosophical discussion with Jozef about God. We'd gone around in circles many times about that subject. "There is some good news," I said. "Anyone who works is going to be able to bring 20 to 25 items of clothing to one of the three laundries." I looked at my shirt and grimaced. A new shirt was out of the question, except on the black market. I remembered Singer bringing a dress for Miriam. I never asked how he got it. He was our 'bad child,' and none of us wanted to know about the risks he was taking.

"I said, Engineer," Heilig's voice disrupted my memory of that beautiful dress, still waiting for Miriam's return, "the laundry does a lousy job. I had to pick dirt off my pants and shirts that wasn't there when I brought it to the lazy bastards."

"What do you expect? They have no hot water, hardly any laundry soap. They have to hang the clothes outdoors where they fall into puddles, or the wind knocks them into the mud. What the hell do you expect?" Pola sounded furious. That surprised me, given we had shared a lovely concert together on Saturday night. I'd enjoyed seeing her eyes closed and her finger keeping time to the music. I'd thought of placing my hand over hers but did not. Perhaps that was what was causing her to be irritable. With the others around, I couldn't ask. When she disappeared, I assumed she went to the bathroom.

"I was wrong," Jozef said.

I thought he was referring to his reaction when he discovered what the rest of us assumed he knew about the used clothing and shoes. "It's okay.

None of us should be held responsible...."

"Not about you. About Pola." He made a wry face. "I thought the addition of a woman to our crew was a mistake. I was wrong. She adds the personal touch we lost from so many months of reading death notices. I feel nothing anymore for those who die from disease, starvation, freezing. Not even suicide penetrates my hardened soul."

"Only murders attract our interest now," Heilig chimed in. "The gorier, the better."

I recoiled at his laughter. His face was so gaunt I could almost see the skull with eyes hollowed out, as in death. "Heilig," I said, hoping not to agitate him, "I think it is natural after a while at such a task to lose our sensitivity."

Jozef said, "We become numb to what others see as horrors in this nightmare existence."

"When Pola returns, let's try to lighten the atmosphere," I said.

"You care about her," Jozef said.

Heilig hissed, "The Engineer cares about nothing but his damn numbers. How else could he do this for so long? Right?"

I was about to answer when the door opened. "Attention," I croaked, forcing myself to my feet.

Jozef jumped up. Heilig rose slower, only coming to attention when he saw the black uniform of the German officer.

The officer stepped toward our table.

I didn't look in his face; my eyes automatically veered to the floor.

"Is no one else here?" He glanced at his clipboard and then searched the room again. "It says four."

"Yes, sir. Four is correct."

"Are you ill?" He asked Heilig, who looked as if he was wobbling on his thin legs.

"No, sir. I am fine." Heilig replied, straightening up.

The officer wrote something on his pad. He then stared hard at Jozef, shook his head, and made another note.

I kept glancing at the door, praying Pola would not return until this inspector was gone. Something about the way he was surveying each of us was frightening. I was grateful Pola hadn't returned. I don't know why I felt this way but hoped she was busy with some female business, or there was a long line at the bathroom.

"You are the leader?" The officer aimed his hard eyes at me. "What do you do here?"

I'd rehearsed what to say with Neftalin. "We few keep the records that enable the factories to produce goods efficiently for the military." I complained that our small crew barely managed to do all that was essential to keep departmental records. I kept it short.

The officer looked skeptical, but our table was filled with stacks of important-looking documents. Our shelves were filled with notebooks and boxes with forms placed there to complete the impression that we were a vital office that could not be tampered with, or the German war production here would suffer.

The door remained open.

Pola might have seen him and stayed away.

The officer grunted, made a military-style turn, and marched from our room.

"And I was worried about matches," Jozef said, letting out a deep breath.

I stared at the door. What happened to Pola?

CHAPTER 36

MONDAY, FEBRUARY 15, 1943

Pola did not return that afternoon nor the rest of the week. I went to the concert on Saturday night hoping she'd be there. *She knows I am here*, I thought, angry and frightened. When the music began, I turned to her chair, prepared to see her silently conducting the orchestra. Where the hell was she? I felt…I didn't know what I felt. I had no right to feel anything, but as much as I tried to fight it, I kept looking at her chair. I wished she'd magically appear.

The walk home, I searched the side roads, the alleyways, behind the dead lampposts. I expected David, or a crony, to grab me and drag my weak body into one of their ratholes. I imagined him interrogating me: "What did you do to her? Where is she?" He knows, I thought. He knows where she is.

Jozef and I were still hardly talking. The frigid cold, in our flat, on our icy streets, and in our workroom, made him even more brittle than before. He now not only snored like a horse but sneezed and wheezed incessantly. When he wasn't making all these annoying sound effects, he complained. His latest complaints were about the high cost of drugs on the black market.

I burst into laughter, irrational, "What the hell do you care about the high cost of anything on the black market? You don't buy anything from those pirates, so stop complaining. You give me a damn headache with your snoring, sneezing, wheezing, and endless bitching."

"And I'm sick of you moping about your Miriam and your kid. All you do is whine and whine. Do something constructive. You should come and pray with me. God helps those who help themselves."

"What do you know about it?" I was screaming when he didn't deserve it. It wasn't his fault. I was distraught that Pola had disappeared. Too many of the people I cared about had vanished, and nobody had answers. Now, Pola too?

"You act as if you're the only one who lost loved ones," Jozef said. "We've all paid the price. That is the one thing we have in common."

He was right, but I was in no mood to admit it. "Why don't you move out?" I regretted saying that the second it escaped my lips. Maybe not? I don't know.

"Yes. You're right." Jozef walked to his side of the bed. "You've been kind. A good friend." He picked up his things from the floor.

I still had Miriam's things in our small closet. I could not move them out. Sometimes, I stared at the dress she wore to the concert, that beautiful dress, and burst into tears. "You don't have to go," I said, but wished he would. I needed a small space for myself. I needed a break from him, from everyone. "I was unkind. Please stay?"

Jozef stopped packing and sat down on the edge of the bed. "I will stay until I find a place." He said it without anger. "But it is time for me to go."

The rest of the weekend, I worked to be hospitable, but a wall had appeared between us. Our conversations were limited to a few sentences. I avoided anything that could spark another argument. In the long periods of silence, I thought of Pola. I regretted not taking her hand in mine during the concert. Then I saw Miriam's hazel eyes...

By Monday, I was eager to be at work. The hike in the cold wind of February was painful. Without fat on our bodies, the wind bit through our skin and struck like icy needles on our bones. Without proper nutrition, rickets was now a problem in the ghetto. I fought to remain erect as I walked the bridge where the wind was more ferocious. I held Jozef up as we crossed over, the streets below prohibited to Jews.

When we reached our building, there weren't any Order Service guards at the door. Two thickly coated Gestapo took our new work cards and let us squeeze by them. Once past the thickly-coated sentries, Jozef heaved a series of coughs and doubled over in pain. I felt guilty that I had caused him more anguish. "Are you okay?" I asked, wiping my snot with my coat sleeve, unwilling to remove my gloves in the bitter cold.

"My ribs hurt. My legs ache." He coughed again. "I don't know how much more I can take."

I put my arm around his waist and guided him through the hall to our chamber. It was so cold our breath rose in gray trails in front of us. "Maybe we should take up smoking," I muttered.

"I used to smoke a pipe," Jozef said.

My hand felt for Rosenfeld's pipe bowl in my pocket. It was comforting to grasp the familiar token.

"I bet his cigarettes keep him warm," Jozef muttered, as we passed the Chairman's office. "I'll bet the Eldest is burning up with a nice coal fire," he continued.

I helped Jozef to his seat. It was like holding up a marionette, his bones moving in odd directions as I tried to lower him to his chair.

"I think I'm getting bedsores," he said and burst into a hoarse laugh. "I have boils on my ass. How they can find space to grow so large on such a bony ass, I will never know."

My coat, slightly thicker than his, insulated my buttocks from the wood seat. My eyeglasses were covered with a mist from the cold. I took off my gloves and stuck them in my pockets. I saw Pola's chair.

"We have a new chief of the Gestapo. They have so many damn titles and medals, I don't know how they can walk." Jozef let out a blast of laughter, which ended in an even louder explosion of coughing. "Dr. Otto Bradfisch is considering banning Jewish women from using makeup and nail polish. Also, from wearing hats."

"No hats in this bitter cold? Next, he'll ban bras and corsets."

Jozef laughed, perhaps imagining our painfully thin women without these essentials, many of which were confiscated ages ago.

The door opened. I barely croaked out my "Attention!" Thankfully, it was Heilig. He looked at us and asked, "What are you laughing at? It is so damn cold."

"We have a new chief of the Gestapo, and he's considering banning women using makeup," Jozef said.

"This is funny?" Heilig sighed.

I said, "Next, he'll ban brassieres. Imagine that."

Heilig didn't laugh.

"You don't think that's funny?" I asked.

"The Gestapo broke into our apartments over the weekend," Heilig said.

"Are you alright?" I asked.

Heilig looked strangely calm for someone who had been rousted by the Nazis during the night. I was amazed he'd escaped their net. "I wasn't home when they broke through the door."

I wanted to ask him where he was, but I did not want anyone to ask me about my whereabouts when I was with Pola at the concerts. "Were they searching for more men for their resettlements?" I asked.

"I don't know. The police did take some residents away. I heard screaming and pleading as I waited on the street. Some people were barely dressed in the cold night. Nobody said anything. No explanations. The chill went into my bones. When I sank to the ground, the armed soldiers did not attempt to make me stand. Perhaps, they were cold and tired too. It was the Gestapo that was breaking through doors and pulling people out of their beds."

"Don't stand," a voice said through the opening door.

"Where the hell have you been?" I blurted before caution stopped me. I studied Pola's face. No bruises, just redness from the cold.

Pola closed the door behind her. "The news is a smuggler was caught by the Order Service trying to break into the ghetto," she said. "The Gestapo has arrested nearly 200 people in brutal raids."

My first thought was that Singer was one of the people arrested.

Pola walked toward me. "This alleged smuggler and his ring were bringing large quantities of medicines into the ghetto. They were our main conduit for supplies to help our sick."

I suspected she was part of this network but had miraculously escaped the net, at least for now. "Do we know who the arrested were?"

Pola shook her head. "The first was a Pole, so the Chairman turned him over to the Gestapo. They broke him. We can imagine how."

At least it wasn't Singer, I thought, understanding the torture methods of the Gestapo and S.S. interrogators.

"If the Chairman didn't turn the Pole over to the Germans, the ring would still be helping us," Heilig said.

"Jews turning anyone over to the Nazis is a sin," Jozef said.

"We don't know everything. The Chairman has no choice," I said.

Pola shot me a cold look. "We need the names of everyone arrested."

I detected a strange tone in her voice. Was it defeat, anger, fear? "You heard her," I said. "As the reports come in, see if you can find out the names of those arrested in this ring."

"No," Pola said. "We need it now. Heilig, search out your informants and get this to me as fast as possible."

Heilig rose from his seat. He glanced at Pola, a smile on his wiry face. Was he grateful she was bringing him back into the fold?

"I'll see if Henryk has the list yet," I said, rising from my chair.

"Stay here, please? Jozef, would you please seek out the Chairman's secretary, Dora Fuchs? See if you can finesse the information from her?"

Jozef gripped the table to help him stand. "I'll do what I can," he said and left the room.

Pola wanted us alone. Why?

"I need to tell you something."

"Is it Singer?" My hand clutched Rosenfeld's pipe bowl.

Pola smiled sadly. "We don't know anything yet."

"He always gets away."

"We all know someday our luck will run out."

I clasped her hand. Was she telling me everything she knew?

CHAPTER 37

SATURDAY, FEBRUARY 20, 1943

The names of those arrested in the alleged smuggling ring did not appear in our records.

"My guess is that our Service Order chief was locked out of this operation," Pola said when by Saturday, we still hadn't received official notice of the arrests.

"I tried Neftalin this morning," I said to her, as we walked into the House of Culture, for the weekly concert. "He looked upset when I broached the issue."

"You have to be careful," Pola said, settling in the chair.

I nodded. "Henryk became agitated when I asked him if any of our friends had been caught up in the raids. He gave me a peculiar look and said the raids were for sanitary purposes."

"That's what they're all saying. Jozef said that Secretary Fuchs was very reluctant to speak about it, but finally said the people arrested were for unsanitary upkeep of their residences."

"Yes. To stop the spread of disease," I said. "Since when do the authorities care about Jews getting typhus and tuberculosis? They certainly don't care about our bones rotting."

"Shhh," someone hissed behind us.

I wanted to shush them back, but Pola had her fingers on her lips and nodded to me, a signal to be silent. The concert was starting. I settled back in my chair. I had not wanted to attend tonight, nor any other of

Rumkowski's concerts, but Pola asked. It was the only thing I could think of as the week passed slowly by.

Bajgelman looked thinner as he aimed his hollow eyes at the audience. "I want to thank the Chairman." He coughed, looked apologetic, and continued, "He is singlehandedly preserving…" He coughed again.

I glanced at Pola.

Her eyes met mine. She slid her hand over my palm. "It will be alright, Bennie. I promise you." Her hand didn't even cover the top of mine.

The same overture. Pola's eyes closed.

"It will be alright, Bennie," echoed in my mind. I leaned back and closed my eyes. In the throes of the music, I drifted back to our office. I saw Pola leaning toward me, her chair next to mine. I looked around us. She'd sent Heilig and Jozef on errands. Was she about to tell me about Singer? Was he one of those caught in the net?

The music was soaring majestically. I felt Pola's fingers tighten on my hand. They were so thin, so small. My eyes closed, but all I could see was Pola in our empty workroom, eyes peering at me as she had said, "Bennie, I have to leave."

"Leave? Now?"

The words made no sense. They were out of context. Pola was going to tell me about Singer, or David…what happened to David?

"Bennie, did you hear me?"

"No. I'm sorry. What did you say?"

Pola glanced at our workroom door. "I'm leaving."

"What do you mean you're…what?"

"Concentrate, please? I'm going to have to leave… soon."

"Where are you going?" I laughed. "Nobody can leave the ghetto." She had to be joking, but she wasn't laughing, not even smiling.

"Things are happening. I can't tell you more."

I stared at her. Her eyes appeared softer than I'd ever seen them…almost hazel. "You're really going?"

"Soon."

"But there's no way out."

"I know. That's why I have to leave now. The noose is closing." She stared hard into my eyes. "Come with me?"

"Don't ask that."

"We can't just let them take us, sheep to the slaughter."

I looked at her hands. They were so tiny. How could someone with such delicate hands fight the wolves? "You can stay with me. Jozef moved out." What was I saying?

Pola looked as if she was considering my offer.

The workroom door opened, and Jozef returned.

Neftalin entered behind him and closed the door. "Our friend is not among those arrested," he said to Pola.

The music stopped. I snapped back to the present. I was dismayed to find myself at the concert. I'd drifted off again.

Pola pulled her hand away as the lights went on. She stood and walked from the aisle. I was to wait until after the Chairman's speech and then meet her a block from the House of Culture. She said she didn't know how much time before she was to leave the ghetto. Uncertainty was a vulture that fed on me. At night, alone, it kept me awake. "Come home with me?" I asked when we met as planned.

"Are you sure?"

Was I? "Yes," I replied.

We walked side-by-side until Wesola Street, where we usually parted. Her flat was half a block away, and I would watch her until sure she was safe. We didn't hold hands, in case others saw us. The smell of the fire that consumed the factory still hung in the air. I summoned my courage and repeated, "Come home with me?"

A couple of men were walking nearby. They were from the orchestra. When I turned back, Pola was gone.

I thought of running after her.

My flat was cold without Miriam and Regina, without any noise other than my own labored breathing from the lonely walk home. Inside, it felt like a coffin, hollow, fit only for the dead. "Pola is leaving...leaving...leaving." It echoed in my head all night. She didn't say when or where she was going, only that she had to leave. There is time to change her mind, I thought, wondering if God would grant me this small bit of solace.

CHAPTER 38

SUNDAY, MARCH 14, 1943

At 7:00 p.m., in a crowded hall at the House of Culture, the Chairman addressed department and workshop delegates. Sunday was no longer a day off for us in the ghetto. Nobody knew why the Germans made this decree. This week, it was difficult for me to be on time the morning after the weekly concert. After Pola confided that she might have to leave at any time, I found it almost impossible to think of anything else. During the day, in our workroom, I felt as if I were suffocating, frequently stealing glances at her, hoping the others didn't notice. When they were out of the room, even for a few seconds, I slid to her, trying to convince her that she had a choice, that she should remain here where it was safe. "We have many new orders from the Germans. The Chairman's plans are working. They need us."

"Bennie, this ghetto is not the world. Jews are endangered everywhere."

"Do you think you can save them?"

"I have to try."

"Why? Why does it have to be you?" She was just one woman against a Nazi wave that was overpowering the most powerful nations on Earth. "You and Singer are made of one cloth. You both think a few Jews can defeat the strongest aggressors the world has ever known."

"We don't think we can defeat them. We know we have to try."

I tried other tacks. "I've already lost Miriam and my Regina," I said, pulling out my 'big guns' to arouse her pity. I had a desperate need for her

161

to stay.

"We all lost loved ones," she said.

"All the more reason why we should help each other."

"Isn't that why you're staying here?"

"What do you mean?"

"You've fought being resettled with Jozef even though it could mean better living standards because you want to be here when Miriam and your daughter return. Isn't that the truth?"

I couldn't argue. Pola knew the truth.

Pola nodded. "I don't hold that against you. I admire the good man you are. Perhaps, that is why I am drawn to you. I was from the first arguments you had with Heilig, from the first kindness you showed Jozef. I know you still love your wife, and certainly, your child." She smiled. "I would expect nothing less of you."

I felt tears welling in my eyes. I was ashamed to be too weak to fight them. "May I still escort you to the concert?" I asked.

"Until the time I must leave, I would be honored," she replied.

And that gave me something to look forward to as we processed more notices of suicides, death from starvation and disease, and worrisome announcements of more forced resettlement actions.

Holding Pola's hand during the musical interludes in our struggle to survive was the highlight of my week. And now, I was aware that any time, even this, might be taken from me. When the lights went on, and she pulled her hand away, my hand felt empty. I sat up as the Chairman approached the stage, leaning on his cane. Tonight's speech was different. At first, I was focused on Pola's face, which appeared to visibly harden as the Chairman spoke. Seeing how intently she was focused on him, I wondered what it was that he was saying that aroused such a reaction.

After a few opening remarks about the "constantly changing situation in the ghetto," he said, "At one time, we had autonomy. But step by step, that autonomy was curtailed, so that today only a few remnants of it remain."

I understood what Rumkowski meant but was surprised he was admitting his loss of power in front of hundreds of people.

"As you know, my brothers and sisters, orders from the authorities are not subject to discussion. There is a war on, and there is total mobilization in the Reich; new factories must be created, for which additional workers must be found."

New factories were good news, but where would workers come from? Our population was dwindling daily, from resettlements, illness, and death. The Chairman spoke of reorganizing the labor force and shifting office workers into more demanding factory work. We were safe, I thought, our skeleton crew barely able to cope with all the records cluttering our room. He then spoke of initiating a survey of all workers. Much of what he said, I tuned out, either because I'd heard it all before or because I was thinking about Pola and how much I'd miss her if she left. I still doubted she would go. I could convince her to stay, even if she knew I loved Miriam.

The speech ended with the Chairman discussing the need to conserve food and tighten our belts. I heard Jozef griping that his belt was as tight as it could go. There was a smattering of applause, but it was not as in the old days when his speeches were met with thunderous approval.

Pola inched her way through the crowd ahead of me. From the rear, in her blue dress, she resembled Miriam in height, but her hair was cropped short, almost boyish. Once outside, I found her walking along the gutter. "He sounds frightened," she said.

"He admitted not having authority anymore. That should be frightening for all of us." I could hear Singer cheering that the dictator had finally acknowledged he was merely a puppet with the Nazis pulling his strings.

"He said that this was a three-month plan," Pola said. "Did you catch that?"

"No." I'd been too focused on her.

"That's not very long."

I mulled that over as we walked toward our customary point of departure. "With all the resettlements and the storming around of Nazi officials and inspectors, he said conditions are constantly shifting."

"I used to think this war would be a hiccup in my life," Pola said.

"Me too."

"I think what bothers me most is the uncertainty, not knowing what tomorrow will bring." Pola stopped at the corner. "It still smells. The fires slowed them down."

I looked questioningly at her.

She didn't reply.

I checked the street. I then placed a small kiss on Pola's cheek. "Thank you. I'll see you at work tomorrow."

She began to walk away and then turned back. She was walking at my side, not saying a word.

I didn't question her. I didn't want to break whatever spell was keeping her with me.

CHAPTER 39

M ONDAY, MARCH 15, 1943
MUCH ADO OVER A HEN
Stern, a commercial gardener on Urzednicza Street, was the owner of a hen, a thing of enormous value in the ghetto, where there is no fowl to be found.

"I was told to report to you," a young man said after knocking on our door.

"Who sent you?" I asked, guessing he was barely out of his teenage years.

"My uncle, Max. He says he knows you."

"I don't know who he is. Did he say how I know him?"

The boy looked uneasy. "He's an Order Service officer. He says that he talks to you sometimes."

I scratched my head. "I'm sorry, I don't know him. What do you want?"

The boy held up his right hand.

"What happened to it?" I grimaced at the sight of his broken fingers.

"My hand was caught in a machine. I can't work anymore." He hid his hand under the table. "My uncle said if I don't work, they will ship me out, away from my family."

"But you can't write," I said. "We need someone who can help write."

"I'm a good reporter," the boy said. "My teachers always said I could tell a story better than Moses." He held up his right hand. "I taught myself to write with my left hand. I need a little more time than most, but I do know a good story and am a hard worker." He handed me a page of his writing. "I think this is unusual."

"It's about some guy who owned a hen? I don't see much important here." I handed him back the page. "I'm sorry, I don't think we can use you here."

The young man's face drooped. "You were my last hope. My father was taken away months ago. My mother lost her other children last September."

I felt sorry for the boy.

"Thank you for hearing me out," the boy said and replaced his cap on his head.

"So, what happened to this hen?" Jozef asked, having sat silently throughout this conversation.

The boy looked uncertainly at me.

I had my mind on other things but forced myself to hear the end of the story.

"Well, you know eggs are selling for 25 or more marks per egg," the boy said. "That's a lot of money. So, his faithful hen was making its owner, a professional gardener, Stern, quite well off."

"Yes, so what happened already?" Jozef asked again, giving me a look that told me he was becoming impatient.

The boy sniggered. "So someone stole his feathered money-maker. He followed the tracks of his beloved hen and arrived at his neighbor's house."

"What kind of neighbor steals a man's hen?" Jozef shook his head. "What is the world coming to?"

I glanced at Pola's chair. It was empty.

"Boy," I interrupted. "What's your name?"

"Szmul, sir. Szmul Hecht." He gave me a smile.

"Well, Szmul, we don't have much time here for long-winded stories, so finish it now."

"Yes, sir. So Stern followed the hen's tracks, and there were feathers outside the neighbor's door," Hecht said.

"Can you believe a chicken thief is caught 'red-feathered?'" Jozef burst into laughter. "This was not a smart crook."

"Most crooks, thankfully, are not terribly intelligent," I said, wondering why Pola was so late. "So the neighbor stole the chicken and had to return it. So what's the big megillah?" I asked.

Szmul looked anxious. "You see, sir, it turns out that the neighbor, Szatan, it was his daughter who stole the hen."

"So, the daughter has to return it," I said.

"Not so fast," Szmul said.

"This whole story is not so fast," Jozef grumbled.

"He's right. Finish it so we can get to work," I said.

Szmul shrugged his shoulders. "The daughter, to hide the chicken, took it to her sister's house. Unfortunately, when Stern tracked the chicken down, it was dead, apparently suffocating on its way."

"That's the story?" Jozef said.

"Not quite. It's going to court. It will be the trial of the century here in our ghetto," Szmul burst out laughing.

"You're insane," I said but laughed at the ridiculous story.

Jozef sobered quickly. "The chicken thief could face the death penalty based on the new laws."

He was right. Almost any infraction, even reading a newspaper, could cause a Jew to face execution. Where was Pola? "So, you uncovered the trial of the century by following an obscure trail of chicken feathers," I said, studying a face that was both earnest and hopeful. I looked at him and smiled. "Very well, I will talk to Neftalin. We need more help." I could swear the boy's entire body sagged with relief. "But you will not tell anyone anything you learn in this room. That is of the utmost importance if you wish to remain employed here."

"Yes, sir. My uncle will tell you I am very trustworthy," Hecht said.

"Here, Mr. Hecht, our lives depend on it," I said. "Now, go to the courthouse and bring back more stories...but no more chickens."

Szmul laughed, clearly relieved that he was working with us.

I couldn't laugh. The reason I hired such a young man was I couldn't let his mother mourn another child when she'd already lost three the same night they took Regina.

Laughter subsiding, Szmul hurried out with deep bows and a promise to fetch me a great story.

Jozef looked at me. "You did a compassionate thing," he said.

"I hope so." I pretended to be absorbed in a stack of documents from the health department, but my mind strayed back to the night of the concert. Pola had followed me home. I didn't speak until we were on my block. "This is where I live," I said, afraid she'd take off. I held the door open. Would she enter or back away? "I'm on the top floor." I led her up the stairs. "Be careful, someone stole the railing. There are no lightbulbs." Her feet barely sounded on the steps. Was she trying to sneak past nosy neighbors? I hesitated by our door and then pushed it open. I was surprised when she stepped in front of me. "It isn't much. I asked for a larger flat for Miriam, and…anyway, we never got it." I shrugged. "The apartment would have been too large for only me."

"Are you nervous?" Pola asked, standing by the door, peering into the one-room flat.

"No. A little." Was I that transparent?

"You're talking a lot."

I clammed up.

"I don't mind. I just don't want you to be nervous." She pulled off her scarf. She was smiling.

"Miriam says I talk too much when I get nervous, so I guess I'm nervous."

"Don't be."

"I've never been with another woman." I kept my voice low, afraid neighbors might hear.

"I know."

"You know?"

"You're a good man."

How can I be a good man if I'm here with someone other than Miriam, I thought.

"I loved my husband very much too." Pola took my hand. "I'm not looking for love. I think, at this time, with so much uncertainty, it is not wrong for people to find comfort with each other."

"You don't love me?" Was I surprised? Insulted? Relieved?

"I said you are a good and kind man." Pola undid the top button of her coat. "I don't know what tomorrow will bring. None of us do. I know I

168

want to spend what time I have left here with you…if you wish that too?"

I could only nod. I was overcome with emotions I didn't understand.

"It is late." She pulled me gently, and I followed. When we got to my bed, she kicked off her shoes.

"I don't know what you want of me," I said.

"I don't know either," she whispered as if there was someone in the room who might overhear.

I watched her pull off her kerchief, and her hair fell slightly above her shoulders.

Miriam's hair had fallen nearly to her waist. I had to stop thinking of that. I removed my cap and brushed back my hair with my palm.

I saw her hand move up. "It is the only coat I have. I must take care of it." She looked at me with her dark eyes. "May I remove it?"

I nodded.

She undid the three buttons that were keeping her coat closed. In the dark, the yellow stars on the right front and rear of her coat blazed. I hated those damn stars and removed my overcoat as well.

She was in her dress. "May I remove it?" she asked. "It is my only one fit for the concerts and I…."

"Yes. I understand." I stood frozen as she undid the buttons.

"Will you take off your jacket?"

Would I? I had no choice. "It is my last one," I said, pulling gently out of the sleeves and draping it on the back of my chair. When I saw the yellow star, I turned the jacket inside out. I moved my body slowly to face her. Was I afraid she'd vanish?

Pola was standing in a slip and bra. Before I could say anything, she sat on the bed and slid beneath the covers. Was she beautiful? I didn't have time to look. I stood by my chair, a fool, not knowing what to do.

"Bennie," Pola said, "Take off your shirt and trousers. You don't want to get them more wrinkled."

She was right, but could I do this? Wrinkled? Every inch of my clothing was soiled and creased.

"Bennie," she said, "It's cold in this bed. Please?"

169

"I don't know if I can do this," I stammered.

"I understand."

I'd wanted this for months, ever since I felt her hand in mine during the concert. *But Miriam, do you want me to do this?*

"You can't stand there all night," Pola teased.

I saw Miriam when she stood in her filthy chemise. I remembered her hair cascading when she pulled off her kerchief...it trailed down her back. Oh, God, what should I do?

"It is only to keep warm," a silky voice penetrated my thoughts. "We don't have to do anything else."

Her voice in the dark could have been Miriam's voice. It was only a whisper, and one whispered female voice sounds like another. I undid my trousers and pulled my legs free. I folded the ragged pants, more to delay my actions than to help their poor wrinkled and tattered soul. I draped them on the back of the chair. In socks and shirt, I stepped toward the bed.

"You may remove your shirt," the whisper came.

I undid the buttons. Singer would have thrown his clothes to the wind for a chance like this, I thought. What is wrong with me? She's leaving soon, she said. Doesn't she deserve a chance to be happy? Do I? She said she doesn't love me... "May I leave it on?" I asked.

"It will be wrinkled."

There was that whisper again. Did it sound urgent? It was sensual coming from the dark, face unseen. My shirt was already wrinkled and filthy. I removed it and placed it on the back of the chair.

"Good. Now come to bed."

In two steps, I would be in the same bed where Miriam and then Jozef had slept. Now, she was here. Who was Pola? When I first saw her in our workroom, I thought she was hard and without feelings, perhaps once a soldier. Her body was thin and rigid, not soft and curved...Miriam. It had taken months before I saw cracks in Pola's shell, depth to her soul. Was she beautiful? No. Miriam was my definition of beauty. Nobody could be Miriam, but as time passed, I saw some form of warmth in Pola's narrow face, something that made me feel there was beauty there. When

170

she smiled, transported to fantasy places by the swells of music, I felt warm inside, a feeling I thought was extinguished the night the Chairman gave my loved ones away. It was only when Pola's eyes opened again, and they were not hazel, that the spell broke.

"Bennie?"

Whispering, she could be Miriam returned to me. I moved to the bed and lifted the coverlet.

Her arms reached up.

"Would you mind turning your back to me?" I asked.

Pola hesitated and then dropped her arms.

The bed rustled as she turned over.

I slid under the coverlet, keeping as much distance between us as was possible in the narrow space. From the rear, in the dark, she could have been Miriam.

"Good night, Bennie," came the whisper.

I didn't reply out loud, but in my mind, I said, "Goodnight, Miriam."

CHAPTER 40

SUNDAY, MARCH 21, 1943
FROM THE POLICE BLOTTER
Three Smart Turkeys
On March 7, a man came rushing into Precinct III and breathlessly reported: "Three birds have entered the ghetto through the barbed wire." This caused some surprise at the precinct. What? In broad daylight and despite the guards? The birds will have to be arrested and brought to the precinct.

I heard Jozef's laughter as Szmul read the report from the police epartment. I visualized the three fat birds wriggling through a hole in the barbed wire...a hole in the barbed wire? I liked Szmul. He brought laughter into the humorless chamber. "Another chicken story?"

Pola's chair was empty still. On Mondays, we had decided she would arrive late, at least until we announced to the others that she and I were at the concerts together. I couldn't tell them she stayed overnight.

"So how did the police react to this invasion by turkeys?" Jozef asked.

Szmul smiled. "The Jewish police were dumbfounded. They raced to the reported site of the hole in the barbed wire."

"Where was it?" I asked.

"In Marysin. Not far from your place. On Okopowa street."

Jozef looked at me. "That's near the cemetery, isn't it?"

"It could be. I don't know."

"Back to the story," I said, hoping for a funny ending.

Szmul nodded. "The police found a bunch of children and questioned them about the birds. They said they were playing with them."

"So, the police found the birds?" I asked. "Did they find the hole in the barbed wire?" Why was I asking this?

Heilig glanced at me. "You're jumping the gun. Let our boy finish his story."

Szmul removed his hat, and his uncut hair fell to nearly his shoulders. "One of the children said that huge ravens with scarlet beaks and red crops had flown into the ghetto." He laughed. "The child had never seen a turkey before."

"Of course. We have no fowl here, so no children would have an idea of what a turkey looks like," Jozef said. "And certainly, not what they taste like. Oy, for a taste of turkey." His eyes closed as if savoring the memory of what a piece of turkey tasted like.

"Did they find the hole?" I asked again.

"Electrified by the news, the entire squadron, with a large number of interested volunteers, searched the entire area," Szmul said.

Jozef sighed. "I imagine their 'hunting instincts' were aroused by the prospect of a juicy tidbit of turkey meat."

"I would join such a hunt," Heilig said, his mouth salivating at the thought of a slice of turkey on his plate.

Szmul nodded. "Everyone was racing all over. Mouths were watering."

I had lost interest in the damn turkeys. I wanted to know about the hole in the fence. Pola's seat was still empty. I'd kissed her goodbye. We did that every morning now when she stayed with me. I kissed her cheek because I knew that someday she would leave me. She'd said it many times, a reminder, perhaps so I would not fall in love with her. "So, did they find the damn birds?" I asked, unable to hide my irritation that our youngest member was, as usual, stretching the story. "We are not all as young as you, Szmul. We don't have as much time for stories as you do."

Szmul gave me a curious look and then said, "There wasn't a trace to be found of those desirable feathered creatures."

Jozef looked disappointed. "After all that, it was a wild goose chase?"

"A wild turkey chase," Szmul said and burst into laughter. "But just imagine all those policemen and resident zombies racing all over to find these mythical birds."

"Was the hole in the fence real?" I asked after their laughter subsided.

Heilig, a Weasel smile on his face, asked, "Can turkeys make holes in barbed wire?"

I dropped the subject. I tried not to let my eyes wander to the empty chair.

Jozef pulled up a typed report from Dr. Hugo Natannsen, a German. "This doctor was assigned to find out why Jews have so many diseases," he said and coughed hard.

"Because the bastards are starving us," Heilig said. "They paid a doctor for this? I can tell them in one sentence."

"Shaa, Heilig," I said. "What did the doctor come up with?"

Jozef looked over the details. "For once, Heilig is right. The doctor says that previously rarely observed diseases such as scurvy, pellagra, edema, abscesses, and others are directly linked to malnutrition."

"A German doctor said this?" Heilig said. "I must be dreaming."

"Heilig, please?" The Weasel had a way of getting under my skin, and today, with Pola still not in our chamber, I was in no mood for his sarcasm.

Jozef jotted something down on a sheet of paper. "He says when food is nutritious, the number of these cases declines."

"What a genius!" Heilig barked.

I ignored him. "What else does he say?"

Jozef read further in the report. "He notes there is an increase in bronchitis and pleurisy. Interesting. He says they are not always in connection with tuberculosis." He let out a short series of coughs. "Ah! He says, and I quote, 'A new and frequent phenomenon is the so-called softening, that is, decalcification of the bones.'"

"That is why we all are starting to walk and look like zombies," Heilig said.

Jozef burst into laughter.

"What is funny? Share. We all can use a laugh," I said.

"He says, 'Sunlight,' and get this, 'sunbathing' are cures."

We all burst out laughing. It was ridiculous. The reality wasn't funny, but imagining a doctor using the word "sunbathing" in the chimney-spewing, factory-choked ghetto was incredibly ludicrous to men who clutched at anything that could provoke laughter. I visualized our zombies in bathing suits lying on beach chairs, the glorious rays of the sun beating down on our skeletal bodies. Pola would have laughed.

When the laughter subsided, as it always did, Jozef said, "This doctor is taking significant risks. He says, 'But since the mass of ghetto dwellers do not have ready access to ultraviolet radiation,' a euphemism for sun-bathing..." He shook his head at the ridiculous notion and then frowned, "the above-mentioned diseases cannot be fought successfully with the means at our disposal." He then goes on to say that sauerkraut, red beets, red cabbage, and turnips, eaten raw, are of some help." He pulled out a filthy handkerchief and coughed into it.

I turned away, not wanting to see him gazing at blood spots, as Cukier had done so many times.

"I'm dismayed he didn't prescribe turkey meat," Heilig said and let out a burst of gobbling noises.

To my surprise, Jozef started gobbling too.

If I didn't follow suit, they would think something was wrong with me, so I jumped from my chair and imitated a pecking turkey, gobbling like a fool. We were all three acting the idiots when the door opened. "Attention!" I screamed.

Neftalin looked upset.

I thought of the holes in the fence, Pola crawling through. I heard the sound of gunshots in my exhausted brain.

Neftalin handed me an official-looking document. "By order of the Chief of the Ghetto Administration, the sacred shrine at the intersection of Brzezinska and Miynarska streets is to be demolished."

I sagged into my chair, relieved. It was not the news I'd feared.

CHAPTER 41

MONDAY, MARCH 22, 1943

"Nothing much in the news today," Jozef said, handing me his entry.

"No news is good news, they say," I said to Jozef after perusing his report.

"Are you alright, my friend?" He asked. "Pola will be alright. She is one tough woman."

Jozef was more insightful than I wished. I stared at the empty chair. "Thank you, Jozef." But he was wrong, something of significance had happened in the ghetto.

Jozef returned to his seat. I was glad Heilig hadn't shown up yet but hoped he hadn't been picked up by the goon squads searching for likely candidates for the resettlements. Had Pola been nabbed? I thought back to our last night together. It was a Saturday night, and she surprised me by saying she didn't want to attend the concert.

"Are you sure? You always enjoy it."

"No. Not tonight. I want to spend the entire night with you."

I didn't know why she'd want to waste her time on me. Even though I liked her, desired her, I had not managed anything more than to wrap my arm around her and clutch her close to me. I found my arm around her that first night, we shared a bed. When I went to move it off her, she held it and whispered, "It's fine." And yes, it was warm and comforting. But I could do nothing more. Night after night, I felt her against me and held to her as if she could give me safe-haven from the waves of conflicting thoughts, fears, in my head. The first night, I couldn't fall asleep, regretting that I'd invited another woman into Miriam's place. After that night, it became more automatic, natural. Pressing myself near her, then later, against her body, I fooled myself into believing all I wanted was to feel warm. When, after each concert, she followed me, it was increasingly easy to settle in behind her. I even lifted the coverlet and cast my eyes on her thin back, the bones of her spine visible through her skin. "Are you sure? You always enjoy the orchestra."

"No. Not tonight. I want to spend it with you. Let's talk."

We lay in darkness. "What do you want to talk about?" I asked.

"Nothing."

"We can pretend we're outside, under the stars," I said, my arm draped around her.

Pola turned over. "Lay on your back," she said.

I turned over, and she nestled herself against my chest. "This is nice," she whispered. "Now, I can look up and see the stars."

We became silent, her arm felt light draped across me. We were both little more than skin and bone. I didn't remove her arm. She kept her fingers and hand still, flat against me.

"I feel your heart," she said.

"Is it beating fast?"

"Slow. As if you are relaxing."

"Yes."

We rested like that for a long while. Then Pola moved her head, and I felt her lips touch lightly on my cheek and then pull away. I said nothing.

"Thank you," Pola whispered.

I lowered my hand and pushed her closer against me. I wanted to feel her with my other hand, but it remained dead at my side.

"I care about you," she said. "When I first met you, I thought you were a good man, but rather dull."

"Thank you very much." I bristled at how she sounded like Miriam.

"Dull is not the right word. I mean, boring. You were all about numbers." She laughed. "I'm botching this up, aren't I?"

"Yes, I think you are." I laughed too. "I know what you mean. I guess I've changed."

She reached up and kissed my cheek again. "Not as much as you think."

"I'm sorry," I said.

"You don't have to be. I understand." She lay back in my arm. "I like this."

"So do I."

"Will you kiss me?"

"I kiss you goodbye every morning," I said.

"I want you to kiss me goodnight." Pola lifted her body. I closed my eyes as she lowered toward me. I let her drop her lips on mine. I felt her gently suck in my breath as she shifted her body over me. Her kiss was not a morning goodbye kiss, but more urgent and unforgiving. It was the kiss of someone who wanted to be with me, to hold me, to love me. It was the kiss of someone who wanted more. Her hand moved lower. Oh, God, I wanted so much to feel her, to break Miriam's hold on me…Miriam. Did I say her name aloud? My hand grabbed Pola's wrist. Her lips were not on my lips. I opened my eyes. Her eyes were staring down at me. They were not angry. I expected harsh words. I wanted her to say them. I needed her to be furious. "I'm sorry," I said, barely able to breathe.

Still hovering over me, Pola smiled. "I said you are a good man."

I expected Pola to lift off my body and turn away from me. Instead, she dropped her head on my chest and curled her body next to mine. After a short time, I moved my hand over her and pressed her against me.

When I woke up, she was spooned against me, my arm in its familiar place around her. "Are you okay?" I asked.

Pola turned toward me and moved her hands to the sides of my face. She then raised herself over me, and I met her lips willingly. When she released me, she asked, "Does that answer your question?"

"I have to leave," I said, "I think we should let the others know soon."

Pola didn't reply. She lay on her elbow as I dressed. "One more hug?" she asked.

I watched her move from the bed. She was still in her bra and underpants. So thin, I thought, so vulnerable. But when she curled around me, her arms encircling me, I felt the pressure and warmth. I wanted to make love to her but held back. I bent to meet her lips and gave her a brief kiss.

"No," she said. "You can kiss your mother like that." She pulled my head down and holding tight, pressed my lips so that I had to respond. I swept my arms around again, but this time, not holding back. I felt light-headed. Lack of nutrition? Passion? She kissed me again and again, and I kissed her back. If only there isn't a Miriam, I thought and was frightened. How could I imagine such a thing? I pushed Pola back. I held her away when she tried to kiss me again. "I have to go," I said, confused and disgusted with myself. "I can't be late."

Pola dropped her arms. "I went too far."

Consumed by guilt, I replied, "It isn't you. I really have to go. I'll see you in a little while. Tonight."

"One last kiss," she whispered. "A goodbye kiss. I promise."

I bent down and gave her a kiss on her cheek. Before she could protest, I escaped.

Heilig's eyes were studying me. "This memo says that the Chairman performed 15 marriages in the House of Culture yesterday. What happened to Pola's weekly report?"

Jozef placed a finger on his lips.

Heilig sighed. "Another one, gone."

I heard Rosenfeld's familiar refrain, "Jews vanish, and nobody can find out what happened to them." Was Pola gone now too? I felt like crying but kept it back. A numbers man never shows his feelings, nor his regrets.

CHAPTER 42

T**UESDAY, MARCH 23, 1943**

It is being whispered that about 1,000 persons are soon to be resettled.

WEDNESDAY, MARCH 24, 1943
NEWS OF THE DAY

Spirits in the ghetto remain low. In the course of three hard years of ghetto life, people have developed a nose for impending disaster...

THURSDAY, MARCH 25, 1943

It was nearly a week since I saw Pola. I was filled with fear and regret. Had my lack of warmth driven her away? She left without explanation, without a goodbye to any of us. The others, our co-workers, stopped asking about her. I couldn't tell them about us. I couldn't tell anyone. That silence, when I wanted badly to tell someone about the thoughts battling inside me, made things more difficult. Jozef seemed to suspect but never opened a discussion. Nobody did. With each new notice of arrests, shootings, and resettlements, I begged I would not find her name.

Heilig burst through the door. "My God! My God!"

Jozef jumped from his chair. "What is it? What's wrong?"

I blocked the door. "Lower your voice. They will hear you."

"I was stopped on my way here. In the market square." Heilig was gasping for air, his hand on the back of a chair. "They took anyone away who did not have papers."

"What?" Jozef's hand was on Heilig's shoulder. "In daylight?"

"Lower your damn voices," I hissed. "They're everywhere now."

Heilig dropped his voice to a low rasp. "There were no announcements. There were women out shopping. They did not have their working papers with them."

"Who did this? The authorities?" Jozef asked.

"Yes. The Germans were rounding up people like dogcatchers."

"Where did they take them?" Jozef asked his hands, gripping the back of a chair.

"I showed my pass to a Service Order man. He was about to grab me, I think, but stopped when he saw my administrator card. He said his name was Max."

"Thank God," Jozef gasped.

"Szmul's uncle. It doesn't matter. I've warned you to be careful," I said, wishing I had warned Pola too.

"They took people even with working papers," Heilig said. "I think they would have taken me too if it had been one of these younger men and not this officer." He took a deep breath. "I asked where they were taking everyone. He said, 'The precinct stations and the guardhouse are storehouses for the 'goods.'' He called them 'goods.' People are 'goods.' Can you imagine?"

"We are not goods," Jozef said firmly.

"I'm glad you made it back," I said.

Heilig looked at me. "You know my photographic memory. The officer's words are etched in my brain. He said, 'The Special Department, the Gestapo, bring in a certain number of heads. Terrified, these prisoners attempt to convince the Order Service to release them by shouting, crying, whining, and begging. But the Order Service has no say in the matter. The situation is in the hands of the Special Department.' He sounded afraid."

I shook my head. "If this is true, we have a new precedent. Do we have any idea how many were taken?"

Jozef stared at me.

I knew what he was thinking. "Jozef, ask Neftalin if he can come to our office for a few moments?"

Jozef looked at Heilig. "Ostrowski is right. You need to be careful. We all do."

"You had quite a scare," I said to Heilig.

Heilig looked at me as if I were his enemy.

I was about to press him for more, but Jozef returned with Henryk following behind.

"I guess you've heard the latest," Neftalin said. "The Chairman is devastated. He asked what was happening to the people arrested, people he needs for work. Dr. Ley, the German commander, sneered, 'A field commission inspected this "human merchandise." This "merchandise" is in miserable condition: worn, bedraggled, gaunt.'"

"We are all guilty of being in poor physical condition," Jozef said. "Even young Hecht is coughing like an old horse." He looked at me. "Is that not what you called me?"

"We are all old nags," I said. "But hear Neftalin. You and I will talk later." I shot him a stern look.

Neftalin nodded. "I will tell you it took until late at night before nearly 80% were released."

"They were freed?" I was unable to believe the Germans would be merciful to any of their Jewish merchandise.

Neftalin nodded. "The condition of these people defies description. They were given no food nor water all day and had no idea of their fate."

"Do any of us?" Heilig asked.

Neftalin said, "No."

I'd never heard him admit that before. It was frightening. I thought I heard a wheeze in his breathing. He did not look well. "Henryk, is the Chairman aware of this new situation?"

"Of course. The Chairman demanded to know when his workers would be released. The Gestapo chief replied —I'll never forget his words—'The commission does its job efficiently. Those men have a practiced eye for the difference between usable material and "scrap."' That is what he called us."

"I am not 'scrap,'" Jozef said.

Neftalin smiled sadly. "Those considered 'scrap' have been removed from the ghetto. Those judged even half-able to work were freed to return to their desperate families." He walked to the door. "Thanks be to God and our Chairman, the Eldest of the Jews. By the way, he just celebrated his 66th birthday. Long-life to Chaim Rumkowski."

"L'chaim," Jozef said.

"L'chaim," I repeated.

Heilig mouthed the words. "To life."

Oddly, I remembered Singer once saying, "Someday, someone is going to shoot that bastard." Thankfully, that hadn't happened.

FRIDAY, MARCH 26, 1943

The action connected with the scheduled resettlement has, unfortunately, not yet come to an end. More people have been taken from their homes in nighttime police raids, most of them unemployed persons in the older age groups or persons with fictitious jobs.

CHAPTER 43

S UNDAY, MARCH 28, 1943
NEWS OF THE DAY
The ghetto's anxiety continues to rise...since the people assigned to this affair are pledged to secrecy, no detailed information is available. The populace is, of course, tormented by all sorts of fears and conjectures.

MONDAY, MARCH 29, 1943

The situation in the ghetto remains unclear, and morale is even lower than before—if that is possible. In the evening, it became known that a meeting of the precinct chiefs has been held at police headquarters. Absolutely nothing has been learned about the purpose of that meeting...

"You were unable to learn anything about this meeting?" I asked Heilig.

He shook his head. "Everyone is on edge since the nighttime raids."

Jozef nodded. "Doesn't anyone know anything?"

Heilig continued, "My sources tell me that approximately 1,000 people are under lock and key. There is a shortage of beds, so many spent the night against the doors and walls or in almost any position to avoid being bitten by insects on the floor."

"Szmul, anything in our police reports about these poor people?" I asked.

"None. The prisoners are in limbo."

Jozef remarked, "We all are."

Heilig said, "Nobody knows what's in store for them. Nobody knows what criteria the authorities used in these roundups. The fact that the

184

internees include all ages and skill levels has increased fear."

"I spoke to Neftalin on Sunday, and he said nothing new has been learned about these roundups."

"Do you believe him?" Heilig asked. "You know everyone involved in this has been sworn to secrecy."

I no longer trusted anyone. "I believe Henryk. Remember, the Chairman wants our document as evidence for the future. He knows someday, he will be judged."

"Singer said we all will be judged," Heilig muttered.

Jozef said a silent prayer.

"How many this time?" I asked. "Does anyone even know that?"

"I've heard rumors as high as 15,000. Nobody knows."

"Or they're not saying," Jozef said.

I heard Rosenfeld mumble, "The Germans know." And then Singer adding, "The Chairman knows."

"I can ask my uncle," Szmul said. He was usually silent at our meetings, perhaps awed by our older workers, as I was in the beginning.

"You just want a chance to visit your sweetheart," Jozef teased.

Szmul turned red.

Heilig was silent.

"Okay. Just be careful. I don't want you taking chances." It was enough that Singer and now Pola were risking their lives. I had tried to talk both of them out of trying to fight against the Nazis. I'd failed even at that.

"I'm going home," Jozef said.

Heilig said, "There is no chance that tonight will pass calmly. You would be wise to stay here."

Jozef stood. "Because I am old and infirm?"

Heilig appeared flustered. "I meant no offense. You are my friend."

Jozef smiled at Heilig. "I am old and ill, but not afraid of the Nazi bullies. You, Szmul, and the Engineer are young and have long lives ahead. What do I care if they send my cold body to the northern farmland? Or anywhere else?"

"No, Jozef," I said, alarmed by his acceptance of whatever fate the

Germans had penned for us. "We know nothing about where our loved ones..." I choked. "Jozef, you can't become a farmer. We need you here."

"God knows what he wants of me," Jozef said. "If God wills it, I will see both of your ugly faces tomorrow. If not, Engineer, and you too, Bernard Heilig, with the photographic memory, have happy lives. And if you have a moment, at some time in the future, tip a glass of schnapps to your old friend, Jozef Zelkowicz."

I watched silently as Jozef straightened and, with great dignity, left our room. "He's a stubborn, old man," I said.

Heilig replied, "He's terrified."

"If he weren't frightened, he wouldn't be normal," I said. "I'm scared too."

Heilig smiled. "Only young men like Szmul, and fools, aren't frightened in the mouths of wolves." He buttoned his coat. "I would have taken Pola from you. I was quite smitten by her when she first joined us here."

I shot my eyes at him in disbelief.

Heilig chuckled. "You forgot I am Singer's cousin. I would have been a far better choice for her than a human calculator. But, foolish girl, she prefers you." He sighed. "Perhaps, she is right. Perhaps, you, with your logical mind, will be the survivor of all this irrational shit." He laughed. "That would be God's ironic twist: to select an atheist to be the last Jew of the Lodz ghetto. Good night, Engineer. Hopefully, we will be here, in our stinking little cell, in the morning."

I remained seated as he left. He liked Pola? I didn't think he liked women at all. "I guess you never know people," I said, gazing up at the square where Rumkowski's portrait had hung on the wall.

CHAPTER 44

WEDNESDAY, APRIL 7, 1943

As expected, the night of March 30 did not pass calmly. Rumors spread that the wolves were coming for anyone who was ill. A great many sick people tried to hide. Because of the curfew, nobody saw that the patients from the hospital infirmary on Dworska Street were taken. Night raids netted 90 more sick people, dragged from their ratholes to the Central Prison. Half-naked people were racing through the streets in vain attempts to keep themselves from being thrown into trucks or marched in bare feet to the prison.

I passed the infirmary and saw it was a barren monument, empty of its patients. Windows were broken. I didn't want to look closer.

I detected a strange sound. A horse? Then I heard an even stranger sound. Singing?

A cart was heading in the direction of the Central Prison, but the captives were singing. I listened closer. They were singing, Hatikvah, "The Hope," the anthem of the Zionists who dreamt of reestablishing a Jewish homeland in Israel.

How can they sing, I asked God, not knowing where they were going. Did they believe the Germans were sending them to Palestine, where the Arabs would welcome the renewal of a Jewish state with open arms? I listened to men and women about to leave our ghetto, raising their voices in song, and hope was rekindled in my heart. The war will end soon, and we will all meet in Israel.

When I got to our office, I searched for any news from Warsaw. I had taken to searching for this, believing Pola may have returned to her hometown. There was nothing. Where was Heilig? The door was a blank wall. Nobody was walking through. Had they been taken? Jozef, with his bent frame and rickety legs, was a more likely candidate for deportation than Heilig, but there was no logic to the German actions. Any of us could be caught up in the hunt at any time.

"I saw at least 20 train cars at the Radogoszcs sidetrack," Heilig said, walking into the room.

A chill shot through me. "Were the cars full?"

"I don't know. They were freight cars."

"They're probably here for the shoes and clothing in our warehouses," I said.

"You mean the used clothes and shoes," Heilig said. "That makes sense."

"Have you seen Jozef?" I asked.

Heilig bit his lip.

"I haven't either," I said. "Any word from Warsaw?"

Heilig shook his head.

The door opened. "Atten...." It was Jozef. I fell back into my chair. "I'm glad to see you," I said.

Heilig rose and helped Jozef to his seat. "I was worried about you," he said.

Jozef laughed. "Me too."

I felt relieved to see them, even the Weasel. "What else is on the docket today?" I asked.

"This memo says the Chairman conducted 17 weddings at the House of Culture on Sunday. He was ill again. God bless him," Jozef said.

I thought of Pola asking me to accompany her to the Chairman's wedding ceremonies. She'd said they filled her with hope for the future. Her eyes brightened when she said that.

Jozef picked up a memo. "Oh, God." He looked at me and read, "Mr. Julian Cukier-Cerski died today at the age of 43."

I grabbed the sheet from his hand. I trembled as I read aloud, "The deceased was one of the first members of our staff and directed the Chronicle from its inception until he was stricken with tuberculosis...."

"Who was he?" Szmul asked.

Julian. I fought back my tears. "I have to go out," I stammered, handing the brief memo to Jozef. "Please add, 'The staff of the Archives mourns the loss of a colleague, friend, and co-worker.' Thank you."

I thought I'd become inured to any loss, but not of Julian. I saw him, his once cherubic face, now hollowed-out by disease, staring with fear in his eyes at the thickening drops of blood on his handkerchief. I saw those eyes, once aflame with hope, grown waxy, and tired from fighting the plague.

I was walking without direction when my thoughts were shattered by wailing and then shouting. How did I get here? I was near the tracks. If I were spotted, I'd be swept up with the others. The Germans had no logical criteria for their roundups. Miriam was right. She said Hitler didn't obey the rules of logic. He didn't care about which people contributed to his cause, not even if they enhanced the strength of his country. As I watched, hidden a short distance away, hundreds, perhaps thousands, of people, some barely able to walk, some hanging onto each other, some too exhausted and sick to even whimper, were herded into freight cars by our police. I didn't want to believe our police could do this, but their armbands and hats were conspicuous in the dimming light.

And not far away, armed with rifles, some with German Shepherds, Gestapo were watching.

I backed away from the surreal scene as the first car doors slammed shut, and locks sealed the human 'baggage' inside. I couldn't digest the panorama of train cars stretching in front of me. Twenty, I counted. Twenty times how many per car? I was held to the scene as if the vehicles were magnetic. *Count them. Count them all.* "Children." Only a few. A girl. Regina. I had to leave.

When I returned to our sanctuary, I pulled out a sheet of paper. I included what I'd witnessed, the brutal treatment of the prisoners by our police. "Chairman, read it. Damn you, read it!" I doubted that he still did.

I had to stop when I saw the note about Julian. The tears were threatening again. "No," I shouted in my brain and typed his death notice. Of the tens of thousands of deaths, suicides, executions, and more, Julian Cukier's was the one that no amount of slamming my fingers on the keys made less painful. Julian's loss even drowned out the cries and whimpers of nearly twenty thousand people forced into freight cars.

I was about to leave when the door opened.

"You look as if you've seen a ghost," a voice said.

CHAPTER 45

"I didn't mean to frighten you."

"I thought you were a ghost. You're alive?"

"You must have lots of questions."

"Are you real?" What a stupid thing to ask. "I thought I'd never see you again."

"Until I saw you sitting in the shadows, I did not believe either."

"Your apartment. It was torn apart. I was there. I saw the bed. It looked as if you struggled? I don't understand." I sounded like an idiot, but he was here. After all this time, Dr. Rosenfeld, my professor, was here. I trembled, unable to fathom what my eyes were taking in. "I don't understand. Didn't they take you? I saw the blood."

"I did fight them. Of course, your poor Doctor was no match for the Chairman's thugs. I was convinced my fate was sealed."

"My dear Doctor Rosenfeld, I cried for you. I mourned you. Where the hell were you?"

Dr. Rosenfeld walked toward me. He was limping. He wrapped his arms around me. "Dear Engineer, I thought I was lost from here forever. A Jewish policeman saw me within a crowd of old men at the prison after they dragged me and everyone from the building. Are you not a doctor?' he asked, peering at my dazed face. I clutched at this glimmer of hope. "Yes, I know you," I replied. He helped me to my feet. "Wait here. We need physicians. I will come back for you," he said. I almost blurted out that I'm not that kind of doctor, but God tied up my lips, and the man was off. One by one, the others around me were dragged from the room. I was resigned

191

that soon I would be called. The rumors said that the weak and infirm were the first to be selected for deportation. I had not been well, as you know. I mustered what strength I had left to convince my interrogator that I was fit for labor and of value to the ghetto. God knows what the wolves do with those who only exist to be fed?"

I stared in disbelief. This apparition was another of God's malicious tricks. "Dr. Rosenfeld?"

Rosenfeld smiled. "Yes, Engineer, it is I. What is left of me."

"Are you really here?" This defied all logic. "Please, be here? I've missed you so much."

Rosenfeld nodded. "I missed you. I never thought I'd see you again."

"But where were you?"

Rosenfeld's hand shook, and he lay it on the back of a chair. "I am returned from the dead, my friend. When the policeman didn't return, I was still on the floor of the Central Prison, cold, hungry, thirsty. They did not feed us nor give us a drink. My turn was coming. I watched man after man being rousted from their daze and lifted to their feet. Some had to be literally held up as they were walked from the chamber." He shook his head. "I vowed to stand on my own. You know how stubborn I can be. I watched the door for the Jewish policeman, praying he'd come back, but knowing nothing would come of it. Then I heard someone calling, 'Rosenfeld? Dr. Rosenfeld?' It was a German officer. My heart sank. I didn't raise my hand. The finger of the Jewish policeman pointed me out. Had he sold me out to the Nazis?"

"The Jewish officer betrayed you?" Anger simmered in my chest.

"No. My fellow Jew saved me. He lifted and supported me as they led me, stumbling, from the holding tank. I was terrified. Why had he singled me out to the Nazis? Others were being interrogated in the hallway. Some were being examined, naked, in front of everyone. How bony everyone looked. I was led past them out into the street. I could barely see in the glaring sunlight. I had been in darkness. A day of terror...mind-numbing suspense."

I imagined what it must have been like.

Rosenfeld's voice was creakier than I remembered as he continued. "A black car had its door open. Only Germans have cars, I thought. I wanted to resist being forced into the rear seat. I had little strength. I heard the sound of men screaming and saw men being beaten by clubs in the street. Shivering like a frightened child, I imagined the worst. The Jewish policeman had handed me over to the Gestapo. Can you imagine my panic?"

"Where did they take you? Why didn't you let us know where you were?"

"In time, you will know all," Rosenfeld said, sitting on the chair next to me. "The car drove to the train station. Freight cars, for livestock, cattle perhaps, were lined up with men being herded through their doors. Again, I heard men being beaten with clubs and much whimpering. Was this to be my fate? I expected to be forcibly extricated from the seat and thrown into one of the freight cars. I waited, urine pressing inside me. I had no dignity left. Only terror."

I thought of Miriam. What had she and my poor Regina felt as they were taken away from me? Rosenfeld was still talking. I had to refocus. I was still shocked, not believing after all this time, he was here.

"The car door closed, and a different German officer sat next to me. He said, 'You are a doctor?' I replied that I was. I'd had enough time to think that was my best course of action. But who knew? He studied me in the dark of the immobile car for what seemed a long period and barked something in German. The next second, the car took off."

"So, you let them mistake you for a medical doctor?"

"I would let them mistake me for Rumkowski. I was so shaken. I didn't know where I was being taken, but I did not want to be thrown into the cattle cars. You can't imagine such a sight, such sounds. Humans forced into crowded freight cars..."

"So, where did they take their Jew doctor?"

Rosenfeld frowned. "It is astonishing. The Germans have constructed massive labor camps. I don't know how many. Thousands of Jews and other 'undesirables' work in these tightly guarded installations. The conditions are deplorable, and many become sick and unable to work. I was taken to one called Buchenwald, where I was assigned to help keep the laborers working. It is their obsession."

"But you're not a medical doctor?"

"One learns quickly when uncertain of the alternative," Rosenfeld replied. "Besides, I was helping my fellow Jews." He looked into my eyes. "My personal mission became to help as many as I could, to keep them working. Once a man could no longer bear his yoke, the wolves had no use for him. Many were taken in trucks to what the Germans said were less taxing work farms." He sighed. "I don't trust Germans. The physical and mental condition of those workers we could not help was so grave I did not think they would long survive without extraordinary care and recuperation. Do our Aryans appear to be the kind of people who would care and nourish sick Jews back to health?"

"So, what do you think they did with them?" I asked, afraid to hear, thinking of the rooms of used shoes and clothing, the thousands of discarded knapsacks.

"None of us knew. Frankly, I suspected the worst, so I did what I could to keep Jews on the work lists."

"How did you get free?" I asked, still not believing he was here.

"It was strange. A few weeks ago, the tone of the German officers and guards changed. Those that had been friendly, at least for Germans, became more close-lipped. Everyone seemed anxious. I sensed something was happening but had no real clues. A few of our medical staff reported overhearing bits of conversation, scraps, that the German troops had failed in their attempt to conquer the Soviets. One of our surgeons reported having to cut away a white suit from a badly wounded German soldier. I recalled the camouflage snowsuits we made here for the Russian-bound forces. Soon, there were more such incidents reported. The dribs and drabs of gossip painted an enticing picture of German soldiers and tanks abandoned as the army retreated from the frozen steppes with Russians burning down farms and fields to keep the half-frozen soldiers from obtaining food."

"Have the Soviets invaded Poland?"

Rosenfeld shrugged. "I don't know. Before I could learn more, we were rousted from our beds and ordered into the backs of trucks. Nobody said where we were going. At first, we were in a convoy. I heard the rumble of other vehicles. Then the noise grew faint. I assumed they were heading in one direction, and we were going in another. Who was better off? Nobody could say. Nobody knew what was happening to us? But the Germans seemed in a panic."

"So, how did you end up here?"

"We were traveling fast. I was rocking in the back of the truck when there was a loud blast. Our truck leaped into the air and then careened to its side."

"My God!" I examined him with my eyes, amazed he'd survived.

Rosenfeld nodded. "Yes, God was with me. I was thrown against the canvas where I lay unconscious, for I don't know how long. When I awoke, my body felt broken. My eyes revealed I was still in the back of the truck. I heard voices. Were they Germans? I felt the pulse of one of the men. His arm was on me. Nothing. Another pulse. Nothing. I closed my eyes. Soon, I would be dead too. I asked, "When, God, will you end my nightmare?""

"It really was a nightmare," I muttered.

Rosenfeld nodded again. "But, as if in answer, I heard someone speaking Polish. At first, I thought it was a German trick. I listened again. It was a female voice. Polish. I had to take a chance. I was injured, barely alive. What more could the Nazis do to a half-dead old man?"

I thought of plenty of things they could do.

Rosenfeld continued, "I banged my fist against the wood beam. No response. I pounded again, my hand broken, the pain shooting through me. The sunlight blinded me when the rear cover was untied and thrown open. A man jumped into the rear of the truck. Scrambling over the bodies, he appeared an ape, but with a long knife in his hand. Terrified, I pretended to be dead."

I didn't think it would be much of a push given his state.

Rosenfeld wiped his brow. "This burly man pushed aside bodies, the knife gripped as if to plunge deep into an enemy. "If you are alive, show yourself. I will not hurt you," he said. What else could I do? I could barely speak. "I'm not German," I squeezed through parched lips. The knife was instantly over my eye. 'Who are you?' the man demanded. A wrong answer would have meant my eye. 'Dr. Oskar Rosenfeld, a Jew from Lodz,' I rasped. Almost immediately, I felt hands pulling me free."

"Who were they?" I asked. "Were they from the Polish army? We heard they were destroyed by the Nazis."

Rosenfeld smiled. "They were Jews."

"Jews?"

"They were a small band of resistance fighters who sprang from the forest and attacked our convoy. They were Jews, who, like heroes of old, are risking their lives to hurt the Germans any way they can."

"But it's hopeless," I said.

"That is what makes them heroes. Singer was right. It is better to die fighting than to die like sheep in a slaughterhouse."

"Did they know Oscar?"

Rosenfeld nodded. "They knew our brother."

"Is he alive?" I hadn't heard from him since our last meeting.

"They said he was with them in the forests for a while but was summoned to Warsaw."

"Why Warsaw?"

Rosenfeld shook his head. "Nobody said. They asked me if I wanted to remain with them in the forests. 'I'm an old man and will drag you down,' I replied. I asked if they could help me return to Lodz...to be with my family...you."

"You're an old fool," I said. "There is nothing but hunger, disease, and misery here."

"This is my home. Where else can I go?" Rosenfeld smiled gently. "All the signs indicate the war is almost over. I want to be here and finish what we started."

"Do you really believe the war is almost over?" I had held onto that hope for so long, but that too had finally slipped away.

Rosenfeld nodded slowly. "Yes, my friend, I truly do. Hitler is on his last legs. And when your wife and child return to you, I want to be here to share your joy."

After I'd given him up for lost, the dike holding back my tears burst open. Rosenfeld's coat wrapped around me. As I cried and cried, it was the greatest sense of joy and hope I'd felt in four years. Thank you, God, I prayed silently, clutching the old professor as if he were my father. Thank you, God. And for once, I believed he was listening.

CHAPTER 46

M ONDAY, APRIL 12, 1943
FOOD SUPPLY
Greater supplies of potatoes had been expected, but since the authorities seem to think that the ghetto has been supplied with mounds of potatoes through the end of April, they do not view the matter as urgent.

FRIDAY, APRIL 16, 1943

Our ghetto is calm. A supplementary ration announced today has raised spirits somewhat. Nevertheless, the general picture is bleak...People can barely drag themselves down the street...

TUESDAY, MAY 4, 1943

The mood has improved substantially with the hope of greater potato shipments. Hundreds of people waited on Pieprzowa Street, in front of the gate to the vegetable yards, since early morning. In spite of the fact that the Order Service was beefed up, the usual commotion prevailed.

FRIDAY, MAY 7, 1943
PEOPLE ARE SAYING

That the amount of potatoes coming into the ghetto will be large enough to allow potato rations for the next few weeks...and the people of the ghetto will have to move their furniture out into the courtyards to make room for such vast quantities of potatoes. This grand-sounding declaration has brought hope to the hearts of 80,000 hungry people...

CHAPTER 46

SATURDAY, MAY 8, 1943

Pola and I were at the House of Culture, the music majestic and soothing. I turned and her eyes were closed, her finger conducting the orchestra. I settled back in my chair. Eyes closed, music romantic, I saw her silhouetted against the white of my sheet, her body waiting for me. I heard the drumbeat of my heart. But it was not my heart. The drums were louder, more insistent. Trumpets joined them. Cymbals crashed. It was getting louder and more forceful. "What are they playing?" I asked. When nobody answered, I opened my eyes and turned to her seat. "Pola, that sounds like Wagner." The sound of guns and cannons echoed violently in the hall. Why weren't people screaming? I veered around. Nobody was moving. I turned anxiously back to Pola. The flesh of her face peeled in bloody strips to the floor. I stared in terror at the empty eyes of her skull. They were all flesh-peeling skulls and bones. A loud explosion and the building split apart, plaster pieces drifting down. Slabs of paint and concrete fell atop the skeletons seated dutifully in their seats. When I looked up, the Chairman was center-stage, conducting the orchestra, his eyes glaring demonically under his wildly flowing hair.

Did I scream? I shot out of bed, peering into the dark. It was hostile, alien.

It took me several long seconds before I was calm again. Hunger triggers nightmares. Pola had protected me in my bed, her thin body pressed into me. I missed the feel of it, how she fit against me. There'd been no news from Warsaw. Not of her, nor of Singer. Rosenfeld said that some mission had sent Singer back to Warsaw. Slivers of gossip circulated, but with radios and newspapers banned, the uprising begun on April 19 in Warsaw was relegated as wishful thinking. The authorities would not let such inflammatory news into their well-guarded Litzmannstadt. "Jews do not fight. Jews follow death like moths to a flame." So, while Warsaw Jews, emaciated and oppressed, were fighting, the Nazis kept their valiant struggle from us in Lodz. How could they allow us to learn that their mighty army had been forced to send in tanks to crush a few Jews? Had I known, I would have worried even more about Pola, whose hands were too dainty to hold a gun. Singer, my reckless friend, a cat with nine lives, would survive all. Thank God, none of us knew.

We knew only of potatoes. They had become our chain to life.

"Is there nothing else happening other than news about potatoes?" I asked after arriving in our cell and being greeted by the latest hopeful news about our spud saviors.

Jozef's nose was running incessantly. "Every time there is a rumor that potatoes will arrive in the ghetto, crowds gather."

Rosenfeld waxed poetic, "Starving children stare longingly at every cart. They run after the carts, pleading with the drivers: 'Give us a potato.' It would be funny if it weren't so sad."

Szmul, twenty years old, rarely spoke, but added, "People are dying from starvation." He covered his mouth with his hand. He appeared to be in awe of Rosenfeld, but we all were, except perhaps for Jozef, who may have resented that he was no longer our senior member.

"You picked up a cough from some of your young friends," I said.

Szmul looked embarrassed.

"As long as that is all our young man picks up from his 'friends,'" Heilig joked.

Rosenfeld shook his head. "Leave Szmul alone. Life is for the young, except in the ghetto where starvation makes us all old before our time."

I was grateful Regina was not among our starving children, but Miriam and my lovely daughter were someplace where vegetables and perhaps even meat was abundant. With the war ending soon, I'd be joining them.

Heilig said, "I saw the Chairman at the potato storehouse with Gertler, the head of his Special Department."

Rosenfeld looked curious. "What is this Special Department?"

"The Chairman appointed Dawid Gertler to establish a unit of our strongest men to perform operations that he believes would otherwise be usurped by the authorities."

"They're goons," Jozef interrupted. "Every dirty task is their assignment."

Szmul looked uneasy. "I have a friend who was selected by Gertler. He remains in the barracks. He acts as if he no longer knows me."

Rosenfeld shook his head. "His police force was not enough for the Eldest of the Jews?"

"The Chairman was forced to create this unit," I said, not fully convinced. "The Germans are sharpening their claws."

Rosenfeld smiled. "My Engineer, you never change."

I would have replied angrily if anyone else had said that, but not to him. "Back to the story. Jozef, why were the Chairman and Gertler at the storehouse for potatoes?"

Jozef frowned. "No one knows, but they were arguing. An Order Service chased me away before I could hear anything."

"The Order Service is protecting potatoes? Ironic." Rosenfeld said.

Szmul replied, "There have been riots just at the rumor that spuds are arriving."

Heilig laughed. "Mobs of adults and children pounce on any potato that falls off a cart. It is madness. Aren't you glad you returned?"

I wondered if the professor regretted his decision.

"Our fine police are reduced to protecting every last potato against these street attacks," Heilig said, sarcasm boiling over. "Not to mention potato peels. They kill for a handful."

Rosenfeld was silent, his wise eyes aimed at Jozef.

"We must have other news?" I was fed up with our obsession with potatoes that never arrived. Be careful what you wish for.

On May 20, 1943, we were compiling our lists of the dead when Neftalin barged through the door. His face told me he was not here about potatoes. "There is nothing sacred anymore," he said. "The bastards went to the cemetery."

"In Marysin?" I had scouted out the cemetery. I had devised a plan to hide there, in case things became desperate. I thought it would be safe.

"Yes. A Gestapo commission went to the cemetery. The bastards dug up a grave."

Jozef broke into silent prayers.

"Why did they do that?" Szmul asked, fear in his voice.

"What were they looking for?" I echoed, worried my plan was doomed to failure if the Nazis thought nothing of desecrating our cemetery.

"The pigs were rooting for valuable objects buried in the graves." Neftalin bit his lip. "God will punish them all."

God was punishing me again. Germans digging up the cemetery shattered my hopes for a possible hideout.

It was lunchtime. Heilig helped Jozef to his feet. Szmul accompanied the Professor, who enjoyed telling the young man of his adventures. I guessed Szmul reminded him of Singer, who also had a special place in the old man's heart.

Neftalin said, "Ostrowski, stay behind a moment. Please?"

The others looked at me. "Go ahead. I will be with you soon." I watched as Heilig, arm around Jozef's waist, left, with Szmul, and Rosenfeld a short distance behind.

"Zelkowicz is not well," Neftalin said.

"He went through a lot. He is fine," I replied, understanding the implication. "We are all starving and exhausted."

"Potatoes are being counted and will soon be distributed to the kitchens."

"Potatoes again? All the news lately is of potatoes." Perhaps I should not have complained.

Neftalin unfolded a yellowed slip of paper. "I wanted to give you this while the others are not present."

I thought immediately of Singer and Pola.

Neftalin licked his parched lips. "I saw you at the concert several times with your female colleague."

I froze. Neftalin knew about Pola and me? I was about to protest his butting into my business but needed to hear where he was going with this.

Neftalin frowned. "A bachelor like me can't imagine the pain of losing a wife." He let out a deep sigh. "A woman succeeded in entering the ghetto at the intersection of Zurawia and Koscielna Streets."

My heart pounded. "Pola?"

"We don't know if it was her."

"You don't know?"

"A large police squad was sent."

"Order Service?"

"No. The authorities failed to find the female."

I sagged back in the chair.

Neftalin dropped his hand on my shoulder. "The same day, three smugglers attempted to enter the ghetto. The soldiers fired shots at the hole in the fence, and they escaped."

"No arrests were made?"

Neftalin shook his head. "I wanted to give you this news in private before you receive the official account."

"But, you don't know if it was Pola."

"She is the only woman we know of who escaped our ghetto," Neftalin said. "That we do know. We also know Singer has been in-and-out of the ghetto as well." He looked at me with a sad expression. "The Chairman fears that such actions risk severe reprisals from the authorities. You understand." He looked hard at me. "The Chairman and I know you are a supporter of his policies that have helped us survive when many Jewish communities are no more." He hesitated. "We can't afford to give the wolves more excuses to usurp what little power we still have. Imagine how much worse things can get if we have more fires and can't stop these smugglers?"

"What are you asking?"

"The Chairman wants to talk to them. He will protect them. He promises that your friends, my friends, will be safe." He leaned closer. "My friend, we must act, or the Germans will."

I nodded. The Chairman had promised to protect our children...where were they now?

"If you hear from them, or from anyone who knows how to reach them—"

"I will inform you." Would I?

Neftalin rose from the chair and closed his coat. "I never thought it would come to this. I was certain the war would be over a few months after it started." He shook his head. "Will you walk with me to the Kitchen for the Intelligentsia? I hear they have potato soup with real potato bits today."

"Thank you. I think I will remain here."

Neftalin shrugged his shoulders and walked from the room.

I felt sick to my stomach. It must have been the potatoes.

CHAPTER 47

S UNDAY, JUNE 6, 1943
 FOOD SUPPLY
 Large shipments of potatoes have begun to arrive in the ghetto since the beginning of May and have accordingly been distributed to the population... Stomachs are full, hunger pangs have subsided, and, after a long period of starvation, people have begun to recover gradually and to gain some weight...

"Aren't you glad to have some good news for a change?" Jozef asked. "Even I am feeling better."

Rosenfeld looked amused. "Who would think humble potatoes could make such a difference? There are sparks of hope in peoples' eyes. They believe the worst is over, and hunger will not return to the ghetto."

Heilig said, "They're fools."

"Why must you always be a pessimist?" Jozef asked. "Summer is finally here. It is a warm and lovely Sunday." He looked at me. "What do you think, my friend, is this not good news for all of us?"

"Yes," I replied, but wondered if people were right in believing hunger would not return. It seemed that every time we got a bit of good news, we got a chaser of much worse.

"You don't sound convinced," Jozef said. "You're becoming as bad a pessimist as our friend Heilig."

"I suppose it's the natural result of what we do," Rosenfeld said. "Our Engineer has been at this a long time."

There was a knock at our door.

"Come," I said, curious as to who would knock.

A woman with a brown kerchief on her head peeked at us from just inside the entryway.

"This is the Archives Department. Are you sure you're in the right place? Come in. We'll help you find the right department."

The woman, in her thirties or forties — everyone looked older from years of neglect, so who could tell ages — remained by the door.

"What is your name?" Jozef asked.

"Henryk sent me," she said.

I didn't recognize the name, and then it hit me. "Neftalin? Henryk Neftalin?"

"Yes." She looked at me again. "He's a friend."

Jozef offered her a seat, even pulling it out for her, but she remained standing by the door.

Heilig rose, and the woman jumped away as he reached to close the door. He quickly sat down again so as not to spook our 'rabbit.'

"Why did Henryk send you to us?" Rosenfeld asked in a gentle voice, always the consummate father-figure.

"He said you would provide me employment."

Not again? Did Neftalin think of himself as my matchmaker? "We have enough workers here," I said, remembering how the German official had sneered when we said we needed four mouths for record-keeping.

The woman said, "Did you hear about the raids on Dolna Street?"

"I heard something. The area was sealed off." I replied.

Szmul leaned forward. "Near Lagiewnicka Street? I saw many people behind the hospital. They were standing in long lines. I hurried past when I spotted German soldiers. Rumors were it was a resettlement raid."

The woman's voice was low. "It was around dawn. The German police banged on doors and ordered everyone into the streets."

"You were there?" I asked, recalling what I'd been through. My jaw where the rifle butt hit still hurt.

"We stood there for hours. I was certain it would be my last day in the ghetto."

"You see, I told you," I said to Jozef. "Good news is always followed by bad."

Jozef waved me away with his hand. "Tell me, young miss, how did you get away?"

"The Germans demanded our working papers and ration cards. Then they let us go."

"They let you go? It wasn't a resettlement raid?" I asked, shivering at the memory of the night Regina and Miriam were taken from me.

"This is unusual," Heilig said. "Do you want me to check it out?"

I nodded. "But be careful. The net is spreading."

Heilig bowed to the woman and left our room.

Jozef again offered the woman a chair. "You must be tired after your ordeal."

She moved to the chair and spread her coat as she sat. Seeing her seated across from me, she appeared younger, her eyes light blue. I could almost see through them. When she removed her headscarf, her blond hair fell to her shoulders.

"Can you tell us anything else about that night?" Rosenfeld asked.

She ran her hand through her hair. Miriam used to do that. She said she was 'fluffing' it.

Rosenfeld leaned closer. "My child, what else did the Germans do? Anything at all may be of help."

Her eyes closed. "I saw them running from building to building. Doors were broken down when we returned."

Oh, God, it was just like that terrible night in September. "Play 'Hide-and-Seek,'" I'd urged Regina, planting her under soiled laundry in the closet. We'd practiced her pretending to be asleep...I wanted to see her face. I saw hazel eyes...like her mother's lustrous eyes.

"Engineer, you missed it," Jozef said.

I refocused on his face.

"Rivka. That is our young lady's name, she says that when the residents went back to their flats, all the closets were open, and everything was thrown around."

"That is normal." They found my Regina in the closet.

Jozef looked puzzled. "Rivka says they searched every drawer and bureau as well. Laundry baskets. Anything that could be a hiding place for valuables."

Rivka added, "The next day, they closed the shops and confiscated all the merchandise."

Jozef said, "Engineer, the Germans don't usually waste the Special Department on such searches and then return the people. What do you think?"

"Only the Germans know." I heard Singer add, "And the Chairman." I noticed Rivka had placed her coat in her lap. "Do you know how to write in German?"

"Yes."

"You may remain, but you should know that if we must lose someone from our department—"

"Oh, thank you. Thank you, kind sir. Henryk said that you were very kind."

I wondered why she called the Chairman's Deputy by his first name.

CHAPTER 48

SATURDAY, JUNE 12, 1943

In the stream of death notices, only a few caught my attention. Executions were still shocking to us. What made them of greater horror was my fear that someday Singer's or Pola's name would spring out at me like some tiger that had been in hiding too long. I held my breath whenever I received such notices. "Are there names?" I asked Szmul.

The young man shook his head. "The first escaped from the ghetto and was hiding with peasants in the area."

I stopped my pen. It could have been Singer.

Jozef said, "The other two escaped from labor camps."

"Rivka, go to Neftalin and see if you can learn their names."

Jozef looked disappointed that I had not asked him to seek out the Deputy. I had not shared my suspicion that the girl was acquainted with our supervisor.

Rivka stood, and I could not ignore the change in her in a week. No longer hidden in a coat, her body looked fuller, her legs firm. As she left the room, her hair bounced on her shoulders. There was an eagerness in her step that her timidity during our first encounter had not indicated.

Heilig was watching Rivka as well. As soon as the door closed, he hissed, "She is a looker. I did not expect that when she first came here."

He looked as if he were sharpening a knife and fork to slice up our rabbit.

Rosenfeld took me aside. "There is something about her that makes me uneasy."

I shrugged. "Well, we need help. While we're waiting, any more news?"

"This is interesting," Szmul said. "A locksmith in the woodwork factory has invented a new material the Germans want."

"To help the Germans make new weapons?" Heilig asked. "Shit! Don't we ever learn?"

"It can be used to make utensils, lamp bases, etcetera." Szmul looked excited. "I wish I could invent something like that. We'd all be rich. I'd share the money with all of you."

"Rich in the ghetto? You're a dreamer," Rosenfeld said.

"It's the etcetera that worries me," Heilig quipped.

A dark look came over Jozef's face. "Our friend, Heilig, may be right. A military commission led by Amtsleiter Hans Biebow conferred with the inventor, Henryk Wosk. There are large orders for this product already."

Heilig shot his finger at me. "You see. I am right. This damn Jew has invented some shit that the Nazis are going to use to try and win their damn war."

"Shut up, Heilig," I ordered.

"You don't believe me? Why else would they come to our factory and spend time with a Jew?" He shot his eyes at Jozef. "What is this super-material made of? We have nothing in the ghetto that even passes for gold, silver, any metal."

Szmul scanned the report. "Well, we have lots of sawdust, and the whole ghetto sits on clay."

Jozef said, "One thing you can say about us Jews is that we're resourceful. Who else could come up with a hundred recipes for rutabaga, potato peels, and now, a miracle material made of sawdust and clay?"

"This schmuck should have shared his invention with our fighters," Heilig rasped, "Not with the damn Germans. What is wrong with us? Don't we realize we're helping our enemy destroy us?" He was gasping for air. "Rumkowski and his like are nothing but collaborators—"

"Heilig. She's coming back. Shut your damn mouth."

Jozef looked shocked.

"We don't know her," I hissed.

"I don't know any of us," Heilig said and grabbed his coat. Before Jozef or I could stop him, he stormed out the door.

"Good riddance," I muttered. "Any more news?" I asked.

"On Friday, the Chairman issued a proclamation that all bicycles must be turned in by June 15, including those used in workshops and departments." Jozef laughed bitterly. "Do they think we're going to attack them on two-wheelers?"

"Shaa," I hissed at him as the door opened again. "You were gone quite a while," I said.

Rivka smiled. "I have what you asked for."

I had no intention of asking her for an explanation of what had taken her an hour. I imagined the Deputy was busy.

Rivka unfolded a sheet of paper. "The man who escaped the ghetto was Abram Tandowski, born 1912."

I breathed a sigh of relief that it wasn't Singer, but two more Jews were killed by the Germans.

Rivka's eyes were on me. "The other two escaped from a labor camp. They were Hersz Fejeglis, born 1920, and Mordecai Standarowicz, born 1914." She looked up, her blue eyes like small lights in our dimly lit room. "Deputy Neftalin said that no other details of the executions are known, but that all Order Service section heads were 'obliged,' the official word, to attend." She looked at me. "Is there anything else you want to ask me?"

I shook my head and went back to my typing.

It was Saturday night. The concert hall was beckoning. I walked home, wondering if I went to the House of Culture, would Pola be there?

CHAPTER 49

T HURSDAY, JUNE 24, 1943
FOOD SUPPLY
The situation is extremely critical. Naked hunger once more reigns
in the ghetto.

"I don't want to write about hunger anymore," Jozef whined. "I thought that agony was over."

Heilig smiled, the smile of the insane man he was becoming. "Yes, we have no more potatoes. No more potatoes today," he sang and then burst into irrational laughter. "I heard this song someplace. I have no idea where."

Jozef was still whining, "How do they expect us to survive on the potato ration they gave us on May 20? They said it was to last us until July 18? 15 kilograms of potatoes? Don't they know they rot? And once the meager ration is gone, they give us rotten lettuce leaves? Are we damn rabbits?"

At the word rabbit, I involuntarily turned toward Rivka's empty chair. She, for some unknown reason, did not appear to be suffering as much as we were.

Heilig held up his hand, a sheet of paper clutched in his fingers. "Here, we go again. Another suicide. If we're going to end our lives, why not do it fighting?"

"For pity's sake! Please, Heilig, just give us the facts?" I said.

"Fine. A woman jumped from the fourth floor at 7 Bazarna Street. She died. Those are the facts." He glared at me with eyes that blazed fire. "Are you satisfied, you heartless calculator? Do you want the truth? Don't you give a shit anymore?"

Rosenfeld looked up from his writing. "Show respect. Our friend has been at this for nearly four years."

"I want the truth," Jozef said.

I kept my anger bottled up. The Weasel was out of control. "Is there more to this tragic story that has you so riled up?"

Heilig glared at me. "Her name was Mrs. Friederike Mukden. She was recently resettled here from Prague. Her husband, Alois Muken, was born on October 15, 1894. He died on November 12, 1942."

So far, there was nothing newsworthy. I remained silent, unsettled by Heilig's raging looks and the challenge in his voice.

Heilig threw the paper at me. "He was an engineer."

I picked up the paper.

"Read on, Engineer, if you can?" Heilig taunted.

"Read it aloud, please?" Jozef said.

I read, "Her 14-year old daughter Emilie Rene, died of tuberculosis today. After the death of her husband, she lost much of her will to live. The death of her child…was the crushing blow." If I knew Miriam and Regina were gone, would that not be 'the crushing blow,' I thought, unable to read more.

"The unhappy woman chose death the same day as her child's death," Jozef said.

"Yet another family wiped out," Rosenfeld said.

"Nobody cares," Heilig added.

Was he right? I was numb. Was I past caring?

The door opened, and Rivka entered, followed by Neftalin. "I have wonderful news." He handed me a short note, which I recognized was in the Chairman's handwriting.

After I read the note, I passed it to the others.

Rosenfeld squinted through his dirty lenses. "He says there are post-cards?"

"So, you see," Neftalin said, sitting across from Rivka, "Our fears for the deportees were unfounded."

"May I see the postcards?" I asked, still skeptical.

"Of course. Here you are." He handed me three postcards with very little writing on them. He smiled at Rivka. "Soon, we'll all be reunited with our loved ones."

I hoped the postcards would confirm his optimism. His suit looked less rumpled, and his hair was regaining its sheen. He walked with a swagger I hadn't seen in days. As he left, he shot Rivka a smile.

It was odd, but seeing Rivka transformed into this attractive woman, who had obviously caught Neftalin's eye, gave me a new sense of optimism. In some ways, her mannerisms and her eyes reminded me of Miriam, not their color, but the flashes of light that shone within them. In their sparkle, I saw life, the possibility of seeing Miriam and Regina's bright eyes again. The postcards, with human scrawls in black ink, rekindled my hope. I was happy to type up an entry for a change:

MONDAY, JUNE 28, 1943

Lately, more and more messages have been arriving here from people who left this ghetto in the course of various resettlements. These are postcards with brief messages that indicate that the senders are not faring too badly. At any rate, it is a reassuring sign that these people are alive and able to work.

When I shared my entry with Jozef, he mimed a short prayer.

"What did you ask for?" I asked after saying amen.

"I thanked God for word from our friends, at long last." He aimed his eyes at me. "Ben, I'm tired of this work, this sad chronicle. I'm sick of the pain of hunger." He smiled, benignly at me. "I'm an old man. I can't take this much longer. Resettlement is a real option. Just read the cards."

If I knew Miriam and Regina were never coming back, I could leave this hellhole, I thought, wishing I'd get just one postcard from Miriam. I took Jozef's hand, bony and shriveled, and said, "Always remember, the devil you know is better than the one you do not."

He gave a hoarse laugh, more a cough. "I'm not leaving. Just considering it."

"You still say that about the devil we know," Rosenfeld said. "But I think you are right."

"That's a first," I said, chuckling, something I rarely did these days, "Someone thinks I am right about something. The world must be coming to an end."

"I wish you didn't say that," Jozef said.

CHAPTER 50

T HURSDAY, JULY 1, 1943

I stared at what I'd written in disbelief. If tearing it up would have changed things, I would have ripped it into tiny shreds. Oh, God, I had such regrets. As I read my words, I felt I was choking, tears welling up in my eyes. How could I be so blind? Had I lost all sensitivity to others?

"It's okay, Bennie, he was very ill," Rivka said.

"I didn't see it coming. I should have."

Neftalin was reading the obituary I'd composed, leaning against the wall. "I did not know this about him. I see why our esteemed Chairman picked him."

I realized once again how little I knew about the people I worked with. I stared at yet another empty chair. "I guess the shock is that I didn't see it coming." When Cukier coughed incessantly, I knew it was tuberculosis. His nose rags gave it away. Rosenfeld? His cold hands and aged face made him a likely target for the Nazi resettlements. I glanced lovingly at the professor, working on his descriptions of ghetto life. Jozef was saying Kaddish, the "Mourner's Prayer." I'd thought he would be the next to go. Heilig? I thought the Weasel would outlive us all. "He was only forty-one. I never imagined him dying so young," I said, realizing he was only a year older than me.

"He had tuberculosis," Jozef said. "He tried to hide it."

"I knew he was ill, but not...."

"I like what you wrote here," Neftalin said. "The death of Dr. Heilig has

216

left a gap that will be hard to fill."

I called him the Weasel, but he was never that. He was not always easy to work with, but which of these opinionated men were? Was I? Miriam didn't think so.

"I also like this part: 'His personal graciousness, his sober demeanor, and his spirit of cooperation also earned him the friendship of many people.' Very nice. You've become quite a writer, Engineer. I guess something good has come of this damn insanity."

"Nothing good comes from this shit," I said.

Neftalin nodded. "I must go." He rose and then fell back on the chair.

Rivka hurried toward him. "Henryk, are you okay?" Her hand was on his arm. Her eyes were glued to his face.

Neftalin rose from the chair. "It was a momentary weakness." His voice softened. "I'm fine. I guess this 'diet' is taking a toll on all of us."

"Do you want me to see you back to your office?" Rivka asked, giving me a questioning glance.

I nodded. Perhaps our female's attention to the Deputy was helping us in some way too. Who was I to judge them?

Neftalin smiled. "Thank you," he said. "I believe I'm fine."

"Go with him," I said, worried about the sudden weakness of my friend.

I watched them leave, her arm on his. Who was I to deprive him of whatever pleasure he might get in these terrible times? I trembled to hear what Heilig might say about this new development, prepared to shout, "Shut up, Heilig." An empty chair. Another empty chair.

"I'm happy for Neftalin," Jozef said.

"We have work to do." I watched Rosenfeld bend over his pad. He was writing the rest of the obituary for our colleague, Dr. Bernard Heilig. "I'm glad we were able to bury him in one day as our traditions demand. It was a nice ceremony, considering everything."

"I have not been to a funeral in a long time," I said.

"Most Jews don't get formal burials anymore," Jozef replied. "The wagons come, and the meat goes. At least our co-worker had a good send-off."

Rosenfeld looked at me and shook his head. "These days, even that is too much to expect."

I began to type: "Weather: Temperature range: 18-30 degrees, sunshine. Deaths: 19. Births: None." I stopped my fingers. It had been sunny at the cemetery, a rare chance to be out in the sun during our 12-hour days of labor. The funeral in daylight was almost enjoyable. Who would not welcome bright sunlight when all they see is darkness?

"Will you say Kaddish with me?" Jozef had asked as we stood at the open gravesite. "Yisgadol vyiskadosh...."

Jozef's mumbled prayers were the buzzing of a bee in my ears. My eyes drifted to the many nooks and crannies permeating the Marysin cemetery. What a wreck, I thought, seeing the holes where iron fences had been ripped away by the Germans, hungry for metal for their munitions. There were craters where tombstones had been removed. The Nazis had aroused great fury when they had dug up a grave searching for hidden gold and silver. Even the Chairman had lodged protests with Biebow, who assured our Eldest of the Jews that this was an unfortunate event that would not be repeated. What ungodly creatures had vandalized these stones, had dug up our hallowed dead? Was the cemetery now safe? Would the Germans keep their promise to protect our ghosts? There were places here where a man might hide...

"Say, 'Amen.' This much even an atheist can do," Jozef barked at me.

"Amen," I said, my eyes on a corner between two concrete crypts that were standing near the much-neglected rear rock wall of the cemetery. A crack in one of the walls was almost hidden by wildly growing shrubs. A man could hide there...or there...perhaps even there...

The door burst open. I jumped to my feet.

"It's a fire," Rivka said. "Another fire."

Szmul grabbed his coat and ran from the room.

"He reminds me of our friend," Rosenfeld said.

"Not at all," I replied, wondering if someday I would tell him the truth about Singer and Miriam.

CHAPTER 51

F RIDAY, JULY 9, 1943

Do we ever become accustomed to living in a cage surrounded by barbed wire? I suppose we do, as we also get used to being hated and kept in a slum by gun-happy sentries with orders to shoot at will. We become numb to death. Very little penetrated my shell these days.

"The ghetto looks different in summer," Rosenfeld said. "The brighter sunlight and colors add a little hope."

"You can almost forget we're starving. No news of more rations?" Jozef asked.

"No. The vegetables promised haven't materialized."

"You see the despair on every face. It is odd to see such unhappiness in such welcome weather," Rosenfeld muttered and then wrote it down.

"Even the kitchens have nothing to cook," Szmul said.

"I think the authorities are doing this on purpose," Jozef hissed. "They are getting ready to close up the ghetto."

"How can they do that? We are essential to their war effort." I couldn't imagine anyone, not even Hitler, being that illogical. "Rivka, go to Neftalin and ask if he has any news about upcoming food deliveries." I looked at Szmul. "That will make our growing boy happy."

Of course, Rivka didn't protest this assignment.

"Do you know there is no sanitation service?" Jozef said.

"Garbage is everywhere," I replied.

"Typhus and rats are the results," Jozef said. "I tell you, something is happening. The situation is more and more critical. I can't believe we would not be better off outside of this hellhole. You should have let me volunteer. A farm would be a welcome change. We can go together."

"I can't leave."

"I have no such ties," Jozef said. "What truly hurts is I thought our starvation was ended. Don't dangle a carrot if you intend to yank it away."

Don't dangle a carrot? Why did God give Miriam, Regina, and Pola to me if he intended to yank them away? If God existed, what pleasure could he get from tormenting me like this?

Szmul interrupted my thoughts. "I have a report about books in the library your friend Neftalin started. Apparently, many ended up as paper in the latrines, but about 30,000 are in the book collection at the Department of Vital Statistics."

"30,000? That's a miracle," Rosenfeld said.

Szmul nodded. "The memo says they even saved a few Torah scrolls."

"Now, that's a surprise," Jozef barked. "The Germans must think they have value. The bastards would sell their grandmothers if they could squeeze out a few marks."

Szmul coughed hard and then said. "The shelves reach up to the ceiling with books that have been handed down for generations...." He looked at me. "I would like to see that before I die."

"Die? You are the youngest of us all," I said.

Rosenfeld smiled. "Young man, you are the storyteller that will turn our struggle into the stuff of legend."

Jozef preempted my response. "My father used to say when you save a book, you save a million lives. I never understood what he meant. Not until...."

The door burst open, and Rivka charged to her chair, crying hysterically.

Rosenfeld bent over her, consoling her.

It's a lovers' spat, I thought and was not surprised when Neftalin came charging in after her. There were flames in his eyes. "It's your fault," he shouted at her. "You brought this on all of us."

Rivka buried her face in her hands.

"Henryk, are you out of your mind?" I asked, never having seen him so enraged. "Calm yourself. It will work out."

"Here," Neftalin barked. "Read it yourself." He stormed out of the room.

I'd never seen him so volatile. "Are you okay?" I asked Rivka.

She swept her arm across the table, knocking papers and pens to the floor, and then ran from the room.

Szmul ran after her.

"What the hell is going on?" Jozef asked, staring at the empty chair. "It must be a lovers' spat, but the Deputy is never like this."

"I don't know." I flattened the sheet of paper, and read it, mouth dropping open.

"What is it? What's happened now?" Rosenfeld asked.

Jozef grabbed the page. "I don't understand," he said, rereading the notice.

I growled, "It says all women and girls employed at our administration are dismissed by order of the Gestapo."

"Are you crazy? Why would they do this?" Jozef turned the page over to see if more was explained. "No motive is given." He tossed the note on the table.

"Every woman?" Rosenfeld stared at the note as if it was on fire.

"Every woman." I looked at Rosenfeld. "It says this takes effect in ten days."

"No women? How will we find replacements?" Jozef pointed to the piles of paperwork. "This is in effect in every office?"

"Yes."

"All of our men are slaving in the factories," Jozef said. "The authorities will have to rescind this insane declaration."

"No wonder Neftalin was so upset," I said. "Why would they do something this illogical now?"

"Only the Germans know," Rosenfeld said.

CHAPTER 52

T UESDAY, JULY 13, 1943
When it was learned on July 7 that the female employees would have to leave Balut Market and be replaced by male personnel, all sorts of conjectures and vague theories about this fact were bruited about. The conjectures seemed to gain plausibility when one of the executive officers of the German Ghetto Administration, Schumburg, was removed from office.

Rivka did not return.

"What do you think of this?" Jozef asked, handing me a brief notice about a German Ghetto Administrator, Schumburg, being removed from his position.

"It's a strange coincidence that a notice banning women from all of our administrative offices is followed by the dismissal of a German Ghetto Administrator," Rosenfeld said.

"Why not ask Neftalin about this?" Szmul asked.

"Are you serious? Did you not see how angry he was? I've never seen him lose control as he did."

"I thought it was a lovers' quarrel," Jozef said.

"It is curious that a German official was removed right after the banning of women," I thought aloud.

Jozef spat on the floor.

"What the hell?"

Jozef laughed. "Don't you see?"

"What?"

"It's obvious. Are you blind?"

My hands balled into fists. Miriam had screamed at me that I was blind. "Oh, God. You think that Nazi bastard was involved with one of our women?"

"It makes sense." Jozef looked disgusted.

"Not her?" Szmul looked devastated.

Jozef looked at me. "Rivka was hysterical, screaming. Neftalin said it was her fault." His eyes opened wide. "She wasn't with Henryk at all! He said it was all her fault!" He stared at the empty chair as if Rivka were still on it. As if she could answer him. As if he wished he could set her on fire. No trial. No publicizing of her suspected sin. If it were true, it was the worst sin a Jewess could commit.

Szmul shot out of his chair. "No. You're wrong. She's a good person. Nice."

Jozef snarled at him. "She was caught up in the roundup. She said that. But she escaped. She never said how."

Szmul looked as if ready to burst into tears. "I don't believe it. It's not true!"

The boy had a crush on her. I'd always suspected something about Rivka, but not this. I felt as if I'd been punched in the brain. It couldn't be right! Rivka was Henryk's girl! We all thought that.

Jozef spat on the floor again. "She was shtupping a Nazi bastard," he said.

"Stop spitting on the floor. We have no proof. It's all conjecture." Even as I said that I suspected the worst. But how could it be true?

Jozef pointed at me. "Neftalin said it was her fault. What else could it mean?"

The idea that Rivka could have been with the dismissed German turned my stomach. I had always felt uneasy about her, but could never put my finger on why. I had misjudged so many people in my life, was I doing that to her as well?

Like many of the phenomena that marred our lives in the ghetto, I never learned what actually caused women to be banned from the Jewish and German Ghetto Administration offices. Who could we ask? The Germans?

I certainly couldn't ask Neftalin. He was in a rare mood. Our only path was to try to forget and do what we could to survive this new calamity.

Amid the gloom of hunger and the loss of our female staff that day, came the report that Dawid Gertler, the head of the Special Department, had been abruptly taken by a black car to Gestapo headquarters.

Gertler, one of the Chairman's most powerful appointees, and his Special Department were in charge of searches, confiscations, and resettlement actions. It was believed he worked hand-in-hand with the Gestapo as part of the Chairman's effort to keep the Germans from completely taking over. Many accused that he'd gone too far, not merely enforcing the occupiers' laws and decrees, but spying for the Gestapo and informing on his fellow Jews. His disappearance sparked rumors that this was a precursor to a full German takeover.

Jozef read my entry silently. "I am ready to leave here," he whispered. "I only pray God makes it easy."

I laughed. "Does God make anything easy?"

CHAPTER 53

T HURSDAY, JULY 29, 1943
A FUGITIVE IN THE GHETTO
German police patrols searched for an alleged Polish fugitive who had fled into the ghetto. The man could not be tracked down inside the ghetto. He had undoubtedly escaped again at some other point on the border of the ghetto.

I closed my eyes. I visualized a man crawling through a hole in the fence. Then I saw flashlights and rifles aimed at him. When the light hit…Singer's face.

"Whoever it was escaped from some other point on the border," Neftalin said. "He was fortunate. The authorities are dealing harshly with smugglers."

I grasped Henryk was warning me that if I heard from 'our friend,' I should pass the warning to him. I was starving and exhausted. I was beginning to think Jozef was right when he said all this was a precursor to the eventual evacuation of the ghetto, but we were all in limbo. Even the Deputy was unable to offer more information about the harrowing events happening to us.

Rivka had vanished too. I honestly didn't care. She was a fantasy creature, a character in this strange melodrama we were living. Neftalin never spoke about her, but there were rumors that one of the women in our offices had been intimate with the German staff. Was it Rivka? Two plus two….

"There was a large crowd at Zawiska and Dworska streets today," Jozef said.

Neftalin nodded, "Our Special Department dispersed them before the authorities got involved."

Jozef fired back, "They were doing no harm. Rumors spread that Gertler had returned and would be appearing. Everyone is curious about his long detention."

Neftalin looked uneasy. "The Chairman appointed Gertler's replacement already, Marek Kligier. The rumors are wrong. They usually are."

"But is Gertler back?" I asked, my curiosity piqued. "Everyone is gossiping about this mystery. Some say he was a rival to our Chairman."

Neftalin was silent.

"What shall we write in the Chronicle about this? He was, after all, one of our most important officials," Jozef said, not letting go of this bone.

"Some say he was to be the next Chairman?" Rosenfeld twisted the knife.

Neftalin stood abruptly. "You may write, 'The rumor of Gertler's return has proven unfounded.'"

"Does the Chairman know where Gertler is?" Jozef persisted.

Neftalin cast dark eyes on Jozef. "Add, 'No authenticated information has as yet been obtained concerning Gertler's whereabouts.'"

Another Jew vanished, and nobody can say where he is. "Have we had any more postcards from our resettled citizens?" I asked, hoping for word from Miriam.

"A few, here and there. The former residents are enjoying the summer months in the north country," Neftalin said.

"It would be nice to have some fresh fruits or vegetables," Szmul said, sounding timid and then coughing into his hand.

"The Chairman is doing the best he can," Neftalin said.

"What about more help? Will women be allowed back since we have no men available?" Jozef asked.

"Women? Unfortunately, no," Neftalin replied.

"There are some women still in the building," Jozef said.

"The Chairman must have his secretary and a few other veteran helpers. It is for the benefit of all our residents that his staff is maintained." Neftalin sounded as if this had been rehearsed. He shot a glance at Jozef and left the room.

"Are you a fool or suicidal?" I hissed at Jozef. "Do you want to antagonize our friend and end up on the resettlement lines?"

"It can't be worse than this," he replied.

I aimed stern eyes at him. "We all will walk out through the fence, arm in arm, when the rest of the world kicks Hitler's ass. It can't be much longer."

Jozef smiled. "I'm sixty-six years old but feel as if I'm one hundred. Why won't you let me leave? Even an old horse can enjoy his last days in a pasture."

"Unless he is eaten by wolves," I replied, wishing we had more information about where our resettled Jews were. Whenever I thought of giving up and leaving, I forced myself to visualize a room filled with old shoes and soiled clothes.

Rosenfeld nodded. "I believe the Soviets have given the Nazis a pounding. The end is near."

I'd heard this so many times, but Rosenfeld saying it made me believe it was true.

CHAPTER 54

S UNDAY, AUGUST 1, 1943

It was a warm day. Fed up with remaining indoors, I walked to the market square. I hoped to find a bit of sausage, a loaf of bread. The stalls had been torn down for firewood, and what wares there were sat on the ground. As I approached, I saw children carrying scraps of old beams, posts, doors, and window frames, most riddled with rusty nails. I remembered the story of apartment residents waking up to discover their stairway had been stolen during the night. Who knows where these objects came from?

Knapsacks begged to be filled with anything their scurrying owners could find. Children, mostly orphans, raced around begging for bread. A Jewish policeman struck one with a stick. "Get out of here, you little thieves," he shouted. Children whimpered, tumbled into the gutters, which smelled like piss. Miriam often accused me of being blind. I wished I were as I walked on.

"He has money," a child shouted as I handed a bill with the Chairman's face to a vendor for a bit of coal. The children crowded me, dirty faces, hands extended with grime-encrusted palms and fingernails.

A girl, arms and legs pencil-thin, was sitting in the gutter. Her hair was wild and stringy. "Regina?"

She looked up. Her eyes...hazel? No. They were mud-brown and dull. She smiled. Broken teeth and gaps. "She is not Regina," I told myself. My daughter is not begging in the street, sitting in a puddle of urine. I reached over to put a bill in her hand, but a boy, too fast, grabbed it from me.

"Hey," I shouted.

He ran in bare feet across the muddy road, other street-rats racing after him.

"They will kill him if they catch him," I said. I turned to where the girl was. Gone. A setup? Rosenfeld often said, "Desperate people do desperate things."

I searched for the girl, but the gang had vanished.

A few denizens of the slum were dozing on the ground in the steamy air. No river, brook, lake, in the ghetto. A half-dry well yielded a few pails of water. I wrote, "Such is ghetto sunbathing and fresh air therapy. Eighty-five thousand people with parched tongues."

I returned to my flat and stared into the dim light of my candle. In the flickering flame, I hoped for a glimpse of the future, but nothing was revealed to me. With little to eat, I fell onto the thin mattress. I had no one to hold. In the dark, I heard Regina gurgling in her crib, and thanked God she was far away from the squalor of a Sunday in the ghetto.

I was almost asleep when something broke the silence.

I stared into the blackness. "Is it soldiers? Are they coming this way?"

I waited for the door to be smashed open, no strength to run, nowhere to hide. The Gestapo and Order Service do not observe Sundays. My jaw ached. A rifle butt had left a permanent reminder. I listened for screams and boots on the stairs. Sweat on my flesh, my eyes waited for the gleam of metal gun barrels, the black of clubs.

No sounds on the stairs.

Another nightmare. I hated sleep. I needed sleep.

The rumors were that the wolves were returning from Russia, their tails between their legs. I prayed every one of them would freeze to death before they reached our ghetto. I wanted to kill them all, even if it was with my bare hands. "Look what you've done to me," I said, staring with wild eyes at a world of swirling shadows and darkness.

CHAPTER 55

SUNDAY, AUGUST 8, 1943

It is a difficult time. Again and again, hunger tempered with hope! In June the word was: July will mean potatoes. In July there was the consoling thought: August will mean vegetables.

The question: How much longer can this go on? is gradually becoming irrelevant. Death is flourishing. There are practically no births. The ghetto is liquidating itself. The Litzmannstadt ghetto is true to its image as "death's corner" in Europe.

July was a time of worry about a morsel of bread, a scrap of food. The sun was blistering hot. There was no rain...no water.

Rosenfeld said, "Imagine a city of approximately 85,000 people without open-air spaces and no bodies of water. It is a rat cage, our ghetto."

I lifted my head from my work. "When it's winter, you rub your hands together and complain of the cold, and when its summer...."

"I gripe of the intense heat." He laughed. "I'm an old man, so let me complain? It's one of the few pleasures the Huns left me."

Jozef wiped his brow of sweat. "It is so hot, damn hot that people are sleeping outdoors, in courtyards and gardens. Some are sleeping in the streets."

Szmul was observing us.

"The Chairman posted more warnings reminding everyone of the nine o'clock curfew," I said. If Singer were here, he'd be breaking that law every night. Would he? Had his relationship with Miriam tamed him? Frequently small reminders drove my mind to think of my wild friend. There had been no word. I could learn nothing about any of my departed friends and loved ones. The Germans blocked all access to those they had resettled. Why? Only the Germans knew. "Has anyone heard anything more about Deputy Gertler?" I asked.

Jozef said, "Since he disappeared on July 12, he has become more popular."

"So, I hear."

"His popularity rivals our Chairman's." Jozef gave me a meaningful look.

"I don't think he was a threat," I said.

"To be honest with you, Gertler's popularity grows the longer he is away." Jozef burst into laughter. "Absence makes the heart grow fonder."

Rosenfeld had been listening in silence. "I would not put it past the Eldest and the Germans to want to eliminate a rival. Remember how Rumkowski came to power."

I shot a warning look at my friend. There were discussions one did not have in the open.

Rosenfeld raised his bruised hands. "Engineer, they can't do much to me anymore. I am on borrowed time."

The door opened. It was Neftalin. "I can't believe our people can be this stupid," he said. "Stupid and selfish."

"More bad news?"

Neftalin opened his jacket. "Everyone knows the authorities are looking for any excuse, any, to take over all areas of our administration."

"So the Chairman states repeatedly," Jozef said, sounding bored.

"Oh, trust me, it's true." Neftalin pulled out a sheet of paper. "Biebow, the German ghetto administrator, pulled an unexpected visit to a rest home—"

"A rest home?" Jozef sneered. "I could use a rest. I didn't know we still have such facilities."

"Neither did Biebow," Neftalin said. "It's a mess that began with something small that became an avalanche." He shook his head. "It started when a group of workers feeding German horses—"

"Their horses eat better than we do," Jozef interrupted.

"That's what the workers said," Neftalin replied. "They asked for a loaf of bread from the German in charge. He referred it to the Eldest of the Jews, our Chairman."

"So, the feeders of German horses wanted more bread for themselves? So, how did this precipitate the avalanche?" I asked.

"Well, Chairman Rumkowski explained to Schwind, the German horse trainer, that we had no extra provisions, that in fact, we were all in the same boat and he had no means to provide a special ration to anyone."

"That is true enough," I said, shooting Jozef a warning look.

"Yes, but when Schwind gave the workers the Chairman's response, the workers grumbled and pointed out that 'certain persons were enjoying unusually long stays in a rest home nearby.'"

"They opened Pandora's box," Rosenfeld muttered.

Szmul asked, "Who is Pandora?"

Rosenfeld said, "Later." He shook his head, which I understood was his dismay at the boy's ignorance.

Neftalin smiled at Szmul, who smiled back. "The doctor is right. They did open a box of trouble for everyone here. When Schwind took this news of a rest home back to Biebow, he decided to see for himself."

"Oh, boy," I muttered.

"You don't know the half of it. Biebow launched a surprise visit to the Director of the rest home, Jozef Rumkowski."

"The Chairman's brother is the rest home's director?" I let out a low whistle.

Jozef grumbled, "Why not? His sister runs the kitchens and others in his family—"

Neftalin shot at Jozef, "Stop! This is what caused the trouble. Instead of thanking our leaders, we grumble at the small compensations they get for risking their lives to save the 85,000 residents here. You should thank God for the Rumkowski family."

"Amen," Jozef said, sounding sarcastic. "What would we do without the Rumkowskis?"

I shot Jozef a dirty look. "Let the Deputy finish. You said Biebow visited the Chairman's brother?"

Neftalin sucked in his cheeks. "Apparently, Jozef Rumkowski has more than one residence."

"What?"

"Yes." Neftalin shook his head. "Biebow smiled like a fox who caught his dinner as he left Jozef's apartment."

Rosenfeld shook his head. "All this from a loaf of bread."

"I don't understand. Why is this significant?" Szmul asked.

Neftalin sighed. "You don't understand? Biebow accused the ghetto leaders of corruption."

"Everyone knows they're corrupt," Jozef said. "We live in shitholes while they have more than one home? We starve while they smoke real cigarettes? Of course, it's corruption."

"Jozef," I said, shooting him another warning glance.

Jozef shot me an angry look but became quiet again.

I turned back to Henryk. "I didn't know about the other houses our leaders own."

Neftalin said. "There will be hell to pay, I'm sure. Damn! Biebow was looking for an excuse. Now, he has it."

"And all because of a loaf of bread?" Szmul said as if trying to understand this chain of events.

After Neftalin left, Jozef said, "Szmul, Rumkowski blames the workers who are starving and not the real cause, the corruption."

"We all know the real cause of our misery. The question is, what can be done now to enable us to survive? That has been the imperative all along," I replied.

Jozef smiled slyly. "Yes, but some survive better than others," he said, patting Szmul on the back as if they were best friends.

I still had faith in our Chairman, but how would he get out of this new complication? Leaders have always been corruptible, so I never expected it to be different here. But more than one house and untold luxuries while we were scrounging for bread and coal? I am blind, I thought, realizing I must have sounded as ignorant as Szmul.

CHAPTER 56

TUESDAY, AUGUST 10, 1943

The ghetto is very depressed. It is unclear whether this is attributable to the state of nutrition or to something else undefinable, in the air. The Chairman has been more nervous recently. This may chiefly be due to the fact that his sister-in-law, Helena Rumkowska, the wife of Director Jozef Rumkowski, is critically ill. After the awkward episode in Marysin, which we reported, Jozef Rumkowski decided to give up his summer apartment...

SUNDAY, AUGUST 15, 1943
  RESETTLEMENT

"Not again," I groaned as I read the notice Zelkowicz gave me from the Resettlement Commission. "When will this end?"

"I think it is just beginning," Rosenfeld said. "The Chairman's brother and his cronies have opened up Pandora's box for the rest of us."

"His brother gave up his apartment in Marysin," I said.

"Too little, too late. The Germans have ordered the Chairman to register all properties. The 'summer resort vacationers' should be very nervous. Hell, I would be terrified." Jozef smiled. "The corrupt are going to get theirs. Mark my words."

"I wouldn't be so happy. If the higher-ups get theirs, we will, too," Rosenfeld said.

The door opened, and Neftalin entered. I had come to conclude that he viewed our room as an escape from his stress as Deputy to the Chairman.

"The mood of the ghetto is depressed, but it's worse in the Chairman's offices. I'm worried. There are all kinds of alarming rumors circulating, and the hunger situation is impossible." He looked at me. "I used to think we could control this. Now?"

"Henryk," I interrupted. "I saw some officials at the cemetery the other day. I believe one was Leon Rozenblat, chief of the Order Service, and the other was Ignacy Gutman. Isn't he the director of the Construction Department?"

"Yes. What is your question?"

"I live nearby. Cars arriving in the cemetery with so many important officials aroused my curiosity." I didn't let on that the cemetery was the focus of my plans for survival. Such attention by the Germans was a threat. "You know the gossip mill."

Neftalin smiled.

"What's going on?" I asked, wondering why commotion in the cemetery could make our Deputy so happy.

Neftalin leaned toward me. "Air raid trenches," he said.

"I don't understand."

He put his hand on my shoulder. "The Germans want to build air raid trenches in the cemetery. It's happening. The Germans are afraid of the Allies bombing us. Don't you understand? If they want to build shelters, the end can't be far off."

"Air raid trenches." I repeated the words as if they were a magical incantation.

Jozef had tears in his eyes. "Blessed art thou, oh Lord, our God, and bless those who are going to bomb the shit out of the Nazi oppressors."

"Amen," Neftalin said.

"Amen," I repeated. "Is it true? Are they going to dig in the cemetery?"

"Yesterday, around noon, people at funerals were told to leave the cemetery as quickly as possible. So, yes, while we don't know exactly what they are planning, something is happening there. Let us hope their fear is not unfounded."

After Neftalin left, Jozef said, "Engineer, do you know what this means?"

I felt tears welling in my eyes. "With God's help, it will soon be over."

Tears burst from his eyes. "With God's help, we made it."

I felt like hugging Jozef, but something was wrong. It was Rosenfeld. He was not joining in the joy. "Doctor," I said, "They are building air-raid shelters."

Rosenfeld nodded slowly. "And movie theaters too."

"You're a pessimist," I teased. I felt so hopeful that I wanted to celebrate. "Doctor, Joseph, will you go to the House of Culture with me? I know you'll enjoy the concert. They play Jewish music—"

A frown appeared on Rosenfeld's face. "Engineer, you didn't hear the news?"

"What news?"

"The Down Quilt Department is now housed in the House of Culture. All the machines, material, and personnel have been set up there." He must have seen the look of disappointment on my face. "I'm sorry, my friend, there are no more concerts there."

The last of our entertainments was gone. I tried to see Miriam's face enjoying the music. I could barely conjure her features after a year. My consolation: soon the Germans, who had taken away our loved ones, robbed us of our music, would quiver at the sound of airplanes and bombs in a glorious symphony that would forever drown out their drums, cymbals, and goose-stepping marchers.

On Saturday night, there was another resettlement action.

CHAPTER 57

MONDAY, AUGUST 30, 1943
NO MORE ALLOCATION OF BONES AND VEINS
Over the course of time, the Chairman has continually granted an allocation of bones and veins to various people—usually one kilogram of bones and one kilogram of veins per week. But as of today, these allocations have been terminated. This measure can be attributed to the sharply reduced influx of meat. Have any potatoes come in?

"What the hell does this entry mean?" I asked.

"Read between the lines," Jozef barked. "It's more corruption."

"Bones and veins are corruption?"

"Some are eating better than others, even if it's just bones and veins. The rest of us can't even get potatoes." Jozef pulled a slip of paper from his pocket. "Do you know what this is? It's a coupon, a damn coupon instead of potatoes they promised us. No potatoes. No vegetables. No meat for months." He bit the slip of paper. "Oh, yummy! I can live on this."

He was right. On Sunday, the only day I could go to the market, all the booths were empty. Rumors were that the black market sellers were also unable to get anything into the ghetto to sell. Anyone carrying food was accosted by dozens of would-be buyers who offered lots of money, but they clutched their meager possessions with throngs of starving children trying to grab it from their hands. The Order Service swung their clubs mercilessly to quell the riots. I understood. If it weren't for the soup in the Kitchen for the Intelligentsia, I would be dead. As it was, the pangs of hunger were blinding me to almost all else, even danger.

Most of us could hardly walk; the lack of food caused the decalcification of our bones. Vigantol, the only medicine that could help that had been available to the privileged few, could not be found anywhere in the ghetto. People were falling to the ground, unable to stand back up again.

Fruit trees at the edges of fenced yards suffered at the hands of unknown thieves. Vegetable beds, the few that existed, were guarded day and night. Hunger drove people outdoors like hyenas, into the open, where something to eat might be found. People were begging, "Have any potatoes come in?" Potatoes meant salvation.

On August 19, God finally answered this prayer after shipments of potatoes arrived in the ghetto.

Rosenfeld wrote, "People accepted their rations like gifts from heaven — silently, wordlessly, neither grateful nor grumbling. Hunger had left them incapable of any powerful emotion."

"Emotions die when one is dying of hunger," Jozef said.

Unfortunately, three kilograms of potatoes, which can allow a person to live, which were supposed to last two weeks, were devoured on the spot.

Rosenfeld tried to explain it to Szmul: "The hungry are oblivious to any 'afterward' or 'later on.' All they can think is stave off hunger, fill your stomach, live now, and let God take care of the morrow."

Szmul said softly, "I guess I'm a fool too. I have nothing left to eat."

Rosenfeld dug into his pocket and handed the boy a small packet in tan paper.

Szmul looked puzzled, but quickly tore the paper and then gobbled the raw potato in a few bites.

Rosenfeld looked at me. "I guess that was a wasted lesson."

I laughed. Szmul had torn off the paper as if it had concealed a precious gift, and perhaps it was.

That evening, I was at the distribution point, waiting for rations. As usual, there were problems, tempers flared. I was walking away when someone whispered, "Follow me, now." When I turned, there was nobody near. The line was long. If I left, I would lose my place. I was also afraid after my last encounters. But what if it was news of Pola, or hope of hopes, Miriam and Regina, Singer? I searched the crowd for the whisperer. Oh, God, had I missed my opportunity? I didn't hear him, I cried to myself, but that wasn't true. My stomach growling...I'd let that deafen me.

On the way home, I kept hoping whoever summoned me would strike again, even if it meant a gun barrel in my back. As I walked past Dworska Street, I noticed the avenue was barricaded and blocked by Order Service. There were trucks.

"Not again," I thought as the policemen raced after patients trying to escape the net. Rifles and machine guns primed, Gestapo, some with dogs near their feet, supervised the roundup of the sick and mentally unfit from the building by the Jewish police. Stretchers were carrying the seriously ill into the trucks.

"Move on," someone ordered.

I thought of holding up my pass, but why risk it? My stomach churned, and not just from hunger. I walked on.

The next day, I learned that 225 people were turned over to the German authorities for transport from the hospital. The news of the brutal removal of the patients sent ripples of fear throughout the ghetto. Neftalin confided that even the Chairman was in an ugly mood, fearing more such actions would be required by the authorities.

FRIDAY, SEPTEMBER 3, 1943
WORKSHOP NEWS: OLD SHOES COMING IN

The shoe warehouse is constantly receiving large quantities of old shoes from outside the ghetto. It will take months to sort this material.

September 5th was the anniversary of the night Miriam and Regina left me. I could not breathe without thinking of them. I doubt if I said one word to anyone on that day. I wished I could visualize their faces. I again saw Regina's eyes looking at me from over the shoulder of the soldier carrying my sweet child to the trucks. As I read the entry for September 3, I shivered. Were Regina's tiny shoes somewhere in that warehouse?

CHAPTER 58

MONDAY, SEPTEMBER 13, 1943
NEWS OF THE DAY: THE BEKERMAN CASE

"Where were you?" Jozef asked. "Did you see it?"

I nodded. How could I tell my co-worker where I'd been? I no longer trusted anyone. "What did you learn at the shoemaker plant?"

"You wouldn't believe what happened. A worker there complained about the quality of the lunch soup, and his supervisor struck him in the face. All hell broke loose. The worker struck him back," Jozef said, looking smug.

"Are you joking?" Rosenfeld asked.

"I wish. A melee ensued, and the manager called for help. The Special Unit arrested five of the shoemakers."

"All from a complaint about soup?"

"The Chairman had to get involved, and according to my informant, 'settled the matter peacefully.' But I have my doubts."

"What about the supervisor?" Rosenfeld asked. "He struck a man for speaking his mind about soup? Surely, he was censured for that?"

"There is a ghetto practice of physical abuse. The Chairman frequently strikes people to vent his anger or to discipline the unruly," Jozef replied, smacking his leg to illustrate his point.

"Yes, but the Chairman is head of the ghetto," I said. "He must apply force at times, or the authorities will."

"But it is now a widespread practice among the managers as well. This method of getting one's way does little honor to the ghetto," Rosenfeld said.

"Jews should be an example."

"I didn't think of that," I said.

"Perhaps if they struck the supervisor, he would learn not to strike his fellow Jews," Jozef said.

"Leave physical punishment to the Germans," I said. "Yes, that makes sense. Unfortunately, as with most situations, the Chairman must, at times, be harsh."

"Now, back to where you disappeared to?" Jozef aimed his tired eyes at me. "On second thought, perhaps I'm better off not knowing. Do you want me to write up the Bekerman Case?"

Thinking it would distract him, I nodded. I needed time to think of all that had happened today. It began when the door burst open. A German officer barged in. I croaked "Attention!" He shouted, "Get out! Get out all of you filthy Jews!" He swung a club hard on the table, and papers fell in disarray to the floor.

Not knowing what the hell was going on, I raced out of the building.

Order Service officials herded us toward the corner of Prosna and Przelotna Streets, where hundreds of factory workers were milling around. Nobody knew what was happening. I glanced around and saw we were encircled by Schutzpolize and soldiers, all heavily armed. "Does anyone know what the hell is going on?"

A voice whispered in my ear, "Bennie, look straight ahead. Don't react. They'll shoot you."

My heart pounded. "It's you?"

"I'm here for only a short while."

"Pola, was that you, in the market?"

"Yes. Don't show you know me. It isn't safe."

"How did you get here? Where were you?"

"Shh."

"I miss you."

"Dawid Gertler, he disappeared on July 12?"

"Yes. Why do you want to know?"

"He never came back?"

241

"No. There's been no sign of him."

"Pola, are you safe? Where are you?"

She touched my hand lightly. "I love you," she whispered.

I turned, and she was gone. I had so many questions to ask her. I tried to see her in the crowd, but petite, she vanished in the mass of people now staring toward the front of the field.

I followed their eyes. "Oh, God, not again?"

A bare wood gallows rose toward the sky over a high platform.

A trio of black cars pulled up. A woman and two children were escorted by two heavy-set men in black, leather coats.

"That's Bekerman's wife and children," a man whispered.

"What's his crime?" I asked, sidling up to the men who wore leather factory aprons.

"Who are you?" The stockier man asked, a hostile look on his face.

I backed away. "I did not mean to eavesdrop," I said.

"Look at him," a second man hissed. "He's as shabbily dressed as we are."

"He could be a spy, one of the Devil's rats," the stocky man said, his hands formed into fists.

"A spy would have simply listened, not pushed himself into the conversation." The second man turned to me. "Everyone's on edge. Nobody believed they would actually do it. His action was minor."

"What did he do?"

"He worked in the Leather and Saddle-makers Department with us."

"Was he a union leader or rabble-rouser?"

The stocky man leaned forward, the smell of burnt leather thick. "The poor sonofabitch is only 34 years old. He needed shoelaces."

"He's being hung for stealing shoelaces?" I asked, almost bursting into irrational laughter. Not even the Germans could think this was justice.

"Just so. The leather was found in this unfortunate man's apartment by the Kripo during a search. Some say it was a tiny piece, a few decagrams."

I glanced at the gallows. A second car pulled up, and the alleged offender was pulled from it by two soldiers. He was dragged to the platform.

"They're not going to follow through on this," I whispered.

"The German authorities state all material is their property and any theft, no matter how insignificant it may appear, is considered sabotage according to military law."

"They say they've warned us and warned us. All appeals for mercy were denied," the thinner laborer said. "Biebow said the punishment is a deterrent against all future offenses."

I heard a microphone crackle and a man I did not recognize, a clerk from the Central Prison, read a brief statement about the theft of strategic materials.

I searched the crowd again for Pola. Where had she disappeared to? There was a collective gasp. I looked. The man was hanging, his legs twitching. I did not want to see his wife and children. I didn't believe even the wolves could commit such an atrocious act.

The Germans began yelling, and the workers trudged back to their warehouses and factories. It was 6:00 p.m., and they still had work to do.

I remained behind, scanning the dwindling crowd for a glimpse of Pola. Just before she'd left me, she whispered, "I love you."

On my way home, I walked past one of the Chairman's warehouses. Sixteen trucks were in a line waiting to be unloaded. It was the warehouse where Miriam had worked sorting shoes, most missing heels and soles.

CHAPTER 59

T UESDAY, SEPTEMBER 21, 1943
FOOD SUPPLY
The crisis has reached a climax. The populace has not been in so
desperate a situation in a long time. There has always been scarcity before each
ration, but the way things are now, one can only speak of catastrophic starvation.
Ridiculously insignificant shipments of potatoes do not permit even a faint hope
of improvement... ersatz coffee is being sold. People are buying it in order to soak
it in water and eat it as mush.

SEPTEMBER 27, 1943
FOOD SUPPLY
Still no improvement in the general situation. The potato shipments remain
catastrophically small...After many hours in the pouring rain, the endless lines
broke up, and people went home with empty knapsacks.

"Has anyone seen Dr. Rosenfeld?" I asked, feeling a sense of alarm that our
professor was not in his seat. He was one of the oldest in the ghetto and, at
any time, could be snatched up in the Gestapo resettlement net.

Jozef looked at me. "You do know your professor is on borrowed time,
don't you?"

"We all are," I said. "Winter is coming, and the departments report that
no fuel has been stockpiled or announced. Something has to happen soon,
or we will freeze to death."

Just then, Rosenfeld entered the room. He looked exhausted.

"Is everything okay?" I asked.

"I'm sorry I'm late," Rosenfeld replied.

"That's fine, as long as you're here." I gave him a reassuring smile.

Rosenfeld sucked in his lips. "Ever since they established a distribution point for injections, the lines are endless. I got there before dawn, but the line was already a mile long. By the time I got to the dispensary, the medicines were gone."

"Perhaps Neftalin can help?"

"Nobody can help," Rosenfeld replied. "The smugglers used to bring in the drugs, but the Chairman and the Germans clamped down on them."

I thought of Singer. "I wish I could help," I said. "We are all skeletons walking."

"Not all," Rosenfeld said.

I knew who he meant. Such a comment was rare for him.

"Did you see that for the High Holidays, the Chairman gave food to his closest friends and staff members?" Jozef said.

"He wouldn't do that," I replied, but heard Miriam and Singer laughing.

Rosenfeld handed me his entry for Monday, September 27, 1943. I read it silently:

Yesterday, for Rosh Hashanah, the Chairman dipped into the reserve supply at his disposal to distribute some vegetables to a few individuals and social organizations. It is said that he will also take this occasion to grant a special allotment to a few close members of his staff and to persons of particular merit.

"You can't include this," I said. "The Chairman won't allow it."

Rosenfeld laughed bitterly. "Do you really think he reads our work? When Rumkowski created this Chronicle, he, like the rest of us, believed the madness would be over in a few months. I never thought it was going to last this long. He's probably forgotten all about us. Did you get a special allocation or invite for the holidays? I damn well didn't."

Jozef smirked. "I sure didn't. I don't know anyone who benefitted from the Chairman's largesse."

The door opened, and Neftalin entered. "Happy New Year," he said, a broad smile on his face.

Jozef hissed, "I know someone who did."

I gave him a disapproving look. "Any news on food or fuel shipments?" I asked.

Neftalin's smile faded. "Unfortunately, no. But our Chairman, God bless him for the New Year, is working on it."

"What about injections?" Rosenfeld asked. He rarely went over my head and asked questions directly of the Deputy, I assumed because he wanted to keep a low profile to not become a target for deportation. "I had to wait on a line for hours before dawn, and they ran out of my medicine." He coughed hard as if to emphasize the point.

Neftalin stared hard at my dear friend. "The Chairman is well aware of this unfortunate situation, but it is out of his control." He leaned toward Rosenfeld and said, "We have many younger people, highly productive people, unable to get medicine."

I wanted to protest his response, but Rosenfeld dropped his hand on my arm. His silence was a more eloquent reply than I could have mustered.

Neftalin must have realized his lack of tact because he added. "Previous resettlements have removed most of our elderly and infirm residents. It is good you are back with us, Doctor."

Rosenfeld remained silent.

I felt Neftalin had issued a barely concealed threat. Rosenfeld's age made him a logical target to be removed from a ghetto that had become a machine where the old and those unable to pull their weight were excised like an abscess. The authorities promised resettlement meant less demanding work and more plentiful food and fuel for heat for our departed. Did anyone believe the Nazis cared about older Jews? Did Rumkowski?

Neftalin stood. "Again, I wish you, my friends, a happy New Year." He smiled and left the room.

I heard Singer hissing, "Someday, they'll shoot the bastard." This time, I thought of shooting Neftalin, and all the elitists, enjoying food and heat while the rest of their subjects were starving, freezing, and dropping dead while waiting for medicines on endless lines.

Rosenfeld said, "Happy New Year, Bennie. Let us pray we are here next year."

CHAPTER 60

S UNDAY, OCTOBER 3, 1943

"I saw the Chairman's coach outside the Carpentry Workshop," I
said to Jozef and Rosenfeld when I sat in my chair.

"There's been much discontent in the factories," Jozef said. "People are
upset still that Bekerman had to pay for a minor infraction with his life."
He looked at me. "I can't blame them."

"I can't either," I said. "But this factory has been given an order to
manufacture munitions crates for the Wehrmacht, an order critical to
the ghetto's survival."

"So, now we're making ammunition cases for the Nazis?"

"Singer...I mean, Jozef, this could preserve the ghetto and is in line with
the Chairman's policies." I was supporting what Singer would have called
collaboration.

"Well, it doesn't matter," Jozef said. "The workers are on a hunger strike."

"What?" There hadn't been a strike in the ghetto since the Germans
brutally crushed the last one. "The carpentry workers get better rations
than almost anyone. Why on earth would they go on a hunger strike?"

Jozef laughed. "It started with that hanging. The manager was absent the
day the Chairman exhorted the workers to avoid the same fate as Bekerman
by not taking even the smallest item from the shop."

"Nobody should take anything," I said, "Especially after witnessing this
public hanging."

"Well, the manager threatened that if anything were taken, he would have

248

no choice but to hold the carpenters collectively responsible," Jozef said.

"Collectively responsible?" Rosenfeld muttered. "That hardly seems fair, but in wartime…maybe."

"That means everyone gets punished?" Szmul asked. "That isn't fair."

I smiled at our youngest member. "You can't always tell who stole something," I said.

Jozef nodded. "That's the problem. The manager, a few days later, noticed two of his workers trading in wood in the hallway of a building. He realized that the wood came from his workshop."

"Oh, oh," Rosenfeld said. "The shit hit the fan."

"Yes. The manager didn't think their infraction was that serious, but since he had threatened the carpenters with collective punishment, he felt he had to stick to his guns."

"What punishment did he give them?" Szmul asked, sounding like a young child.

I was grateful I was not in that manager's position.

"He withheld their supplementary soup."

"He held back their extra ration of soup? That was the big punishment that led to a strike?"

"That was it. The workers said if they were not given the supplementary meal, they would refuse to accept any soup." Jozef laughed. "Such fools."

"And that became the basis of the hunger strike," Rosenfeld muttered. "So who backed down?"

"The workers," Jozef said. "In the end, they sent a delegation to speak to the manager and demand he should make up for their lost rations. But, of course, he could not. He argued that when he threatened the workers with collective punishment, no one spoke against it, so he felt justified in following through on his threat."

"So, that's why the Chairman was at the Carpentry Workshop today?" I asked. "The workers should know better than to obstruct such an important order. Don't they realize any interference in productivity will invite the authorities to charge in?"

Rosenfeld held up a report from the police. "I think they'll get the message now," he said. "Leon Winograd, the manager of the woodwork factory, was summoned to Biebow's office and is now in Central Prison."

"I know him," Jozef said. "Why did this happen?"

"According to the Chairman's report, the authorities had received various complaints about defective deliveries from customers as well as Nazi officials."

"What kind of defects warrant Central Prison?" I asked.

"It says a German woman injured her hands on a washboard they manufactured," Rosenfeld replied. "There were also complaints about cribs."

"A washboard and cribs?" This was ridiculous.

"It was because Winograd is accountable to Biebow for his plant that this serious punishment was meted out. He even went to court, where he accepted full responsibility." Rosenfeld handed me the arrest report. "He's still in Central Prison. I'm sorry, Jozef, you said he's your friend."

"I thought he was one of our most reliable managers."

"He might have been," I said. "It just goes to show you the Chairman is right. The Germans have zero tolerance for any mistakes. I hope the workers realize this."

Rosenfeld smiled sadly. "I can almost hear Singer laughing," he said.

"I wonder where our rascally friend is," I replied.

Rosenfeld shrugged his shoulders and went back to his writing.

Nobody knows anything, I thought and turned back to the endless stream of memos that, in the end, were meaningless.

CHAPTER 61

S UNDAY, OCTOBER 3, 1943
TOTAL POPULATION 83,672
MARRIAGES

The Chairman married 15 couples today in Marysin...

It was Sunday, but we were at work. I had just recorded another suicide. Hungry, tired, and lonely, I needed something to distract me from all the disheartening news. "Isn't there anything happening?" I asked.

Rosenfeld, already rubbing his hands from the cold, laughed. "You should be grateful there were no events of any significance this week. Perhaps the ghetto is at long last settling into a routine that will be uneventful until the end of the war."

Jozef burst into laughter.

"What's so funny?" I asked.

Jozef could hardly speak. "The chief of the Order Service fired some of his men, and they are being punished by being forced to remove excrement from the streets."

"Shit," I blurted.

Jozef got hysterical with that. "Yes, shit. They're shoveling it."

Now, I laughed. "What did these policemen do to earn this promotion?"

"What else? Smuggling. Everyone who can is smuggling these days. It's the only way to get anything."

"That, or work in the bakery, where you can eat all you want while the workers starve," Rosenfeld said.

"I'm tired of this," I said, standing and feeling the room closing in on me. "I'm going out."

"Where are you going?" Rosenfeld asked. "There is nowhere to go. We must all appear to be working, or be resettled."

Jozef sighed. "Would that be so terrible?"

Rosenfeld shook his head. "You don't want to find out. When I was in Central Prison, awaiting resettlement, I feared what was going to happen to me. It was the uncertainty of what lay ahead that was most terrifying."

"I never knew you were taken there," I said. "Had I suspected that I would have begged the Chairman to free you."

Rosenfeld leaned toward me. "Do you really believe a Jew has such power over the Germans? Singer was right. We are deluded, and our Chairman is the biggest fool of all."

I didn't want to argue with the dear doctor. "I'll see you after Yom Kippur. The Chairman has declared there will be no work in the factories."

"Something is wrong. For the first time in the history of the ghetto, Yom Kippur will be a holiday," Jozef said. "Bless our Eldest of the Jews. Amen."

I hated his sarcastic tone.

"Amen," Rosenfeld said, but sounded half-hearted. "So, Engineer, where are you off to?"

The idea had come to me after reading a short announcement that the Chairman was going to perform fifteen weddings in Marysin, not far from where I lived. That conjured up the day Pola asked me to accompany her when she was to report on the first wedding ceremonies. I declined, uncertain, feeling guilty that I was even considering being with a woman other than Miriam, my wife...a wife I hardly knew. "I'm going to report on the weddings our Chairman is conducting today. I want to feel the optimism of young husbands and brides. It may be contagious."

Rosenfeld coughed. "Yes. It is a blessing that young people are getting married even in this hellhole."

"The Chairman takes great risks in performing these ceremonies," I said.

Rosenfeld looked thoughtful. "Yes, I suppose he does, but it affirms his authority. I think he persists in this to demonstrate he is still in charge."

Jozef said, "He's clutching at straws. It's false hope."

"For once, let's avoid the political wrangling? Just let me go and enjoy young people starting their lives together?" I rose from my chair, my back aching.

Rosenfeld looked at me with his scholarly eyes. "My friend, everything in the ghetto is political. You, our most logical member, must know that."

I didn't want to be logical. In fact, totally illogically, I hoped Pola would be at the ceremony. She had loved being assigned to cover this rare joyful experience, so I hoped she'd miraculously appear. I thought of what I would say to her... that I missed her...that I no longer remembered what Miriam looked like...that I longed to curl my body behind her and feel her tight against me. I still loved Miriam, but Pola, more my age, more aligned with my values, had given me the calm my young wife could not. Did I love Pola? I didn't know. I regretted not giving myself the chance to find out. If by some miracle, she was at the wedding, I would ask her to give up what she was doing and take a chance for what happiness we might find together. In my mind, I'd already granted Miriam the freedom to experience love with Singer. I loved them that much.

As I observed fifteen brides and grooms filled with an aura of hope, I closed my eyes and prayed. I still didn't believe in God but swore if he brought me Pola, I would bless him for the rest of my life. Pola was right, the ceremony gave me a rare interlude of calm.

As the Chairman ended the ceremony, he said, "I don't know how much longer I will be allowed to bring such joy to our people, but as long as I have breath, I will try to do so."

I believed in him again. He seemed so grandfatherly, his white hair such a contrast to the black and brown hair of the young grooms, his withered hands on their shoulders offering a paternal sign of his affection. He cares, I thought, it is a miracle. He still truly cares.

Unfortunately, God did not believe in miracles. After watching the happy couples kiss and then leave with their new partners, I walked home to my flat, more lonely and confused than ever. Back on the streets, guilt that I wanted Pola simmered inside me. Fear that she would never return was far worse.

CHAPTER 62

MONDAY, OCTOBER 11, 1943
YOM KIPPUR IN THE GHETTO
Very few people in the ghetto realize that without the efforts of the Eldest, their worship service would have been impossible. It was not easy to obtain permission from the authorities...to make up for it, factories will operate on October 10 with a 10 percent increase in the rate of production...

TUESDAY, OCTOBER 12, 1943

There was a hopeful mood in the ghetto. For the first time since the ghetto's inception, Yom Kippur had been a real holiday. Very few people in the ghetto knew the Eldest of the Jews had managed to get permission from the authorities to shut down the factories and warehouses for the holiest day in the Jewish religion, the Day of Atonement. I wondered if Rumkowski had worked this miracle because he had so much for which to atone.

"There were so many people out walking, some in clothes I had not seen since God knows when," Jozef said.

"We had steamed potatoes for dinner," Rosenfeld said. "Even our stomachs had a little holiday."

"Yom Tov, my friends. Good holiday," Neftalin said, smiling as he entered our room. "I hope everyone had a fine day of rest. The Chairman promised the factories would be ten percent more productive today if the authorities granted him the Yom Kippur holiday, so the machines are chugging and smoke is billowing."

"It was good to see windows with candles glowing," Rosenfeld said.

"I prayed last night," Jozef said. "I saw many people praying." He looked at me accusingly. "It was good to pray for the end of our pain and suffering. It was good to hear the ancient prayers, the Kol Nidre, after such a long time."

"Yes, prayer is good," Neftalin said. "It keeps us going, does it not?"

I didn't reply.

"Everyone wore their best; even children wore what they could. Most had shoes," Neftalin said. "Things are looking up."

"My friend Aaron even carried a small Torah scroll. In the streets! Who would believe such a thing would again be possible?" Jozef said.

"It is an illusion," I muttered.

Neftalin looked shocked. "My poor friend. Did you not have anyone with whom to share the holiday?"

"He is an atheist," Jozef said. "I invited him a thousand times to pray with me."

Neftalin smiled benevolently. "I thought your fatalism was based on your grievous loss." He sighed. "On Yom Kippur in the year 1943, thousands of prayers, accompanied by memories and sighs, were directed toward heaven from prayer halls and private residences."

"And God heard none of them," I said. "We are still here."

Rosenfeld said, "Yes, Engineer, we are still here. That is the answer to our prayers." He looked at his gloves. "Every year, we, the survivors, call out the names of those who died. This year, the list would have been too long. The last four years have seen 30,000 plus persons, a figure unlikely to be bettered anywhere in the world, placed in our cemetery. But, in spite of everything, we are still here."

"That is enough for you?" I shook my head. "30,000 is a large number for such a short time."

Rosenfeld nodded. "You are still our numbers man. But, my son, the Yom Kippur atmosphere has magically evoked a bit of the Jewish beauty that is still alive somewhere outside, among our brothers and sisters."

Neftalin looked uneasy. "I must go. Ostrowski, I know what you have suffered, but my friend, you must make peace with God. You must believe there is a reason for everything."

"You really believe there's a reason for all this suffering?" I asked.

Rosenfeld replied, "I do."

Jozef stood. "I don't know what reason God would have for this." He looked as if he was about to cry as he handed me a half sheet of paper.

I read it silently and then, feeling as if my legs were going to collapse under me, read it to the spirits hovering in our room:

TUESDAY, OCTOBER 12, 1943
A DEATH

Today, a young member of the Archives staff, Szmul Hecht, died at the age of 20.

"Oh, God," Rosenfeld said, gripping the table. "Why him? He is so young, and I am so old. Why not take me instead?"

Neftalin sat. "Your young helper?"

"Yes. During the resettlement from Wielun, he lost his mother and sister. His father died two weeks ago here," I said, still stunned by the news.

"The young man was shattered, spiritually as well as physically," Jozef said, tears in his eyes.

"He was sickly when he arrived," Neftalin said. "Did he not have tuberculosis?"

"He was starving," I said, unable to hide the anger in my voice. "How could he get well without food or medicine?" I looked at Rosenfeld. "How can your God justify this?"

Neftalin stood. "Don't blame God for what man does. We have free will." He turned to leave and then turned back to me. "I'm sorry for your loss," he said.

I crushed the paper in my hand. "May I include an obituary in the Chronicle?"

Neftalin nodded and left the room.

I wrote a short notice about our youngest member and ended it with,

"He was an exceedingly likable, quiet, modest man whose memory we will honor."

Rosenfeld leaned back in his chair. "I wonder what you will write about me when I am no longer here."

"I wonder which of us will be next," I replied.

CHAPTER 63

MONDAY, OCTOBER 18, 1943

During the past few days many postcards from Terezin (Theresienstadt-Getto) have arrived in the ghetto, with news from relatives of those from Prague who have been resettled there.

FRIDAY, OCTOBER 29, 1943

I reluctantly attended a conference held in the kitchen on Zgierska Street at Neftalin's request.

"I am working on the food situation, so I appreciate your attending this critical meeting," Neftalin said earlier that morning. He settled back in a chair. "I know you will give me an honest report."

When I first arrived at the kitchen, I was a bit frightened. The mood was tense. In fact, I was surprised the Chairman, who arrived at noon, was unaccompanied by his guards. He's a courageous leader, I thought, knowing that our workers were upset by recent events.

After a cursory inspection of the kitchen, the Chairman addressed the worker representatives. "Friends, ghetto workers! I greet you who have appeared in such large numbers, demonstrating that your instincts are sound. I bear no grudge."

He took a conciliatory tone. That is good, I thought, still standing by the door to make a quick exit if necessary.

But the Chairman hadn't finished. "I do not bear a grudge against those who have not appeared...nor against the ailing workers, who, unfortunately, could not come, nor even against those who foolishly let themselves be misled into not coming...."

That is different, I thought, noting dark expressions on faces around me.

The Chairman then said, "I wish to speak to you frankly and honestly, as is Rumkowski's habit...."

I almost choked on that last sentence but stifled my skepticism. I felt as if I were watched by suspicious eyes. I focused mine on the Chairman.

Rumkowski apologized for the lateness of the food and then said, "I would like to make one thing clear. I am, God forbid, not your enemy, but your friend, and a friend must, above all, be understood, or at least, trusted." Before they could react, he sweetened it by giving each man three cigarettes. Then he ordered the food to be served.

I could almost hear Rosenfeld sigh, "What I wouldn't give for some real pipe tobacco."

I fingered the broken bowl of his pipe in my pocket. I had taken it from his apartment when I thought I'd never see him again. It was silly, sentimental, but I hadn't returned it. Food certainly helps the atmosphere, I thought, as the men seemed calmer, many smoking their cigarettes.

The Chairman sat at a front table with the worker leaders. Perhaps my worry was for nothing, I thought, as the tone seemed congenial, and the Chairman appeared in firm control of what I feared could have been an explosive confrontation.

I kept my surprise to myself when the food arrived. Each man was given a bowl of soup. It was steaming hot, smoke trails rising from the table. It smelled delightful, creamy. I sat down at a vacant seat. It was a tasty soup, such as I hadn't had in months. I savored every spoonful. I thought that was the end of the meal, but my eyes opened wide when side dishes of potatoes, cabbage, pickles, relish, and fresh bread were served. We also had knackwurst, which I hadn't seen in a year. "It was a modest meal," I would say later to the others, not wanting to raise a tumult over what might be construed as a bribe to the labor leaders, more evidence of corruption.

I reasoned the Eldest had to give them a decent meal to get their support. But where did it all come from? Was food like this still available to the chosen few? I heard Neftalin arguing, "Don't you understand the pressure he is under?"

"I agree," I replied in my mind, but was dismayed by the array. The meal did seem to lessen the tension. I was hopeful the labor unrest which threatened all of us with German interference had been calmed. I felt a bit more at ease and remained at the table with several workers from the pressers. When one asked who I was, I replied that I worked for the Records Department as a bookkeeper. I had no idea how they would react if they knew my actual task.

The Chairman ended the meal with compliments for the workers' hard work.

I saw that was appreciated by the workers around me, but then he added, "The pressers here have always considered themselves the elite as if they were the only craftsmen in the ghetto."

There was a murmur of disapproval from multiple corners.

The Chairman continued, "In the past, I had supervision over the workshops and, if anything went wrong, well — after all, I'm a sly Jew — I simply turned a blind eye."

There were more angry expressions and murmurs. A few men lay down their utensils.

I pushed my chair back, worried, understanding the Chairman was warning the workers they couldn't 'monkey- around', thinking he could help them if they got caught by the authorities. That was a fair warning, I thought, but didn't know if it was the best way to phrase it.

"He is realistic," Neftalin would have argued. "The game has changed."

Singer would have shot back, "It changed long ago. None of you will admit it."

I focused on the Chairman, as did all the men. He looked sternly at the front tables and said, "The very appearance of sabotage must be avoided, for I need not elaborate on the consequences of such an accusation."

Someone mumbled, "Bekerman."

I had the flashback of a young wife and children staring at a man dangling from the gallows for taking a few scraps of leather for his shoelaces.

The Chairman went on to say, "You all know that I am no liar or speechifier, and therefore, I tell you candidly: I will not permit even the slightest irregularity in the workshops that might be interpreted as sabotage. And in this matter, I will do anything I have to do."

"Another threat," a man at the next table muttered.

There was an audible rustling in the room, but the Chairman continued, "Your so-called leaders, who talk you into believing they are your friends, are in reality misleading you, and I will be forced to put them out of business."

I remembered Rumkowski saying in an earlier speech, "good people have nothing to fear." I felt like crying, "But sir, I'm a good, loyal soldier, so why did you take my child from me?"

A man poked me. "He's threatening us. That's a mistake."

The Chairman continued, "This is your enterprise as much as it is mine and that of all Jews in the ghetto who want to live just as much as the pressers do."

That is true, I thought, we all want to live. And that means the factories must continue to function smoothly.

The Chairman raised his hand. "To sustain the ghetto and protect it from disaster, I will — let me say this openly — show no consideration either for individuals or groups of workers! I will remove the troublemakers and agitators from the ghetto, not because I tremble for my life, but because I fear for you all."

"God bless our protector," someone said in a tone dripping with sarcasm. And others added, "Amen."

I was ready to leave, fearing an uproar.

"No." The Chairman said, "You have to be protected; as for me, my hair is white as snow, I walk with a stoop. My life is already behind me!"

Was he sacrificing himself? He made it sound as if all he cared about was protecting them, not himself. Was it true?

Rumkowski had more to say. "I have my finger constantly on the ghetto's pulse, and I will continue to do so. I have guaranteed with my life that the ghetto will work, and that order will be maintained. I will be forced to eliminate any persons who stir up trouble."

Someone said, "I thought he wanted to have a friendly meeting."

Another hissed, "The wolves are at our door."

I feared an argument would break out, but the Chairman was still speaking. He made it clear that the tailors, like everyone else, had to accept there were limits to what he could do and that no workers were entitled to special consideration.

I'd heard.enough. I pulled myself out of my chair and left the room before there was trouble. I wondered if the Chairman had taken the right approach with the workers. I understood the urgency of quelling anything that could undermine his authority, their productivity, but threatening them?

Later, in our chamber, after my report, Neftalin said, "He had no choice. He has to appear firm and in control or labor will run rampant."

I couldn't answer him.

Jozef said, "Don't you think it is better to strive for cooperation rather than intimidation?"

Neftalin sighed. "Our Eldest of the Jews has repeatedly tried that, but time is not on our side." He turned to me. "Thank you, Engineer, for your honesty. You will report this for the future, my friend, that our Eldest of the Jews made it abundantly clear that nobody in the ghetto deserves better than anyone else."

I could hear Singer laughing like a jackass. But what else could I do?

After Neftalin left the room, Jozef and Rosenfeld were silent.

I was about to scold Jozef for his attitude endangering all of us when the door opened again. "Attention," I shouted.

"Oh. I'm sorry," Neftalin said, seeing us stand. "I forget to knock. I am getting old and forgetful. I came to see you all with some great news. We've just gotten a large number of postcards from Teresezin, from relatives of those from Prague who were resettled here."

None of us reacted.

Neftalin looked confused. "Is this not wonderful news? This should end the terrible rumors once and for all about our resettled friends and loved ones." He held the cards toward me. "Please, look for yourself. We are starting the New Year with good news."

I perused the cards. They looked genuine. I passed them to Rosenfeld, who examined them quickly and then handed them to Jozef, who barely looked.

Neftalin retrieved the cards. "There are many more like this. I know we are all naturally skeptical, but, please, my friends, this is hope. Let's never extinguish hope." He nodded to each of us and left the room.

Rosenfeld said, "Still no word of Miriam?" He smiled. "I pray for her and your Regina every day. You'll see, God will bring you together again very soon."

I replied, "We have work to do."

CHAPTER 64

T UESDAY, NOVEMBER 9, 1943

"Why are you late, Jozef?" I asked when Zelkowciz charged through the door, out of breath. "Are you okay?" I hurried to his side, but he waved me back.

"It's a riot! They're striking, and it's spreading." He sounded excited, almost happy.

"What are you talking about? The Chairman met with the worker leaders the other day and gave them a sumptuous lunch—"

"I don't care if he gave them champagne and caviar, they've had enough."

"And you think this is good? Haven't you been listening?"

"I listen to everything. It is you who are deaf and blind."

"Goddammit, stop saying that!" I rose in a fury, fists raised. "The Chairman has warned us time and again what will happen if we don't pull our weight. He has to break up these demonstrations or the result will be catastrophic. I want you to go back and find out exactly what is happening."

"I don't have to go back. I was there. It began in the Metal Workshop II."

"That is one of our most important workshops," I said. "What started all this? The Chairman just met with them."

"A manager slapped a teenage worker," Jozef said.

"Not that again.," Rosenfeld, who had been silently observing as was his habit of late, interjected. "The Chairman has warned the managers to avoid such behavior, but do they listen? Do any stubborn Jews listen? So why did he hit this kid?"

"Who cares?" Jozef exploded. "There is no good reason for striking any worker. That's why they all refuse to work until they get a good explanation."

"That sounds like a reasonable request," Rosenfeld said.

"At any other time and place," I said.

"The manager called in the Order Service and had everyone arrested from the shift. When the second shift arrived at 3:00 p.m. and learned of this, they staged a strike as well."

"A house of cards," Rosenfeld muttered.

"At that point, the manager called the Chairman." Jozef laughed. "I would like to see his face when he arrives."

"I think that's a great idea."

"What is?"

"I want you to go back to the metal workshop and see how this affair ends."

Jozef looked shocked. "You know this could result in violence."

"You said you wanted to see the Chairman's face."

"I did not mean literally." Jozef looked worried. "These men are angry and rightfully so. It could become explosive."

"Are we not reporters?" I asked. "The future will want to know how the Chairman handles such difficult situations. You'll be safe. Stand with the Order Service if they are there."

Rosenfeld lifted his head. "I can go. I have less to lose."

I had lost him once and had no intention of risking him being nabbed in a net by the Gestapo because of his age. "No, I've made up my mind. Jozef will go."

Jozef rose from his seat and buttoned his coat. He glared at me. "You're becoming just like them," he said.

My fists tightened. I felt like slapping Jozef's leering face for all the insubordinate things he'd said for so many months, and, of course, for all the endless complaining. I stood and pointed my finger at him. "We all have work to do. This is ours. As long as I am in charge, we will do what the Chairman needs doing."

The door slammed shut.

Rosenfeld looked at me with his weary eyes. "You're beginning to sound like him," he said and ducked into his work.

"Oskar," I said. "This is war, and Rumkowski is our general. If he fails, we all fail."

Two hours later, Jozef reentered our room. He was oddly silent.

I decided not to question him. I'd shown him who was boss and, hopefully, he would not need another demonstration of my power.

From time to time, I glanced at Jozef and saw he was writing on his pad. When he finished, he announced, "You were right." He then handed me his paper and left the room.

"He said you were right," Rosenfeld said. "I've never heard him say that before."

I read his report. "The strike spread to another workshop," I said. "Just as I predicted."

"It will continue to spread," Rosenfeld said.

"I don't know. The Chairman arrived on the scene and ordered the release of the workers. He promised to settle the matter himself. He made the workers responsible for the time they had missed and ordered them to work past their midnight shift." I looked up. "They have to work until 3:00 a.m.. He promised a full investigation."

"Did the workers return to work?"

"The Chairman's personal appearance in both plants seems to have done the trick. I added a line to Jozef's report."

"What did you write?" Rosenfeld asked.

"I added, "We can be certain that the Chairman will take vigorous action to establish better relations between management and labor in these important workshops.""

Rosenfeld smiled, "You manage to put a positive spin on everything."

I thought of the promise the Chairman had made to protect our children and replied, "Not everything."

Rosenfeld passed a report to me from the Registration Bureau. "Here's something else you may not be able to put a positive spin on. Biebow visited the Registration Bureau, and the department head believes it is very likely that an official commission will soon be inspecting our department."

I saw a look of resignation on his face and said, "Don't think you are getting out of working here so fast, my old friend." But I did not like the implication of all these inspections by the authorities.

CHAPTER 65

T UESDAY, NOVEMBER 9, 1943
A COMMISSION ARRIVES IN THE GHETTO
WEDNESDAY, NOVEMBER 17, 1943
THE LAST DAY OF KOLACJA (EVENING MEAL)

The lines are hundreds of meters long. The atmosphere in the kitchens is utterly macabre. The staff members are silent. The people waiting in line are mute. They crowd toward the entrance, fearing that the only meal they are to enjoy in their fourteen-day rotation may be in jeopardy—in the ghetto, anything is possible. People eat quickly, knowing that thousands wait outside...All that is certain is that everyone is hungry and bitterly disappointed and that, as of tomorrow, the kitchens will be closed.

I was standing next to an Order Service officer on the line that led to the kitchen. It was difficult to imagine thousands of people, many barely able to walk, standing in mute silence, stunned at the possibility this could be their last meal. I, a member of Rumkowski's inner circle, was still able to dine in Kitchen 2, the Kitchen for the Intelligentsia, but rumors were rampant that even this last bastion of better dining was being forced to close by the authorities who were cracking down on all forms of what they claimed were unequal benefits. While I agreed with Singer that nepotism and favoritism were corruption, unfair to the populace, I felt these were little enough compensation for the responsibility and risk the closest supporters of our Chairman took upon their shoulders.

The officer I stood near spotted a fracas further back in the line and was gone before I could follow. I was facing forward when someone whispered, "Follow me."

I turned, but the figure darted behind a building across Zgierska. A chill shot through me. Hoping I wouldn't be noticed, I moved out of the line and shook my head as if disgusted with waiting.

"You there!"

I turned, grasping for an excuse.

The officer shouted at two men glaring belligerently at each other. Apparently, one had jumped ahead in line when the other, emaciated and filthy, had stumbled.

I took advantage of the distraction and headed across the street.

A door was slightly open.

I remembered David and the knife at my throat. Did I dare open the door?

A thin hand opened it for me.

"Pola? Thank God! It's you!" I hurried inside and pushed the door shut, plunging us into darkness. I couldn't see her face. Why didn't she throw herself into my arms? Why wasn't she kissing my cheeks, my lips? "Where are you?" I asked.

"You'll get accustomed to the dark," She whispered. "I needed to see you."

"And I want to see you," I blurted. "Please, may I hug you?" I reached for her in the dark. "God, I missed you so much." Leaning down, I found her cheeks with my lips. "Please, tell me you are staying? I want you to." I felt her pull away. I dragged her back and pressed her lips with my hungry mouth. I felt her rise up to meet me. I wouldn't let her go. When she tried to move back, I refused to let her. She was all I wanted from our God. I would not surrender her. But finally, weakened by hunger, unable to fight, I released her. "Tell me you're staying," I said, praying silently to God that this one small thing he would do for me.

"Bennie, I wish I could stay. There's so much I want to tell you, but my time is short." She ran her hand lovingly down my face. "Something strange is happening here. Biebow paid a surprise visit to the Registration Department. Our informant told us that a high-level commission arrived from Berlin two days later. We don't know what they wanted."

'You want me to find out?" I was terrified. "Why are you involved in this? You can stay with me, and we'll have a good life. You said...you love me."

"I did say that."

"Didn't you mean it?" I knew some people said this at the drop of a hat. I didn't think she was like that, but I was finding it difficult to trust anyone these days.

"Yes. I meant it, but I can't stop now. Things are happening that sealed up in this ghetto you know nothing about. We need your help. We've learned Deputy Neftalin was ordered to present a report to the Chairman and the Commission. We need you to find out what was in his report."

"You're asking me to spy on a friend? The Deputy has been good to me. How can I do this?"

"Rumors are flying that the Germans sealed all the registration files from the ghetto."

"Why would they do that? It's just a rumor. There are stupid rumors every day."

"Bennie, they did this in Warsaw too...before they sent 300,000 from the ghetto—"

"Warsaw? You were in Warsaw? Did you see Singer there?"

"Bennie, please, find out if the Germans have all the registration forms. That's all you need to do."

"How will I find you? Please, stay with me? Please?" I was about to tell her I loved her, but she pushed herself into my chest, her lips reaching for my lips. I felt her in my arms, her lips pressing urgently against my mouth. "I can't lose you too," I gasped.

And just like that, she was gone. Had I said the wrong thing? Fool! Imbecile! Idiot! I was panting for air, searching in the dark, having seen the door open, a shadow pass through and then vanish. I lost her again. How could I be so stupid?

As it turned out, I didn't have to use subterfuge on Neftalin. On November 17, a large group of high-ranking Wehrmacht and SS officers led by a general arrived in the ghetto. They inspected the Metal Department, then the Boot, Leather, and Saddlery Department. They then drove to the Tailoring and the Carpentry shops.

I thought Neftalin would be shaken when he came into our room, but he appeared jubilant. "The commission was impressed by our factories. It is certain the Nazi officers revised their opinions about the productivity of Jews." He laughed. "They could not get over their astonishment. Their comments and the expressions on their faces were clearly saying the same thing: 'And this really was done by Jews?' Yes, we pulled it off, my friends. The Chairman's actions this month to get the labor forces in line has ensured that our ghetto will endure until the end of this war."

"So, the Germans did not take your registration records?" I asked.

"Why would you ask that?"

"There have been rumors that all our records are in possession of the authorities and that this is a precursor to the total evacuation of the ghetto."

Rosenfeld and Jozef looked up from their work.

Neftalin looked surprised and then burst into laughter. "Engineer, you are the most logical man I've ever met. Would I report as I have on the German inspections today if this rumor was at all reliable? It is just yentas with nothing better to do. Now, I must leave and let you get back to work." He walked to the door. "Gentlemen, let us pray for more good news in the coming days."

I prayed that this news would calm Pola's suspicions, that she'd see that there was no need for fear. I'd ask her to move in with me. I'd tell her that I would find some way to tell Miriam that I now understood why she could never love me, not as she loved Singer. Yes, now I could give my young, obstinate wife to Singer. Perhaps, that was the reason for all this. Jozef says, "God always has a purpose." I couldn't wait to tell Pola and feel her in my arms again.

CHAPTER 66

TUESDAY, DECEMBER 7, 1943

Pola didn't return. I assumed she and her band had gotten the information she needed from better sources. I was optimistic still, and then rumors surfaced that Biebow and the Chairman had argued. It allegedly began when the German ghetto administration took over the food distribution from the Chairman's committee. There had been heated exchanges between the Eldest of the Jews and the Amtsleiter before, but the wresting of the food distribution made it visible to all who was the weaker. It was a worrisome development, yet based on the positive reports of the German commission's visits, our fears of the dismantling of the ghetto were calmed. I was taken off-guard when Neftalin sent an Order Service officer to bring me to his headquarters.

The Deputy's room was as cold as ours. He wore his coat over his suit. Winter was upon us, and the Germans did not favor our administrators, as the Chairman had, with extra lumps of coal for heaters. Neftalin was pacing the floor.

"Henryk?" I wasn't sure he was aware of my presence.

Neftalin waved me to a seat and tossed a report to me. "You remember the Commissions that inspected us? We expected great things, a new plan to enhance services. Well, on November 26, Biebow returned from Berlin." He pointed to the top sheet. "Unfortunately, the high hopes pinned on this trip weren't realized. He was unable to accomplish much in Berlin, which he claims was in a 'period of crisis at the time.' He would not elaborate."

273

I was at the edge of the chair. "Do you think the war is going badly for the Germans?"

"The Chairman believes so, but literally sealed off from the rest of Poland, it is difficult to tell. As far as we know, and this is uncertain, we may be the last bastion of Jews in Poland, thanks to Eldest of the Jew's firm grip on the ghetto."

"Amen." It was automatic.

"You pray?" Neftalin laughed. "I guess the end of the war is coming when our atheist prays."

I did not tell him what I prayed for.

Neftalin became serious again. "I summoned you because 400 department heads were invited to the House of Culture for a scheduled assembly. I was surprised when Amtsleiter Biebow and several uniformed German officials entered through the stage door."

"That must have caused a stir," I said.

Neftalin sat down behind his desk. "It was unprecedented. Biebow addressed his captive audience for an hour and a half. My report is in front of you. I will go over some points with you, partly to clear my head by sharing with a trusted friend." He gave me a weak smile. "Biebow began in a benevolent tone, acknowledging the services of the Eldest of the Jews and our factories." He pointed his finger to the papers. "It's all there. He spoke then about many items in no particular order, heaping praise on some functions in the ghetto, but also talking of the abuses that he and the commissions had found."

From Neftalin's face, I suspected he was under tremendous pressure. I thought it best to remain silent, to act as his sounding board.

Neftalin sighed. "A great deal of his speech dealt with the new food regulations. Food will be given only to those who work at least 55 hours per week. He declared war on those in the ghetto who are not productive…he threatened the death penalty for any abuse."

"The death penalty?"

Neftalin nodded. "Since the Amtsleiter prohibited note-taking and no stenographer was present, no transcript of his speech exists. I wrote my report strictly from memory." He pointed to the sheets of paper yet again. "I was surprised Biebow appeared to reinforce the Chairman as the ghetto authority, stating it was the Chairman's task, and the Order Service's duty, to maintain order and productivity in the ghetto. I didn't expect that comment after the severity of his earlier remarks. I suppose the next few days will answer our questions." He stood. "Please, take my notes and include them in your entries. You may go now. Thank you."

I thought he looked as if he wanted to say more. "Sir, is there something else?"

Neftalin nodded. "There was one more thing, but until it materializes, I want you to keep it to yourself."

"Of course."

"Somewhere, in the middle of his long speech, Biebow went off on a tangent. He mentioned that the workers in Terezin had failed on an important project that might be coming to our ghetto. He said it would require 5,000 able-bodied workers and that this project had been assigned to us by Speer, one of the highest officials of the Reich."

"Another large order is a good sign," I said.

Neftalin smiled. "If this is approved, it could mean many months of work for a number of our factories. They want us to build temporary housing for families left homeless by bombings."

"Amen," I said, daring to hope.

"Amen," Neftalin repeated. "You must tell no one, but the failure of the workers in Terezin, which Biebow blamed squarely on the ineptitude of their Jewish leaders, is a gift from God for Lodz. Nothing must distract us from this contract if we are given the go-ahead."

As I left his office, I thought I heard the sound of aircraft nearby. We'd heard explosions in the distance at times, but this order for temporary housing was our first official confirmation that the Germans were at long last being bombed. "God, give them hell," I prayed as I hurried back to our workroom, eager to hear air raid sirens.

CHAPTER 67

FRIDAY, DECEMBER 17, 1943

NEWS OF THE DAY

It has been learned from Balut Market that the investigating commission is still occupied with the current food supply question. Balut Market is expecting the commission's arrival from the city. The Registration Bureau also remains on alert.

The ghetto is completely calm. The Chairman assures us, as before, that this matter implies no danger whatsoever to the ghetto.

I'd learned that when God gives, he also takes away. After my meeting with Neftalin, I felt hopeful the war was ending. The Allied forces were causing damage in Germany to the point that Speer needed temporary housing for people displaced by the bombs. Though the prospect of bombs raining down on us from aircraft was frightening, the alternative, that Germany might win the war, was far worse. If we could only hold out a little longer…

And then we got devastating news. The ghetto had not known such a grave hour since the loss of our children.

Neftalin burst through our door. "I don't know what's happening. 9:30 this morning, an automobile from the Secret State Police roared into Balut Market. Two men, one in plain clothes, the other in uniform, entered the Chairman's office and demanded, "Are you the Eldest of the Jews? The rest of you, out! Get out now!" Their demeanor terrified me. We stood in the corridor, the door blocked. The meeting lasted an interminable two hours. Then the Chairman, looking shaken, asked for documents from his secretary, Dora Fuchs. He then asked for population statistics from me. I went to fetch what we had. I thought everything was fine until Dora ran into my office, shouting that the Chairman was driven from the ghetto in the Gestapo's car."

Jozef sounded upset. "He was driven from the ghetto at 11:30? It is now 7:00 p.m. Has he returned?"

Neftalin shook his head. "No. I'm worried. Everyone is."

On my way home, groups of people were whispering about this new crisis. Rumors were that the Chairman had been taken to Poznan and, like Gertler, would not be returning. "Rumkowski is the father of the ghetto," someone said. Fear was in everyone's bones. I realized that never before had people felt so profoundly the undeniable fact that "Rumkowski is the ghetto." Fear festered that the ghetto was in imminent danger. Sleep was impossible. The anxiety became worse when it was learned Biebow had also been summoned to Gestapo headquarters.

Just a few days ago, Neftalin had such hope, but now he said, "All we can do is wait. Wait and pray."

It was not all I could do. My mind flashed to the cemetery. Was it time to go into hiding?

In the morning, the cold air kept the streets nearly empty. Factories spewed smoke in the frigid dawn. After arriving at Balut Market, passing sentries, I headed to Neftalin's office. I was prepared to tell him I needed a change, that I could no longer accept the stress of my position. I imagined his face when I told him where I wanted to work. He would never believe anyone would request a transfer to the Gravedigger Department, but eventually, he'd give in. I knocked on his door and stepped inside.

"Good morning, Engineer," Neftalin said with a broad smile. "The Chairman returned from the city last night at about 10:30. People were sitting vigil at his apartment. They saw him step from the tram and spread the word. Some woke others with the joyful news. Today, we may all breathe a sigh of relief."

I sagged into a chair. "Is the Eldest alright?"

"Yes. Our hard-working leader was back in his office before seven this morning. Of course, he was tired. He was in German headquarters all day, eating nothing." He leaned over and confided, "Most of all, he said, he missed his beloved cigarettes. He is a heavy smoker." He gave me a broad smile. "Already, many people have congratulated him on his return."

I shared their relief. "Did the Chairman say what it was all about?" I asked.

"He refuses to discuss the purpose of the investigation, other than it concerned food supply problems." Neftalin tapped his fingers on his desk. "He even refused to fill me in on the specifics but did say that he was told that he bore full responsibility, his words, for everything that went on in the ghetto. I could get nothing more out of him." He handed me a few sheets of paper. "I will tell you that it is typical of the Chairman's amazing vitality that, on his first day back, he already intervened at the shoemaker's factory where a strike was reported."

Labor unrest had become a significant challenge for the Chairman. He had called in his Order Service force many times, often with brutal results.

Neftalin said, "A few minutes after the Chairman's intervention, the authorities arrived at the plant. Thank God, by then, the incident had been resolved. I tell you, my friend, I would not want his responsibility." He stood. "I sometimes ponder throwing all this away and taking on a job in a factory where my brain can get a much-needed rest. I'm sure you know what I mean."

I nodded. If only I could rest my brain from all the conflicting thoughts that plagued me.

I left Neftalin's office, headed to our room when a man grabbed my arm. "Steer clear. They're taking Kinstler, the director of the Food Supply Department."

I looked down the corridor. German soldiers were removing file boxes from Kinstler's office.

Later that day, I read a note from Neftalin. It said the Commission was still focused on the food supply situation, but "the Chairman assures us, as before, that this matter implies no danger whatsoever to the ghetto." Only to Kinstler, I thought.

CHAPTER 68

SUNDAY, DECEMBER 19, 1943

S "Doctor, I admire your ability to capture the ghetto mood so well,"
I remarked on reading Rosenfeld's account of the status of crime
in the ghetto. "I particularly like your opening, where you bemoan the fact
that the ghetto has no access to newspapers and 'the daily chronicler is
dependent on word of mouth and, if they are available, on the reports of the
Order Service.' We are, in an authentic sense, blind to all else." God, I hated
that damn word, but how else could I describe our current condition? We
were blind to what was happening in the outside world.

"Thank you. Sadly, crime in the ghetto is unique. I would say that ninety
cases of one hundred involve the theft of food. They are crimes of hunger.
Making off with fallen potatoes, radishes, or other vegetables, all in the
open. These are desperate people, not criminals."

"I suppose we could debate this for days, but the authorities view these
actions as serious crimes."

"Engineer, on one day alone, six cases of potato theft were reported. Six
cases, but at bottom, one motive: hunger."

"We are all hungry, exhausted, and freezing. Imagine the anarchy that
would ensue if these so-called 'minor' larcenies went unpunished? You're
hungry. I'm famished. Yet we obey the law. Even our Torah, the foundation
of Jewish law, says the poor man must be found guilty if he commits a
crime."

Rosenfeld sighed. "A man, nearly sixty, his wife and four children, victims of the recent resettlement…an elderly woman, undernourished, feverish, consumptive…a widow, suffering from disease, in a ragged dress, looking after a starving child who had no hot food…an old man, decrepit, trembling, an image of woe — these are our criminals."

I understood his sympathy but could not let it go unchallenged. "My dear doctor, I would be the first to applaud your emotional response to the plight of our fellow human beings. But for the general welfare of the ghetto, we must not allow our sympathy to conceal the truth, that these are violations of the law, both ghetto and German. They must be dealt with, or conditions will become far worse. These people have no respect for the police or the court. They make their own laws and risk all of our lives."

"Singer was right. You are a pragmatist." He smiled sadly. "But I see your insides and know that you are hurting for these poor souls as I am. You cannot hide this hurt forever. It will crack through your heart and someday explode."

"Until that day, you will depict these acts as violations of the law," I said, trying not to sound like a dictator, but having to remind him of our duty to the Chairman. "Doctor, the ghetto is sick, but if we do not stop the infection, the lawlessness will become a contagion beyond our control. The authorities will enforce a cure that is worse than any we may administer."

"But sending these people to the Gestapo?"

"If the Chairman sends Jews to the Germans, then you know that what I am saying is valid. I'm sure that is the last thing he wants to do."

Rosenfeld nodded.

The door opened, and Jozef entered. "I have terrible news. Our hospital on Dworska Street—"

"Not again?" The Germans had emptied our hospitals before. The rumor still circulated that all the patients in the mental hospital had been trucked into the forest and executed by rifle fire. That wasn't confirmed, but nobody ever found out what happened to those patients, so any actions on the hospitals sent shivers of fear to all the ghetto residents.

"The Chairman is letting this happen?" Jozef asked.

"The Germans demanded 100 beds be freed immediately for Aryan patients," Rosenfeld said. "Jewish doctors have been ordered to combat typhus for these Aryans from Poland."

"Is this a fact or another wild rumor?" I asked.

Rosenfeld replied, "It is a fact. The ghetto is faced with a mass importation of typhus sufferers, and a large number of Jewish patients will have to be discharged from the hospital to make room for the Aryan patients."

"When this gets out, there will be an uproar," Jozef said.

WEDNESDAY, DECEMBER 22, 1943
THE HOSPITAL ON DWORSKA STREET

Today, Jewish patients were discharged from the hospital on Dworska Street to vacate the beds required for the Polish children with typhus...

There wasn't any uproar about the hospital. Those patients with families were brought to their homes. The Chairman placed others where he could. Those who had no one, or who were too ill, were left in an untended rest home or hostel. We had no resources to spare.

The cold of winter chilled us as we trudged before dawn to our daily tasks, and as we struggled to get back to our unheated hovels hours after sunset. The fifth winter of war in Poland, the fourth in the ghetto. Most ghetto dwellers felt that freezing was far worse a way to die than starving. I asked Rosenfeld his opinion.

Rosenfeld rubbed his hands, cold even in gloves that Singer had given him, now with holes in their fingers. "Freezing is a terrible, slow way to die, but so is dying from hunger. That is why each day we record so many suicides that we no longer mention them in our journal."

Jozef said, "I've had enough of this. The new year is about to begin, and winter will show its teeth. We've seen the postcards. They have food and warmth. We have typhus and frozen limbs."

I wrapped my scarf around the bottom of my face. "Go home," I said. "See you tomorrow." I headed toward the door.

Rosenfeld said, "The day after tomorrow is Christmas and Chanukah, both on the same day. It is also the Sabbath. A great omen."

Jozef laughed insanely. "Merry Christmas, you damn Germans. I hope you choke on your goddamn Christmas dinners." He then looked at me. "Happy Chanukah, Ostrowski."

I felt tears as I thought of another Chanukah without my sweet Regina. Another year was ending, and I still didn't know where Miriam and my child were. Was I never to find out?

CHAPTER 69

MONDAY, JANUARY 3, 1944
Today, at 10 A.M., in the former sanatorium at 55 Lagiewnicka Street, the Chairman celebrated the Bar Mitzvah of his legally adopted son, Stanislaw Stein. Some thirty persons close to the Chairman were invited...The Chairman, gracious as always to his guests, created a warm and intimate atmosphere despite the frugality of the meal.

SATURDAY, JANUARY 8, 1944

New Year's Eve passed in loneliness. I could not even drown my sorrow. The Germans were strictly regulating our food, and alcohol was only available on the black market. I thought of the New Year's Eve when Singer had me chasing him into the dark. I had wanted to save him from being shot in an escape attempt, though I'd thought of killing him for what I believed was his betrayal with Miriam. God, I missed them both, loved them both. In the desolation of my flat, alone on my mattress, I prayed they'd find each other. They deserved to share what little happiness was left to them on this cold, winter-lashed planet. And then I thought of Pola and wondered with whom she was sharing the start of the new year.

When Neftalin entered our office early the next morning, I expected him to be of good cheer after attending the Chairman's Bar Mitzvah celebration for his adopted son. I was prepared to record the details, but his face showed worry. "What is wrong, Henryk?" I asked, thinking it was his health, with our barely life-sustaining rations and the bitter cold.

Neftalin stood by the door. "Early this morning, an automobile of the Secret State Police appeared. They seized the Chairman again." He shook his head. "They demanded all of our food distribution records."

"This is becoming nerve-wracking," I muttered.

Neftalin sighed. "In a recent speech, the Chairman said, 'one must be prepared to atone even for the sins of others and that, in a position such as his, one must be ready to sacrifice one's life at any time.' He is willing to sacrifice himself for us, our noble Chairman. God bless him."

After Neftalin left, I thought of the terror if, at any second, Germans could whisk me away to some unknown destination. Could I persist as our Eldest of the Jews was doing? I thought of the night Miriam left me. Struck by a rifle in the gut and face, I had crawled in the mud, a worm. Could I have done more before she climbed into that truck? I'd wrestle with that question and more for the rest of my life.

After nearly unbearable suspense, the Eldest returned at four in the afternoon of January 4. He was left to walk from the Police Precinct in the Aryan section of Litzmannstadt to his apartment, where he spent the day with his brother, Jozef. Even Neftalin, his Deputy, claimed he was not privy to any information about this interrogation, other than that the Chairman refused the food that was offered to him. How could he, so battered by his years of service, physically and mentally withstand what the authorities were now doing to him? Though far younger, I would have cracked with the suspense that any day I could be tortured or executed for others' actions.

Rosenfeld stood. He looked alarmed.

I'd been lost in a reverie but quickly shouted, "Attention!" I found myself nearly eye-to-eye with Dr. Bradfisch, the Commander-in-Chief of the Gestapo.

The Commander had an ice-cold expression on his face as he surveyed our workroom. A husky guard, with a rifle, stood statue-like at the door.

We'd had visits before, almost all unannounced, but this man's predatory glare made me uneasy. He picked up a document from my pile and held it up to our lightbulb, then tossed it back on the table.

I remained at attention but saw his icy blue eyes were scrutinizing Rosenfeld. It looked as if Bradfisch was about to say something to the doctor when Neftalin thankfully popped in at the door. "The Chairman has the documents you requested," he said in a loud voice.

The Gestapo chief turned and left the room.

The guard closed the door.

I fell into my chair. "This is getting to be a bad habit," I muttered.

"I wonder what he wanted?" Jozef said, sagging like an empty bag of potatoes.

"Only the Germans know," I said. And, as I often did, I heard Singer's voice taunting, "And someone else too."

The next day we received Proclamation No. 406 signed by Chaim Rumkowski. I read the order aloud, "*Citing my memorandum of June 3, 1942, and the memorandum, addressed to all Departments, workshops, and factories of June 3, 1942, I again emphatically point out*

that all ghetto inhabitants (male and female) must unconditionally and un-prompted salute all uniformed personnel and all German officials (civilians)in the street as well as in the workshops and factories."

Jozef interrupted. "Are you joking? This is the most important matter today?"

"There's more." I continued reading, "*It makes no difference whatsoever whether the uniformed personnel or German civilians are in the ghetto on foot or in an auto.*"

Rosenfeld laughed bitterly. "It is not enough we have to risk our bones on ice and hold our coats and scarves around us with frozen fingers, but now as we slip and slide and risk breaking our necks, we must keep one eye out for German cars?"

"So it seems." I read more: "*There thus exists a rigorous obligation to salute. Failure to observe this order will result in extremely severe penalties.*"

"We went from 'severe' to 'extremely severe.'" I grunted. "It's ludicrous."

"I suppose we must practice our salutes?" Jozef taunted.

"Well, the Chairman states, 'everyone must rise from his seat at the command, 'Achtung!' and when all the visitors have entered, work cannot continue until the same person orders, 'Weiterarbeiten.' (Continue work!).'"

"With all the shit we have to put up with," Jozef said.

"The proclamation says, 'The manager of each workshop must delegate a specific individual to call out the above orders, 'Achtung' and 'Weiterarbeiten' at every inspection or visit.'"

"It's specific that a specific person must say these specific words." I burst out laughing.

"You're finally as insane as the rest of us," Jozef said.

"I don't know anymore who is sane," Rosenfeld muttered and proceeded to mime lighting a pipe he no longer had.

I laughed at the old man's antics, his broken pipe bowl still in my pocket.

The door opened.

I yelled, "Achtung!"

Neftalin jumped. "You scared me half out of my wits."

I burst out laughing again. "We were late last time," I said.

Neftalin got serious. "Biebow has not returned from his 'vacation.' Nobody knows where he is."

The real problem was nobody knew who was taking over. The devil you know is better than the devil you don't....

CHAPTER 70

*J*ANUARY 13, 1944

Amtsleiter Biebow arrived in the ghetto today and immediately resumed his duties...he instructed the Eldest to provide him immediately with various statistical surveys...A commission of two men has arrived in the ghetto. No information can be obtained about the purpose or nature of this commission.

Two shots.

I ran for cover to the side of a building.

A sentry looked down at the body and cursed. He aimed his rifle along the street.

The victim was too far to see a face. I thought it was a man from the size. Had Singer attempted to enter the ghetto again? Was he trying to escape? I was tempted to approach the barbed wire but heard a vehicle approach.

A Kripo officer exited a black car. There was talk. Then one of the men laughed.

I walked away as if nothing had happened. The details would come later. Perhaps not. Shootings were not news.

When I arrived at our workroom, Rosenfeld smiled. "The Chairman married seven couples Sunday."

Pola loved reporting about the weddings. I thought them ridiculous ceremonies in the middle of our deprivation, but now admitted she was right. As long as young people were marrying and children were being born, there was hope.

Jozef entered, followed by Neftalin. "The Chairman has ordered all departments, workshops, and factories immediately to provide a list of all workers, male and female, and all juveniles under fourteen. The order came from the German authorities. Nobody knows the purpose of this directive."

"The Chairman knows," Rosenfeld mumbled.

"The Chairman doesn't know," Neftalin countered angrily. "I can only tell you that a discrepancy was discovered in the food distribution."

"A discrepancy?" Jozef looked puzzled.

"Yes. The authorities discovered that 3,000 more ration cards were issued than required by our population."

"3,000? That is a discrepancy." I anticipated how the authorities might view such a costly error.

"Always the numbers man," Neftalin said. "The Chairman argued that the problem was caused by the chaotic conditions after the September '42 resettlement. They want us to make good on the unlawfully obtained food."

"How the hell can we do that? We have no money." Jozef laughed. "This is getting crazier and crazier. How do we repay for something we never got with money we don't have?"

"This is collective punishment," Rosenfeld said.

"How do they expect us to pay back something we didn't benefit from?" I asked.

Neftalin handed me a thin sheath of paper. "The authorities are calling for a seven percent reduction in our food allocation—"

"Seven percent? I suppose we should thank God it's not ten or twenty percent," Rosenfeld said. "How do they expect us to survive on even less food than we get now?"

Neftalin smiled bitterly, "They don't. That's the point." With that, he left the room.

"I never heard the Deputy sound so defeated," Rosenfeld said.

"That's because now even our elite are in the same boat as the rest of us," Jozef said. "The Germans don't play favorites as our Chairman does."

"No, they want all Jews to suffer equally," Rosenfeld replied. "You know, Jozef, at least when our leaders were fed, we had some optimism that we would be as well. Now, what is left when even our leaders are losing hope?" He handed me a sheet of paper. "I'm sure you will be happy to learn that children who have reached the age of nine have been assigned to work in the factories."

Jozef frowned. "Nine years old and slaving in the factories? No, that doesn't make me happy. What children we have here are mainly orphans who have suffered enough."

"They have to work," I said. "It's the only way the Chairman can protect them. The Germans won't feed anyone who isn't working. Anyone who is not their slave will be resettled. The Chairman knows children are a target, so he is protecting them…." I couldn't finish. I was angry he hadn't come up with this kind of scheme to protect our children more than a year ago, to keep my Regina with me. But maybe she was better off away from this slum and starvation.

Rosenfeld shivered. "As if we haven't suffered enough with typhoid and tuberculosis," he mumbled behind his handkerchief.

"What's wrong?" I asked, seeing he was visibly shaking.

"As a doctor, I would diagnose I have the flu."

"You should see a doctor and get a prescription…."

Rosenfeld laughed. "Look where we are! We have no medicines, and the few physicians we have are swamped. The last time I stayed home, I ended up in the net for a labor camp. No, I'll stick it out right here."

1944 was the winter of the flu. Forty percent or better suffered from influenza. Most kept working. They continued to work even when the public facilities for gas cooking were shut down, and the Germans discontinued the distribution of coal. In my entry, I wrote, "The situation is hopeless—utterly catastrophic." Bodies lay in the streets, but we barely paid them any attention.

CHAPTER 71

SATURDAY, JANUARY 22, 1944
To its surprise, the Department of Gas Kitchens has received an order to reopen a few of its kitchens...it appears that the gas kitchens were closed as a punitive measure for excessive gas consumption.

"Not that there's much to cook," Rosenfeld said. "Even the cats are starving."

"You and your cats. I read your entry, 'The Privileged Cats,' from last Saturday and would have laughed if we were not living this tragedy with your feline friends."

"What I don't understand," Jozef interjected, "is why we were feeding cats meat when we haven't had meat in the ghetto for humans in months."

Rosenfeld chuckled. "Well, you know we have no pets and horses, but a few shopkeepers and food distribution points were given the right to keep cats."

"Another one of the Chairman's gifts to the privileged few," Jozef said.

"Not at all. Without cats, the ghetto would be overrun by mice and rats, the only meat we have an abundance of. They chew up sacks of flour, rye flakes, peas, and get into marmalade, sugar, and what little bread we have. The cats must work as do all employees of the ghetto."

"So, the mouse-catchers get imported meat while we starve?" Jozef said. "There's an irony for you."

"You need not gripe. Now, there is no meat for the good little cats, either. As I wrote in my entry, 'Their heads droop, their tails drag sadly. A pitiful sight. The cats accept no other food; they are slowly perishing.' As we all are."

"Enough of cats," I said, waving a new decree by the Germans. "This proclamation demands the obligatory registration of all musical instruments. So much for culture." I thought of Pola and how she had become transformed from the aloof woman I'd assumed her to be, to a human being with closed eyes and finger weaving rhythmically with the music swelling around us in the House of Culture. It was the music that brought us together. Surely, God would not let the Germans take our instruments away now too.

"At least this action does not affect our stomachs," Jozef said.

Rosenfeld sighed. "This last vestige of happiness is now taken away." He looked at Jozef. "I suppose you can't imagine what it means for a professional musician, a virtuoso, to be forced to give up his beloved violin. The few homes still possessing an upright or rickety grand piano, which consecrated them as temples of art, will now be soulless. Beethoven, Mozart, Chopin, Schumann, fall silent in the ghetto."

"You must write your entry like this," I said.

"We have much worse crap to consider," Jozef remarked.

"You are right. The street will notice nothing. Harsh life will go on, but to the torments of hunger and cold will be added the unappeased craving for music." Rosenfeld began to hum Beethoven's ninth symphony.

I could almost see Pola's finger conducting the orchestra.

Jozef's voice broke into the interlude. "Shit!"

"Now what?"

"The bastards are stealing our hospital and using it for Germans only. They're sealing it off from the ghetto with barbed wire."

Rosenfeld laughed. "Their wire makes for a nice noose around our throats, always getting a little tighter until there is no ghetto left."

"But the Chairman goes on and on," Jozef said. "Though he is bedridden, tomorrow he plans to perform a wedding ceremony in his private apartment." He looked at me. "Have you ever been to his private apartment?"

I recalled how I'd gone to the Chairman's apartment, hoping Pola would be there. Would I ever see her again? Rosenfeld was right. The noose was getting tighter.

CHAPTER 72

SUNDAY, JANUARY 30, 1944
"COULD I TROUBLE YOU FOR A LIGHT?"

Day and night one can observe...a person suddenly comes dashing out of some apartment and through the dark hallway holding a burning scrap of paper or pinewood. He has just "borrowed a bit of fire" from a neighbor who happens to be cooking. Even if he still has some matches to light, one would be unforgivably frivolous. It won't be long before some resourceful person starts tending an eternal fire and charging money for a light. There is no flint or torchwood in the ghetto; nevertheless, the Stone Age has returned.

Was not the Eldest of the Jew's refusal to stop performing weddings one of the most significant stands he was taking against the Germans? Of course, it was. So it was my duty to attend the wedding rituals when possible. Hope doesn't die easily.

Sadly, unable to waste a precious match, it was impossible to neaten up as much as I should for a wedding. I put on my ailing shoes and left my flat. The thawed street water penetrated my worn soles. "No wonder everyone is sick," I muttered, heading for the better streets of Marysin.

The cemetery was on the way. A black car was parked by the entrance. I had hoped the authorities would neglect our graveyard, overgrown with weeds and wild bushes. Ah, well, when the time comes, it will remain the best option. There were many places to hide if the Germans just left things alone in our sacred grounds.

The Chairman's coach was stationed in front of the brick building where his apartment was located. His horse was missing, most likely being fed or given water. The last time I'd seen the animal, it looked sad and emaciated. Didn't we all?

I climbed the steps and entered the lobby.

An Order Service guard raised his club.

I unwrapped the shawl around my face and held up my I.D. card.

"Administrator, of course." He whispered, "He's about to perform the wedding. You must be quiet."

As I approached the door, I felt the heat from inside. I undid my scarf but left it on my shoulders. I walked silently to the back of the reception room.

The Chairman, leaning on his cane at the front, cast an annoyed look in my direction. I'd interrupted the ceremony.

It was difficult to hear the Eldest of the Jews from the back of the room, but I saw six couples nodding their heads in unison to his words. There were no sporadic bursts of laughter. No sign of the joy I expected. Everyone seemed aware that even this minimalist ritual might be ripped away from us at any time. Grooms reached for the brides' hands, but there were no gold or silver rings, so they just held their beloved's hand and recited their vows.

When the Chairman announced they were married, to save glass, he stepped on one vessel and said, "Breaking this glass is a wish for good luck in your future. I do so with great optimism for your lives together." The grooms and brides kissed.

Miriam and I did not have a religious ceremony. Her parents gave her to me to protect. I failed. When Singer offered to help us escape, I turned him down. I didn't want to risk working with his underground 'associates.' What a fool I was then and now. No Pola. God had disappointed me again.

I pulled my coat closed and tied my scarf around my neck. It was late, and the wind whipped around me. I could barely see but discerned a shape rushing toward me. Was it Pola? I broke into a trot, and she was in my arms, embracing me. "Your house," she said and grabbed my arm. "Hurry," she said, pulling me with her.

"Are you here for a while?" I asked. A glance revealed the automobile was no longer at the cemetery.

Pola didn't reply.

"I miss you," I said.

She squeezed my arm.

I walked fast, but she kept up. I saw her eyes over her scarf. They were darting from side to side and then ahead. The wind threw ice at us, and my coat was not much protection. "I hoped you'd be at the wedding," I said as we approached my building.

"I hoped you'd be there too."

"It was no accident? You showing up?"

"No. I knew if there were a chance, you'd be there."

"And what if I weren't?" I asked, pushing the door open for her.

"God wanted you there."

We were upstairs, in my flat, no light.

Pola turned and pressed her hands to both sides of my face.

I tasted her breath just before her lips reached mine. In the dark, she prodded me toward the wall, her knee inserting itself between my legs, her arms holding me, her lips not leaving me. There was no time for talk, our mouths locked together. My eyes closed, but I still saw her, not Miriam, only Pola. I didn't care it was wrong. What I was feeling, still shivering from the frigidity of a Lodz winter night, was a fire I hadn't felt inside me for a long time. I couldn't let go of her. We clung to each other, my back against the wall for what seemed a long time.

"It's too cold like this," I said, hoping she would not break away from me as I led her to the bed.

Pola pulled away.

I didn't know what to do or say.

She pulled off her scarf and then her coat. "It's freezing in here."

"There's no coal. I'm sorry."

She pulled off her dress and draped it on the chair. "Damn, it's cold. You better hurry."

Hurry? How could I move while watching her slide into my bed? When

I saw she was safely ensconced under the thin coverlet, I pulled my feet from my shoes and dropped my coat and scarf to the floor. "My pants?" I asked, feeling stupid.

"Hurry. You could rent this as an icebox."

Leaving on my shirt, I almost jumped into the bed. "I can't believe you're here," I said, silently thanking God.

Pola wrapped her arms around me.

I pulled her body so close that not a stray breeze could find its way between us. "I wish I could hold you like this forever," I finally said minutes later. When she didn't speak, I suspected that it was not to be.

Sometime later, Pola's head resting on my chest, she said, "I have something to tell you."

"Not now. Tomorrow." I knew there would be no tomorrow. That's what I was thinking about.

"Bennie, Singer...is gone. I'm so sorry."

God gives a moment of joy and then tears it away. "No. He always survived before."

"I'm sorry."

My body trembled, my eyes wanted to burst into tears. I fought it, fought it as Singer would have wanted. "I loved him," I said.

"I know."

We were silent for a while, her head on my shoulder, both looking up at the ceiling we could not see in the dark. I pretended to see stars. I began to cry.

Pola must have felt me crying but didn't move. "I don't know much. He went back to Warsaw."

"He always wanted to go back. Is that where he was?" Saying that was painful. How would Miriam react when she heard? How could I tell her I was in love? "God, you're a monster. I'm happy at last, and you curse me with guilt?"

Pola sat up. "Oscar and a few brave men and women staged an uprising in April of last year."

"An uprising? In Warsaw?"

"You didn't know?"

"No. You know we're almost completely sealed off. No radios, newspapers, nobody allowed in or out without strict supervision. Hitler wants nothing to threaten his hold on our factories."

"That's why I'm here," Pola said. "Bennie, you've got to warn the others. Warsaw, all the ghettos, are being emptied. You've got to warn them."

"What good will it do?"

"What do you mean?"

I sat up. "Let's say it's true."

"Bennie, it is true. Jews are disappearing all over Europe."

"So, what can we do about it? We're trapped here. There's nowhere to go."

"But people have to know."

"Do they? This terrible news will only panic people. They'll become more desperate, and lawlessness will be worse than it is now. If people lose their faith in the Chairman and his plan, there will be work stoppages, and the authorities will charge in. No, Pola, I can't tell them what will only lead to disaster."

Pola pulled her hand away. "In Warsaw, they fought against the Nazis—"

"And died. Good men and women, like my friend, Oscar, who had so much to live for. No, fighting the Germans is impossible. Only the Chairman's strategy can save us. The war will end soon. Hitler can't win against the entire world."

There was a noise. A truck?

Pola jumped from the bed. "I have to go."

I reached for her. "Stay? Please stay? We are safe here. The Nazis need us."

Pola was dressed. She bent over the bed and grabbed me to her. "I pray you're right. I love you. With God's help, I will see you soon."

I jumped to the floor. "I love you," I whispered, afraid a soldier might be waiting for someone's voice to shatter the peace of night. At the bottom of the stairs, barefoot, in just my shirt, I stared at the empty street. I prayed to not hear rifle shots if Pola tried to escape through the barbed wire closing in around us. Only the thin smoke trails rising from our factories stood between Lodz and the wolves.

CHAPTER 73

S ATURDAY, FEBRUARY 5, 1944
AIR RAID DEFENSE
The street construction unit of the Department of Special Affairs has been assigned the task of digging air-raid defense ditches in the ghetto.

"It's happening! The Nazis are running afraid." Jozef exclaimed, wild with excitement. "They're getting their asses kicked. I know it. Why else this rush for air raid ditches? It's happening, my friends. At long last, we will see the end of this damn war!"

The door burst open. A German in uniform entered.

"Achtung!" I shouted it loudly, so Jozef, lost in joy at the imminent destruction of our oppressors, would hear it.

The German threw a sheet of paper on the table and left.

"What the hell was that about?" Jozef asked.

Just then, Neftalin entered our chamber. He coughed into a handkerchief and, in a strained voice, said, "Today, at two in the afternoon, the Chairman was instructed by Amtsleiter Biebow to vacate Balut Market."

"What the hell?" Jozef asked.

Rosenfeld stared at his gloves, material worn at the fingertips.

"Henryk, why are they doing this now?" I asked, alarmed by this demand.

"They want our premises available for the German Ghetto Administration by Monday."

"This Monday?"

"Yes. February 7."

"Surely, the Chairman told them this is impossible," Jozef said.

Neftalin replied, "The Chairman issued the orders." He picked up the paper that the soldier had dropped so unceremoniously on our table. "Your copy."

"How can he move everything by Monday?" I asked.

"All furnishings and equipment will remain," Neftalin replied. "The Chairman only took his files."

"Will he have an office?" I remembered Pola's warning. Was this the beginning of the end for our ghetto?

Neftalin nodded. "Our new offices will be at the Vegetable Distribution Center, which has been ordered to vacate the premises immediately."

"This is insane," Jozef grumbled.

"There are no vegetables, so why do we need a Vegetable Distribution Center?" Rosenfeld asked in a disturbingly calm voice.

I looked at my old friend and saw a ghost of the man he had been when we first met. At the time, I thought he was going to be my major problem, stuck-up and snooty. "You may call me Dr. Rosenfeld," he'd said. Now, I wanted to rush to him and crush his weary bones in my arms, to hold him close to me, so nobody could take him away again. "You've become quite a fatalist," I said, giving him a warm smile.

The doctor returned a weak version of a smile. "The yentas are gossiping about resettlements again."

"They're also talking about air raid ditches," I reminded him.

"Yes. That is hopeful."

"Yes. That is hopeful," I replied.

MONDAY, FEBRUARY 7, 1944

Today, the ghetto was visited by a relatively large commission consisting of officers from air-raid defense. ..The air raid defense ditches around the city proved to be unsuitable, since water was reached at a shallow depth, and it is feared that the clay soil could easily collapse.

Amtsleiter Biebow ordered the Eldest to have air raid defense ditches dug on the cemetery grounds and to have these ditches buttressed with gravestones.

300

Not even the buried were safe.

CHAPTER 74

T UESDAY, FEBRUARY 8, 1944
TOTAL POPULATION 79,777

     I was thinking of Pola when the door burst open. "Achtung!" I hated shouting that German command, but we couldn't take a chance since the authorities were now regular visitors. "We should set up a special knock for you," I said half-joking, seeing it was only Neftalin.

"This is not a day for laughter. 1,500 young male workers must be sent for labor by orders of the Labor Office in Poznan."

"Again, the rumors are true," Rosenfeld muttered.

Neftalin continued, "Since key departments, essential to the authorities, such as coal and transportation, are exempt, the burden falls on administrative offices."

"Shit," Jozef let out.

Neftalin nodded. "The Chairman said, 'If we do not solve the problem ourselves, you know what the practical consequences will be.'"

Jozef mimed slitting his throat with his hand.

I gave him a disapproving look, but he laughed it off. I was convinced he was insane.

Rosenfeld was examining a hole in his gloves.

Neftalin continued. "The exact wording of the requisition was, 'fifteen hundred men, of sound mind and body, fit for training in a specific line of work.' Look around you. How can we dig up even ten men so fit?"

"The Germans always expect the impossible. And if you disobey, the penalties are severe," Jozef said.

"Henryk, we don't have anyone that meets these requirements," I said.

Neftalin brushed back his hair with his hand, which now looked boney. "I must provide a list of candidates by tomorrow morning."

"You?" Would I obey such an order?

"I have no choice. Rumkowski also assigned Leon Rozenblat—"

"The head of the police?" Jozef said. "Of course, when the public gets this 'wonderful' news, they will panic. Those selected won't show up. Our Jewish police will have another 'roundup.'" He mimed bashing down on escapees with his fist. "Clubs will swing—"

"Stop, Jozef," I barked. "Our friend, Neftalin, is upset enough—"

"Who cares if he's upset? He and our Chairman are doing the Nazis' dirty work."

I jumped up. "Get out! Get out now!"

Neftalin raised his hand. "No. He's right. But there is no choice. As the Chairman said, the consequences of not complying are much worse."

I heard Singer arguing again that we should have fought the bastards from the start. I knew that's what Pola and hundreds of others were doing. "The hopeful thing here is that the Germans want men able to learn a trade," I offered, still grateful my name was not included. As I often said, "The devil you know is better than the one you don't."

"Yes, that is hopeful," Neftalin replied, "as are the many postcards we've received of late from friends and relatives that have been previously resettled. But the fear persists, and many refuse to show up for their medical examination. Their failure to report precipitates the sometimes brutal roundups. It's a miserable predicament. I hate it. If only we could obtain solid proof that our citizens are well off in their new locations."

Are they well off? I thought of the truckloads of used shoes and clothing, the nightmarish image of rooms stacked ceiling-high with unmentionables. I pictured our girls sitting at tables, running their hands over shirts, pants, underthings, ripping seams and pockets, finding jewels, coins, paper bills. What did these nightmare visions portend? I wondered why I'd had no word from Miriam. "We have no such proof," I said. "Do we?"

"No, my friend, we have no such proof." Neftalin stood. "I'm sorry. I know you are suffering."

"May I ask," Rosenfeld said, "Did the Chairman try to prevent this? Did he speak up and tell Biebow we don't have this manpower?"

"Yes, professor. He explained all this, but the Amtsleiter said he would need it in writing to present to Dr. Bradfisch, the head of the Gestapo. We know what that means."

"What age will the resettlement cover?" Jozef asked.

"It was to be from 18-40, but we don't have enough men of this age to fill the order, so we are now up to age 50." Neftalin handed me the German order. "We urged the Chairman to make this order public, so people understand it is not our doing. The Chairman says it will cause a panic. Even though conditions outside the ghetto may be better, most men do not want to be separated from their families at this hopeful time in the war."

I knew what that felt like. I missed my little Regina so much that it hurt. The thought of it made tears come to my eyes. I was too exhausted and frustrated to hide them. "I'm sorry, sir." I covered my face with my filthy sleeve.

Neftalin did something he'd never done before. He put his arm around my shoulders. "My friend, do not apologize. I wish I could ease your pain. I feel your loss as my own. We have all suffered so much, but if the Germans need so many of our workers, think of it as a good sign. They must need every able-bodied man for their war. I truly believe it is a signal that they are losing at last." He tried to make a smile, but it wasn't fully formed. "My friends, we are going to survive. I am positive. God has heard our prayers at last."

After Neftalin left, I turned to the routine news of the day. There was another German commission expected to inspect our workshops. The price of potato peels and rutabaga scraps was soaring. Tuberculosis, typhus, and other diseases were spreading, and more suicides were reported. Why, with all this depressing news, was I praying not to be resettled? The Devil you know....

CHAPTER 75

WEDNESDAY, FEBRUARY 9, 1944
    Machines from an evacuated buckle factory in the Jewish camp near Lublin have arrived in the ghetto.

FRIDAY, FEBRUARY 11, 1944
    The work of the commission is dragging on. Last night, too, people were pulled out of hiding.

When I read that large machines were coming from an evacuated Jewish labor camp near Lublin, I thought of Singer. He'd been smuggled into Lodz in a shipment of sewing machines. Pola reported he died fighting the Germans in Warsaw, so I no longer held my breath, hoping that he was concealed in this new shipment. He wasn't coming back. Pola said it, so it must be true.

I was walking home on Zgierska when I sensed someone was following. I turned, expecting Pola. "Henryk, are you following me?"

Neftalin, taller than me by half-a-head, said, "I respect you. Things are bad. The Chairman is wild. He is cutting off the ration cards of anyone who dodges the medical examinations. I pray this works. I'm frightened, my friend. If we fall short, the authorities will act."

"Nobody wants to leave the ghetto because we don't know what awaits us."

"The Chairman has been assured that these men are being sent out for labor, as occurs in the rest of the Reich. They are even being outfitted for manual labor."

"But the terrified ghetto dweller's memory of neighbors being rousted from beds and chased into streets can't be wiped out," I replied.

"Then our fate is sealed," Neftalin said. "The authorities have made it clear they will intervene if the Jewish leadership can't meet their demands."

"So, the Chairman now wants to starve his subjects into submission?"

"What can he do? The authorities are poised to pounce on us with claws sharpened. Do you realize what will happen?" Neftalin raised his coat collar. "The streets will be red with Jewish blood. Nobody will be safe. We must prevent this."

"What can we do?"

Neftalin's eyes narrowed. "Contact the resistance leaders and tell them to assure the people that this is not like earlier resettlements. Let them use their influence to calm things, so the Chairman can maintain control—"

"Do you think I'm Singer? I have no connections with the underground or any other movement. If I did, do you think I'd still be here, a worm waiting for the Germans to crush me into the mud?"

"You're well-acquainted with Pola."

I stared in shock. What was Neftalin implying? "I have no idea where Pola is. You hired her."

Neftalin grimaced. "It doesn't matter. If you can't contact them, the Chairman will just have to tighten the screws."

"Henryk, why doesn't the Chairman try talking to the labor leaders again?"

"He has. He spoke to a gathering of the managers and department heads. He told them that he needs 1,500 men, but they've gone into hiding. He said he cannot predict what will happen if these men do not report. He said, and these are his words, not mine, 'this is a dangerous game,' and accused that some of these fugitives are hiding in the warehouses themselves."

"He accused the managers of being accomplices?"

"Engineer, the Eldest is desperate to avoid the Germans exacting retribution on all of us. You and I will not be safe." Neftalin glanced down the street. "His exact words were, 'families are also in danger. I have no choice.'"

"He will punish families?" My God, what have we done? We've supported this dictator, and now he is threatening families with punishment."

"He has no damn choice! He told them, 'I cannot endanger the entire ghetto for the sake of 1,500 men. This is no time for mercy.'"

"So, why are you telling all this to me?"

"I care about you. You're in peril if you, or anyone you know, is involved in any of this."

"I resent your accusation," I said. "I'm going home."

"Heed my warning. Be careful, my friend. None of us are safe." He handed me a sheet of paper.

"I can't read this in the dark."

"Our new regulations. They will be strictly adhered to."

I squinted at the sheet of rules:

1. All food distribution points, clinics, and public institutions will be closed during working hours.

2. I order those who work at home to remain there and work continuously under all circumstances. Loitering in the street, on whatever purpose is prohibited.

3. I regret that I, a 67-year-old man, must give the ladies an order concerning cosmetics. But I exhort them. Get rid of your makeup, powder, and lipstick!

"Oh, the ladies are going to love that one," I said.

"There's more," Neftalin replied.

4. The factories will remain hermetically sealed from 7:00 a.m. to 5:00 p.m.. No one will be permitted to leave his plant. All persons on the official roster of a plant must, in fact, be there.

5. I order a regular inspection of apartments. A campaign against the filth in apartments!

"How can we clean our apartments when we work all day and are dead-tired when we trudge home? It's impossible—"

"The Chairman insists it must be done to fight the disease that is crippling our population—"

"His factories, you mean."

Neftalin scowled. "The managers didn't understand either. The Chairman warned them again that if the Germans inspected their plants and workers were not fully accounted for, both the workers and the managers would soon understand 'which way the wind is blowing.'"

"I think we're all beginning to understand that," I said.

Neftalin shoved his hands in his pockets. "Remember, my friend, I warned you. The wind has grown rough, but those of us who learn to ride with the wind for just a short time longer will survive. Those who fight the wind..." He turned and began to walk away.

I saw snowflakes falling from the sky and cursed again that they were not allied bombs.

TUESDAY, FEBRUARY 15, 1944
THE 1,500 WORKERS

Only, if the deadline is postponed will he be able to produce the required number of 1,500 by starving them out. The families of men in hiding have had all their rations cards invalidated...

THURSDAY, FEBRUARY 17, 1944

The number of workers to be dispatched was today raised to 1,600.

CHAPTER 76

F RIDAY, FEBRUARY 18, 1944
PROCLAMATION No. 411
RE: Total Curfew on Sunday, February 20, 1944

In connection with the dispatch of 1,600 workers for labor outside the ghetto, a general curfew is hereby ordered... Street passes will be issued only in emergencies and only by me personally.

To forestall the necessity of punitive measures, I, therefore, advise every ghetto inhabitant to obey this order scrupulously. Litzmannstadt-Getto

Ch Rumkowski

The Eldest of the Jews in Litzmannstadt

SUNDAY, FEBRUARY 20, 1944

The sound of trucks rumbling in the street below my apartment sent chills through my body. I flashed back to the night those sounds heralded the clatter of boots on our stairway. My eyes shot to the closet. Regina wasn't here...no reason to hide her.

The familiar sounds of boots. "Open your doors!"

I stood at attention as an Order Service officer almost slammed into my photo identification card.

"I must search your flat," he said, sounding almost apologetic. "You have no one in hiding?" He glanced around the flat and then held the candle up to my face. "I know you. We've talked."

"You're Szmul's uncle? Max?"

He nodded.

"I'm so sorry for your loss. Szmul was a good boy."

Max looked down the stairs. "I must check. You understand."

"Yes. I understand." At least it wasn't the Germans, and I didn't hear gunshots. Jewish police were not allowed weapons other than clubs. I watched silently as Max peered around my apartment. He pulled open the closet and poked at my clothing on the floor. He did it without disturbing my meager property.

"I see there is no one here. We are cordoning off whole blocks. A few men have surrendered due to the cold and hunger, but many are missing. I apologize for the intrusion, but you would not want the Gestapo doing this." He removed his cap. "I will tell you the truth because I know you. The police are as exhausted as everyone else. We know some of the escapees and their families." He wiped his hair with a cloth. "I can't say more. You understand."

"I understand," I said. What Jew would enjoy rounding up other Jews, friends, and neighbors? "These are dreadful times."

Max replaced his hat. "I have a family. If not, I could not do this." He walked toward the doorway. "Szmul said you were kind to him. Thank you. I'll mark your door. You will not be disturbed again, at least not today. Who knows what the future will bring?"

I remained at attention, eyes aimed at the door. Miriam and Regina were taken from me on such a night. Were the police gone? No gunshots. The Chairman was keeping his word. This was his action. He would have to answer for it when he was judged. "Thank God, it won't be me who will have to answer for this," I said.

The curfew. What could I do? Hungry and aching with fever, I headed for my bed. "Am I becoming ill?" The thin mattress beckoned to my tired brain. I was safe. Nobody else was coming. I pulled off my shoes and pants. Folding them onto my chair, I caught the smell of my shirt. I fumbled with the buttons and set it on the chair as if it was being worn by the wood frame. I extinguished the candle.

The bed creaked as I settled under the coverlet. "Damn, I'm cold," I said, turning sideways, my eyes closing. It was still quiet. Maybe, this really was a different kind of resettlement.

I was nearly asleep when I thought I spotted a shadow moving. My imagination? When my blanket lifted, I tensed. The intruder wasn't imaginary. I didn't move, pretending to sleep, but ready to knock away a knife or club if it was a burglar.

"Bennie, don't move." Pola slid her body against me. "Is it okay if I stay here with you?" she asked, her breath warm against my ear. "I saw them search—"

I whirled on her. "You're crazy," I whispered. "Do you know what danger you're in?"

"I need a place to hide. It isn't the Gestapo this time. It's his police."

"So, that's better?" I looked at her face. "They'll turn you over to the Germans if they find you. Me too, as an accessory."

"Do you want me to leave?"

Did I?

"I'm sorry. I'll go." Pola pulled away.

I reached for her arm. "No. Stay. I want you to stay. Not just because it's too dangerous for you out there." I squeezed her hand.

"No?"

"No. I hoped you'd come back."

"I wanted to, more than you know, but I don't want to endanger you."

"I think it's safe. Szmul's uncle searched here. He marked my door. The searchers won't be back."

Pola smiled. "Is the only reason you want me to stay because it's too dangerous out there?"

I met her eyes in the dark. "I wish it was the only reason. But you and I both know that's no longer true." I wrapped my arms around her and pulled her toward me.

"Are you sure?" she asked. "This is more dangerous."

"Yes. It is much more dangerous." I reached for her lips.

CHAPTER 77

MONDAY, FEBRUARY 21, 1944

When I woke the next morning, Pola was gone. I expected it but was still disappointed. Both of us had been exhausted, and I could not shake off that I was married, and a father to a darling daughter. So, like teenagers, we nestled against each other, felt warm and happy to be close, but soon slept. If she had asked me to make love to her, could I? Perhaps. She did not, and I did not. We were content, or so I believed. Was I blind again?

I wanted to ask Pola where she had been since last we were together. I was afraid if I asked, I would lose her. She let out that the labyrinth of passageways that ran through the ghetto was damp and uncomfortably cold but offered a myriad of hiding places. "I thought you went back to Warsaw?" I said.

"Warsaw is empty."

"Empty? That's impossible. How do you move so many people in such a short time? Where did they send them?"

"The Germans have built labor camps throughout Europe."

"Is that where Miriam is? Do you know where my Regina is?" Was that why Pola returned? "Please, tell me? I'm ready for the truth."

"We know very little. The Germans are close-lipped about what happens in these camps."

"What about the truckloads of used clothing? There are children's and baby clothes...." I choked up. I didn't want to know.

312

Pola took my hand. "We fear the worst. I'm sorry to have to tell you."

I sank back onto the bed, my eyes closed. I saw the stacks of baby clothes. "It's impossible," I said, fighting the horrifying visual. "How can it be accomplished?"

"Accomplished? A strange word for…We don't know exactly. Nobody is allowed in the camps, and none of our people have been able to infiltrate. You do know that your Chairman has ordered Neftalin to integrate every child born in 1935 into the workforce?"

I stared at her. "The Chairman thinks it's going to happen again? The Germans want our children?"

"Bennie, we are getting terrible rumors about the fate of our people. That is why men are in hiding for so many days—"

"Fourteen," I interrupted. "It's been fourteen days since this last action."

Pola frowned. "You're still the numbers man? Well, you have a man who lived on nothing but ersatz coffee and another who the Order Service goons found half-frozen in a soup cauldron in a public kitchen. Our leaders are terrified because we suspect what the Germans are doing—"

"The end will come soon," I said. "Won't it?"

"Yes, the world finally realizes what a monster Hitler is. The war is going badly for Germany, but will the end come for the war or for the Lodz ghetto first? Only God knows."

I didn't want to hear more. I anticipated Pola would ask me to leave with her, but she didn't. She whispered, "I know you still love her." She never said Miriam's name. "I still love my husband. That will never change." She clutched me tightly. "I did not intend to love another. I thought one love in life was a blessing that could never be repeated."

I waited for her to say that she loved me. I was ready to admit that I loved her too. She became silent. "You know I must leave."

I didn't reply. Nothing I could say would stop Pola. How could I bind her to the uncertain fate of the ghetto? I believed we were going to survive, but Pola did not. She deserved to live. I had to remain. For Miriam and Regina, I had no choice.

So, we remained together, her arm wrapped around me, each cloaked in our own thoughts. I knew she'd be gone by morning.

In the darkness before dusk, I joined the zombies trudging back to the factories. There was no joy, no laughter. The manhunts had gone on all night.

I saw Rumkowski's light was on as I passed his office. Always working, I thought, admiring how he was trying to come up with a new plan to keep the ghetto going, to save whatever he could.

I thought of stopping in Henryk's office but was afraid my face would reveal the night of happiness I'd enjoyed with Pola, someone he viewed as endangering the Chairman's strategy.

Rosenfeld handed me his entry as I sat down. "It's a nightmare," he said.

I read what he wrote in silence. A man almost starved to death living on ersatz coffee.

My dear, old professor was engrossed at work, his hands on top of the table. They were always cold. Pola had mentioned a fugitive nearly starving, who survived by living on ersatz coffee. I skimmed farther down his entry: "Another man was found in a cauldron, half-frozen." That's odd. Pola had said almost exactly the same words. "Excuse me, Professor, may I see the police reports that you used as the basis for this entry?"

Rosenfeld said, "I wrote this based on other sources."

I read the final paragraphs, fighting my suspicion:

Many others keep changing their hiding places by night, from one district to another, one step ahead of the patrols. Since all parts of the ghetto are interconnected by open courtyards and a labyrinth of passageways, the fugitives can evade the manhunt fairly easily.

Pola had said she was able to move through the "labyrinth of passageways," to hide within Lodz. I stared at Rosenfeld. I'd suspected Jozef as our link to the underground, but the doctor? Our oldest member? I read the last sentences, still not believing this was only a coincidence:

Their families, though, cannot hold out in the long run; and so every day, emaciated men, in a state of nervous exhaustion, are turning themselves into Central Prison. A hunger blockade in the city of hunger. This is hunger to the nth degree.

"Doctor," I said, "How do you know all this without police reports?"

Doctor Rosenfeld's hands were flat on the table, his voice soft. "Dear Engineer, you already know the answer." He looked at me with a slight smile on his lips. "Singer was right all along. I had to do something." He dove back into his work.

I was mulling this over when the door creaked open.

CHAPTER 78

I jumped to my feet and shouted, "Achtung!"

"Relax, it is only Neftalin," Rosenfeld said. "What is it, my friend? You look distressed."

Rosenfeld had never called Henryk his friend. This was a whole new world I was hurled into. All this time, I thought Jozef was the link to the forces combatting the Germans. Could it really be the old man? It was as if he were taking charge, and I had become a mute observer. "You may speak freely," Rosenfeld said.

Neftalin nodded. "You must tell them the Chairman is trying to protect the children by employing as many as possible. He put me in charge." He handed the tersely written order to Rosenfeld. "He fears a repeat of last September's action, but can only protect children old enough to work. Tell them to get the others out."

Not children again? I returned to the night my Regina was taken from me. The parents too stunned to react. The night filled with shivering, shocked parents, unable to grasp their loss. I was one. Would more parents now suffer? I could barely attend to the conversation, grabbing snatches until Rosenfeld replied, "Henryk, our people already know."

Neftalin nodded and said, "The campaign to secure 1,600 workers is not complete. The Chairman is now looking for women to fill the quota. There will be a 'surprise operation' to obtain women. You must pass it on."

Rosenfeld replied, "All the women likely to be considered will go into hiding."

"Then, the hunt for them will begin." Neftalin bit his lips. "Tell them I don't want to do this."

"You have no choice," Rosenfeld said.

"But I hate all this," Neftalin replied.

"It will be over soon." Rosenfeld smiled benignly at Neftalin.

Neftalin looked at me. "Things aren't always as they appear, my friend." He nodded to Rosenfeld and said, "God bless you."

"And you," Rosenfeld replied.

When Neftalin left, I felt Rosenfeld studying me. He said softly, "You have a wife and daughter. You have much to live for. The less you know, the better."

"I can help," I said, still too stunned to fully understand.

"There is little we can do. You helped Pola and David…before he was taken." Rosenfeld gave me a sad smile. "We all agreed, we did not want to risk you."

"Where were you when I was mourning you?" My hand clutched the bowl of his pipe.

"After I was freed by the resistance, I traveled with them to Warsaw. We thought we could spread the uprising to Lodz. Of course, the Germans, with the help of the Chairman, made that impossible."

"Is Singer gone?" I stumbled over the words.

"Our brave friend died as he wished. The small group of Jews held off the Nazis for a month, but then the tanks crushed them with brutal force. For a month, our people in Warsaw were again the heroes of ancient Israel. They were a small, courageous group of Jews fighting with a few handguns, homemade bombs, bare hands, and ingenuity against a far better-equipped army. Warsaw will go down in history as a glorious sacrifice for freedom."

"Why not here, now?" I asked, still uncertain if I was willing to give up my life, my dream of being reunited with Regina and Miriam. With Singer gone, she would need me. I would take care of her, as her parents had entrusted.

Rosenfeld put on his gloves. "You already know the answers. You, an engineer, so logical, know that the Germans sealed us in like sardines in a can. Smuggling weapons was impossible. Infiltrating through Lodz proper was dangerous because it has been totally Germanized. To control us, the Germans starved and enslaved our people, bound us to their factories. They kept us too hungry and weak to fight against them." He smiled sadly. "They had a secret weapon here that did not take hold in Warsaw: hope. They, and the Chairman, gave us hope that if we obeyed and worked for them, we would survive." He looked toward the door. "Unlike Warsaw, we could not muster the support we needed. We had to limit our work to minor acts of sabotage, labor protests, and helping those slated for resettlement, to hide."

"All of which the Chairman crushed," I said, wondering if things would have been different if our leader was as weak as those in other ghettos.

Rosenfeld nodded. "It's a paradox which history will judge. Rumkowski's policies and actions turned us into a high-value asset for the German military, which may save some of us. But it also made it easier for the authorities to control our actions. His police force and policies hampered any concerted effort to mobilize the ghetto."

"I believed in his policies," I said.

"I did too," Rosenfeld said. "Until I learned of the truckloads of used clothing and shoes."

That frightening image. How many times had I seen it? It sent chills through me. "But we received postcards—"

"Forgeries. Perhaps forced. We don't know."

"Why would the Germans do that?" I couldn't imagine German guards forcing Jews to write false postcards to our residents.

"Think about it," Rosenfeld said. "It's in their interest that they keep us calm and working until they use us for whatever purpose they want. With the Chairman's police enforcing their laws, they did not need to send in massive forces as they did in Warsaw."

"A few postcards?"

"Gave our people hope, the Nazi's most potent weapon. Without it, perhaps we could have managed an uprising. We'd have been destroyed as in Warsaw, but that may happen when the Nazis have the manpower they need to take over our factories."

"Meanwhile, we're helping their military."

"Sadly, that is true. At least Lodz has survived as the last Jewish bastion in Poland, perhaps in Europe."

I was unable to take all this in. "Tell me, how do you think our Chairman will be judged?"

Rosenfeld smiled. "That's what this Chronicle is all about. I don't know. I suppose history will be the ultimate judge of all our actions. I don't know how much Rumkowski knew and when he knew it. The future will judge that too."

"And that depends on who wins this war," I said.

Rosenfeld nodded. "God help us if the Germans don't lose soon."

The door opened, and Jozef entered. "They're hunting women now," he announced.

Rosenfeld feigned a surprised expression.

I pretended I was surprised too. I realized Rosenfeld did not want Jozef to know of his clandestine work. The war had proven once again that you couldn't trust anyone.

CHAPTER 79

THURSDAY, FEBRUARY 24, 1944

The ghetto was electric with fear. Night after night, the Order Service was in action, hunting both men and women. Neftalin had been put in charge of checking the family situations of the captured women, but the Gestapo was officially in charge. Biebow was summoned to Berlin. His relationship with the Chairman was stormy before this trip, generating more fear. Rumors were that his return had been delayed by an automobile accident. "The devil you know is better than the devil you don't," so I hoped he would return. God knows what monster might replace him.

Walking to work, I showed my official pass with its photo of my face to the Order Service guards scavenging the crowd for people on their resettlement lists. Each time I held up my pass, I feared they would take me anyway.

Rosenfeld was waiting for me in our chamber. "It's happened. The Chairman has ordered that children born in 1935 are to be employed. The whole ghetto is alive with fear of new separations. The Chairman told Dr. Bradfisch of the Gestapo that this will involve 5,000 children."

"5,000 born in 1935? How is that possible?"

"Apparently, our brave leader is trying to escalate the number so he can include younger children as well. There are less than 2,000 children left in the ghetto. Our population growth can't account for 3,000 more but he is trying—"

"So, the Chairman is now playing the numbers game with the Germans," I said.

"Neftalin says the Chairman plans to do the same with any younger children who are physically fit." Rosenfeld looked to the door. "Jozef is our weak link. He will be easy for interrogators to break. That is why he has been excluded—"

As if he heard, Jozef charged through the door. "How can you sleep at night? The police are everywhere, even dragging women from their beds. The screams are shattering my nerves. I can't stand much more."

Rosenfeld shot me a look that said, "See what I mean?"

I studied Jozef visibly trembling and agreed the man was falling to pieces.

The door opened, and Neftalin entered. "Happy birthday, Engineer," he said and handed me what looked like a cake. "Did you think we forgot?"

"I forgot," I said, thinking that what I wanted for my birthday, a visit from Pola, was impossible. "How did you get a cake?" I asked, knowing the Germans had removed all 'special allocations.' We're all starving."

Neftalin laughed. "I asked a friend. Can you imagine how many hours it took for her to pick over potato peels for your birthday cake?"

So, we gorged ourselves on ersatz coffee and a birthday cake made of 'select' potato peels. For a few minutes, we were not co-workers enslaved in a stifling room, but friends celebrating my special day. I was 35 years old when the Germans and Poles chased Miriam and me into this barbed wire corral for Jews. Now, I was 39, an old man clinging to life for but one purpose: my young wife's and my daughter's return.

I thought about that, and Pola, as I made my way back to the flat I hated. In the dim light of a candle, I sat in my chair, hoping the door would open, and I'd see...Regina. Miriam? Pola?

I rose from my chair. I pulled open the closet. In the corner lay a crumpled blanket. It had covered my child that night. "Play 'hide-and-seek,'" I'd said. Regina was so good at our game. I picked up the ratty clump and walked back to my chair. The blanket clutched to my heart, I slept.

TUESDAY, FEBRUARY 29, 1944

The operation still looms over the ghetto like a thundercloud. The rain of deliverance will not fall. The ghetto is buzzing with all sorts of rumors...

CHAPTER 80

TUESDAY, FEBRUARY 29, 1944
THE CHAIRMAN'S APARTMENT
As previously reported the Chairman will have to vacate his apartment at 63 Lagiewnicka Street by March 15, 1944...

WEDNESDAY, MARCH 1, 1944
NEWS OF THE DAY: THE 1,600 WORKERS (1,610)
The quota of workers to be dispatched was raised by ten yesterday...The situation has basically not changed.

SATURDAY, MARCH 4, 1944

"Is this a game they're playing with us?" Jozef shouted. "Wednesday, they wanted ten more bodies. Yesterday, they were hungry for another one hundred! They're cannibals, ravenous for more Jewish meat."

"If they were cannibals, they would want to fatten us up, not starve us until we are skin and bones," I said, wondering where Rosenfeld was.

There was a knock at the door, so I didn't shout my "Achtung." It was Neftalin.

"I remembered to knock," he said, glancing around. "Rosenfeld?"

I shrugged. "Any news on the resettlement?"

Neftalin slammed his hat on the table. "We thought the Chairman had managed to reduce the number. He was shocked when instead, the quota was increased. It is as if they are punishing us all for our people who are

323

dodging the action. I tell you it's damn frustrating."

"Does anyone know where they are being sent?" Jozef asked.

"No, but we've been assured that conditions will be far better than they are here."

Jozef closed his eyes. "I'm so tired, hungry, and cold."

"Neftalin, is it true two doctors died?" I asked.

"Sadly, yes. Doctors can also get typhus and tuberculosis, especially now that everyone is on the same starvation diet."

"Typhus and tuberculosis," Jozef repeated. "Can matters get worse?"

Neftalin shot him a concerned look and handed me a sheet of paper. "This is Proclamation No. 414. It is self-explanatory."

I read the proclamation signed by Rumkowski. The first word sent a chill through my being: "Warning!"

WARNING!

Since various persons have still not reported to Central Prison despite my repeated warnings, I am making a final appeal to them to report without fail to Central Prison immediately after the posting of this proclamation.

Those still in hiding are wrong in believing that the cancellation of ration cards will be rescinded after the transport of workers has been dispatched.

I must expressly point out that this assumption is incorrect, and that after the labor transport has left, the persons in question will have to report to Central Prison along with their entire families.

When applying at Central Prison for reinstatement of ration cards, those who had previously been in hiding will be arrested and detained there; they will be forced to reveal where they have been concealed, who aided them in concealment, and who supported them with any sort of food during this period—so that those people too can be called to account. Ration cards will not be reinstated before this is done.

Those who are still in hiding but who turn themselves in at Central Prison without delay after the posting of this proclamation will be exempted, along with their families, from the measures described above.

Ch Rumkowski

The Eldest of the Jews in Litzmannstadt

Jozef sagged into his chair. "I was prepared to volunteer until this ultimatum by our leader. Why must he resort to such harsh measures if there is no danger at the end of this transport? Oh, God, it only gets worse." He began to sob.

I placed my hand on his shoulder. "That is why we must do what we can to remain here. We can only speculate as to what is at the other end of the train ride."

Neftalin picked up his hat, straightening the brim.

I looked at him. "It is obvious the Chairman is desperate, and even more draconian measures may follow."

Neftalin nodded. "The first group of workers, at 5:30 this morning, were marched to Radogoszcz Station where freight cars waited—"

"Freight cars?" Jozef asked.

Neftalin must have sensed Jozef's fear. "Unlike previous resettlements, an official from the company requiring these workers assured the Eldest of the Jews that our people would be sent to comfortable quarters and receive five days of rest before they were put to work in textile or metal factories. He also assured us that food would be better and that as long as they did decent work, they would have nothing to complain about."

"And you believe this?"

"To be honest, I don't know to what extent this man was in a position to make such a promise. He says the workers will live in a camp and—"

There was a knock on the door.

Rosenfeld entered. He nodded to Neftalin. "I apologize for the delay. I was talking to an Order Service officer." He looked at Jozef.

I suspected Rosenfeld was trying not to reveal too much in front of our co-worker who he called our 'weak link.'

Rosenfeld undid his coat. "This officer just returned from the station."

"Where the workers were taken?" Jozef asked, a tremble in his voice.

"He says everything went smoothly. No one was beaten or roughly treated. The Order Service handled the entire affair."

Neftalin smiled, obviously relieved. "That should ease our fugitives' minds, so they turn themselves in and make things easier for the rest of us."

Rosenfeld glanced at me.

Neftalin walked to the door. "The end is in sight."

"Amen," I said, noting Jozef had closed his eyes and was asleep. I did not have the heart to wake him.

Rosenfeld slid himself into Pola's chair. "All is not as it seems," he said softly.

Jozef snorted and woke up, eyes wild. "I had a terrible nightmare."

I laughed. "What could be worse than what we are suffering now?"

Rosenfeld didn't laugh.

CHAPTER 81

TUESDAY, MARCH 7, 1944

The hunt for the fugitives continued, but now women were mainly taken. We didn't have enough men to fill the quota. Our nights were shattered by the hunters, but the mark on my door kept me safe. I'd thank Szmul's uncle for that. If I ever saw him again.

Rosenfeld was reading silently when he exclaimed, "Good! They got that bastard!"

I'd never seen the old professor so riled up before.

Rosenfeld snarled, "They got Mosze Boms at last."

"Who?"

"The rat. We've been on his trail forever. He was one of the vilest creatures here. He was a German Police informant. He denounced countless Jews in the ghetto—"

"He informed on his fellow Jews?"

"Not anymore. During the search for fugitives, the Order Service visited his apartment. Boms flaunted his high-level connections in the Kripo, but was taken anyway." Rosenfeld winked at me. "When the Kripo learned their rat was taken, they declined to intercede. It would have meant admitting to relying upon a Jewish spy."

"God forbid," I interjected.

Rosenfeld nodded. "Instead, the Kripo left his fate to the discretion of the Eldest. So, he and his entire family were taken, as were any others found in the building."

"So, they were all put on the transport? I don't like collective punishment, but in the case of this rat, it seems appropriate."

"The family is still in prison. Boms tried to pull strings to avoid being deported, but justice, for once, has been served."

"Being shipped to a labor camp from this hellhole is justice?" I asked.

"Oh, no. Before Boms left, word spread. It is hardly surprising that some could not pass up a chance to slap and kick this rat with their pent-up fury."

"They beat him up?"

"Not only did they beat him, but they refused to allow him into their cars. He was so desperate to avoid being shipped out with his fellow Jews that he opened an artery. In the end, this rat had to be stowed in the baggage car. I hope he gets what he deserves. Thus to all traitors."

This was definitely a different Rosenfeld. I settled back into my work. I was reading a report about a new kind of commerce in the ghetto. I called it "Traffic in Human Flesh." Apparently, although many were terrified of what lay at the end of the transports, some starving souls were offering to take the place of others for a fee. "Professor," I said, surprised by this news, "have you heard of this business where some of our people pay others to replace them on the transports?"

Rosenfeld looked up. "Desperate people do desperate things. I've told you this many times."

"But this is immoral. It's wrong."

"Engineer, you are too logical. When people are starving, they will sell their souls into bondage, even to die for the right compensation. Why pray for tomorrow if you can have a good meal today?"

"It says that some are paid two loaves of bread and one kilogram of sugar."

"I suppose these poor souls reason that conditions can't be worse on the outside, and at least now they can fill up on bread for a few days."

I asked him to write a report about this new type of barter. Rosenfeld's final sentences were haunting: "When terror, hunger, and misery exceed all bounds, two loaves of bread and one kilogram of sugar can buy a human life." As I reread it, I had to admire again his eloquence, the power to make our horror almost poetic with his words. I was about to read it aloud for

Jozef when I recalled his chair was empty. "Have you heard anything about Jozef?" I asked.

Rosenfeld shook his head.

I pulled out another report from the Order Service. It was from Monday, March 6, describing another night where men, and now women, 350 persons in all, most unmarried, were forced from their lodgings. Neftalin said the Chairman was making an effort to reduce the pain by having the commission designate only younger singles whose departure "will not inflict emotional and material hardship on families." And, of course, selecting no one whose disappearance would impede the productivity of his factories.

Jozef's chair was still empty. Would his disappearance impair productivity? Did any of us in this room really matter to the Germans? If anyone was guilty of this traffic in human flesh, it was the Nazis who valued us only for as long as it fed their lust for death and power.

Rosenfeld leaned toward me and said, "He was complaining about hunger and cold."

"God, no."

Rosenfeld's eyes were gentle. "A story reached me the other day. A replacement was given four loaves of bread, a kilogram of sugar, and a half kilogram of margarine in exchange for taking someone else's place in the resettlement. The replacement, after gorging on the food, said he wasn't this well-off in years. He was eager to go to a different job with better conditions. So what can go wrong?"

"I have no idea," I said.

Rosenfeld chuckled. "Well, the next day, the replacement was summoned for his interview. An official says, 'You work on the excrement removal crew. You can't leave. You're essential to the survival of the ghetto.' In other words, my good friend, this worker was saved from an uncertain future by shoveling shit."

I burst into laughter.

Rosenfeld laughed as well.

When we both sobered, I remarked, "You're right. We can't survive without excrement removers and gravediggers."

"Chroniclers? Sadly, my friend, only the Chairman, in his wisdom, knows why he needs us," Rosenfeld said.

"He said for the future." I wondered if any of us would have a future. If this war didn't end soon, the freezing cold and starvation would do Hitler's work for him. Maybe that was the Nazi plan all along?

FRIDAY, MARCH 10, 1944

Early this morning, the second group of 850 workers left here to perform manual labor outside the ghetto. Their destination remains unknown.

CHAPTER 82

TUESDAY, MARCH 28, 1944

I had barely enough strength to walk from my home to our office. People were dying from hunger and disease. We were surviving on a diet of soup, watery, with potato peels. If lucky, we had ersatz coffee. God knows what that was made of. A favorite joke: Two boys are chatting. Boy 1 asks, "Did you eat your lunch today?" Boy 2 replies, "No, I've only eaten my coffee." Isn't that funny? Hunger made us laugh at such nonsense because otherwise, we'd cry.

Jozef hadn't returned. I was too exhausted to traipse over to the flat he shared with four others to see what was keeping him home. I was beyond caring about anyone vanishing from the ghetto, but then news broke that even I couldn't ignore.

Neftalin summoned me to his office. I was ready to accept that it was my turn to leave. I had a plan, a place where I might hide. "Henryk, you look worried."

"This is a blueprint the Chairman just received from the authorities." He spread it out on his desk, sweeping everything to one side. "The Chairman has been ordered to tear down a section of the ghetto from Drewnowska to Podrzeczna Streets."

"Tear it down?" I studied the map.

Neftalin pointed to a large cluster of black rectangles and squares. "There are rows of buildings in the best condition here, in which a large number of our doctors, and most important officials, live with their families."

I hadn't realized such distinctions in housing existed. Miriam had argued this, but I didn't believe it. "There are enough apartments for at least a few thousand families here."

"You are the numbers man. I've been assigned to find apartments for 2,000 people who lived here. They will take this news very hard, especially when they see where they will now live."

I felt little sympathy for this privileged class. I'd been blind again.

Neftalin was still talking, "The project is going to seal this area off from the ghetto. The Germans estimate it will take 500 of our workers to demolish these buildings." He looked at me. "What do you think? Is this an accurate assessment?"

I leaned closer to the blueprint. "My eyes are not what they used to be. I'm unable to get new eyeglasses."

"We all make do somehow." Neftalin held up a tattered sleeve of his once immaculate jacket. "My father's favorite expression, 'Necessity is the mother of invention.' I miss him saying that. It's never been truer."

I was almost nose to map, hardly listening. "Henryk, this will chop a major portion of irreplaceable housing from the ghetto."

"Goddammit! I know that! Unfortunately, we can't stop it! The Chairman fought with Biebow." Neftalin calmed down. "Can this be done with fewer than 500 men? That is what the Chairman is asking you."

"It has been a long time since I studied such plans—"

"Dammit, Engineer, I need an answer now! The Germans insist we use our best workers on this monstrous task. We're struggling to fill their orders now. You know what will happen if we fail."

I straightened up. "Henryk, you do understand what this new project portends?"

"Of course. I'm no fool. The Chairman feels we need only a little more time before the war ends."

"God! How many times have I heard this, and the war hasn't ended yet."

"I know. I know." Neftalin looked hard at me. "Do you want to supervise this project?"

Was he kidding? Didn't he understand the risk? "No. I am no longer the engineer I was." I did not want to face German bosses every day. I was spent, barely hanging on. "My advice, let the authorities run with this. It's a huge undertaking."

"It must not be interfered with," Neftalin said. "The authorities have sent a large commission, led by Gestapo chief, Bradfisch. He informed the Chairman that any suspected sabotage would be met with unprecedented measures."

"I'm sure the Chairman will make that clear to everyone."

"He already has charged his police force with strict orders." Neftalin approached. "I hoped you would help us meet the German timeline on this." He sighed. "There are times I believe even the Chairman, God bless him, wishes he had not accepted this office." He walked to the door. "Thank you for your unstinting support. It has been noted."

Unstinting support? I didn't know anymore if I could support all of the Chairman's actions. I still didn't see any options. I left the office wondering if Neftalin knew that I would pass this alarming new information to Rosenfeld. Was that his ulterior motive in sending for me? Was I now a pawn in this life-and-death game they were playing?

CHAPTER 83

SATURDAY, APRIL 22, 1944

I was walking home lost in thought when a terrible stench reached my nostrils. "Where is that smell coming from?" When I turned the corner, the moon was over the horizon, and what appeared to be a pack of wolves was silhouetted scurrying across a small field. But they weren't wolves, nor rats. What were they?

The vampiric scene lured me closer. I was startled that the creatures mauling the ground was a swarm of children. Some were armed with makeshift spades and sticks. Others were digging with fingernails pulling voraciously into the sandy earth. "What's going on? "What are you doing?"

The boy closest to me, dirt-encrusted hands and face, teeth missing, replied, "What do you care?" He glared at me, a wild animal.

Another boy, a bit younger, scooped something into a bag.

"What did you find?" I asked, trying to sound friendly.

"It's mine. You can't have it," the urchin replied, clutching the bag.

"I don't want it. Have you found some treasure? Is that what you boys are doing here?" The stench was overwhelming, so only a stray piece of jewelry, a jewel or coin, would have justified digging into what smelled like a garbage dump.

"You won't take it from me?" The boy clutched the bag tighter.

"He found something," someone hissed.

The boys looked over, but perhaps seeing an adult, they kept their distance. Some resumed their digging. Others were all eyes, vicious, hungry

334

eyes.

I bent lower. "Now, tell me, boy, what did you find?"

The boy looked uncertain and then, barely moving it past the lip of the bag, held up a shriveled piece of potato. Just as quickly as he'd raised it, he put it back in the bottom of the bag as if it were a precious treasure.

"Are they all looking for food?" I asked, concluding they were digging up a mound of garbage that had been covered over by sand to keep the noxious odor in check.

The boy nodded and went back to digging, a foot clamped down on his bag.

The mix of odors they unleashed from the mound, and the sight of what once were children now transformed into some form of mutant animals, drove me away. My hunger made their savage tearing up of the trash mound understandable, but these were children. I heard Miriam whisper, "You see, Bennie, I was right. How can we bring children into a world such as this?" Tears in my eyes, I pulled myself the short distance to our apartment, the smell of the rotting garbage still with me, the sight of the small wolves etched in my brain.

The next day, I wrote of stumbling upon this scene that made me grateful Regina was not here. I read my entry to Rosenfeld:

"...anything edible in the garbage, anything consigned to the dump was truly unfit for consumption. And there it was covered with fetid rubbish, excrement, and sweepings; no one would ever have imagined that people would grub in this abyss of misery, undaunted by the obnoxious stench, the ghastly pestilence. And yet every tiny remnant is extracted with the fingers, carefully checked, and collected in a little sack or bowl.

This is not simply hunger; this is the frenzy of degenerate animals. This is unbridled madness, a shame and a disgrace. This must not be, this cannot be."

Rosenfeld let out a deep sigh. "I know the area. It was the Chairman himself who ordered it covered with sand to quell resident complaints about the toxic odors. And you say boys have discovered this mound of buried garbage?"

"I can't get over the sight of so many children digging into that stinking pile like rabid dogs. Their bones were visible, eyes satanic. I felt frightened. I'm glad Regina is safe with Miriam, far from here."

Rosenfeld stared at me. "Of course, she is safe." He nodded slowly and picked up his pen. "I'm adding a sentence: 'Perhaps someone from the Sanitation Section will pass this way, hold his handkerchief to his nose for a moment, then bring some chlorinated lime there and drive these degenerates away — to save them, at least, from death by poisoning.'"

"Do you think the Chairman will see this?" I asked.

"I wonder if he still reads our entries. He must notice they have changed, not as positive as they were." Rosenfeld smiled. "Even you have changed your perspective."

"I expect the Eldest to come charging in here at any time, hair flying, eyes blazing, harsh voice screaming at our disloyalty." I laughed. "Singer would be proud of us."

"I don't know if we can ever come far enough for our friend," Rosenfeld said. "He was one of a kind." He gazed at his empty pipe, now merely a prop. "I miss him terribly."

"I do too." I wondered how much Rosenfeld knew about Singer and Miriam. I understood how in a time of terror and deprivation more intense than any in history, my young wife would clutch to a kindred soul, grasp at what little joy was available. I could not be that for her. Rosenfeld was right. I had changed. To save my wife and child, I would claw the hard earth with broken fingers for buried scraps of fetid garbage. I would kill.

CHAPTER 84

TUESDAY, MAY 2, 1944

Again, the ghetto is in a state of nervous anxiety. A notice has been posted on the bridge near the Order Service post: "Wanted: volunteers for labor ..."

I thought Rosenfeld would be surprised by the notice I'd seen on my way to work. Instead, he leaned toward me and said in his calm way, "The Order Service collected people with criminal records and brought them to Central Prison."

"How many?" I asked.

Rosenfeld chuckled. "Perhaps, in one way, you have not changed. Eighty or so. What is most disturbing is that the Chairman initiated this roundup without prior notification of last night's actions. It's strange because the news from outside the ghetto has been encouraging, and hunger and disease here are taking a terrible toll."

"So why do you feel Rumkowski ordered these brutal actions?"

"That is the question. Rumors are that not all is as the Germans would like us to believe in the labor camps. Some claim that the smoke from the factory chimneys has an odd odor." Rosenfeld removed his glasses and rubbed the dents on either side of his aquiline nose. "It is far-fetched, but there are those who believe the smokestacks are burning human flesh."

I almost burst out laughing, but the horror of what he implied, within the context of all the Germans had unleashed upon us, made even such a horrific nightmare plausible. "It is possible they are incinerating those who die of disease to stop the contagion. That would be logical."

"Yes, that would be one explanation."

One explanation. The other was too inhuman to contemplate. "Not even Hitler, this Satan, who hates Jews and other 'undesirables' with such fury could come up with a method to kill so many people for his chimneys to spew such smoke." I laughed uneasily. "Do you know of such a means?"

Rosenfeld replaced his glasses. He transformed from the cunning spy to the old professor again. "There is some talk of the Nazis working on a weapon of mass destruction, a gas—"

"Achtung!" I shouted and grabbed Rosenfeld's sleeve to help him stand. "Oh, damn."

"I forgot to knock," Neftalin said. "There is trouble in the Metal and Carpenter departments. Agitators are spreading propaganda."

I thought of Pola, who had talked of fomenting unrest to inhibit work for the Nazis. I wondered what Rosenfeld knew of this.

Neftalin's eyes were fixed on me as he described how May 1st was the perfect day for labor unrest. "We will have to see whether there is solidarity among the workshops. The consequences will be quite unpleasant." A hawkish smile appeared on his face. "Anyone who knows the Chairman is confident he can cope with the situation."

After Neftalin delivered his message, I turned to Rosenfeld and said, "So, what do you think?"

The professor smiled at me and said softly, "Anyone who knows the Chairman knows he can cope with the situation."

SATURDAY, MAY 6, 1944

Managers of several departments reported that increasing numbers of their workers were refusing to eat the soups provided for lunch.

"It's quite ingenious," Sam Walfish, a manager said, as I stood with him at the door of the Leather/Saddlery plant, the smell of leather quite pungent. "The agitators convinced the young workers they could take this action without fear of punishment because it does not impact production. They were wrong, of course. I took firm action. I disciplined several boys and dismissed those I considered the ring leaders."

I studied the workers toiling away at their stations. "They look young," I said.

Walfish sneered. "They are naive. This won't last. A few beatings with a stick, a few dismissals, and all will be back to normal."

"You beat them?"

Walfish looked at me with dismay. "If we don't act, the Chairman has made it very clear the Germans will."

I took another look at the boys beating leather, sewing at machines, and was glad to be able to walk away.

I was writing my entry when Neftalin knocked on our door. "Those fools!"

I was startled by his anger. "Who?"

Rosenfeld was still at lunch, or so I thought.

Neftalin roared, "You have a bunch of boys who are causing no real harm. So, they refuse to eat soup. Who cares? The Chairman didn't respond because he knew that would last one day, maybe two. Boys get hungry, they eat. Right?"

I nodded.

"So, what does the manager do? The tyrant dismisses some of his boys. But these are not old men who are fearful of more dismissals. The beatings, which the Chairman forbade, and the dismissals, for not eating soup, enraged the other workers. Now, like a fire, the strike spreads, and even the promise to bring the dismissed workers back is not stopping it."

"Is the Chairman stepping in?" I asked.

"Rumkowski is far too smart. He does not want to inflame things. He is trying not to apply severe measures, but one hopes that these demonstrations cease before they attract the attention of the authorities. That is the name of the game. Biebow and the Chairman, as you may know, are at odds, and the vulture is waiting to swoop down on us."

"The beast will find very little meat on our bones," I said, breaking into a hoarse cough.

"Are you ill?" Neftalin asked. "Nearly everyone is sick." He coughed into his hand. "The ghetto is a petri dish. How bacteria can grow without food is beyond me."

"The germs feed on us. Hungry, malnourished, we haven't the strength to fight them off."

"I will make you laugh," Neftalin said. "The gravediggers are demanding a third bowl of soup each day. Without it, they claim they are incapable of handling their 'flourishing business.' Is that not funny?"

I paid attention when he said 'gravediggers.' "Will the Chairman give them their soup?"

"What choice does he have? As the Eldest said, 'Without this soup, the living cannot bury the ghetto's dead.' All hell will break loose without grave workers."

After Neftalin left, I sat in my chair. Was it time to execute my plan? I had theorized long ago the gravediggers and sanitation workers would be among the last to be taken from our paradise. Even the Germans were afraid of the diseases that would attack them if these essential workers were removed. I looked at my hands, free of blisters. Could I become a gravedigger to remain in the ghetto?

CHAPTER 85

M ONDAY, MAY 15, 1944

The morning began badly. Neftalin asked me to go to the Metal Plant, where the workers had again gone on strike against the soup that didn't 'suit them.' "Do they imagine that anyone else can be satisfied with this soup?" I wasn't.

Neftalin frowned. "The Chairman decided he has no choice but to take things into his own hands. He is on his way there now. I am working on demands from the last commission, so you will go as Head of the Archives and report back to me."

I was not thrilled about the danger of the workers exploding in their frustration, but had to obey my superior. I saw the Chairman's coach at the factory entrance and hurried inside. He was already addressing the workers. He sounded calm but firm. "These soup strikes are senseless; I can't put any more than I have into the soup. So who is this demonstration against? Against me? I'm just a servant of the authorities; I have to bow my head and do as I'm told."

Was he really just a servant for the Germans? I recalled the first time I saw his portrait hanging over the desk in his office. It was larger than life, eyes imperiously staring at something mere mortals could not see. He did not look like anyone's servant, but an emperor surveying all he owned. Now, he looked older, more bent, cheeks hollow, complexion gray, but in tone and eye, he did not look like a servant, nor a victim. He still had that authoritative presence that commanded the stage.

Rumkowski lowered his voice. "No strike of yours can force me to make thicker soup, for I have nothing to thicken it with. Do you intend to strike against the Ghetto Administration?" He shook his head, still thick with wild white hair. "Do you believe that the authorities will be intimidated by you? The Jewish authorities are doing everything that can be done. I do what I can, wherever possible. I hope that the situation will improve soon."

Did he really believe things would improve, or was this more showmanship, snake oil salesman propaganda? It sounded so convincing. I wanted to trust him. I had to trust him.

Without waiting for questions, the Chairman turned to the manager. "Give me four of the ringleaders."

Walfish pointed out four adolescents.

The boys, caps in hand, were herded toward the chairman by an Order Service guard. "Come with me," Rumkowski said and left the room, the boys casting uncertain looks at all those fortunate enough to be left behind.

I soon heard the sound of soup being slurped. The strike was broken, at least for now.

I walked outside.

The boys were cowering in front of the Chairman and the Order Service officer.

The Chairman surveyed the alleged ringleaders with grandfatherly eyes. "I know this is the fault of agitators, but you chose to show your heroism in defiance of the common good of the ghetto." He addressed the officer. "Take them to the demolition site. They will work there from now on."

The boys looked shocked. One dared speak up, "Sir, we are metalworkers."

The Chairman turned his back on the boys, and his driver helped him into the coach. Covering up with a thick blanket, his eyes spotted me.

I felt my blood chill under his gaze but worked to show no fear.

The Chairman pulled a cigarette from a silver box, and the driver quickly lit it with a match. The small flame illuminated the Eldest of the Jew's face.

My God, he does look like the devil. Despite my effort, I felt as if my legs were going to fold under me. I bowed my head as his coach drove slowly by.

When I turned back, the boys were being marched away from the plant. There was a stick in the policeman's hand. Three of the boys walked with eyes defiant. The last had his head bent to the ground and was sobbing.

I had to get home before the curfew. I walked quickly.

There was a rumbling noise.

Alarmed it might be Germans, I moved to the side, raised my hand to salute.

A pair of automobiles raced by.

Not far away, I saw an Order Service detail marching a ragged line of our people toward Central Prison.

A chill shot through me. Another resettlement. I had to bypass the line or risk being caught up. Where could I go?

The cars had the intersection blocked.

I heard another vehicle approaching.

Panic set in.

Gestapo officers stood by the black cars.

I heard shouting. *What the hell is going on?*

The head of the Order Service was being berated by Biebow.

I wanted to hear what was being said. I stepped closer.

"Bennie. Here."

"Pola?"

"Get out of here," Pola hissed.

I followed quickly as Pola ducked into a nearby door. "What are you doing here?" I pulled her toward me, finding her lips.

Pola broke away. "Are you crazy? This morning, Kligier, the head of the Order Service, was ordered to bring 50 men in for manual labor. You were walking into it."

"The Chairman didn't announce it," I said, trying to see her in the dark.

"Rumkowski's ill. Kligier took this on himself. He sent a squad to surround the demolition site and had the workers line up. The men selected were to be put aboard a tram. Many escaped. Ghetto residents can smell a rat."

I suspected they had help but kept my thoughts to myself. "So, that is why the cars and soldiers are racing around?"

"Only three made it to the train station. The roundup had to begin again." Pola made a wry face. "All we can do is delay the inevitable. After the others escaped, the rest of the quota was made up of workers forcibly removed from another workshop." She shrugged her shoulders. "We can't predict their moves, and there are too few of us—"

I took Pola's hand. "You've done more than enough."

She pulled her hand free. "I must do more. What happened at the Metal Shop?"

"You know about that?"

"We haven't heard from our boy there."

"The Chairman sent four alleged ringleaders to work at the demolition site with the Germans."

"Damn him."

I didn't argue. I didn't want to spend our few minutes together debating the policies of the Eldest of the Jews. "Pola, it is so dangerous what you are doing." I forced myself to speak what was in my heart, "The war must be nearly over. You...we...we could have a good life together." I put both her hands in mine. I waited for her to ask me about Miriam, but she remained silent. "I think... I love you. I miss you when you're not with me."

"I miss you, too."

My heart was pounding. "I want us to have a life together. It is possible." I hesitated. What I was about to say would be very difficult. "When Miriam returns...I will tell her. She will understand." How could she not after falling in love with Singer? She never truly loved me. I was far too old for her, a different generation. I was her protector. I didn't know what else to say. "Please, Pola? We deserve to be happy."

"Bennie, dear Bennie. The ghetto is doomed. Now, after five years of war, just before the end, Jews are being deported allegedly for labor outside the ghetto. Deported? Dragged off somewhere. God knows where—"

I interrupted, "You said it. The war is nearly over."

"The captives weren't even permitted to say goodbye to their families —

wife, children, parents." She reached for my face with her hands and kissed me. "Don't tempt me. You must live for your Miriam and Regina. They will need you when they return."

I trembled. "You always tell the truth."

"I'm not a propagandist, a writer, like you." She laughed and then kissed my lips again. "If I can, I will try and come to you when it is safe."

"Not tonight?"

"Is that what you want?"

"More than anything."

Pola glanced through the door. "It is a moonless night." She pulled me into the street. "At least if I walk you home, I won't have to worry about you walking into a roundup."

TUESDAY, MAY 23, 1944

NEWS OF THE DAY: LABOR OUTSIDE THE GHETTO

Today, again, there have been volunteers to perform manual labor outside the ghetto. It is reported that eighty persons are to depart on May 30, and that the required number has been raised to a total of one hundred forty...

CHAPTER 86

WEDNESDAY, MAY 24, 1944

If someone feels ill and wishes to stay home from the workshop, he needs certification of his illness from a physician. The physician fills out a certificate excusing him from work for a specific number of days. This certificate also entitles the worker to continue receiving the workshop soup. And since soup is his basic nourishment, the physician's excuse is a question of "to be or not to be" for the patient.

...nothing can be done. Always the same story in the ghetto. One family after another is destroyed. Son, father, mother, sister. Always the same story...

TUESDAY, MAY 30, 1944

LABOR OUTSIDE THE GHETTO

At 8:30 A.M. today, another group of sixty people was sent from Balut Market to perform manual labor outside the ghetto...This seems not to involve industrial, but agricultural manpower, which is now required on small farms for the planting season. The workers must be in the immediate vicinity...Since there have not been any reports, nothing definite can be said about this matter.

"Doctor, your entries of late sound bitter. I don't blame you, not after all we've been through, but you're walking dangerously close—"

"A whole family was destroyed, Engineer. Unlike you, I feel emotion—"

"I feel things. I share your anger."

"Do you?"

I felt like screaming at him, but this was Rosenfeld. "My concern is that

346

the Chairman is being driven to the wall by the strikers, the Nazis, especially Biebow. The war is almost over. Why risk the Chairman's displeasure now?"

Rosenfeld laughed and then burst into a body-wracking fit of coughing. "I will never see my Rosalie again." He held up his handkerchief.

I trembled at the stains…blood red. "I'm sorry."

"You have nothing to be sorry for." Rosenfeld's fingers gripped the rim of the table. "I can barely lift myself from a chair."

"You need only to hold on a little longer." I could not be alone with the burden of these endless entries. "Doctor, please?"

He looked at the door and lowered himself back onto the chair. "My poor friend, I have tuberculosis. It is everywhere in our ghetto. We are incapable of containing it when the ill know if they do not appear for work, they will be shipped out. At any rate, it is too late for me. I am ready to leave."

"No. We hear the bombs. They are close."

"The numbers man clings to illogical hope?" He smiled. "Love can fool us into euphoria. The ghetto is doomed. Every day, more poor souls are being deported."

"Sent for manual labor," I corrected.

"That is what they say."

"Chief Muller of the Gestapo said to the Chairman, Neftalin told me, that upon completion of this seasonal work, the workers will return to the ghetto."

"The Germans are not to be trusted," Rosenfeld said. "You know this."

"Which is why you must not volunteer," I said.

Rosenfeld burst into laughter and then coughed. "Volunteer? That is a funny one. But, for your sake, I will stay until I am 'volunteered.' Will that make you happy?"

I knew to keep my friend alive, I was giving up on my survival plan. The cemetery where I planned to hide until the war's end would have to wait. I prayed the war would be over before tuberculosis, the scourge of the ghetto, killed him. The sound of bombs exploding, barely audible in our ghetto, sounded like God coughing.

CHAPTER 87

T UESDAY, JUNE 6, 1944

I could tell something had happened. Pola had warned me to stay away from the factories where hundreds of young workers were refusing to eat their soup, the only food now available in the ghetto. I did not ask her how she knew, nor if she was involved in orchestrating these disruptions. I was grateful to have her with me if only for a few hours. Was it love? Whatever it was, we clung to each other because we understood it might be for the last few minutes.

"Engineer, are you listening?"

"Yes, Henryk, you were saying the Chairman appeared at the Metal Workshop, and the strike ended immediately."

Neftalin aimed his eyes at Rosenfeld as if measuring him. "Word spread quickly that our Eldest sent sixteen youths, the ringleaders fingered by the managers, to Central Prison."

"That's a bit severe. These are children."

Neftalin shook his head. "This sends a clear message that no more nonsense will be tolerated. He threatened to suspend all ration cards of the families if this disobedience reoccurs. That should put an end to this once and for all."

"But Henryk, how will the future judge such harsh actions? Sending our own children to prison for refusing to eat soup—"

"Stop! Do you really believe these are spontaneous actions?"

My thoughts swung to Pola, and whoever else was instigating these actions. "They appear to be—"

"Nonsense! We all know these strikes are instigated by leftist agitators who are exploiting these young workers."

"Henryk, these are soup strikes. Minor actions—"

"There is nothing minor! You should understand by now. The Chairman must ensure order. He must resort to stringent measures, not only because he is personally responsible for maintaining order but because he is responsible to the populace for averting the crises that would result from German intervention."

"I know these arguments well, but Henryk, once this war ends, and it will soon, the victors will judge him."

"They will understand he had to maintain control at all costs."

Our door burst open, and two Gestapo officers charged in.

"Achtung!" I jumped from my chair, as did Neftalin and Rosenfeld.

The officers searched our faces and then walked quickly around the room. Hands dipped into various boxes and pulled through our piles of papers. As abruptly as they entered, they left.

I remained standing. I looked at Rosenfeld. "What are they searching for?"

The professor shook his head.

Neftalin looked shaken.

"Henryk, what are they looking for?"

"I don't know. This was totally unannounced." He left the room.

Rosenfeld smiled. "Whatever it was, they looked worried."

By nightfall, everyone in the ghetto knew there had been arrests. No one knew why. When Pola did not appear, I feared the worst.

CHAPTER 88

T HURSDAY, JUNE 8, 1944
The ghetto is still reeling from yesterday's unfortunate arrests. The event is discussed in whispers everywhere, and fear for the lives of these people has a stranglehold on everyone who knew them...

I was desperate for news of Pola, but there was a sense of excitement racing through the ghetto that caused some of our residents to forget where we were and who we were dealing with. The rumors had penetrated our barbed wire enclosure, and our people, eager for any scrap of positive news, forgot to keep on their poker faces. "Have you heard? The Americans have landed in France," spread through the grapevine, igniting the hope that tomorrow the friendly forces would bang down Lodz's doors. Fools! Jews, who should have been more circumspect, were out in the streets embracing and congratulating each other...smiling with hope, all in front of the wolves. Somehow the slaves had gotten wind of the invasion. But how could such reports be known by their captives, hermetically sealed away from the world for five years?

Neftalin kept his voice low. "The authorities are many things, but they are not fools. We are. Those who celebrated an American victory prematurely precipitated yesterday's arrests. The Germans put two and two together and surmised that the only way this news could have become known was by radios hidden by some of our residents."

"Radios?" That would explain how so many of our rumors proved to be true.

"We did not even know of these devices since their owners were discreet and kept news within their family or in their extremely close network. I'm told most of the receivers were primitive and could only pick up stray broadcasts from German stations. One or two were able to reach British stations."

"All this time, we had radios, and the Chairman didn't know?"

"No. Not until the news of the American landing made the owners careless. They actually printed the story on paper."

"So, the authorities found out."

"Oh, yes. The Gestapo arrested a man named Altszuler on Wolborska Street. They then proceeded in a borrowed vehicle, to disguise their arrival, to 9 Mylynarska Street, where they caught a man listening to his radio."

"Do you have this man's name? For my report."

Neftalin closed his eyes. "Tafel. The fool was actually caught in the act. But that was not the end of it. The authorities did not find a radio at Altszuler's apartment, but his son, sixteen, was also arrested. He confessed where the radio was and divulged the names of two of his father's co-workers. One, Szlomo Redlich, was arrested immediately, but the other, Chaim Widawski, escaped."

"Did that end it?" I was fearful I would hear Pola's name.

Neftalin shook his head. "The Order Service was given strict orders to bring in Widawski. The police also arrested a man named Lubinski, of Niecala Street, and three brothers, Jakow, Szymon, and Henoch Weksler of 61 Lagiewnicka Street." He peered at his notes. "Oh yes, they raided Tatarka's barbershop and arrested Richard Beer. He's a former newspaper editor from Vienna. He had transcripts in his coat. Can you believe it? Fools! God knows what hell will rain down on us for this."

I stopped writing. Were these men fools or brave men who wanted to bring hope to our savaged populace? "Any women?" I asked.

Neftalin shook his head. "I feel sorry for these unfortunates. We can guess how the authorities will treat them. I only pray that this does not reflect back on our Chairman." He aimed his index finger at me. "With the Americans so close, his policies have kept us alive. Nothing must endanger that. Nothing." He walked to the door. "Two radio sets for 150,000 people. They could be our death sentence."

After Neftalin left, I stared at the empty chairs in our room and then completed my entry:

Two radio sets were discovered. A closed city of some 150,000 people! Perhaps these were receivers left in the ghetto by Poles, perhaps they were even primitive ghetto contraptions. No one had known whether there were actual radio sets in the ghetto or whether information came in through the barbed wire fence, but one thing is certain: the ghetto had always been filled with all sorts of rumors. Now it turns out that a few persons were daring enough to listen to the news right in the ghetto and to pass on what they had heard.

As I walked home, I prayed Pola would appear at my side. The news was that the young Widawski had not been found. Everyone was alive with the announcement of the Americans landing. Widawski could remain in hiding until the Germans were no more. Hope was mixed with high but was tinged with an awareness that the Germans were not quite finished with us. With the Americans and Soviets so close, I waited for any word about Pola. It would be my luck to lose her just when liberation was finally near.

FRIDAY, JUNE 9, 1944

I'd grown inured to reports of our people ending their suffering by various methods. I rarely bothered to include this epidemic of self-destruction among our nearly 1,000 entries. I had not known this young man, but he quickly became a legend in the ghetto. Widawski's escape from the Gestapo and their inability to capture him had become a symbol of hope for all of us. I anticipated he would be among the first to greet the Americans when they soon marched onto our streets. I did not know him, but something about him brought tears to my eyes as I finished reading the police report:

Widawski remained in hiding until today but realized how hopeless his situation was and decided to take his own life. He swallowed a fast-acting poison (probably cyanide) in the gateway of a building on Podrzecna. Then he went out to the street and collapsed.

The end is so near! Goddammit! Why couldn't you hold on a little longer? I was angry, furious, that when I needed him to live as my hope, he had given in to the easy way out. How many times had I been tempted? Cyanide? Where did he get it? No answer here. A pill...fast-acting...painless? You were supposed to be my hero, our hope? I am the real hero. I will not surrender, not until I have Regina back in my arms. Not until I fulfill my obligation to Miriam.

I put down my pen. The police report said Widawski left a note for his relatives. I wondered what he wrote. What could I write to Regina and Miriam? What could I leave them if I were taken from the ghetto before they returned? A young man defying the cruel authorities had become a legend, while I, an engineer, who could have built the Taj Mahal, Eiffel Tower, or an apartment complex for the crowded population of the ghetto, spent four years of my life with meaningless scribbling. What did the Chairman do with all our work? Most probably, our propaganda — Singer had been right in calling it that — was lost in a file cabinet, or more likely, burnt for fuel in the Chairman's fireplace. Widawski, barely a man, was lauded as a hero, while I, and all those who had set our pens to this endless chronicle of a dying ghetto, were merely bookkeepers, the devil's bookkeepers.

On Sunday, June 11, 1944, Chaim Widawsi was buried. By order of the Chairman, only family members were present.

CHAPTER 89

T UESDAY, JUNE 13, 1944
NEWS OF THE DAY
The Chairman, who felt ill yesterday afternoon, is staying in bed today. He complains of heart trouble.

AIR RAID DEFENSE

The Ghetto Administration has ordered slit trenches to be dug immediately in all gardens within the ghetto's center...

The news of immediate attention to constructing air-raid defenses would be alarming to most people, but the ghetto dwellers, already electrified by the news reports of Allied assaults on France, took this as another proof that our ordeal was nearly over. Those digging the trenches by hand let smiles escape as they toiled at back-breaking work.

Even the news that our Chairman was ill in bed did not set off alarms as it would have a few weeks earlier. Our eyes were on the sky, and though all we saw were the billowing smoke streams, we sensed in every part of our deprived bodies that the sky would soon reveal hordes of black dots as the air war finally reached us.

Neftalin was the only one who did not appear rejuvenated by the news of the American invasion. If anything, he seemed depressed. He spent more time in our chamber as a refuge from his duties as the Chairman's Deputy, but he'd become close-lipped about his assignments.

"Jews are inventive," I said, hoping to lighten Neftalin's mood with a different kind of report. "A resident has solved two serious problems with one unusual solution." Neftalin's facial expression showed no interest, but I persisted. "As you know, we're all starving. Our supplies have become worse as the war created a new urgency for the authorities."

Neftalin still showed no reaction.

"And we have little water for the few home gardens some far-seeing residents have planted."

Neftalin looked angry. "The Chairman does what he can. I'm sick of the endless moaning and groaning—"

"Wait. Someone came up with a marvelous idea." I could barely keep from laughing. "He covered the roof of his building's toilet with soil. Then he planted radishes and leeks—"

"On the roof of his latrine?"

"Yes. Whenever this agronomist wishes to water his crop, he climbs down a short ladder from his apartment window to the latrine roof and sets to work." I burst into laughter.

Neftalin sighed. "You're making this up."

"No. It's really ingenious. Nobody will steal from his garden. There is an odor, of course, but when you are starving...."

"Not much longer," Neftalin said.

"Amen," I said without thinking there might be a double meaning to his comment.

Neftalin rose from his chair. "Not much longer," he repeated and handed me a single sheet of paper. He then left the room.

The poor man must be drained, I thought, grateful I did not have his responsibilities. He'd said the Chairman was ill in bed. Also understandable after all he'd been through. It was natural for his body to demand a respite when the good news was finally about to lift the burden from his shoulders. He had saved us. Almost single-handedly, the Eldest of the Jews, often against harsh opposition, both by the authorities and his own people, had brought us to safety. He deserved a day in bed. He deserved to be blessed by every one of us, the survivors, every day of our lives.

I then read the sheet of paper Neftalin handed me:

PROCLAMATION No. 416

ATTENTION!

Re: Voluntary Registration for Labor Outside the Ghetto.

I hereby announce that men and women (including married people) may register for labor outside the ghetto.

If families have children old enough to work, the children may be registered along with their parents for labor outside the ghetto...

What the hell was going on? "Volunteers?" "Children?" Who was the Chairman trying to fool? Recent 'requests' for volunteers had set off brutal hunts where residents were snatched from their beds. Would this be an attempt to recruit volunteers or more nights of terror? I crushed the sheet of paper in my fist.

CHAPTER 90

S ATURDAY, JUNE 17, 1944

The shock of the new proclamation raced through the ghetto. With the news of the Allied invasion filtering in, the cork in the bottle had popped. The zombies had come alive with expectation, but this new proclamation raised specters of recent violent roundups of Jews. I was debating this with Rosenfeld, who had become painfully thin and hacked into his handkerchief. "They call it voluntary, but we know better," I said, concerned he might volunteer.

"I will not argue with you on this. Our information was that only 500 people would be drawn, but we now believe that was only the start," Rosenfeld said.

"Do you have any idea of the actual number?" I asked.

The Professor did not give his usual chuckle when I asked for specific numbers. "Only the Germans know."

"Neftalin said the new crew is being sent to Munich to clear away debris."

"I hope from Allied bombs," Rosenfeld said. "I hope they bomb the crap out of them."

There was a faint knock on the door. Neftalin entered, his face ashen. "It's happened. Something terrible." He fell into a chair.

"What is it, Henryk?" I asked, fearing anything that could bring such despair into my superior's face.

"Biebow appeared without announcement and ordered me and several others to leave the Chairman's office. I heard the door lock. I never thought he would strike the Eldest of the Jews in the face."

"He struck Rumkowski?" *What the hell did this mean?* There had been bad blood between them, but this?

"Biebow's aides tried to calm him, but he attacked our Chairman. I'd never seen him in such a rage. The Chairman was taken to the hospital." Neftalin looked frightened. "Never before has Biebow laid hands on the Chairman. Yes, there has been conflict, sometimes stormy. But who would believe he would dare touch, not only the leader of 80,000 Jews still in the ghetto, a man of nearly seventy?"

"What caused this?" Rosenfeld asked.

"There is no way of learning what precipitated this outburst. I do know Bradfisch, the Gestapo Chief, demanded 600 more laborers, and the Chairman agreed without asking Biebow." Neftalin handed me the latest manpower requisition. "Biebow's primary concern is keeping the factories producing for the military, so the loss of so many men may have set him off."

"Six hundred more?"

Neftalin nodded. "The Chairman is under medical care at the hospital but decided that several workshops will be closed to meet the quota."

"Factories are closing?"

"Yes, but the authorities claim, and this is a quote, that they 'do not plan to liquidate the ghetto, because business orders are still coming in and there is an interest in maintaining the factories here that are vital to the war effort.'"

"So, how many are leaving?" Rosenfeld asked.

"You're the numbers man now?" I teased, but it did not lighten the mood.

"The truth," Rosenfeld said. "What are we facing?"

Neftalin shrugged. "Ten to eleven thousand."

Rosenfeld took his empty pipe from his mouth. He stared at the bowl for several seconds and then said, "Thousands of tragedies are in the making."

Neftalin nodded his head slowly. "I had high hopes we would lose no more of our labor force before the Americans arrive. We must pray." He pulled himself from the chair. "We must all pray."

After Neftalin left, I turned to Rosenfeld. "I guess we have to wait and see whether the Chairman can maintain productivity with such a large labor reassignment."

Rosenfeld looked stunned. "Don't you understand? This is the end for us."

"You're being a fatalist again."

Rosenfeld pointed the pipe at me. "A realist. The commission is closing some factories completely. All of their workers are listed for resettlement. Their ration cards and that of their families are already suspended. Only the managers and their families are exempt."

"How do you know all this?"

Rosenfeld reached into his pockets. "Singer gave me these. I no longer will require them since I won't be here this winter." He handed me the two knit gloves with the love he might have shown two furry kittens. "Like me, these 'friends' have aged, have worn fingers, but at heart, are still of use." He let out a chuckle. "That's a worthy analogy. You didn't write it down?"

I was unable to reply.

Rosenfeld handed me a few sheets of paper. "I signed a few of these damn entries. Who knows? Perhaps, some professor may want to know what happened to the Jews—"

"Enough!" I exploded. "You need these damn things. I stole the first pair from a corpse, and you're keeping this pair if I have to shove them down your throat!"

MONDAY, JUNE 19, 1944

The Chairman is still in the hospital.

Volunteering has given way to conscription. The authorities need around ten thousand people...the machinery is in motion.

I read Rosenfeld's entry:

"A few thousand Jews are to enjoy the blessing of laboring outside the ghetto, of leaving the ghetto, the Jewish residential area, through the barbed wire into golden freedom. What a marvelous prospect! After four hard, torturous years

filled with anxiety and distress, they can go out into the world again and see a patch of land that is not surrounded by barbed wire, they can receive food other than ghetto rations. In other words, they can be human beings again. And yet, few people, very few, regard this prospect as a stroke of luck.

Was it? "Do you really believe being taken by force is evidence that our people are fortunate in being so honored?" I asked the Professor.

"Read on, Engineer, if you want to know my innermost thoughts."

I continued to read his entry:

How deeply must skepticism be ingrained in the souls of the Lizmannstadt ghetto's Jews if they fail to jump at such a chance, if they prefer to remain in the utterly bleak and hopeless condition of the ghetto. They would rather remain in the familiar circumstances of the ghetto with their families and friends than go outside."

"The devil you know is better than the devil you don't," I said.

"Not when the devil is destroying you," Rosenfeld countered. "Resistance, my friend, has failed to gain a foothold here thanks to the actions of the Chairman's police and the German authorities. All our people have been taken."

"Pola? Is she gone?"

Rosenfeld nodded. "I'm sorry, my friend."

I fell back against my seat. Not again? Oh, God, not again? "Do you know where? Is she in prison?"

Rosenfeld's lips trembled. "They're all gone. They 'volunteered.'"

I was about to beg for more when there was a knock on the door.

Neftalin entered. Lately, he'd been depressed, so I was startled that he had a smile on his face. "I want you both to know, there is some good news. I've been entrusted with supervising the sale of goods from those being sent for labor outside the ghetto."

"Why is this good news?" I asked. "The Chairman has arranged for such sales of goods before since the deportees no longer need the few items they have in their possession once they are rehoused in the Polish farmlands."

"You don't understand. Before, those resettled were paid in Lodz ghetto money, worthless outside of our realm. This time, Amtsleiter Biebow has arranged for them to be paid in German marks. This is the first time in the history of the ghetto that the German authorities have made arrangements for our workers to take German currency with them."

"That is good news," I said, realizing this signified that our people would be able to use this money to buy items in their new locations.

"I am to take charge of this, and, of course, will need to retain most of my staff to manage such a massive operation. That is good news for you as well."

After Neftalin left, I turned to Rosenfeld, a hopeful smile on my face. "You see, dear Professor, we are safe here. Neftalin assures us that he needs us."

Rosenfeld wasn't smiling. "Beware of Greeks bearing gifts," he said.

I gave him a puzzled look.

"We've had many requests for volunteers before, and they've evolved into brutal manhunts. So now they want 10,000 workers and don't care if they are men, women, or children, so why are they suddenly offering us German currency?"

"Do you have a theory?"

Rosenfeld tapped his pen on the pad. "Perhaps it is far-fetched, but what is the effect of such a gift to our suspicious people?"

I had to think about that for several seconds and then said, "It would calm them, assure them that the rumors about the ultimate destination of these transports are false. Giving money to condemned human beings would make no sense."

"The Germans are struggling to obtain manpower from us. They are using soldiers and Gestapo officers in futile efforts to root 'volunteers' from our labyrinths and ratholes. As I said, 'beware of Greeks bearing gifts.'"

I looked at the Chairman's Proclamation 417 announcing this new offer and said, "Beware of the Chairman's men bearing gifts as well."

Rosenfeld nodded. "You understand, at last."

CHAPTER 91

WEDNESDAY, JUNE 22, 1944

"What the hell is that?" Rosenfeld shouted as the room filled with the screeching sound of sirens.

The door swung open.

I was about to shout my call to attention, but a young man, Order Service by his armband and cap, shouted, "Air Raid! This is not a drill! Get out! Get out!"

I grabbed Rosenfeld, bones wobbling on atrophied legs, and pulled him along with me. "Can you make it out of the building?" I shouted in the din of sirens and people screaming instructions. I held him up, but he was a marionette with a body held together by thin strings.

Germans were streaming out of the building and heading to conveniently located bomb shelters, recently completed, on the premises. "We need to get to Lagiewnicka Street," I said, pulling the professor behind me.

"Leave me here. Save yourself." Rosenfeld tried to pull away.

"Why are you always so obstinate?" I gripped his waist tighter.

The sirens were deafening. The smell of bodies crowded into the makeshift shelter reminded me that it had been weeks since I had bathed. As I glanced around the crowded room in the former kitchen, I saw none of the more essential administrators. Did they have deluxe shelters too? This brick building with boards nailed to its glassless windows would hardly withstand a bomb, but it was better constructed than most of our neglected structures.

"Is it for real this time?" an elderly man asked the air-raid warden.

As if in answer, we heard a few explosive sounds that sounded distant. "Are those anti-aircraft guns?" I asked Rosenfeld.

"I hope they miss." He cocked his head. "Shit. They've stopped."

The warden shouted, "Everyone, remain where you are."

"I don't hear any more shots," I said.

"I was hoping to hear bombs," Rosenfeld replied.

The all-clear signal came at 12:40.

Feeling disappointed the air assault was over, but relieved to be alive, I helped Rosenfeld to his feet. "I guess it was a false alarm," I said.

An Order Service officer overheard me and whispered, "No. It was not. Some of us who remained above ground saw a large squadron of planes, perhaps 300, flying east." He smiled.

"Were they German?"

"No, my friend." Something caught the guard's eye, and he sped off, but not before whispering, "Hang on a little longer. The end is near."

As we walked back to Balut Market, I heard Rosenfeld mutter, "No bombs. No bombs. Why no bombs?"

THURSDAY, JUNE 22, 1944
DEPARTING WORKERS

The ghetto is haunted by the imminent bloodletting. People generally suspect that a gradual liquidation of the ghetto is underway...

I stopped Rosenfeld from reading his entry. "But we're still getting orders from the Germans," I said, clutching to hope.

Rosenfeld shook his head and muttered, "We are living in limbo."

I was unable to shed the images of Germans racing through our apartments, pulling women and children from their beds to fill their stomachs with Jewish bodies. There was no longer any doubt in my mind that the liquidation of the ghetto had begun. From this point on, I would have to be extremely careful if I wanted to remain here.

CHAPTER 92

F RIDAY, JUNE 23, 1944
NEWS OF THE DAY
Labor Outside the Ghetto

The first transport of 562 people left Radogoszcz Station this morning at 8 A.M. Before their departure, Gestapo Commissioner Fuchs made a few reassuring remarks. He stated that they would be working for the Reich and that decent food would be provided. For lack of passenger cars, they would initially be loaded onto freight cars but be transferred to passenger cars en route. No one had anything to fear.

Naturally, the news of this speech spread through the ghetto like wildfire and had a somewhat calming effect...

"No one had anything to fear," I repeated from Neftalin's report.

"Then why are those drafted for outside labor hiding like frightened mice in the labyrinths of the ghetto? Why are the wolves hunting and dragging them kicking and screaming to the train station?" I asked Neftalin, who had served as the Chairman's representative at the station, and witnessed the Commissioner's speech. It was Henryk who transmitted Fuchs' assurance that "no one had anything to fear." Was he joking?

Neftalin replied, "This time, it was different. People were treated correctly. The loading of the transport went smoothly. There wasn't any violence. Families were not broken up."

"You witnessed this yourself?" There had been so many horror stories of the brutal handling of people before this resettlement action that I found

366

this difficult to believe.

Neftalin nodded. "Unfortunately, the Chairman is still in the hospital. So, yes, I was sent in his place." He handed me his report.

"Were passenger cars used this time?" I asked.

"Fuchs apologized that the passenger cars were unavailable but said the freight car floors were now covered with straw."

"Straw?"

"So the passengers did not sleep on wood," Neftalin said, again looking uneasy. "It is wartime, you know."

I decided to shift to another topic before he decided to cut off the meeting. "I understand there was an assembly today of all department heads and factory managers at the Metal Department," I said, pulling out a blank sheet of paper to take notes.

"That is correct."

I was ready to launch my 'missile.' "I understand those administrators in attendance were instructed to compile lists of people—"

Neftalin interrupted. "Oh, I forgot. Today, a large quantity of material arrived for the tailoring workshops." He handed me the report from the authorities.

"Henryk, this is all very good, but the word from this meeting is that the Germans want 25,000 more of our workers. Is that true?"

Neftalin stood, paced the floor, and then shrugged his shoulders.

"Is it true?" I asked again, praying the information was incorrect.

Neftalin nodded. "The managers were instructed to compile lists of people for dispatch from the workshops and departments and turn them over to the Chairman's commission at Central Prison... 25,000 new workers." He lowered his voice. "I don't know how much longer we can survive like this. This news will panic our people."

It was odd how I felt nothing as I watched Neftalin smile sadly and walk from our room. It was almost time to leave for the day, but I wrote my entry: "Today, considerable quantities of raw material for the tailoring workshops arrived at Radogoszcz station. The ghetto again concluded that it will not be liquidated..."

As I walked home, the streets were nearly deserted. I came to the corner where Jozef had usually left me to join his friends, who prayed in a secret hovel for God to help his Jews. It was also here that Pola had, at times, appeared. I sensed someone approaching. I turned, expecting to see my shadowy lover, but an Order Service officer, a head taller than me, was blocking my path. I reached for my identification. "I'm an administrator," I began.

"I know who you are."

His raspy voice frightened me. "What have I done?"

"Listen. A note was found in one of the freight cars."

"I don't understand."

"Shut up. Listen. It said the train went only as far as Kutno."

"That's less than 35 miles from here."

"Something is very wrong."

"Did you see this note yourself?"

"No. Nobody has confirmed it. But you need to investigate this. We need to find out what is happening to our people." He hurried off.

The next morning, I included his report in my entry, hoping Neftalin or the Chairman would read it. I ended it with, "It is hoped that we will soon learn what is happening with these people." After I finished my entry, I went over my notes from my last meeting with Neftalin. 25,000 more people would be leaving the ghetto…but at least they'd have straw to sleep on in the freight cars that were racing back and forth. To where?

With each day, the struggle to save a few Jews in this crumbling ghetto until the Soviets or Americans arrived was becoming a race against the coming and going of the trains. Who would win? God only knew.

SATURDAY, JUNE 24, 1944

NEWS OF THE DAY

A Minor Panic

The ghetto is agitated because the railroad cars that carried off yesterdays' transport are already back at Radogoszcz station. People infer that the transport traveled only a short distance, and a wave of terror is spreading through the

CHAPTER 92

ghetto.

CHAPTER 93

S UNDAY, JUNE 25, 1944
Ghetto dwellers are now being shipped out of the ghetto to perform manual labor. One transport has already gone off; the second will leave the ghetto tomorrow. Today is Sunday, June 25. A Sunday of sunshine and drifting clouds, of calm and storm and rain showers...

"As always, you write beautifully," I said, relieved Rosenfeld was back. He said he'd been ill. The news that 25,000 more Jews were to be conscripted had forced him to return to work. "Why did you break up your report with the weather?" I asked, skimming the first paragraph of his entry again.

Rosenfeld coughed into his handkerchief, no longer examining the red stains. "Were you not the one who argued so many ages ago that weather should be included?"

"It does seem lifetimes ago."

He coughed again.

I felt sorry for him. "Let me finish writing this for you. Please, dictate what you witnessed."

The Professor spoke softly, the soiled cloth blocking my view of his face. "The streets leading to Central Prison were teeming with people of all ages and both sexes. Even children and the aged were hauling suitcases, knapsacks, and cloth bundles on their bony shoulders. There was also much bedding, striped pillows, and garishly-colored blankets." He looked at me. "Are you getting all this?"

"Garishly-colored blankets. Yes, continue."

Rosenfeld closed his eyes as if envisioning the scene. "There were curious stares from workers heading to factories. You can say, 'Life as usual. And yet, there is a pall over the ghetto.'" His voice trailed off.

I had to bring him back. "They announced twenty-five transports..."

Rosenfeld's eyes snapped open. "Twenty-five transports have been announced. Everyone knows that the situation is serious, that the existence of the ghetto is in jeopardy." He lowered his handkerchief. He was trembling.

"Do you want that included? I know it is true, but this will be our first confession of what we have suspected that we've hidden from others... for some time."

Rosenfeld nodded sadly. "No one can deny that such fears are justified. The argument that not even 'this resettlement' can imperil the survival of the ghetto now falls on deaf ears." He bit his lip, tears in his eyes. "For nearly every ghetto dweller is affected this time. Everyone is losing a relative, a friend, a roommate, a colleague." He looked at me. "Did you get all that?"

"Yes, dear Professor, I got it."

Rosenfeld pulled his empty pipe from his pocket and studied it as he had done so many times before. He then gave me a smile. "Add this: 'And yet — Jewish faith in a justice that will ultimately triumph does not permit extreme pessimism. People try to console themselves in some way. But nearly everyone says to himself, and to others: God only knows who will be better off: the person who stays here or the person who leaves!'" He let out a deep sigh. "I'm done. You may sign this with my initials." He burst into a fit of coughing, held up his hand. "My last friend, it is now a race between the Germans and our rescuers. If they do not arrive soon, the Chairman will have lost his battle, and history will ask why Jews, the scions of legendary warriors, fell in line with their German captors." My friend lifted himself painfully from his chair. "God bless you, dear Engineer."

My hand dipped into my pocket and cupped the broken bowl of his pipe. "I will see you tomorrow," I said, and added, "God bless you, my oldest and dearest friend."

Rosenfeld stopped walking and turned, a rare twinkle in his eye. "A blessing from an atheist? Yes, I guess we all turn to God in the end." He put on his hat and, leaning on his cane, left the room.

I typed his entry as he had dictated. It was amazing how he had captured the emotional state of the ghetto in a few paragraphs. Tears welled up in my eyes. Exhaustion and loneliness. I felt empty…is there such a feeling?

That night, I said goodbye to the flat that held too many memories of Miriam and my precious Regina. I executed the first step of my survival plan. I packed up the few things I would need and closed the door of our apartment for what I believed was the last time. I hefted the misshapen bundle on my shoulder and walked toward the abandoned streets of Marysin. A basement in a vacant building, a neglected crypt in the cemetery. The freight trains had straw bedding. I slept on concrete, clutching Regina's blanket.

MONDAY, JUNE 26, 1944

Today, Transport II, with 912 persons, left the ghetto.

CHAPTER 94

WEDNESDAY, JUNE 28, 1944
NEWS OF THE DAY: LABOR OUTSIDE THE GHETTO

Early this morning, Transport III departed with 803 people.

I thought of remaining in my new rathole in a crypt in the cemetery, hiding until the end of the war. I concluded that the best option was to return during the day to the Jewish headquarters, where I could keep tabs on the latest developments. While many ghetto residents were suspicious about the transports carrying nearly a thousand people, of all ages and gender, out of our paradise daily, others were happy they were leaving to promised new homes, better food, and jobs outside the ghetto. I was grateful each day that Rosenfeld was still with me.

Neftalin's visits were less frequent. He was occupied compiling the lists demanded by the authorities. These resettlement and work orders were posted on walls in the factories and departments. "People are flooding me with pleas for exemptions," he complained, "It is a zoo. Everyone is trying to pull strings."

Rosenfeld said, "Doctors' offices are mobbed by people who claim to be sick and by healthy people who want to be sick at any price."

Neftalin made a wry face. "Doctors are making a fortune from people trying to be exempted from the work details."

"So people aren't buying the German line of promises?" I asked.

"Shady deals that involve human lives are negotiated everywhere. The workshop managers are corrupt and manipulate the lists trying to keep their workers, knowing their own survival depends on their factories still being able to function: "You cross out my Jew, and I'll cross out yours. If you list my Jew, then I'll list yours." It is so frustrating. Immoral intrigues and vendettas are rampant. The Chairman is at wit's end—"

"Do you blame them? How can we trust the wolves when they have lied to us so many times?" Rosenfeld asked.

Neftalin shook his head. "It's a mystery how any of our workshops can still function." He glanced at Rosenfeld. "The Chairman, ill as he is, works ceaselessly to protect us."

I picked up a report I'd received from the police. "People are still selling themselves as substitutes. A human being's life is worth three loaves of bread, a half kilogram of margarine, one pound of sugar."

Neftalin sighed. "Add shoes and some items of clothing. It is a mess, but the Chairman is determined to do what he can to keep people here. The factories must keep functioning."

"I hope the Germans agree," I said.

"Why else would they keep sending in orders and raw material?" Neftalin asked.

Rosenfeld, barely audible, replied, "Only the Germans know."

Neftalin rose from his seat and said, "The Chairman knows what he is doing."

"The next days will tell," I said. "Goodbye, Henryk." It was the first time I dismissed him.

Neftalin looked dismayed for a second but rose from his chair. "You'll see, Chaim was right. History will record that his actions preserved the ghetto."

After Neftalin left, Rosenfeld handed me his entry: "After four years in the ghetto, we leave the old home without shedding a tear, abandon the furnishings you worked so hard to acquire…these are the slogans of all ghetto dwellers who have received a departure order…Now the ghetto dweller has to give up the very last of his possessions."

I had left everything I owned in our apartment, making it appear as if I still lived there. It hadn't bothered me one bit. Night after night, I clutched Regina's blanket, my last treasured object. "Doctor, the Germans confiscated all our money, jewelry, furs, sewing machines, photographs, stamps, bicycles, irons, carpets, crystal, even our musical instruments. They took every electrical appliance. What are the departed saying goodbye to?"

Rosenfeld replied, "I walked by the Main Purchasing Agency's storehouse on Koscielny Square. Pillows, blankets, bedding of all sorts lie packed in bales in the courtyard. Buckets, dishes, and linen are stacked up around the tables of our officials appraising and purchasing all these belongings. Lines of people are waiting with their hands out for a little money to buy food for the journey and their ultimate destination."

"Are they still paid in German currency?" I asked, reaching for any scrap of hope.

Rosenfeld gave me a curious look. "Actually, they receive a voucher made out for ghetto marks and Reich marks. The Reich marks are paid at the Central Prison."

"Another way to ensure they report for the resettlements," I said.

Rosenfeld said, "Thus do people bid farewell to the last of their goods. No tear is shed, no harsh word spoken. Fatalism prevails. People think: 'It's the final stage. Now nothing more can be taken from us. We are as poor as when God created us.'" He winced with pain. "The clothes on our bodies and a few remaining necessities — this will suffice until then."

"Then?" I asked, moved by the Professor's words and tone.

"Then is the moment when fate chooses between life and death," Rosenfeld said.

I replied, "You've made it that the Main Purchasing Agency is a symbol of these days of anguish."

"Days of anguish?" Rosenfeld smiled. "Yes, you have become quite a writer," he said.

I browsed through my pile of reports and found one that noted the departure of 803 people from the ghetto on Transport III. It said, "For the time being, no difficulties worth mentioning have been encountered in the requisition of human resources." The suspension of ration cards had done its job. Threaten to starve the victims and their families...

The door opened. Dora Fuchs, the Chairman's long-time secretary, charged in. Even she appeared to have lost significant weight. Her hair had turned iron-gray, and her attire looked worse for wear. "The Deputy wants you to record this. Transport IV just left with 700 more people." She handed me a small sheet of paper with numbers for each of the four transports and leaned closer. "It's not in writing, but there is worry about shortages for the next quotas. More raids are to be carried out." Her eyes darted to Rosenfeld. "Henryk wants you to know." She rushed from the room.

SATURDAY, JULY 1, 1944

The commission is beginning to encounter difficulties in supplying the human resources required for the next transport...

The agencies involved are aware of how dangerous it would be to fall behind in supplying the quotas required.

CHAPTER 95

SUNDAY, JULY 2, 1944
NEWS OF THE DAY: LABOR OUTSIDE THE GHETTO
Tomorrow's transport V has already been filled. The ghetto still has no idea where the transports are headed.

"Where the hell are they sending all these people?" I asked Rosenfeld.

He shrugged. "Since the train is always back on schedule for the next dispatch, it must be shuttling to somewhere close."

I studied a map. "The distance is no more than 35 miles from the reports we've received."

Rosenfeld nodded. "It is odd though that the first shipment left nine days ago, yet the ghetto has not received any news about the deportees."

I had received no news about Miriam, Regina or Pola. How was it possible that Germans could keep us in the dark about where our loved ones were now living. My logical mind came up with the only answer I could accept: the war had created such chaos that all record-keeping was impossible. It was a breakdown of communications. "I wonder when these resettlements will stop?"

"Only the Germans know," Rosenfeld said.

I heard Singer saying, "The Chairman knows."

MONDAY, JULY 3, 1944
NEWS OF THE DAY: LABOR OUTSIDE THE GHETTO
Early this morning, Transport V left Radogoszcz station with 700 people.

...people are whispering about a new demand for 3,000 able-bodied men, but official sources know nothing of the matter.

FRIDAY, JULY 7, 1944
NEWS OF THE DAY: LABOR OUTSIDE THE GHETTO
Early this morning, Transport VII left the ghetto with 700 people.

Each morning began with Neftalin handing me an announcement of yet another shipment of Jews from the ghetto. "How is the Chairman filling these quotas?" I asked the Deputy, who had become less communicative as the resettlements threatened our existence.

Neftalin replied, "The quotas must be filled."

"What do you mean?"

Rosenfeld shot in, "When starving those selected and their families fails to force them to report, then the Chairman's police pull them out of bed at night and drag the victims to the staging area at the train station. Isn't that right, Henryk?"

Neftalin looked about to answer but gave our eldest chronicler an angry look and stormed from the room.

"It is not like you to provoke him," I said.

"Have you seen them? Our 'volunteers.' Sad figures with bundles on bent backs, makeshift bags on their feeble shoulders. Old women, starving children crying for their parents—"

"Stop! Stop!" I gripped my chair. "Please, stop. My friend, no more."

"This is tearing out my heart," Rosenfeld said and placed his hand on my arm. "Here is my entry." His hand shook as he handed it to me. He'd signed it with his initials.

I signed it with my tears.

There were almost no volunteers now. People were hiding where they could. I was ensconced in the cemetery as the nightly roundups continued.

The Order Service had been ordered to clear occupants from yet another area of the ghetto. This area was ordered to be demolished, and a barbed-wire fence was moved to separate it from what was left. The noose was closing. I felt it choking us.

MONDAY, JULY 10, 1944
NEWS OF THE DAY: LABOR OUTSIDE THE GHETTO

Today, Transport VIII left the ghetto with 700 people.

CHAPTER 96

THURSDAY, JULY 13, 1944

The last nights were disrupted with raids by the Order Service, clearing out entire blocks of apartments with the same scenes of anguish repeated. The commission, according to Neftalin, was coping with the ghetto's precarious situation by more of these gruesome nighttime raids. In my rathole, a small burrow covered by trash, I grabbed sleep clutching Regina's blanket, protected by the cemetery where only I and the dead resided.

In the dark before dawn, I crept from the hole and made my way to the hall of horror, as I now called the building where large swastikas had been painted over the stars on our entry door. As I walked through the corridor, I saw only vacant offices. Even the administrative departments were feeling the tongs of resettlement grabbing off their workers. Shreds of hope lingered that our liberators would soon arrive, so we hid like rats in every nook and cranny, even in the stinking cellar of a crypt in the cemetery.

I sifted through the dwindling reports from the few still operational departments. Transport IX had left the ghetto with 700 people. My mathematical brain calculated that the total now had risen to 6,496. I looked at the report's date: July 12, 1944. Yesterday.

The door opened.

I no longer cared; no longer jumped to attention. We were rarely invaded now by the authorities. They had more crucial preoccupations:

the resettlement actions and news of the war which they kept from us.

Rosenfeld, in his coat, always cold, even in July, shuffled in. His walk was more of a stumble than the authoritative gait of a few years ago. A dirty nose rag had replaced his pipe as a constant prop in his hand. "You are here?" It was a question that could have been, "You haven't been taken?"

"Good morning, Professor," I said, grateful for his appearance.

Rosenfeld lowered himself to his chair. "There were raids again last night. I passed crowds at the prison."

"I don't see how the Commission can make its quota," I said.

The door burst open, and Neftalin charged in. "Ostrowski, now! The Labor Bureau."

Rosenfeld stood.

"Not you," Neftalin said. "Only the department chief." He then shot out of the room.

"What do you think that was about?" Rosenfeld asked.

"I have no idea, but I'll find out." I got to my feet and straightened my jacket.

Rosenfeld laughed. "You look dapper, for someone who has not bathed in weeks." He wrinkled his nose.

I laughed too, yet rushed from the room, fearing more bad news. The Chairman's door was open, but he wasn't inside.

I headed for the Bureau of Labor farther down the hall.

"In there," an Order Service sentry directed.

I was surprised to see approximately seventy people milling around. "What's happening?" I asked, searching for Neftalin.

I got a bunch of shrugs, and a "you know as much as I do," from a burly man whom I recognized as the head of the gravediggers department, a function that had been left untouched by the resettlements. The health of the ghetto depended on its operations.

There was a sudden silence as two Order Service officers entered, followed by Neftalin and, to my surprise, the Chairman. Leaning on his walking stick, he looked as if he'd been ill. There was a slight discoloration of one side of his face, presumably where Beibow had struck him. "Gentlemen," he began, "I am in a difficult situation. I am battered by two hammers, one on my heart, the other on my brain."

I had no idea what he was driving at, but his tone was of a man who had indeed been beaten by hammers.

Neftalin assisted the Chairman to sit on a chair. Once settled, he spoke again. "My heart refuses to grant what my mind demands, and yet the difficult problem must be resolved. I realize that I must show some special consideration, and I will do so to the best of my ability." He stood, shook his head, and then leaning on his cane, walked into an office door at the far end of the room.

It was true. The Chairman was playing favorites. I caught Neftalin's eyes, and he gave me a quick smile and wink. If I stayed in good favor, I was safe. Did that mean Rosenfeld was included? I watched as Neftalin called individuals into the office. I assumed to be interviewed by the Chairman. Most smiled as they left. One woman was crying as she walked away. I stopped her. "What is wrong?" I asked.

"Are you anyone?" She asked. "Can you help me?"

"I don't know," I replied.

"Then, don't bother me. My name was called, and he says he can't help me." She walked haltingly, looking back, as if headed for her own funeral.

Another potential suicide? There was nothing I could do. I didn't even know her name.

"You're next," Neftalin said. "Don't worry." He prodded me toward the front office where Rumkowski was seated behind a desk, a thin sheath of paper in front of him, a pencil in his hand. "Sir, you remember Bernard Ostrowski?"

Rumkowski skewered me with his eyes. They reminded me of the picture I'd seen of a shark, its eyes hypnotizing in their iciness. As I drew closer, his stare loosened. "The engineer?" He nodded. "My Deputy has praised your loyalty often." He coughed into a handkerchief. "You have done well." He waved his hand at Neftalin. "I have no questions. His function is still needed." He made a checkmark on his page.

"Come, Ostrowski," Neftalin said and gripped my elbow. "You are safe."

"What about Dr. Rosenfeld?" I asked.

The Chairman looked up. "Oskar is with you." He scanned his list and looked at Neftalin. "He is not on my list. You left him off?"

Neftalin stood at attention, not replying.

The Chairman closed his eyes and then opened them again. "I will try," he said.

Neftalin pulled me away.

"Rosenfeld?" I asked again, once clear of the door.

"Be happy you got this," Neftalin replied.

"Rosenfeld has been with me from the start. He is loyal," I persisted.

Neftalin glared at me. "Don't you know what is going on? There is no way we can fill the demand for 25,000 workers. You know about the night raids."

"They're horrible," I replied.

"Of course they are, but we have no choice." He leaned closer. "The names on the resettlement lists have gone into hiding at night, but many still show up for work during the day. The Chairman has authorized new raids." He leaned closer. "In the daytime."

"At work?"

"Yes, at work." Neftalin hissed, "You are naïve. Do you wish to witness such a raid?" He signaled an Order Service officer. "Take my friend to the textile factory," he ordered. "You will not be so quick to criticize."

"I need to return to work," I said.

Neftalin snarled, "You need to witness what our fugitives have forced upon our Chairman." He waved to the officer. "Take him."

The officer, a burly man without a smile, prodded me outside with his club on my back.

I felt as if I'd been arrested as the club urged me toward the end of an intersection bordering the factory. I saw an Order Service detail walking to the opposite intersection.

Suddenly a whistle sounded, and the police cordoned off all access roads. A squad of men burst through the factory doors blocking escape.

The workers were lined up by the officers.

A manager with a megaphone demanded the men display their registration documents. Several officers advanced down the line, sending workers back to their stations or to a second line along the far wall. Guards with clubs stood ready as the fish captured in the raid were marched off to Central Prison. A few of the captives, mostly young men, were crying, but many appeared numb and emaciated.

My guard was silent, but after it was over said softly, "Jews hunting Jews like wild game. But there is no choice." He lowered his club. "Go with God," he said, and just like that, exited from my life.

Not believing I was still free, shaken by what I'd witnessed, I scurried back to my workroom. It had been a surreal scene as if I'd been watching myself from some distant and foggy point. Those poor boys.

The transports grew more frequent and turbulent. I suppose those named who refused to report believed, as I did, that the resettlements, with the war getting closer to Lodz daily, would end. Hide for a few more days. Hide...

On the 13th of July, the day before a new transport was scheduled, people were trudging through the streets to the workshops, factories, markets, wherever, when without warning Order Service squads burst in on them from all sides, herding together everyone who happened to be present.

FRIDAY, JULY 14, 1944
This morning Transport X left the ghetto with another 700 people.

CHAPTER 97

SATURDAY, JULY 15, 1944

I just trudged from the cemetery to our office when Dora Fuchs rushed in and shouted, "It's over! God bless him! The Chairman is riding around and announcing that ration cards are to be issued and conscriptions are canceled." She let out a laugh. "I thought I was next. People are embracing and kissing in the streets. We made it. Thanks to our Eldest, we are safe."

Rosenfeld spoke calmly, "No one is giving thought as to whether this is a temporary or permanent halt."

Dora laughed again. "You're an old pessimist!"

"We have a right to be skeptical," I said.

Dora replied, "Henryk ran to the train station to verify this for the Chairman. Nothing is being readied. Even the most doubting are coming to realize that it is over. My friends, the threat is no longer hanging over us."

I felt like crying. No one can imagine the sense of relief.

"I will wait and see," Rosenfeld said.

Why did he have to spoil it by being so damn logical?

Later that day, word came that the group to be deported had been released from Central Prison and were moving back to their apartments. Though these people had sold all their belongings and were now forced to sleep on bare floors, they were grateful to have escaped the net.

Rosenfeld's reaction was, "The ghetto dweller is like a cat, he always lands on his feet; he can cope with anything."

So frustrating. Everyone was celebrating, and we were still dubious, waiting for solid confirmation.

An hour later, Neftalin exploded into our room. "You've heard the news! The Commission is doing its final accounting and then kaput!"

Rosenfeld unbelievably still looked doubtful.

Neftalin slapped Rosenfeld on the back. "My old friend, this is a day of joy such as the ghetto has never known."

Rosenfeld, though his back must have ached with pain, let out a tentative smile.

If my beloved colleague finally believed it was over, then so could I. I wrapped my arms around my dear friend and we rocked each other with hearts filled with joy and relief. "We made it, my old friend," I said, thinking how brittle he felt.

For once, he didn't disagree. His head on my shoulders, he trembled.

That night, I returned to my flat, and for the first time in many nights, slept in a bed. It took a while before I fell asleep. I was straining to visualize Miriam's face, but time had vaporized much of what I had viewed so fondly. I only saw eyes, hazel eyes…ghostly, tender, hovering over me. The only thing that could have made this night better would have been feeling Pola's body inching its way against me.

That did not happen.

The next morning, I wrote my entry: *Never has the ghetto been so happy. Today toward noon, the Eldest was instructed to halt the resettlement. The Chairman himself immediately telephoned the Rations Department and ordered a reinstatement of all ration cards.*

CHAPTER 98

WEDNESDAY, JULY 19, 1944

The ghetto was a manic-depressive, reacting to rumors of Allied advances and bombings as if liberty were hours away, but then cowering in fear at the least suggestion that the resettlements were about to resume. We were lifted by surges of hope, then slammed down by anything that signaled the liquidation of the ghetto.

Rumors reached me that Neftalin had been ordered to compile a list of the entire population of the ghetto. Rosenfeld was concerned. He asked that I interview the Deputy about these rumors. I expected Neftalin to laugh and promptly refute them as false.

Neftalin closed the folder on his desk when he saw me at the door. "I'm sure you are celebrating like the rest," he said.

He did not look as if he were in a celebratory mood. "You look like you have much work to still do."

"There is always work."

"Perhaps, I may help?"

"That is good of you, but no, I am assigned to do this with my commission."

"I thought you were almost finished?"

"Biebow wants data on our able-bodied workers, by year of birth, sex and...frankly, Engineer, he says the Gestapo wants this. We told him we don't have this data readily available, but he insists."

"Why do you think the Gestapo wants this now? The resettlements are terminated."

"I don't know. The Chairman is stalling. He and the Amtsleiter are not on good terms."

"People are spreading rumors again about the liquidation—"

"There are no grounds for concern. Biebow merely wants this data on hand."

"So, this has nothing to do with restarting the resettlements?"

Neftalin stood. "It is understandable that this work being done in the Department of Statistics might give rise to such rumors. But they're false."

I studied his face. "No sooner do people hear the word 'list' than they jump to the conclusion—"

"There is not a word of truth in any of this."

That was the message I included in my entry. Did I believe it? I wrote it knowing Rosenfeld would read what I wrote.

As I walked to my apartment, several people were staring at the sky toward the east. I turned my eyes and in the distance saw billows of smoke rising from the Earth. I thought I saw yellow and orange bursts of light and more smoky columns drawing closer.

SATURDAY, JULY 22, 1944

At this point, the chronicler cannot possibly ignore the events that ultimately concern the entire world and that, of course, are not without influence on the ghetto...The times are certainly critical, and ghetto dwellers await the coming hours with mixed feelings. All thoughts, considerations, hopes, and fears ultimately culminate in one main question: "Will we be left in peace?"

All eyes were on the east.

The excitement was tangible as word spread that our liberators were near. The Germans were packing boxes of documents. Their cars raced through our streets. Signs of change were everywhere. The Americans were coming. We had survived.

But it wasn't the Americans heading our way.

CHAPTER 99

SUNDAY, JULY 23, 1944
NEWS OF THE DAY
The mood in the ghetto is rosy. Everyone is hopeful of a speedy end to the war.

The ghetto was electric with rumors that the Soviets were in Kutno, the terminus for the trains. This explained the end of the resettlements. Our few remaining factories were still functioning under the Chairman's unstinting control. Neftalin stated, "The Chairman's policy in these critical days is not to allow discipline to slacken under any circumstances, to avert danger for the ghetto."

I felt this was wise since human nature being what it is, many of our long-suffering residents would go wild and leave their positions prematurely, risking intervention by our oppressors who were still a threat. New orders from the military were additional evidence that the Chairman's policies had succeeded. The mood in the ghetto was rosy.

Food continued to be a critical issue. For weeks, no vegetables were delivered to the ghetto and no potatoes. Suddenly, wagonloads of cabbages came rolling through the streets. At first, we were relieved, but they kept coming. We had cabbage soup three times a day for our 60,000 people. As Rosenfeld declared, "The ghetto wallowed in cabbage. The ghetto reeked in cabbage." He grew even more eloquent: "Stomachs revolted. Nor were the intestines better off. Diarrhea set in. Nausea was a common symptom. Every ghetto dweller suffered in some way from overindulgence in cabbage.

People drank cabbage soup by day and passed it spasmodically by night. It was hard to get a good night's sleep." He ended the entry with the following, "The last week of July in the ghetto year, 1944, was dominated by the hope that the Eternal, Praised be His Name, would liberate the ghetto from cabbage soup, soon, in our days." He signed it, O.R., and laughed as he slid it to me.

I would have laughed too but was trying to fathom a note in my hand. It was a report that Commander Rozenblat was ordered by the Kripo to have 200 members of the Order Service at Marysin cemetery at 4:00 a.m.. The last line read, "The purpose of the squad is not known." I typed the entry, relieved I had abandoned my hideaway in the cemetery before this order. I hoped they wouldn't find the few items I'd stored there in case I'd still need them. I prayed they wouldn't find Regina's blanket. I intended to retrieve it as soon as it was safe.

Neftalin knocked on our door, interrupting my search for more details about the cemetery gathering of Jewish policemen. He reported that the Chairman had inspected several departments, and all were functioning as well as could be expected with severe manpower shortages.

Rosenfeld smiled. "It is good to see the Eldest of the Jews is active again."

"He is rejuvenated by the news that the war is nearly over," Neftalin said. "He wants me to pass on that the authorities are imposing a permanent blackout now."

"They know the bombers are coming." I had to conceal my anticipation, but everyone was tingling with excitement. We were going to be bombed! Liberation was near!

Neftalin smiled. "We've received 31 postcards from Leipzig where apparently many of our residents were sent. They indicate our people are doing well."

I asked to examine some of the cards.

Neftalin handed the cards to me. "Families are together. This should address our concerns."

I read the postcards and gave Rosenfeld a smile as I handed a bunch to him.

Rosenfeld leafed through the cards and peered more closely.

"What's wrong?" I asked.

Rosenfeld muttered, "The postmarks. It is probably nothing. They're all dated July 19."

Neftalin gathered up the cards. "It's war still. It may be difficult to get mail sent daily."

Rosenfeld nodded. "Yes, of course, that explains it."

He still looked doubtful. I had another question for the Deputy. "The Corset and Brassiere Sewing Workshop manager reported he was ordered to prepare raw goods for shipment out of the ghetto back into the Reich. Are you aware of that?"

Rosenfeld said, "That's a coincidence. The Clothing and Linen Department has been ordered to send all of their machines back to Germany." He pulled out another memorandum. "The Boot Department is also shipping out its machinery."

"What's going on?" I asked Neftalin.

"The suffering is nearly over," he replied.

That had two very different meanings, I thought, as Neftalin left without explaining. "What do you think he meant?" I asked Rosenfeld.

He frowned and said, "The suffering is nearly over."

CHAPTER 100

S UNDAY, JULY 30, 1944
    WEATHER
    Temperature range 22-38 degrees; sunny, hot
DEATHS
One
BIRTHS
None
TOTAL POPULATION
68,501
NEWS OF THE DAY
One can see the war gradually approaching Litzmannstadt. The ghetto dweller peers curiously at the motor vehicles of various service branches as they speed through; for him, though, the crucial question remains: what is there to eat?

I wrote this entry anticipating our ordeal would end in hours, a few days at most. I sensed the changes coming by the frantic actions of the Nazis. Their vehicles raced around, scooping up boxes of documents, removing them from the ghetto. The cancellation of military orders fueled our hope and fear: hope the hunters were about to become the hunted, and fear that once the requisitions stopped, we would no longer be needed.

The German eyes and ever-present weapons affirmed we were still targets. We were their emaciated, nearly dead prey, but now they had more pressing concerns. Rumors everywhere made me believe it was only a matter of time before the liberators arrived. Being logical, I feared the

Germans might do something unthinkable in a desperate frenzy to hide the evidence of their savagery. The die could be cast either way. Time was running out. I had to make a painful decision. "We must hide," I said to Rosenfeld. "I know a place—"

"Where can an old man with tuberculosis hide? My logical friend, you know how this will end." Rosenfeld chuckled. "You have a wife and daughter. You hide."

"I won't go without you."

"You're sentimental? Then today is my last day of work. I quit."

"You can't quit. Where will you go?"

"I will find my sweet Rosalie. She has waited long enough for me to come home." The professor stood. "It has been the greatest honor in my life to work with you."

"No. It is my greatest honor to have you as my friend and mentor until this war ends."

"No, however this ends, I'm done here." He smiled. "Do you think anyone will ever read this chronicle we slaved over so long?" The professor closed his coat.

"I hope so. As the Chairman told me a long time ago, it is a message in a bottle for the future."

"If there is a future for the Jews? Let us pray so."

"Amen."

"Yes. Amen, dear Engineer." Rosenfeld started for the door.

I wanted to stop him but had no strength. "You're a stubborn old man," I called after him as the door closed.

That was the last I saw of my friend.

On August 2, 1944, the Chairman issued a proclamation in German and Yiddish that all workers were to report for resettlement out of the ghetto.

Why now? From the sound of artillery and bombs, I estimated the Russians were only a short distance away. All I had to do was hide for a few days. I went back to the cemetery. There were no longer burials to threaten my being discovered. The Nazis were too preoccupied with their urgent matters to bother with our weed-clogged cemetery, yet I shivered in fear I would be found.

During the day, I sought out the few administrators and workers still visible and learned that Rumkowski commanded his police to round up all Jews not essential for the governance of the ghetto. Naturally, many escaped his net, so the Germans took control of the roundups on August 9. They surrounded one block after another, ordering the Jewish police to drag out everyone they could find. The Gestapo threatened that anyone found hiding in the ghetto after August 18 would be killed. I had to risk it, to be here for Miriam and Regina's return.

The Germans ordered the Chairman to assign 700 people to clean up the ghetto. I begged Neftalin to let me be among that crew.

"But you're safe with us. You're one of our Chairman's inner circle."

"Are we so blind?" I asked.

Neftalin bit his lip and extended his hand. "I have no strength to argue."

I shook his hand, and then he pulled me toward him and wrapped his arms around me. "God bless you for your loyalty, my friend."

I pulled away and said, "God bless you."

Neftalin sighed. "Only the future will judge if we will be blessed or cursed for our actions, eh, Engineer?"

I nodded and left him, wishing I could offer him some solace.

During the day, I worked at various locations, packing boxes of documents, and cleaning out offices. At night, I snuck back to my crypt, starving and exhausted, grateful to survive one more day without being shipped out.

On August 28, I returned to the Chairman's office. It was empty. The entire building was abandoned. I learned from others the ghetto administration had been disbanded by the Germans. Rumkowski and whoever was left of his upper echelon were no longer needed. The ghetto ceased to exist.

Panicked by this blow of the Nazi fist, I went into permanent hiding. Like a rat, I scrounged bits of food wherever I could find them. I slept fitfully on the dirt floor. If only I could hide a little longer...a little longer.

On August 29, before dawn, I was shaken awake by the roar of trucks.

"But they're driving away," I said, unable to believe the sounds were fading in the distance.

After waiting several minutes, I emerged from my hiding place, a rodent peeking from a rathole. I saw the dust trail as vehicles sped away. Suspecting a trap, I crawled back inside and into a corner, Regina's blanket in my hands.

Several hours later, the ground rumbled louder, and I emerged for another peek.

A tank rumbled by.

I ducked back into hiding.

Soon more tanks and vehicles arrived, shaking the ground.

It wasn't long before soldiers entered the cemetery. Russians.

We'd been warned many Russians harbored rabid hatred of Jews. But I was starving and exhausted. I raised my hands over my head and left my safe haven among the dead.

A rifle aimed at me. I could barely stand. I pointed to the star on my jacket.

"You are safe," the soldier said in stilted Polish.

I sank to my knees, my hands in the dirt.

The soldiers gathered those of us left and made us sit on the ground in Balut Square. Soviet flags were everywhere.

Still frightened, thinking these were my last minutes of life, I asked God, why not the Americans? Were we to be sacrificed now to the Communists?

The look of pity in the soldiers' eyes and the food they provided surprised me. In my weak, disbelieving state, I couldn't stop crying, even as I savaged the bits of bread and meat they gave me.

The few hundred survivors were all either crying or too numb to feel anything. I barely heard the Polish translators telling us again and again that we were safe, that for us, the war was over. We had survived.

It took several days for Soviet officers to interview each of us. What were they looking for? Criminals? Nazi collaborators? Was this the judgment day I'd feared so long? I limited what I revealed. "I was only a bookkeeper. I knew nothing of what the administration did." No longer blind, I trusted no one. That part of me was dead forever, a casualty of war.

As the Soviets firmed up their control of Poland, they left us to stay or leave the ghetto. I was one of the few who remained. Since I'd been hidden, I asked others what happened to Neftalin and the Chairman. Nobody knew more than that the Chairman and his entourage left on the last transport. I prayed Henryk was safe. I was positive Rumkowski and his family had been secreted away to a secure location by the Germans they had served so long.

As the days passed, I learned the magnitude of the nightmare Hitler unleashed on the Jews of Lodz. In the four years the ghetto existed, more than 250,000 men, women, and children suffered within the Nazi barbed wire noose. 43,500 died in the ghetto, most from starvation and various diseases. More than 77,000 were sent to be executed in the Chelmno death camp between December of 1941 and July of 1944. In our recent resettlements, those I'd escaped, more than 72,000 people were deported to Auschwitz-Birkenau. Almost all were murdered within hours of their arrival. Auschwitz? I'd never heard of this death camp. There had been times during the resettlements when I suspected the worst, but given the logistical impossibility of such mass murder, the reality came as a traumatic shock. I couldn't imagine how anyone, even Hitler, could manage such a genocide. Poison gas? Unheard of. Unbelievable. That any human beings could have such hatred for others that they devoted their resources and minds to engineer the extermination of millions was beyond my understanding. Who could accept such a heinous thing? Who could believe a civilized people could committed such an atrocity?

I was still in Lodz when they announced Hitler was dead, and the war, thanks-be-to-God, was finally over. But it was not over for me and for the rest of the Jews waiting anxiously in the nearly deserted ghetto. Each day, I begged for any word of Miriam and Regina. I skimmed the newspapers and the records, lists of the victims, from the labor camps, the death camps. I cornered the battered people returning to Lodz and echoed the universal plea, "Has anyone seen my wife or child?" I asked about Pola, Singer, Rosenfeld, Neftalin, and all the others, souls lost, unaccounted for. People were shell-shocked and adrift, locked in their own desperate searches for loved ones. We, the survivors, were grateful to be alive but tormented by our lack of knowledge about those we sorely missed. Everyone asked each dusty passerby, "Please, has anyone seen my wife or child? My mother? My father? My children?"

Rumors circulated about Rumkowski. It was said the Germans offered him, his family, and top administrators permission to remain in the ghetto supervising the cleaning crew. He declined that offer, perhaps believing the Germans were sincere in telling him Jews were being moved away from Lodz to keep them safe from the Soviet bombings and ground assault. The Chairman, his wife, adopted son, brother Jozef, and his closest friends were placed on a separate train car. Did they know the destination was Auschwitz? Did they know what fate awaited there? Nobody could tell me what happened to Rumkowski once he left the ghetto that he had kept going longer than any other in Europe. A few survivors of Auschwitz, barely more than skeletons, said the Chairman, the Eldest of the Jews, was killed by some of his fellow Jews shortly after he arrived in the death camp. They said Rumkowski and his family were strangled by the hands of his enraged laborers. No one was ever able to confirm this.

Was Rumkowski the savior of the Jews of Lodz or the devil who collaborated with the Nazis for his own benefit? I could never decide. But I did owe him my life.

Years later, after endless searches, I confirmed that Miriam and my precious Regina were murdered within hours of arriving in the death camp, Chelmno. I had hoped until the last. There weren't any bodies. No headstones. A few fading photos and my memories were all that remained. And guilt that I survived when Miriam, my innocent Regina, and so many others did not. I also learned that my dear Professor Rosenfeld was killed almost immediately in Auschwitz. What a loss to the world. Of all the chroniclers, I was the only survivor.

I remained in the ghetto until late October of 1946, hopeful Miriam, Pola, anyone would return. Still weak, and no closer to answers, the Soviet consolidation of power forced me to make a painful decision. With Regina's blanket, a few personal items, and a ragtag group of other Jews, I left the Lodz ghetto. But before I passed through the hated gates, I had one more thing to do.

I stole to the cemetery and dug up the first batch of papers where I'd buried them under a headstone. I then went to 13 Lutomierska Street, the site of the ghetto Fire Department, and recovered the second batch in the horse stall where I'd buried them under the dirt floor. A third batch had been buried at the Jewish cemetery, but I learned the Germans forced the director of the cemetery to reveal the hiding place. I was grateful that so many of our bulletins were recovered. I vowed to preserve them as the Chairman had wanted, as my dear friends deserved.

We walked west, a group of fearful, dazed wanderers, bound by our tragic past and the desire to escape from the Soviets. We were also tied together by our obsession to learn whatever we could about our families and friends. We refused to accept that so many were dead. It was impossible to believe. So-and-so had to have survived. We just had to find them. At every city, to every passing Jew, many meandering aimlessly, still shocked at the enormity of the death and decay, we begged for any scrap they could provide about those we lost. "Yes, I saw him. I don't know what happened to her." But mostly, "I'm sorry. I wish I could help. Did you know my brother...sister...child?"

Trucks drove by. Many were filled with Russian soldiers.

I lowered my eyes and kept walking. The news bantered about in low voices about Stalin's repression wasn't encouraging. I was afraid someone might have discovered my recovery of the Chronicle pages and was hunting for me. The war turned me into a paranoid, fearing every approaching sound.

We heard the Americans were west. If we could keep walking, we might reach them.

Many vehicles passed us. The Soviet stars emblazoned on their metal skin reminded me of the yellow stars that had branded us in the ghetto. Some soldiers waved. A few sneered or shouted curses, but most paid little attention to shabbily-dressed Jews stumbling along the roadways. Who cared if the Jews stayed, left, or died?

I cast a wary glance at a small column of trucks and walked on.

"It stopped! They're coming for us," someone yelled when one of the trucks had passed slowly by and stopped.

"Oh, God," others exclaimed.

A few scattered to the nearby woods. Most, out of breath, barely alive, waited with heads down for whatever new ordeal God would unleash on us.

I thought of running away. I was exhausted. I could barely hobble, let alone escape from armed soldiers. If the Soviets wanted a Jew, they could have me. I waited for the soldiers, my eyes aimed at the ground. My humble aspect would convince them I was not worthy of their attention. Just another pitiful, worthless, Jew. I prayed they wouldn't inspect my knapsack where the Chronicle pages were hidden under smelly laundry. It would be my bad luck to be killed by a Russian after surviving the Nazis. *Why were they taking so long? Keep walking.*

The truck didn't move.

When I didn't hear a command or a gunshot, I lifted my eyes.

The sun was blinding.

A blurred figure walked toward me. "It is you. I searched all of Lodz. I was afraid I lost you."

"Pola?" I peered at the apparition walking toward me. "My God! You're real! You're alive."

Pola placed her hands on my face and smiled. "Bennie, I love you."

I never kissed anyone more gratefully. I couldn't believe she was alive. As we kissed, I silently thanked God for letting us survive. I held onto her…held on…held on…I never wanted to let her go. I still didn't believe she was real.

As Pola helped me into the back of the truck, she whispered, "Bennie, we made it. The nightmare is over."

I wanted to believe her. But Pola was wrong. For the rest of my life, even in America, where Pola and I would find freedom, a new life, and a new family, the nightmares returned. They would never end.

WHAT HAPPENED TO THE LODZ GHETTO?

A t this point, the novel ends. Ostrowski is left with many unanswered questions, because even today, many questions about the ghetto my parents miraculously survived, remain unanswered. I urge you to read the actual *Chronicle of the Lodz Ghetto*, translated and edited by Lucjan Dobroszycki, (Yale University Press,1984). I've never read a more chilling account of what the occupied Jews suffered than these largely anonymous entries that build to a tragic conclusion. My novels are historical fiction, based on what are, unfortunately, documented events. I lost my grandparents, and most of my relatives, in the ghetto and concentration camps, and still don't know their exact fate. There aren't any tombstones. Most of the survivors are gone. The Holocaust is the shadow that haunted me all my life and compelled me to devote years to telling this story.

SUNDAY, JULY 30, 1944 is the final known Chronicle entry:
   population 68,561.
   ...the crucial question remains: What is there to eat?

Among the less than 5,000 survivors of the Lodz ghetto were a young woman and man destined to become my parents. They never said how they survived. I was too frightened to ask. I knew almost nothing about their ordeal until I read the *Chronicle*. I hope my novels honor them and all the victims and survivors. Only knowledge can prevent history from repeating.

Thank you for sharing this experience with me. Please invite your friends and family to learn more so we may all say, "Never again to anyone, anywhere."

NOTE: About *The Chronicle of the Lodz Ghetto*

My historical fiction series follows the timeline of events detailed in *The Chronicle of the Lodz Ghetto*, translated and edited by Lucjan Dobroszycki, (Yale University Press, 1984). While the names of some characters are real, any resemblance to actual persons is fictitious, unintended, and should not be inferred. The exception is Chairman Rumkowski, whose policies and actions are still hotly debated. Rumors were that his fellow Jews strangled him when he arrived in Auschwitz. That has not been confirmed.

While this work is fiction based on real events, I've attempted to retain the tone and style of the original entries as they appear in the *Chronicle*, including grammatical and formatting errors and irregularities: e.g., the inconsistent formatting of the titles. I decided to include these excerpts and titles because, on their own, they present a grim outline of the steps leading to the ghetto's demise. I selected those fragments that best fit my dramatization. I didn't want to 'touch one hair,' fearing to dilute the 'chill' factor I experienced reading them. The *Chronicle* is an invaluable document that miraculously was saved when the only surviving author, the real Dr. Bernard Ostrowski, no spoilers, recovered copies of many of the pages that had been hidden from the Nazis. Some, unfortunately, were not rescued.

The *Chronicle* raises many troubling questions. When did the ghetto residents know the fate of the deportees? Why did so many of the entries lack emotion? Who wrote each of the entries? What did the writers actually think of their leader? What would we have done in Rumkowski's shoes?

Was Rumkowski a savior or a greedy collaborator, the Devil? As Rumkowski said, "Someday, I will be judged." A critical question is when did he know the fate of the deportees. One final clue comes from a footnote by Dobroszycki:

It is not known whether Rumkowski, as the Eldest of the Jews, or someone else in the Jewish administration was aware when issuing Proclamation No 416 of June 16, 1944, that this time "voluntary registration for labor outside the ghetto" marked the beginning of the action to liquidate the ghetto. It is also not known whether M.C. Rumkowski or someone else in the Jewish administration of the ghetto knew that all the transports that left the ghetto from Radozoszcz station in Marysin between Friday, June 23, and Friday, July 14, 1944, were sent via Kutno to Kolo and from there to the death camp in Chelmno (Kulmhof) on the river Ner.

I leave it to the reader to decide.

My parents never talked about what they survived in the Lodz ghetto, so writing about the ordeals so many suffered was an eye-opener. It was also an emotional experience. There were many decisions I had to make. One, in particular, I debated until the end: should I use the real names of the chroniclers when I was unable to learn much about their personal lives? I chose to do so for several reasons, including to honor their memory and lend authenticity to the events described in this saga. I wish I had the staff and ability to translate German, Polish, and Yiddish, to have researched each character, but then these books might never have been written. I hope by including their names, I may pique the curiosity of others to learn more about these courageous figures. As Dobroszycki says in his introduction, "They are like the invisible men of history." I hope my novels have brought their names back to life and breathed new interest in their amazing work, *The Chronicle of the Lodz Ghetto.*

If nothing else results from the years of work I've put into this trilogy, I hope my children and future generations of my family will have some idea of what a miracle their survival is. At least, they will know this indelible part of their heritage. I owe it to them.

Please, share these books with your family and friends so we may end hate and assure this never happens again to anyone. If you enjoyed, (wrong word), this incredible story, please add your reviews, so others may share the experience. I hope it touched your heart and soul and haunts you as it still haunts me.

Thank you,

Mark

BIBLIOGRAPHY

Dobrosyzycki, Lucjan, *The Chronicle of the Lodz Ghetto 1941-1944*, (Yale University Press, 1984), 550 pp. Incredible anonymous entries documenting the daily ordeal suffered by the nearly 300,000 residents of the second-largest ghetto in Poland, under the leadership of its controversial leader, Chaim Rumkowski. You feel the noose tightening.

Adelson, Alan, Lapides, Robert, *Lodz Ghetto: Inside a Community Under Siege*, (Viking Penguin, 1989) The sourcebook for the award-winning documentary film of the same title. An eye-opening view of the ghetto: "Listen and believe this. Even though it happened here. Even though it seems so old, so distant, and so strange." Jozef Zelkowicz

Grossman, Mendel, Smith, Frank Dabba, *My Secret Camera: Life in the Lodz Ghetto*, (Gulliver Books, 2000) A picture book with photographs taken by a concealed camera at the risk of his life.

Sierakowiak, Dawid, *The Diary of Dawid Sierakowiak*, Daily diary of a young man who died at age 19. The Anne Frank of Lodz.

Trunk, Isaiah, *Lodz Ghetto: A History*, translated by Robert Moses Shapiro (Published in Association with the United States Holocaust Memorial Museum, Indiana University Press, 2006) Most complete sourcebook for researching the Lodz ghetto.

ADDITIONAL RESOURCES

Photographs of the Lodz Ghetto by Mendel Grossman, Henryk Ross, and other clandestine photographers helped provide background information for this book. Google "Lodz ghetto photographs." Many of these photographs were taken through holes in the photographers' coats, risking their lives.

United States Holocaust Museum: Visits to the museum helped provide the physical elements. I'm proud to be a supporter and invite you to join in their effort to combat hate and genocide for all people.

NEVER AGAIN TO ANYONE ANYWHERE

More from NCG Key and Newhouse Creative Group

Inspiring the readers and writers of today and tomorrow!

Visit NewhouseCreativeGroup.com for more from NCG Key and the rest of the Newhouse Creative Group family of authors.

About the Author

Mark was born in Germany to Holocaust survivors from the Lodz ghetto and Auschwitz but lost his grandparents and most of his relatives during this horrific time. His novel of love and courage in the Holocaust ghetto his parents survived, *The Devil's Bookkeepers,* won the Gold Medal Historical Fiction and Best Published Book of the Year in the Florida Writers Association's Royal Palm Literary Awards competition. The sequel won the Bronze Medal for unpublished Historical Fiction by the Florida Writers Association.

Mark's humorous children's mysteries, *Welcome to Monstrovia; The Case of the Disastrous Dragon; and The Case of the Crazy Chickenscratches,* received Benjamin Franklin, Readers' Favorite, Royal Palm Literary, and other awards and are being developed for a movie or television series.

Founding president of Writers League of The Villages, Top Cat of Writers 4 Kids Club, he writes Village Neighbors magazine's "Writing Bug" and is a Director of the Florida Writers Association, and Chairperson of the Florida Writers Association Youth Program and Conference Chairperson. A former Long Island teacher, SUNY at Old Westbury adjunct instructor, he was honored as Teacher of the Year by the New York State Reading

Association, among other honors. The proud father of two sons, he married his English bride on the 4th of July and it's been 'fireworks' ever since. Learn more and contact him at www.newhousecreativegroup.com. He thanks you for reading his books and appreciates your kind reviews.

Made in the USA
Columbia, SC
01 June 2020